CITY OF SHADOWS

JAMES DALTON

TOR®

A TOM DOHERTY ASSOCIATES BOOK
NEW YORK

This is a work of fiction. All the characters and events portrayed in this book are either products of the author's imagination or are used fictitiously.

CITY OF SHADOWS

Copyright © 2000 by James Dalton

A Tor Book
Published by Tom Doherty Associates, LLC
175 Fifth Avenue
New York, NY 10010

www.tor.com

Tor® is a registered trademark of Tom Doherty Associates, LLC.

ISBN: 0-812-58957-2

First edition: November 2000
First mass market edition: May 2002

Printed in the United States of America

0 9 8 7 6 5 4 3 2 1

"*City of Shadows* chronicles the late-'60s and early-'70s 'wilderness of mirrors' where nothing is as it seems, and the book itself is a conundrum. Even the author's name requires decoding. The pseudonym credited on the book's cover, 'James Dalton,' belongs to a veteran fiction writer whose real first novel was a best seller made by Hollywood years ago into a stylish, successful, and critically acclaimed espionage thriller. . . . *City of Shadows* deserves the attention of both casual readers in search of a crackerjack political thriller and serious historians seeking a greater understanding of the turbulent Nixon presidency."

—James Rosen, *The Washington City Paper*

"A wild, entertaining tale that involves—among other things—the Vietnam War, Watergate, and the antiwar movement."

—*The VVA Veteran*

"Action-filled. . . . [Filled with] menacing deep-Beltway insider gossip, suggesting that there might be still more to the dark deeds inside the Nixon White House."

—*Kirkus Reviews*

"The terrifying tale he weaves of corruption, abuse of power and secret deals made and broken in the political shadows is geared toward political thriller junkies who can keep a multitude of characters straight and will enjoy weeding out the facts from the fiction."   —*Publishers Weekly*

"*City of Shadows* is a turbo-charged roman-a-clef that soars a lot closer to the truth about Watergate than Woodward & Bernstein ever did—or even imagined. It's all there—the Pentagon spy ring that targeted a suspect president; the Mob-connected hookers and their high-powered Johns; the conniving Dean and the sinister McCord. And if that isn't enough, there are tag-teams of spooks from Langley and the Bureau—and half-a-dozen people that you probably never heard of, but have Need To Know."

—Jim Hougan, author of *Secret Agenda*

"I haven't been so excited by a crime novel since I read James Ellroy's *Black Dahlia* years ago. James Dalton's *City of Shadows* has the power and narrative drive of Ellroy at his best, plus a brilliant premise, epic scope, terrific suspense, superbly drawn characters (about whom I came to care deeply) and a sense of place (Washington) and period (the Watergate era) that are absolutely stunning. Please take note: this is a major debut!"

> —David Hunt, bestselling author of *Trick of Light* and *The Magician's Tale*

"*City of Shadows* gave me a perspective on both the city and the [Watergate] scandal I'd never had before. James Dalton's breakthrough novel is a multilayered, action-packed, chillingly believable exercise in high-tension political paranoia. The novel is populated by good people you feel you know and bad people you hope you never do, and since it rings so true, you're never sure which is which and who's going to be left standing at the searing, devastating end. CITY tells it like it was, and even scarier, how it might have been."

> —Mark Olshaker, bestselling co-author of *Mindhunter* and *Journey into Darkness*

"James Dalton has concocted a thrilling and intriguing spies-and-coppers caper, set against the intricate twists and turns of Watergate. He knows his history and has produced a daring and action-loaded what-if that both illuminates the darkest recesses of the nation's worst scandal and probes the secret territory of behind-closed-doors Washington."

> —David Corn, author of *Deep Background*, Washington editor of *The Nation*, Edgar nominee

"A thrilling and thought-provoking journey into America's worst excesses of power. It grabs you, shakes you, and leaves you gasping. It sends a message you will not forget."

> —Ethan Black, author of *The Broken Hearts Club* and *Irresistible*

FOR BONNIE

CHAPTER 1

Smoke from a hundred fires filled Washington, D.C. Gunshots and sirens ripped the April 1968 air. On Seventh Street, a line of cops faced rioters. The mob surged into a liquor store. Two men carrying a TV set staggered up the road. Flames licked an overturned car.

A black man stood in front of the police to yell at the chaos: "This isn't what Martin wanted! Be cool! Dr. King didn't want this!"

A police cruiser parked behind the lawmen's formation. A sergeant climbed out, conferred with the senior patrol officer, then marched to the young white cop on the end of the line.

"What's your name?" asked the sergeant. A bottle shattered beside him.

"Pig motherfuckers!"

The young cop kept his eyes straight ahead: "Officer Quinn! Badge 779!"

"Son," said the sergeant, "I asked for your name."

"John Quinn."

A fire truck blared through the intersection behind Quinn.

"How old are you?"

"Real close to twenty-three, sir—I mean, Sergeant."

"How long you been out of the academy?"

"Today's Friday. We graduated on Tuesday."

"Hell of a shift to break your cherry."

"I stood crowd control Wednesday at the rally for Bobby—for Senator Kennedy."

Behind them, the blue police academy bus ground to life. The senior patrol officer shouted, *"Attention!"*

But the sergeant told Quinn, "You stand firm."

"Right face!"

"You got a lot going for you, Quinn. The liquor store's been picked clean, furniture place burned up. There's a corner store behind us, but they hung a 'Soul Brother' sign in the window. So there's nothing much to bring them down this way. Toward you."

"Forward . . . march!"

The line of his fellow officers pulled away from Quinn.

"We need those men elsewhere," said the sergeant. "We need you here."

Glass shattered. Quinn's fellow cadets snaked into the blue machine.

The sergeant led Quinn to the middle of the road. "Wish we had a radio to leave with you. But you'll be OK, as long as you have the baddest fuck-you face on the street. Work on that."

"Yes, Sergeant."

The sergeant licked his forefinger and held it up: "We're lucky. The wind is on our side."

The blue bus rumbled away.

"Wait one," said the sergeant. He went to his cruiser.

Quinn watched a wild-eyed trio jeer the man who kept pleading for the brothers and sisters to cool it, to honor Martin, to stop. The boldest of the trio swung an open bottle through the air. Gin whipped over the peacemaker like the lines of a cross. The mocked man wept. Vanished.

The sergeant fired a tear gas grenade to the left of the mob. He dropped a second grenade on their other flank. A third canister skipped off the pavement beside a burning Ford.

"Sorry, we ran out of masks," said the sergeant.

"But it'll be OK because the wind's on our side—right?"

"Orders of the day are secure and protect. Be sure nobody innocent gets hurt. Back them down. They don't stop, run. They truly come after you, shoot the motherfuckers. Whoever they once were, now they're all blood crazy."

The two cops heard coughing, shoes scuffling away in the caustic gray gas and black smoke.

The older cop looked at the rookie, dropped his command tone. "Kid . . . how you doing?"

"Feel like a freight train is roaring straight toward us."

"Appears to me it's already here." The sergeant shook his head and put muscle back in his words: "Officer Quinn, you *own* this street."

Then he drove away. Riot echoed through the urban canyon.

John Quinn, who was real close to twenty-three, stood in the middle of Seventh Street.

Alone.

Don't back down, he ordered himself. Flames licked the mangled Ford. A red high-heeled shoe stood on the road amid a million glass diamonds. He felt the smoky breeze. He heard distant sirens, his pounding heart. *OK, it's going to be OK!*

A burglar alarm clanged behind him.

Secure and protect. If he turned one way and exposed his back to the other . . . If the clanging alarm meant a citizen was having a heart attack, being robbed, raped, murdered . . .

You got the badge you always wanted, he told himself. Go earn it.

The clanging alarm came from a mansion chopped up into ghetto apartments. A cardboard sign in the door glass read: SISTER MARIE SAINT JAMES—PALM READING AND FORTUNES TOLD.

Quinn pushed the door open with his nightstick.

A stairwell zigzagged up bare-bulb shadows to where the alarm rang. He slipped the nightstick into the steel loop on his belt, drew his revolver, and started up the dark stairs.

A shadow loomed over the third-floor railing. A man bellowed: "Run, motherfucker!"

"Don't move! I'm—" Quinn saw two flashes and heard a double crack of gunfire.

The cop shot back before he knew it.

The man screamed, fell to the second-floor landing. His impact filled the air with dust.

For a moment, Quinn heard only the clanging alarm and

his own frantic breath. Then from the second floor came: "Oh, shit!"

The chocolate-skinned man Quinn found sprawled there wore a corduroy sports coat over a brown sweater, dark pants and moccasins. His left leg zigzagged at a painful angle.

"Police!" yelled Quinn. "Don't move!"

"*Police!* You're the fucking *police*?"

"You're under arrest."

"You broke my leg! You stupid cop! I thought you were one of those gone-wild people!"

A crowbar and a gym bag lay close to the injured man. A pistol lay by Quinn's new shoes.

"A starter pistol? You shot at me with a damn cap gun, no-bullets starter pistol?"

"It's supposed to scare you off! I ain't no killer! No evil jive for me. Damn, my leg hurts. Ain't you even gonna say you're sorry?" A dark smear the size of a quarter dampened the man's shoulder. A jagged sliver of wood poked into the dark spot. The man stared at his wound. "You ain't much of a shot."

"I hit you, for Chrissakes!"

"The hell you did! Your bullet hit the rail and split that hunk of wood into me. If you hadn't made me fall and break my damn leg, I'd've beat feet all over your sorry blue ass."

"Let me look at your wound." The splinter moved when Quinn touched it. He eased the wood free. The man yelled, but his trickle of blood began to clot.

"You're a heartless son of a bitch," the man told Quinn.

"And you're a burglar," said Quinn.

"You should have read me my rights by now."

"You probably already know them," said Quinn. "Lay still. I'm going to pat you down."

"No tickling."

They laughed. Tension flowed from both of them.

Outside, a fire truck Klaxon roared past, then vanished.

"What's your name?" said Quinn. "Come on: I should at least know who I caught."

"Damned if you shouldn't: Cyrus Watson." He sighed. "So

do I call you 'Officer' or 'Yes, suh!' or 'honky mother-fucker'?"

Quinn told him his name. "Now I have to figure out what to do."

"You the man."

Quinn knocked on the nearest door.

"Ain't nobody home," said Cyrus.

"What about upstairs?"

"If there was anybody up there, why would I—*ay!* Damn, my leg hurts! All you'll find up there is Mary James's place, and she's long gone."

"Sister St. James?"

" 'Saint,' my ass. 'Marie,' my ass. 'Gypsy,' my big ass. But, hell, she knew 'nough about the future to run away today."

A new chorus of sirens sounded faintly beyond the clanging alarm bell. Both men saw a vision of the burning city.

Quinn whispered, "Why did somebody kill him?"

But they both knew the answer.

"I'm sorry," said Quinn.

"You think one damn apology to some random black man will—"

"I'm sorry for all of us," said Quinn. "Not just for you. Not just because King was black."

"*Too,*" said Cyrus. "Black, *too.* Black like me."

The walls muffled a distant explosion, but they both heard it.

"Black like them," said Cyrus.

"Can I ask you . . ."

"Don't be so shy, John. You got the gun, the badge, pure, white snow skin."

"Don't hand me that shit, OK? I wouldn't give it to you."

"Maybe *you* wouldn't. But don't expect me to say sorry for thinking you *might.*"

Quinn nodded. "Why are they doing that out there?"

"What the hell else they gonna do? What the hell else works?"

"That's not what he thought."

"Well, probably he was right. But he's stone dead today."
Cyrus said: "Folks got to do something, or they get it done
to them."

"We've got to do something," said Quinn. "I mean about
this, now."

"I currently gots some limitations."

"There's gotta be somebody home, some phone I can use."

The alarm bell clanged as Quinn climbed the stairs to the
third floor. The first two apartment doors there were bare. A
crucifix surrounded by a garland of garlic hung on the third
floor. That brown surface also boasted a Star of David, a
pentagram, an all-seeing eye, the yin-yang circle. Chunks of
wood were pried away from the doorjamb's five locks and—

Raindrops tapped the brim of Quinn's uniform hat.

What? Quinn ran his fingertips over his brim: they
smeared red. He lifted his flashlight from its loop, threw its
beam up. . . .

A wet crimson stain marred the ceiling.

Quinn ran down the stairs.

"The voodoo spook you up there, Officer?" Cyrus laughed.

"It's OK," said Quinn. "Everything's going to be OK."

"Easy for you to say. You probably ain't going to jail."

"Jail's not so bad." Quinn knelt beside the man on the
floor. "Sit up. Let me help you sit up."

Quinn's hand on Cyrus's back touched a warm ooze the
size of a tennis ball. Quinn imagined the movie: Cyrus
leaning over the railing, firing. Quinn snapping off a wild
shot. The bullet hit Cyrus by his shoulder. Small entry
wound. Blew out Cyrus's back below his shoulder blade.
Gore splattered the ceiling. The splinter stabbed Cyrus as he
spun over the rail.

Cyrus saw the red smear on Quinn's sleeve. "Oh, man, I
am fucked."

"No, you're not! We're going to get you to the hospital,
get you to a doctor."

"How you know that, man?"

Quinn tore off his white shirt. Badge and all, he pressed

the shirt over the wound in Cyrus's back, lowered the man to the dusty wood floor.

"I know because you gotta go to jail. You're my first arrest."

"Oh, yeah. Sure. Forgot to read me my rights."

"That's right, you'll walk; you and your buddies gonna laugh at me." Quinn wiped his mouth, realized he'd smeared it with blood. "You'll be OK. I'll find a phone."

The alarm bell clanged. Quinn ran downstairs, pounded on apartment doors. Nothing. He ran back up to the second floor, to the third floor. Banging on doors: "Anybody home? Open up!"

Quinn kicked a door open. Inside: cheap furniture, an unmade sofa bed. A picture of Grandma tacked to one wall. Jesus smiled down from another. Pots on the stove. But no phone.

The alarm bell clanged.

In the hall, he grabbed the doorknob on the other apartment—the door opened effortlessly. That apartment was totally empty.

"Hey, Quinn! Think I heard somebody. First floor."

Quinn banged on every first-floor door. A voice yelled at him from beyond Apartment 2's solid wood: "I gots a shotgun!"

"Mister! Thank God, you gotta help us! Open up, I need to use the phone, a man's—"

"Get away from here! I seen the shit you been doing up the street! I got a shotgun! Leave me alone, or I'll blast you!"

"This is an emergency! You've got to—"

"Get away or I'll call the police!"

"I am the police!"

"You be dead, you don't get away and leave me 'lone!"

Quinn begged and pleaded and threatened for two minutes, but the voice inside the door said nothing more and wouldn't open up.

"Cyrus! That Sister Mary: She got a phone?"

The voice that floated down the stairs seemed weaker: "She's in the Yellow Pages."

Back up to Cyrus. His chocolate skin seemed gray. "Getting cold in here for April."

Quinn draped his T-shirt across Cyrus's chest, said, "Almost there."

He grabbed the crowbar, ran upstairs. Ripped the wood around the solid door with Cyrus's tool. Splinters flew as he pried the doorjamb off, but the door stayed shut.

"Son of a bitch!" Quinn beat the crowbar against the solid door. The crucifix fell, the garlic garland tangled around the crowbar. "You fake gypsy bitch, why'd you have to be so paranoid!"

Quinn put the muzzle of his service revolver inches from the first lock. He fired. The muzzle flash burned his eyes. The roar drowned out the clanging alarm. He zeroed the next lock, closed his eyes, fired. Lead slammed into wood and steel. Bullet fragments sliced Quinn's bare chest. He lined up the gun and fired again, then again, and then again on the final lock.

The door stood closed.

With a scream, he hurled himself against it. The wooden slab fell back, flipping him head over heels into the apartment.

Red, everywhere was red, beaded curtains and junk, dead incense, chairs—on a lamp table by a stuffed armchair: a phone.

Quinn dialed 911: busy.

He called the police academy and listened to the no-answer peal for thirty rings.

Zero, dial zero: "Due to the unusually heavy volume of calls, all operators are temporarily busy. Please hang up and—"

Phone book, there had to be a phone book in the—found it. What were the names of the hospitals in this strange damn city and why had he quit college and moved here, should have gone to work in the steel mills back home. Quinn grabbed a Yellow Pages, found *H*. . . .

The phone was dead.

The alarm bell clanged.

Back downstairs, Cyrus stared at him with soft eyes. Quinn tucked his T-shirt around the wounded man's chest. Cyrus's skin felt wrinkled.

"Just hold on! I'll be right back!"

Quinn ran to the center of Seventh Street, a half-naked, blood-smeared berserk white cop, screaming, "Help me! Somebody! Anybody! Help me! Help us! Help him! Help him!"

Nobody came.

"Cyrus," panted Quinn, kneeling beside the man.

"Don't leave me, man! Don't leave me alone!"

"I won't! I won't leave you! We're in this together." Quinn gently shook the man, whose eyes had glazed. "Cyrus!"

"Don't hug me so tight, John. 's our first date."

"Can you hot-wire a car?"

"I'm just a burglar, man. Don't steal nobody's ride." A thin smile came to Cyrus. " 'Sides, if you could fly us downstairs to the street, we wouldn't need to steal a car."

"I know. I know."

"That feels good."

The cop realized he'd been rocking the man he cradled.

"We almost all square now," said Cyrus. "You doing your job, I doing mine. All this just what it costs."

"Shh. Rest easy."

"Don't you shush me, John-boy. I know what's what. Maybe you can lie to yourself, but you can't lie to me, and I know what's what and you owe me one thing."

"Anything, whatever you want, I'll do it, get it while you're in the hospit—"

"They're not gonna take me to no hospital. You do this one thing for me, we be square."

Quinn rocked him and felt the tears trickle down his own cheeks. They'd turn red when they rolled over the blood on his face, disappear when they dripped into the scarlet lake surrounding him. He wanted to wipe them away, but he wouldn't let go of who he held.

"You tell my mother, Doris Watson, office manager over

at the Agriculture Department. Tell her it was OK, tell her didn't hurt none. Tell her she done ever'thin' right, it's all on me. Tell her wasn' her fault. Sorry! Oh, Jesus, tell her I'm sorry!"

"You tell her! You'll get OK, I'll get you free, a job and—"

"Got a job, man, an' it's killing me." Cyrus laughed. Spit blood. "You promise me that? Even though you the law?"

"Yes! I promise! I promise!"

Cyrus rolled his eyes up to the man who held him. "Why'd you wanna be a cop?"

The alarm clanged. John heard the sigh inside the man he cradled, and he knew, but he sobbed and yelled the answer to ears that couldn't hear: "Somebody had to! Somebody had to!"

CHAPTER 2

Nine days after he shot Cyrus, John Quinn went to Mrs. Doris Watson's house. She made him stammer his apologies and message through the iron bars over her door. She told him nothing.

The police department ruled the shooting of burglar Cyrus Vance as justifiable and kept the riot statistics lower by deeming Quinn's police action unrelated to the chaos following Dr. Martin Luther King's assassination. After the Board of Inquiry, Quinn shuffled through clerical assignments while he waited to be assigned to regular uniformed patrol.

After the riot, good apartments were easy to find. Quinn snagged a place with a view of a park. He lifted weights in the police gym, thought about going home, bringing his motorcycle back to D.C. from Lorain, Ohio, but settled for phone conversations with his mother. They talked about his father, who'd died young of a heart attack. Quinn got an auto-squad detective to teach him how to hot-wire cars and shimmy locks.

Gotta know more than how to squeeze the trigger. Gotta know what I might hit.

Late one June night Quinn's black-and-white TV flickered live reports from Los Angeles, where a crazed gunman blasted presidential hopeful Robert Kennedy. Quinn thanked his lucky stars that it hadn't happened on his watch; wished he had been there, badge and gun, to stop it.

Richard Nixon, the only politician besides Eisenhower that Quinn's father ever revered, won his Republican Party's presidential nomination at their August Miami Beach convention. Nixon picked Maryland's unknown governor, Spiro Agnew, as his running mate. After the GOP's show, the Democratic Party descended on Chicago, where Vice President Hubert Humphrey won the nomination President Lyndon Johnson had declined to pursue so he could concentrate on the Vietnam War, which had been killing Americans since 1959. The streets of Chicago surged with a police riot as the bastions of law and order clubbed hundreds of anti-war protesters, who saw the TV cameras that brought them into Quinn's living room and chanted, "The whole world's watching." The *Washington Post* quoted Chicago Mayor Richard Daley: "Get this straight once and for all. The police isn't there to create disorder, the policeman is there to preserve disorder."

Quinn cut that quote out of the newspaper and taped it to his refrigerator.

August also gave Quinn to Jimmy Duvell, who on Quinn's first day of street patrol said, "The brass want you to have a training officer who can break you in right."

"Me, too," said Quinn.

Jimmy Duvell leaned on their cruiser. "You wanna be a cop, this is what you got to know: Don't piss off your sergeant. Do your paperwork so it says what it's supposed to. Carry mints. Never snooze with nobody watching your back. What goes on with partners is sacred. If you don't know the play, get out of Dodge. Don't taste no other cop's honey. Volunteer nothing. Catch the *can't-be-sure's-I-forget's* if you bump Internal Affairs. Keep the coloreds cool. They got a new strut to 'em since they burned the town down, but remember: nowadys, don't leave no bruises on 'em. Most of all, make the right numbers every year."

Quinn took thirty seconds to find something to say. "That's an amazing load of shit."

Jimmy Duvell waved his hand. "You'll pick it up."

They were assigned to the Second District, milk-white neighborhoods where the police were welcome—within limits—and a rookie who'd had a bad baptism could ease into the job.

"God bless women's libbers," Jimmy Duvell said as they cruised past Georgetown's chic bars and boutiques. "Them getting rid of bras makes their bullshit damn near bearable."

Quinn said nothing, but he, too, watched the women flow past the cruiser.

Jimmy Duvell chased fire trucks. Explored burned-out buildings. Once Jimmy Duvell emerged from a smoldering shop with an electric typewriter he locked in the cruiser's trunk.

"This is my score," he told Quinn. "IBM Selectrics are big stolen property stats. All those government buildings get picked like cotton. Guy whose place burned down won't miss this. Eat up duty time with 'Assist the fire department.' Hammer and chisel the serial numbers, and presto: one officer-recovered stolen typewriter, one statistic in the plus column for yours truly.

"Remember," he told Quinn, "get your own deal. I'll cover you, you cover me. This is why you get a year of OJT."

"A whole year," muttered Quinn.

By September, Quinn wondered who he was going to shoot: Jimmy Duvell or himself.

Quinn drove past the girl on the Wednesday afternoon the leaves began to turn to gold. She had a sweet smile, tie-dyed blouse, cut-offs, and a pink suitcase by her sandals as she stared at a telephone pole above Georgetown's hip commercial strip. Quinn drove a block before he realized she looked fifteen and school was open. He U-turned. His partner yawned. The girl was still there, staring at a psychedelic poster for a rock band. As they cruised past her, Quinn noticed a van idling across the street. The van driver was a bald man; his eyes stroked the blissful girl.

Two blocks later, Quinn again made a U-turn.

"Go easy," said his partner. "I got an IBM in the trunk!"

Quinn kept his tone even. "Don't worry about that."

"What are you pulling over to the curb for?"

"I want to check her out. She doesn't belong out here now."

Jimmy Duvell sighed as they parked. "Why you always gotta get involved in shit?"

As the patrolmen stepped onto the sidewalk, Quinn smiled at the girl: "Hi."

"Wow, you, too?"

Quinn laughed; so did she. "I'm John. What's your name?"

"Carrie. Like, you're a cop."

"Yeah, but that's just the uniform."

"Oh. OK."

"You got a driver's license, Carrie?"

"Am I driving?"

Jimmy Duvell swore. "She's high as a kite. Forget it. You start this white knight shit, you're on your own!"

He climbed in their cruiser and slammed the door.

"Ca-thunk!" said Carrie. "Doesn't that make a great noise?"

"You are absolutely right."

"That's what pisses my folks off."

"I'll bet. Where are they?"

She shrugged. "Where they always are. You know, you're not a white knight. You're like . . . a jillion colors."

"How did you get so lucky to score Owlsey?"

"I didn't," she said, but before Quinn could figure how else to fish for which hallucinogen she'd taken, she said, "It's windowpane. The best. It's what LSD is all about.

"Win-dow-pannne!" She swirled her arms in a slow-motion arc that widened her eyes. "I just got it! Window-*pane*: you go through the window and there's no *pain!*"

She pondered her revelation while Quinn opened her suitcase, found blouses, jeans, a book of poems by Leonard Cohen, a Walt Disney change purse stuffed with baby-sitter dollar bills and her driver's license. She was sixteen, with an Albany, New York, home address.

"How did you get here, Carrie?"

"I hitched. But like, this isn't San Francisco."

"Almost. Did you come in that van?"

"No. It's yellow."

"Yes, it is." Quinn felt the eyes of his partner and the bald van man boring holes in him as he led Carrie to a call box. The switchboard patched him to Missing Persons, where a Sergeant Madison promised to wade through the stack of bulletins to see if the D.C. cop machine cared about a sixteen-year-old Albany girl who'd hit the road. He told Quinn: *"Be nice to get one back all OK."*

"Why are you putting her in the car?" yelled Jimmy Duvell as Quinn eased Carrie and her luggage into the cruiser's backseat.

"I squared it with a sergeant." Quinn told himself: Keep cool.

"She's some daddy's little girl! You can't be serious about busting her!"

"You're right, that wouldn't do anybody any good." Quinn made a U-turn and parked behind the van. "But get your head up. This guy's got a bad smell."

"Who gives a shit? Let's go!"

"Wow," said Carrie. "You two sound like my mom and dad."

"Oh, shut up!" snapped Jimmy Duvell. "And you, *partner*: don't forget who's the boss!"

Skin tightened on Quinn's head. He lifted the radio mike for a records check on the van.

The radio blared: "Officer needs—officer in trouble! Newton and Seventeenth! Offic—"

The radio cut off.

Quinn thumbed the mike: "Scout Nineteen responding!"

Jimmy Duvell yelled: "That's in three-D! Not our job!"

Quinn punched the gas, hit the siren and lights. Inertia pushed Jimmy Duvell and the girl back in their seats. The van fell out of the cop's mirrors as other cars swerved to get out of the way of the speeding cruiser.

Once, Quinn swore to himself as he skidded around a corner, just once before they can me, I'm gonna be a real cop! Buildings whizzed past his open window. The wind raced through his hair and felt great. He fishtailed past the German embassy.

Jimmy Duvell's feet mashed the floorboards, his hands pushed against the dash. All the blood in his face spun in the cruiser's flashing red lights.

In the backseat, Carrie rolled from side to side, wailing a joyous duet with the siren: *"Wooo! Wooo! Wooo!"*

Quinn felt electrified. It flashed through him that perhaps this was how the stoned girl *wooing* and bouncing around the backseat felt: absolutely *there,* alive in the moment at light speed.

Tires cried, brakes burned as the car careened down Seventeenth Street toward Newton.

An empty wheelchair rolled toward the skidding cruiser.

The two vehicles stopped inches from a collision.

Three men struggled ten feet beyond the empty wheelchair. The uniformed policeman lay sprawled on his back. One of the cop's arms was locked around the neck of a legless fat man sprawled struggling on top of him. The cop's other hand clung to handcuffs snapped on one wrist of a ragged man. The ragged man stretched out from the cop, and his frantic efforts to escape dragged the cop and the legless fat man over the asphalt.

Quinn yelled for Jimmy Duvell to watch the girl and swung the ragged man into a hammerlock, kicked his feet out from under him. Quinn finished cuffing the ragged man, pushed him to the pavement, jerked the legless man off his fellow police officer.

Jimmy Duvell charged out of the cruiser, yelling, "I'm the senior officer!"

The ragged man staggered to his feet: his skull met the senior officer's face. Blood spurted from Jimmy Duvell's nose. Dazed, panicked, the ragged man spun around, ran.

Carrie opened the cruiser's back door smack into the ragged man. He fell like a tree.

"I got you, Fat Paul!" screamed the rescued cop as he pulled paper bundles from the amputee's shirt. "Six months I know you been selling smack and now I got you, you mother—"

A crimson tide flowed through Jimmy Duvell's hands: " '*y 'ose! 'roke 'y 'ucking 'ose!*"

"Wow," said Carrie, "what a rush!"

Sirens screamed closer.

Like a bullet to the brain, Quinn envisioned his chance.

"Thanks," the rescued cop told him. "Fuckin' Fat Paul sucker punched me!"

"That guy," said Quinn, pointing to the ragged man. "Can I have him?"

"He's just the junkie making a buy, he'll cycle through—"

"I'm in two-D, Quinn, I got your junkie, gotta get my partner to the hospital, he's hurt. That's all you tell the brass: we got the junkie who was making a trade for the dope."

"What trade? Man, I saw cash!"

"Yes, but he had stolen property nearby, too, OK? And the girl was never here!"

Quinn stuffed his bleeding partner into the backseat and pushed Carrie in beside him; muscled the handcuffed junkie into the cruiser's front seat, raced around to the driver's seat and tore away, red lights flashing, siren blaring as three other cruisers reached the scene.

The last impression the dealer-busting cop had of his rescuers was a receding feminine voice screaming, *"Woo! Woo! Woo!"*

"Carrie!" yelled Quinn. "We have to turn off the siren!"

"Wow, blood is *so* red. You're getting it all over you. Your mother is going to be *so* pissed."

" '*uck you! 'uck you 'oo, Q'in! My nose!*"

"Carrie," said Quinn, "are you OK?"

"Sure. But it was, like, close."

"I know, I'm sorry I had to drag you along on the officer-in-distress call, but—"

"Like, *so* close! Freaked I would come down at the wrong time, so I dropped a half—"

"You took more acid?" yelled Quinn.

"Do it right or why bother, that's what my dad says. I still got half a tab. You want it?"

"Oh, man," moaned the junkie. His eyes were yellow. "My head is boomin'."

"You want the hit?" Carrie held a tablet over the car seat.

"Acid'll mess up your mind." The junkie drooled.

Quinn tossed the tab out the window. "Just sit back, Carrie."

"Can I be the siren?"

"No. Be the lights."

Quinn raced to a hospital, unloaded Jimmy Duvell and Carrie. Quinn took Jimmy Duvell's belt; the cop's pants sagged under his Sam Brown rig, but his protests drowned in bloody sputters. Quinn looped the belt around the handcuffed junkie's neck and cinched him to the car door.

"Stay!" Quinn led Jimmy Duvell and Carrie into the ER. The injured cop held his bleeding nose with one hand, kept his pants up with the other. The stoned girl drifted through a warm sea.

The admittance nurse said, "Is this going to be a lot of paperwork?"

"I'll handle it!" Quinn steered his charges to the benches. He grabbed the nurse's phone, called Missing Persons. Sergeant Madison agreed to get to the hospital as soon as possible.

Quinn told the nurse, "I need to talk to my partner before you start work on him."

"Go ahead. You got plenty of time."

"No, I don't."

All the other waiting patients had moved away from the

bleeding cop, who told Quinn, "You are 'otally fucked! 'inished!"

"Maybe, but I'm the rookie. What hits me smears my training officer, so you can either sit there and bleed, or you can do what I say and come out of this with good numbers."

Jimmy Duvell's eyes narrowed.

"We were on patrol," said Quinn. "We spotted that junkie carrying a typewriter; you wanted to check it out to see if it was stolen. He dropped it and ran toward Newton Street. You—"

" 'ewton Street's two 'iles from our two-D li—"

"Bosses buy what works. You recovered the typewriter, then we heard the officer-in-trouble call. We had a hunch, rolled on it, saw our suspect involved, and you got hurt in the apprehension. The girl doesn't exist, she was never there."

Jimmy Duvell's bloodied grin was smug. "She isn't 'ere now."

Quinn whirled: Carrie had vanished.

He ran to the admissions desk. To his left were the glass doors, and through them he saw the cruiser where the belted-in junkie was the object of critical, police-brutality stares. Beyond the driveway waited the September city street, where anything could happen. Quinn whirled to his right: Carrie, drifting down a white corridor toward a steel door beyond which glowed bright light.

"This bracelet is so you won't get lost," said Quinn as he handcuffed her to a wooden bench. She stared at a No Smoking sign.

Outside, Quinn used tissues stolen off the nurse's desk to mop the junkie's brow while critical bystanders watched. Quinn whispered, "You got one chance."

The junkie licked his lips. "Say what?"

"Here's what happened. You stole a typewriter—"

"Man, I was only lookin' to score some personal-use skag!"

"—and you were going to trade the typewriter for dope when me and my partner rolled up on you. You dropped the typewriter and ran to Newton, tried to score from Fat Paul—"

"I never seen that cop! Fat Paul, he didn't see him till—"

"If you go with my story, you can sign off on Disturbing or another nowhere charge. You fuck me, I'll write you up for assaulting an officer, resisting arrest, escape, possession—"

"Shit, man! Life's a raw deal."

"So you going to play or pay?"

Yellow eyes met Quinn's: "Where'd I steal the damn typewriter?"

"You're a junkie," said Quinn. "Nobody gives a shit."

Back inside, he saw Carrie still cuffed to the bench, his partner waiting to see a doctor. Quinn flashed Jimmy Duvell a thumbs-up, got a raised middle finger in reply.

But you'll go with it, thought Quinn, you have to.

Three police uniforms marched into the ER. The cop with the gold bar on his collar growled at Quinn, "Talk to me."

A thick man in a bad suit hurried down the corridor toward the ER, and Quinn just knew. "Sir, can I finish up with that detective sergeant while you interview my training officer?"

"Hell," said the lieutenant, "you dealt it, play it out."

Quinn diverted Sergeant Madison toward Carrie. "Her suitcase is in my cruiser. For the record, I found her here, not in the street, then I called you."

"No sweat." Madison gave Quinn his card. "You're closing a case for me and her ass just stole home. We gotta stay in touch."

Carrie stood with her forehead pressed against the white-tiled wall. "The hard is, like, *right there*. Straight into my head."

While from the corner of the ER, Quinn heard, "It's the truth! Good bust. I got the numbers, just ask him! But I ain' never, never no more gonna ride wit' Quinn!"

CHAPTER 3

"You got a new partner," said the desk sergeant when Quinn showed up for duty the next day. "Buck Jones himself, waiting in the lot. No complaints, either: you both bought this ride."

The desk sergeant glanced beyond Quinn, saw a cruiser parked in the district commander's private slot. Out of the car climbed a lieutenant, two captains and a deputy chief.

"Oh, shit!" The desk sergeant straightened his tie. "Get out of here! And get a haircut!"

Buck Jones stood like a pillar of ebony fire in the lot where cruisers waited for their cops. The sleeves of his white uniform shirt bore scars where sergeant's stripes had been. He nailed his eyes on Quinn. "I hear you are a troublemaker."

"I've had my moments."

"Apparently so. Why do you want to be a police officer?"

"I already wrote that essay for my jacket at the academy."

"And if your sorry ass dies in the line of duty, the brass might release your heartfelt words to the newspaper so the citizens will shed a tear and vote our budget. Don't give me a company line, I want what you whisper to the mirror."

Risk it, thought Quinn. "I want to make a little justice."

"Forget that noble shit. Justice is a dream, a nightmare. If you decide you're doing justice, we'll all pay for your arrogance. We are the dogs of law and order, we are the guns of peace."

"You don't want my bullshit, don't give me yours. You want to know why I come out here in the heat, tell me why you do."

The black cop looked toward the horizon. "Honor."

"And you told me to forget justice?"

"Learn this, rookie. Honor is how you do what you can. Everything else is blind luck."

"Where have you been all my life?"

"Right here." Buck led him across the yard. "What did our fearless leader tell you?"

"Where you were standing."

"As if he knew. They harbor some hope for you, they can't get rid of me. We are part of a new tactical program. City-wide patrol. Plus, on the books, you are a white rookie being commanded by a black officer. My, but won't we look like equality on these city streets. And, if you put all your trouble in one can, it's easier to keep it in your sights." Buck nodded to a dented cruiser with a cracked rear window and no air-conditioning: "This is a present from my fans in the department. This is our chariot of fire."

"Hell, the bad guys will fall down laughing when they see us."

Buck reached for the decrepit cruiser's door handle.

"Let me try something," said Quinn.

He found the visiting brass clustered around the desk sergeant. Quinn spotted a familiar face: "Excuse me, Lieutenant, but we've got a problem."

"You have your orders, Officer!" snapped the desk sergeant.

"Yes, sir, and I got no problem with that, but it's not going to look good for the department."

"Talk to me," said the lieutenant.

"You stuck me with Buck Jones—"

"So that's what happened to him," said the lieutenant.

"And public relations–wise, him and me crawling the streets in the oldest, beat-up cruiser—"

"It meets the department's standards!" said the desk sergeant.

"But how will it look—sir?"

The brass turned to the desk sergeant for the answer.

Ten minutes later, Quinn jangled keys in front of Buck and led him to the newest cruiser.

They rode the city. Broke up two armed robberies. Arrested three men for wife abuse and made charges stick once. Locked up a rapist with acceptable arrest injuries. Busted four nickel-bag heroin dealers. Chased down a stolen car. Rolled on three murders, and at one, tripped up a witness in a street interview that let homicide detectives close the case. A dozen times, half by following requests from Sergeant Madison, Quinn pulled teenage runaways off the street.

Buck took Quinn to Jake the Jar, an ebony slug who never crawled out of his clapboard row house a pistol shot from the Capitol dome. Buck and Quinn sat across from Jake in his yellow kitchen, where the cabbage boiling on the stove failed to hide the stench of fermenting moonshine.

"Elma!" yelled Jake. A woman shrunken inside her coffee skin eased closer. Quinn saw her bruised and bloodshot eye. "Elma! Fetch the boys a glass o' cold beer."

"We aren't here for hospitality," said Buck.

"You come to Jake, 'cause I knows what's what and who's who." Jake winked at Quinn. "Them crime boys in the street think I got half your force iced to keep from bein' busted, they thinks that's why you guys drop in here all the time and never take Jake out in no handcuffs."

"This is the Sixties," said Quinn, who'd been given the pass to speak his mind from Buck. "Nobody believes you make enough money off homebrew to fix more than the beat cop."

"I loans a little cash to those who needs it. I'm just a poor man trying to get by in—"

"Shut up, Jake." Buck sounded almost pleasant.

"Ain't you heard?" said Jake. "We in new times. We got us a *revolution,* no more . . . pigs comin' into the black community—"

"You being black only proves that God's got a twisted sense of humor," said Buck, the heat of the kitchen baking a sweat on his ebony skin. "And you got zero community."

Then he squeezed Jake until the slug gave up a burglar who'd trashed eight middle-class homes. When they left, Elma closed the door behind them.

One night Buck steered their cruiser to a rubbled block

between Capitol Hill and the White House. Buck parked under the streetlight. A dozen skirted figures melted into the shadows. He rolled down his window, lit a cigarette. Beeped the horn.

They came in turn to the open window of the cruiser, ebony butterflies drawn to the glow of Buck's cigarette, their heels clicking on the sidewalk, their perfume flowing into the car as they gave Buck names and *don't know*'s, studied Quinn's face. Eventually, a willowy beauty with flowing locks leaned on Buck's door and said, "Hey, baby, how you doin'? I missed you."

"Madeline, why are you working this low-rent strip? You should be in Georgetown."

"Don't I know it! *Oooo!* Your new partner here looks just like a tall Steve McQueen. If only he looked like Warren Beatty! Wasn't Warren completely divine in *Bonnie and*—"

"Madeline—"

"Sure, I know, forget about it, someone like me looking for stars in the night."

"Madeline!" said Buck. "Somebody's rolling johns. You heard anything about anything?"

The crimson lips frowned. "No. Well, that awful Dwayne Rogers is back. He's a brute."

Buck sent her back to the shadows to complain about how Mr. Po-lice had given her a rough time for not having a valid ID. As he grilled the next prostitute, Buck groused about Madeline's lack of papers to bolster the lie.

Buck pulled the cruiser away from the curb, already talking about ways to track Dwayne Rogers. Then Buck said, "Tell me about this strip, how it stands up next to the stroll on Fourteenth."

Quinn shrugged. "The women back there were all black. On Fourteenth, you get a mix."

"There ain't no mix back there. There ain't no women either."

Quinn stared at the block vanishing in the electric night. His partner laughed; told him to learn to look at the size of hands, at throats for Adam's apples. "Sin gets specialized in this town. And not much is like it looks."

One day after their shift, the older cop drove Quinn through the city's fading light to the Maryland–D.C. border near the old Greek and Jewish blue-collar neighborhood of Silver Spring. Buck spun a number on a pay phone.

"Let it ring twice, hang up," said Buck, doing so. "Somebody answers, hang up. Call right back, ring three, hang up."

"Then what?"

"Get in the car."

They drove past a closed soft-ice-cream store guarded by twin statues of polar bears to Fort Stevens, one of 461 memorial sites and parks in Washington, D.C., a grassy knoll near the urban Maryland–D.C. border where Abe Lincoln in his stovepipe hat had stood to look out at Confederate soldiers. Commuter traffic whizzes past the few remaining battlements of the "fort"; its horseshoe trench hides visitors from the eyes of the city.

The acned man waiting for them with his back against those earthworks wore a buckskin coat, blue jeans and cowboy boots. His blue eyes drilled Quinn: "Whathafuck! Who's he?"

"Easy, Alvin. John here's my right arm, so he has to know at least one master criminal, and you, Alvin, are the master."

Cowboy boots shuffled in the snow. "Don't shit me, Jones. Whathafuck, I been good to you!"

"Alvin knows chop shops and hot-deal used-car lots from Atlanta to Boston," said Buck. "He gets a customer's order, pops a car, delivers the machine, gets his cash and catches the bus home."

"Cut this 'all the news' jazz! My biz is my biz, and you ain't the only law game in Dodge!"

"No, now there's John Quinn here, and you're his bitch, too."

"You can't pimp me out!"

Buck ignored the crook to lecture Quinn. "Alvin here lives with his mom and they live real well. Not like Al Capone, but enough for the IRS to wonder. Plus, he's been a wheelman and mechanic for hijack crews up and down the Jersey Turnpike—"

"I never give up guys like that! Whathafuck, man! Dead, I do nobody no good."

"Yeah, it'd be a shame if it got out all of us were friends." Buck flashed a greenback in front of the pockmarked cowboy. "Yo, Alvin, we're just tugging your chain a little. Here's a ten spot from John and me. Just for coming out in the cold."

The bill waved in the evening chill, until Alvin plucked it for his pocket.

"You guys: blackmailing my ass, ready to sell me out to the feds or the wise guys, winking at my scores, slipping me chump change, pimping me. . . . You're supposed to be the good guys!"

Quinn shrugged: "Whathafuck."

THAT NOVEMBER'S ELECTION was Quinn's first chance to vote. He pulled the lever for Nixon—a vote that would have made his father smile. Besides, Quinn believed Nixon truly had a "secret plan" to end the war in Vietnam.

Nixon won.

Quinn pulled crowd duty for Nixon's January 1969 inauguration and saw nothing of the chilly event but a sea of bundled bodies. Though, from a bystander's transistor radio, he heard Nixon proclaim: "When we listen to the better angels of our nature, we find that they celebrate the simple things, and the basic things, such as goodness, decency, love, kindness."

In April, Buck took two weeks' leave to move his mother-in-law back down to North Carolina: "Gonna miss the quarrelsome old gal. Her gone from the house, our kids wrapped up in teenage jive, me and the wife gonna have a lot of the got-nothing-to-say's around our dinner table."

Buck's leave coincided with their cruiser's servicing. They put Quinn on solo foot patrol.

Spring filled Washington with a clean zest. Walking a

downtown beat, Quinn directed lost tourists, waved to a
school bus and pretended not to see the middle-finger response he got from a boy in the back row. A passing car
with its windows rolled down tossed him a radio blast of
"Aquarius/Let the Sun Shine." Quinn hummed the refrain
as he walked toward Fourteenth Street's sinners' strip. He
breathed deep, stepped easy and smiled at life.

Then he saw the Cadillac.

The grill of that gold Detroit money machine hung over
the corner's curb; its taillights stopped just short of the awning for a strip club called The Silver Mirror. Quinn saw the
fire hydrant blocked by the car and the wiry black man in a
sports jacket sitting on the Caddy, his pencil-mustached face
turned up to the spring sun.

Too nice a day for trouble. Quinn put a smile in his voice
when he walked up to the man on the Caddy. "Excuse me,
sir. Is this your car?"

Mr. Mustache opened his eyes slow and easy. "Say what?"

"This Caddy—is it yours?"

"Why the hell do you care?"

"Let's try this again. I'm a cop, you're sitting on a car
parked in front of a fire hydrant."

Mr. Mustache winked at Quinn. "But that ain't all, so you
best just walk on."

"Get the fuck off there."

Mr. Mustache's eyes flashed as he obeyed Quinn's order.

"What's your name?"

"You forgot to say *boy*."

"Are you pushing the direction you want to go?"

"David Strait. *Mister* David Strait."

The D.C. driver's license Quinn demanded matched that
name.

"Is this your car?"

"No, man, I'm just watching it."

"Where's the owner?"

"In the club."

Maybe because it was an invigorating spring day, maybe
because Quinn sensed that he was dealing with an attitude

powered from outside the insolent man in front of him, maybe because *whathafuck*, Quinn took his badge past the street, stalked inside The Silver Mirror.

The bartender polishing glasses didn't look up. "We're closed."

Quinn said, "I'm looking for the owner of the gold Caddy."

The bartender flicked his gaze into the blue shadows where five shapes huddled around a table. Two of the shapes were women. The men with them shifted to face the cop by the bar.

Quinn caught a pinky ring sparkle as one man moved. Quinn saw his face, an absolutely smooth countenance, a head that had lost its hair before its due, a flat, emotionless face with hooded, dull eyes that had lost all time. Ringman glanced to the man who sat opposite him, a jovial guy. Ringman scraped his chair away from the table—

But the third man stopped him by raising a shadowed hand. The third man sat between Ringman and the jovial guy. A red and white Pall Mall pack lay crumpled like an origami sculpture beside the third man's drink. Quinn caught only a blue-shadowed impression of his heart-shaped jowly face and the red coal of a cigarette.

The shadowed man sent Mr. Jovial to deal with the cop. "Hey, how you doin'? Ricky, get my friend here a beer."

"Do you own the Caddy parked in front of a fire hydrant?"

"Forget about it." Mr. Jovial flashed a gold Metropolitan Police badge. "Billy Bruce. Drink your beer, go keep the Afros in line. This in here is covered."

"Covered?"

"Nothing happening, just a little ongoing investigation work."

"What squad?"

Detective Bruce lost his jovial face. "Me, I'm with Morals, but that don't matter: my gold shield says you gotta mosey when I say, I say that now is when."

Quinn felt the chill off a beer the bartender placed beside him. He smelled Detective Billy Bruce's leather aftershave.

Back in the indigo smoke, Quinn saw the glow of embers.

As he walked out, Quinn heard chuckles and a hacking cough.

"You get what you were after?" said David Strait when Quinn reentered the sunlight.

Quinn filled out a ticket and stuck it under the wiper blades.

"You're kidding!" said Strait.

Quinn handed Strait a second ticket.

"What the—you giving me a ticket for *loitering*?"

"Have a nice day, Mr. Strait." Quinn walked on.

Sunday, when he was off duty and knew a certain sergeant in Administration would be working, Quinn showed up at headquarters.

"Do me a favor? I want to check on two citations."

The sergeant tapped keys on the department's brand-new computer. "They've been cleared."

"Cleared? Paid?"

"No, Administrative. You could have done it, so could have any traffic clerk."

Quinn got a printout of this trivial bureaucratic maneuver, and got the sergeant to run the owner of the Caddy: Joseph R. Nezneck, a D.C. address.

Monday, Quinn ran Joseph R. Nezneck through Records: arrests dating back to Prohibition, jail bits for petty theft, a murder beef with a jury acquittal. In 1963, Nezneck was arrested in suburban Maryland for illegal gambling; local prosecutors stetted the case—postponed it indefinitely. A 1965 arrest for illegal gambling equipment ended in a mistrial. In 1967, Las Vegas police notified D.C. badges that they'd detained Nezneck for "investigation."

"Hello, asshole," said Quinn. He stuck the report on Nezneck in an unmarked file with a photocopy of his citation stubs from his ticket book, and the computer report showing those citations cleared. He kept the file in his squad room locker and a duplicate file at home.

Quinn ran David Strait through Records: the mustachioed man came up clean of convictions, but had two nol-pros

arrests, both for assault, and a supplemental charge, also
dropped, for carrying a prohibited device that coded out as
a switchblade.

On Tuesday, Quinn pulled photostats of Joseph R. Nezneck's driver's license.

Joseph Nezneck. Born September 13, 1915. Five feet eight,
174 pounds. A listed home address on 4312 New Mexico
Avenue, Apartment 9, an expensive apartment building
called the Colonial. The blurred photocopy showed a hollow
grin on a handsome face, thinning hair. The eyes were black
dots.

Wednesday night, it rained.

Quinn knocked on the door of the apartment across from
his, where a pudgy grad student who'd nodded her way into
his acquaintanceship lived. She let him use her manual typewriter; made him coffee while he tapped out a report of the
Caddy, the tickets, a paragraph detailing Detective William
Bruce ordering a foot patrol officer to ignore criminal offenses. He signed his report, tucked it into a manila envelope
along with photocopies of the citations, their clearance, and
the Records runs on David Strait and Joseph Nezneck.

Rain beat down on the grad student's windows. She sat
on the couch reading *I've Been Down So Long, Looks Like
up to Me*. Quinn went to the bathroom, found a flat pack of
birth control pills on the sink. When he came back to the
living room, he noticed that his hostess wasn't wearing (anymore) a bra under her sweatshirt. "Mr. Tambourine Man"
played on her stereo. She said something, he said something
back, she laughed, so did he. She fingered the manila envelope. Her hair was close to his face. Their fingers brushed
and she didn't pull away. When she turned her face up, her
eyes were closed. He kissed her, slid his hand up under her
sweatshirt. She said, "Why not, it's raining."

Thursday morning, his badge polished, his shoes spit-
shined, Quinn strode down headquarter's tiled corridor to the
fogged-glass door labeled INTERNAL AFFAIRS DIVISION.

Quinn marched into IAD, closed the door, let the two faceless detectives playing cribbage skim past his eyes, noted a

third detective on the phone, swung his gaze over the squad room.

In the shift commander's office, seated behind a desk with a nameplate that read LT. C. GODSICK, sat a man with an absolutely smooth countenance, a head that had lost its hair before its due, a flat, emotionless face with hooded, dull eyes that had lost all time. On the little finger of his left hand glistened a diamond pinky ring.

Godsick's hooded eyes saw Officer John Quinn standing at the rail of his Internal Affairs policers-of-the-police squad. Godsick's lips curled in something like a smile.

"Hey!" Quinn heard one of the faceless detectives say. "You need something?"

"Sorry," said Quinn, "wrong door."

And he walked out, the manila envelope burning in his hand.

CHAPTER 4

One Friday in May 1969, Quinn caught the bus home to Lorain, Ohio, to visit his mom and bring his motorcycle back to D.C. Saturday afternoon he hurried downstairs to get to a send-off party for a drafted buddy who was on the path to a land mine in Vietnam. Quinn's mom stopped him by the front door: "There's people here I got for you to meet."

On their living room couch sat a woman with dark hair. A small boy in blue jeans and a clean shirt pushed a toy truck on the carpet near her shoes.

"That poor woman goes to our church, she hears my son is a big-shot policeman in D.C.—"

"Mom!"

"Mrs. Gennie Dawson. Her husband ran off after Korea. She has a daughter and a cute little guy for a grandchild—

and she's younger than me! They got trouble, I don't know what, down there in Washington, godforsaken place. Why my own son would want to—"

"None of the other departments hired me."

"So go in there. Maybe all you can do is listen. But maybe you can do some good."

"You already made her a bunch of promises, didn't you?"

His mother shrugged.

Quinn sighed. Followed her into the living room where he played as a child. He and Mrs. Dawson let Quinn's mother direct them through a skit of shaking hands. The boy watched the adult ritual from the floor near Mrs. Dawson's ungrand-motherly sleek legs.

She leaned down. "Dion, say hello to Detective Quinn. You know how to shake his hand."

The boy stood frozen in front of the man-giant reflected in his eyes.

"That's OK," said Quinn, letting his untouched hand fall back to his side. "Guys don't always need to shake, do they, Dion?"

Nothing.

Quinn squatted to eye level with the boy. "Are you really nine years old?"

The kid wouldn't fall for it.

His grandmother cut in. "He's four."

"Know what, Dion?" said Quinn's mother. "If it's OK with your grandmother, would you help me find some cook-ies in the kitchen?"

As Quinn's mother led the boy into her sunlit kitchen, he heard her say, "I always bake chocolate chip and peanut but-ter when my Johnny comes home because they're his fav—"

That door closed.

Quinn sat across from the woman with bloodshot eyes and silver streaks in her dark hair.

"I know you're busy," said Mrs. Dawson, "so straight to it: my Pat is missing. She lives in Washington. It's been three days."

"Three days isn't—"

"It's too much. Pat calls us every day. Sometimes twice a day. Maybe she's late one day a month, but nothing for three days? Never. So she's lost or in trouble or . . ."

"How old is she?"

"Twenty-five last January."

"She's not a kid, then. Maybe she, you know . . ."

"I know too much." Gennie Dawson's hands shook as she lit a cigarette. "I always know too much and not enough. When you're a parent, you walk around scared to death that you screwed up and then your kid is going to pay. My daughter, Pat, she's no angel. She never was. My fault, probably."

"No," soothed John, sneaking a look at his watch, reminding himself to go easy at the party, that he had a brutal ride tomorrow. "Kids are somebody besides who their parents made them."

"I got pictures of her."

Quinn took the snapshots from the woman's shaking hand and forgot about the party.

Pat Dawson: great hair, a wide mouth and big eyes at her high school graduation. A Polaroid of her in a bikini mimicking a *Playboy* cheesecake spread, heavy breasts and long legs. A shot of her on a balcony, a cityscape spread out behind her. In every picture, even when holding a happy baby, Pat dazzled the camera's cold lens.

"She's not bad," said her mother. "She's half-smart, half-lucky. Wants it all and that's too much for people like us. She can waltz into any room but she can't read the writing on the wall, especially if it's not what she wants to believe."

The mother's smile was wistful. "She has violet eyes."

"What about a husband?"

"No." Mrs. Dawson lit one cigarette off the ember of another. "Never did, so I guess it's not quite like mother, like daughter. Fred Ellis was Dion's father. Big deal in high school, big nothing as soon as they handed him that diploma, but Pat couldn't see that, even after she'd been to New York. Or maybe it was pity. Nostalgia. Doesn't matter. She wouldn't have married him even if he'd had the decency to ask, which he didn't. Two years ago, he wrapped his car around a telephone pole, left nothing to nobody. We didn't even go to the funeral. God bless her for not having an abortion or giving away my little guy, but . . ."

"But it's hard."

"You have no idea."

"Maybe she needs a break from everything, so she just hasn't called."

"Hardest thing she ever did was to leave Dion home with me. She said she could kiss the devil easier than she can kiss him good-bye. That's her half-good part. The half-smart part is her believing she can do better than what she's got. Make it big or strike it rich or get way ahead and get enough to find some damn better life. Scoop up Dion and live happily ever after. She's half lucky enough to . . . but she'll be damned if she doesn't want it all. You know what I mean."

"Sorry," said Quinn. "I don't know her."

"Sure you do. You just never met."

"Where does she work?"

"My daughter makes her living off men."

"Excuse me?"

"I know what I know. She's a model, but that doesn't pay, not in Washington. New York, maybe, but she didn't make it there, no more than a million other girls. She says Washington is a smaller town and . . .

"Don't make me say words I don't want to. She's got a nice apartment and a car, lots of clothes. Flies places. Calls us. Postcards. Envelopes with money for Dion. She's got a hundred men she knows and not one boyfriend. Don't make me put out words I don't let myself think."

"Mrs. Dawson, don't tell my mother, but these days . . . it's not like when you were—"

"You think people didn't screw around before you kids and all your 'free love'?"

"It was a different world before penicillin and the Pill."

"Maybe those were the good old days. But you're a man."

"Women are equal."

"Are we?" The mother's smile held no joy. "Maybe we're equal, but we're not the same."

Quinn shrugged.

"You got a lot to learn about women. Forget about your free love. We aren't talking about love. When she came home for Christmas, all those damn fancy presents, Pat told me if she ever . . . wasn't there, something bad might have happened, and I should call the police."

"You said it's been only three days. Have you done anything?"

"I went downtown here to the cops. Men still like helping me. I filed a missing person's report that they sent to Washington."

"Then what you have to do is wait."

"If I wait, then waiting is all I got. Don't treat me like that. Don't let Pat get treated like that, even if she's . . . You'd understand if you were a parent."

"All I am is a beat cop. Not a detective—yet."

"I didn't know your mother, my neighbor does; she goes to church, not me. She knew about Pat, so I came to you. Whatever you can do, whatever you want—"

"No, hey, it's OK. I'll try, see what I can do. But before I go back, I bet Pat will call you and Dion, and we'll all forget about this. It'll be OK."

"Yes, that's just how things always are, right? All OK." They smiled at each other and pretended not to notice that Mrs. Dawson had to drop her cigarette to keep from getting burned.

She gave him a set of her daughter's keys and called for her grandson.

"I've got some postcards in the car you might want to look at," Mrs. Dawson told Quinn as her grandson led Quinn's mother toward them.

Dion, who was four *not* nine, turned his face up to Quinn. "Are you really a policeman?"

Quinn let the boy touch the silver badge in his leather folder.

"Wow!"

Quinn felt huge.

"Are you gonna get to go see my mom?"

The two women shared a look, then stared at Quinn.

"Maybe," he said. "Tell you what: I'll try."

"Really?"

"Sure. Really."

"She loves me."

"I know. She'd have to."

"Tell her to come home, OK?"

Quinn found no help in the women's faces.

"Please?"

"OK," said Quinn.

"Promise?"

"Promise."

Dion beamed. "She'll have to. You're a policeman."

His grandmother said, "We have to go now."

Quinn moved with them toward the door. Dion enfolded the policeman's Mr. Pointer finger with a butterfly grasp and walked beside him like that all the way to Grandma's car. He waved and waved and waved as they drove away, as the policeman stood on the sidewalk, his finger aglow.

Sunday morning Quinn left before dawn, his duffel bag and a lunch pail of his mother's cooking strapped on the Harley-Davidson motorcycle. Quinn zipped himself into his father's World War II leather jacket. He wore wrap-around sunglasses and no helmet; he was never, ever going to crack up. In his duffel were postcards from Pat Dawson to her son from Chicago, Texas, New York, the Bahamas and Miami, places Quinn had never been.

Been yet, he told himself as the Ohio Expressway rumbled beneath his two wheels. He was returning to a place where he was somebody besides his father's son, on his way back to the real world, a badge in his shirt pocket and the wind blowing free in his hair.

Pat Dawson had to be OK, woman like that, kid like that. Might have some trouble, but her mother was wrong about the bad stuff. Kid like that. Woman like that. God, how she shone in those pictures! Couple years older—so what? Got a kid—but a great kid, so what? So what, so nothing, so just a fast favor, a promise. Can't expect anything even when it turns out OK. Like the mother said, there were a million girls who had all the . . . *promise* that a man could wish. One of them would look at an Ohio boy with a badge and a bike, and see such promise, too. All Quinn had to do was do it all right. That's the great promise: a man works it right, puts it all on the line, proves it, then he gets the great, right woman.

Quinn roared toward the capital of his country, his motorcycle throbbing against his loins.

Monday he and Buck were on the four-to-midnight shift. Quinn called Pat Dawson's number: nobody home. He called her mother. Dion answered on the first ring but Gramma grabbed the phone: her daughter hadn't phoned. He drove to Pat Dawson's apartment building. A confident look let him stroll past the security guard and knock on Pat's seventh-floor door.

Nobody answered. He entered the apartment of pink and yellow. The air was stale.

A telephone and answering machine set on a table next to the couch. Only rich people and businesses can afford answering machines, thought Quinn. How come she's got one? The answering machine counter showed fifteen messages. Hang-ups, a male-mumbled "Wrong number," four "Call as soon as . . ." messages from Mrs. Dawson in Lorain. And between beeps, Dion: "Hi, Mom! I miss you! Where are you? Mommy, how come you haven't called today? I love you, Mommy, honest! Please come home now, OK? . . . Mom, it's me. Please call. You promised."

Promise, thought Quinn. Only that.

Dust covered the TV screen, her stereo. Quinn scanned the few record albums: bossa nova junk, Sinatra, Elvis's sound track from *Blue Hawaii*, Tony Bennett—older-generation stuff except for a worn greatest-hits album from Dion and the Belmonts.

Fashion magazines. Paperback novels, romances, a Le Carré spy thriller. A desk held paid receipts from the phone company and stores. The bottom drawer sheltered two scrapbooks with carefully mounted photos: Dion in the hospital nursery. Dion in his mother's arms as she carried him into a house. Dion's first birthday, Mom and Grandmom and two smiling strangers. Preschool playground, on the potty, in the tub. Dion in front of the camera held so often by someone who wasn't Mom. Quinn slid the scrapbook back in its drawer. He found a portfolio haphazardly stuffed with photos of her—including one studio nude shot. A few clippings of her as an anonymous model for a local department store cut from the *Post* and the *Star*. He found a picture of her and a blond woman, smoking at a restaurant or bar booth, smiling for the camera. Something made him add that snapshot to his Pat Dawson collection. He ached to take the nude picture. But he didn't.

He found no pictures of men.

Her bedroom was tidy. Clothes jammed her closet, filled the bureaus. Her bras and panties were lacy, black and white and red. He found a black garter belt that looked *nothing* like the foundation wear his mother had abandoned when panty hose was invented. Pat Dawson's bedside table drawer had a dozen condoms, a squeezed tube of KY jelly, and a jar of pills Quinn was sure were uppers and downers. Liquor bottles stood sentry on a cart.

All that plus an answering machine: "Ah, shit."

In her bathroom, amid drawers of makeup, he found a stack of birth control packets—including one with half its pills poked out.

The pudgy graduate student told Quinn that she never left home without her contraceptive pills; she'd told him that to confirm her power, not so he wouldn't worry about unwanted babies.

Pat Dawson's dishes looked unused. Her refrigerator held beer, wine, cheese, spoiled milk.

He found an envelope with $1,753 hidden in her hall closet.

She had five empty suitcases.

He found a palm-sized, pink, plastic-covered address book stuffed inside cheerleader sneakers. *The book is one of those items you always mean to throw away but don't. Why'd you use it and hide it?* Quinn took it. In the lobby, he badged the security guard.

"You finally after her for them parking tickets?"

"Something like that. You seen her lately?"

"Naw—and I notice."

"Anybody been by looking for her?"

"You'd think so, all the men she's got. But nobody's asked about her—until you."

"She have a parking place? A car?"

"Sixty-seven Camaro, blue. Cool. Ain't here."

"What's she like?"

"You mean besides us both wanting to fuck her eyes out?"

So that's all you know. Quinn passed the guard his department business card. "You see her again, call me. Try me at home, too, it's on the back."

By 10 P.M., he and Buck were cooling their heels in the precinct after they'd collared a burglar. The detectives wanted the arresting officers to stick around, so around they stuck.

Quinn sat at a detective's empty desk, spun around in the swivel chair and decided that felt just fine. He fished Pat Dawson's pink book from his back pocket, matched names and addresses to its local phone numbers and initials.

Two *A* notations gave him names and addresses that meant nothing to him. "Heidi" turned out to be Heidi Ryker, with an address near Foggy Bottom, the trendy neighborhood close to the State Department. The first number for "Mel"— the one next to a penned star—was registered to Melvin Klise, a business phone on K Street in his name, and his second number was registered to the American Association for Justice. *Knowing somebody who worked for a group like that, no matter what she did, maybe she had a warm spot in her heart for guys who carried badges. P* had three listings: The first number was for the Freedom Wig and Beauty Shop, Inc., on F Street in the "old" downtown, the kind of place a model probably would know. The second two numbers were listed to women, the first one to Heidi Ryker (again), the

second one to Marjorie Bell, both phones located at 4312
New Mexico Avenue, Unit 9.

Two minutes later, Quinn stood at his locker, staring into
his file that confirmed 4312 New Mexico Avenue, Apartment
9, was the driver's license address for Joseph Nezneck.

When he checked off duty at midnight, he called Pat Dawson's number.

"Hi!" said her message machine. Her voice was a smooth
tenor, not cutesy, not coy, not anything but a warmth he
couldn't touch. "Sorry I'm not here, but you can leave a
message."

Quinn hung up.

Eight A.M., sharp, he was in the Missing Persons office.

Sergeant Madison had circles under his eyes. Said, "I'm
crazy for your help."

"Why?"

"Two eleven-year-old girls, regular families, coming home
from Catholic school, only they never get there. Maybe they
ran away to the hippie streets you watch."

Madison showed Quinn two photos of smiling innocence.

"Can you peel a hungry eye for them? Today? I got a sick
feeling about this."

"Do what I can," said Quinn, "but I need a favor."

"Like you said, do what I can."

"You got a report on a Patricia Dawson?"

"Her again? You and Buck roust her for hooking or
what?"

"Why do you ask that?"

" 'Cause a Morals detective asked if we had a file on Dawson. I'd called her apartment, checked the hospitals, no
big—"

"What vice cop?"

"A sergeant name Bruce, Billy Bruce."

Quinn went cold. "What did he want?"

"Said he was checking a lead. Hotshot read the file, shot
the shit, left." Madison pulled a brown case jacket out of the
stack on his desk. The first page in it was the referral Tele-

type from Lorain, the second and last page was the D.C. paperwork.

"Do me a favor," said Quinn. "Work this for real."

"I got two kids freshly gone; that woman is a consenting adult who hasn't called her mother. You figure the priorities."

"OK, but . . . you get anything on Dawson, call me right away!"

The detective sergeant frowned at the young cop, but nodded.

"And do me a favor: don't tell Bruce anything about anything, especially about me being here for Pat Dawson!"

None of the impound lots Quinn called had Pat Dawson's Camaro.

Traffic Enforcement showed no citations written on the Camaro: if Pat Dawson had gotten D.C. traffic tickets like the security guard wisecracked, they'd been cleared.

D.C. Motor Vehicles said Pat Dawson didn't have a Washington driver's license. On a hunch, Quinn called the Ohio state police: Pat was a licensed driver in the Buckeye State, with her residence listed as her mother's Lorain address.

Home, thought Quinn. All these years getting away from it, New York, D.C., you still won't give up that link. Not just for Dion, either. Hungry for someplace better, you still refuse to surrender the last evidence of where you came from. *I know how you feel.*

The auto squad detective who'd taught Quinn to hot-wire cars and pick locks agreed to put the Camaro on the alert sheet.

Outside, Quinn straddled his bike, checked his watch through the lenses of his sunglasses: ten-thirty. Take Buck aside when they signed on at four, give it all up: The Silver Mirror, the two cops in the cigarette smoke, Nezneck, Pat Dawson and Dion and the promise. But until then . . . He felt a little boy's warm grasp around his trigger finger. *Kick the bike to life and go.*

*   *   *

"WHATHAFUCK!" WHINED ALVIN when Quinn joined him in Fort Stevens's trench. "You woke me up. Where's Buck?"

"You got me on this," said Quinn.

Alvin wore a Hawaiian shirt, jeans, cowboy boots. He glared at Quinn's twenty-dollar bill.

"I'm looking for a car. A blue sixty-seven Camaro."

Three children from a nearby day-care skipped beneath dark clouds on the top of the earthworks. With instincts that have kept mankind from extinction, the four-year-olds ran back toward their teacher the moment they saw the two men standing below them.

Alvin shrugged. "Why come to me?"

"That's a prime machine. If a pro popped one, you should know. Or you can find out."

"You looking to make a bust?"

"No. Just looking for where it is, where it's been."

They heard the teacher call to the kids. They heard the hum of traffic, noise muted by the grassy knoll and the earth battleworks.

"Sixty-seven Camaro." Alvin rocked on his boot heels. "Choice machine."

And you're the right man, the man who knows. "Give."

"Whathafuck. Sixty-seven Camaro, blue, mag wheels, pussy automatic tranny." Alvin grinned. "I popped one this weekend."

Quinn rattled off Pat Dawson's license plate number.

"Denomination numbers on green is all I remember."

"What did you do with the car?"

"This was a gimme, an insurance job. A guy calls a guy calls a guy calls me, tells me where and when I can find a sweet machine good to go. I do the pickup, the plate switch hit a chop shop up Delaware way, then I'm on the bus with a pocket of green."

Pat Dawson knew lots of men, her mother said. One of them could help her scam the insurance, front her the cash from the stolen car settlement. *But she had cash hidden in her closet.*

"Where'd you pick it up?"

"Driveway of a shack in the woods. Nowheresville, P.G."

Prince Georges County, a Maryland suburb of D.C. Quinn coaxed a better description of the house, its road and an address number: 23227.

"Who called you to pick it up?"

"I don't give up my business over one lousy car! Fo'get about it. I'm going back to bed."

Forty-five minutes later, Quinn was lost in the rural bedroom lanes of P.G. A delivery van driver, wary of the outlaw biker, kept his foot on the gas pedal as he gave Quinn directions to a gravel road. A battered mailbox at the gravel road's entrance bore the number 23227. Quinn parked the Electra Glide when he saw the outline of a house through the trees.

He crept across somebody else's land. From the trees, the house looked quiet: one story, peeling white paint. No garage. No cars. Door shut. Shades drawn. No dogs barking.

P.G. County. Out here, his badge was no good. Trespass on private property put him over the line of the law.

Pat Dawson. Smiling Detective Sergeant Billy Bruce. Joe Nezneck.

Hell, thought Quinn, no law against knocking on the door. He walked out of the trees.

CHAPTER 5

No one answered Quinn's knock. The door was locked tight.

Gravel crunched underfoot as he made his way around to the back of the house. Shades covered each and every damn window. A screened back door creaked when he opened it. He knocked on the inside door—just in case.

Deserted, he reasoned. One could presume—one could argue—that a reasonably prudent officer of the law in search of an officially missing individual whose vehicle may have been at the deserted premises could, acting under exigencies including that said missing person could be incapacitated and struck mute, legally enter said premises for the purpose of—

If you're going to do it, *do it.*

The knob on the back door turned. Quinn pushed it gently—

The door froze. Through the half-inch gap, Quinn saw the steel line of a hook-and-eye lock.

Go home. Or go all the way.

A twig through the crack, and the hook came out of the eye, the door swung open.

A kitchen, rust-spattered linoleum and a wheezing refrigerator, a rickety kitchen table.

A stench of burned metal, cold ham and cabbage.

Kitchen sink in front of a blanket-draped window, the cabinet doors underneath the sink yawning wide open, a wrench and a screwdriver on the floor in front of their maw.

Flies buzzed past Quinn. He waved his arm and they buzzed him again. Forget about them.

"Hello?" He imagined facing the polygraph doctor, saying, "Yes, I did verbally attempt to announce that I was entering . . ."

Leave the flies in the kitchen. Slide down the hall toward the living room.

Past a half-open door, see a dirty sink below a mirror— bathroom, must be empty.

Past an open bedroom door—couple of cots, some boxes, closet closed, nobody there.

Living room—a card table, folding chairs, a radio, a fireplace filled with charred junk.

Nobody here but me. Quinn relaxed.

He used his pen to poke through the fireplace ashes. A blackened husk of paper crumpled to cinder dust as he moved it aside. He stirred up a brass clasp: Purse? Pocketbook? His pen tapped a bump on the fireplace iron. Quinn gently blew away a layer of gray powdery ash, found a glob of melted plastic the size of a half dollar melted onto the black iron. Colors smeared through the plastic's gray glob, colors and a wavy line of blue letters: *OHI*.

Writing on plastic? Something tossed into a fire.

No: writing on paper *covered* in plastic. Laminated—driver's license.

OHI: what was left of *OHIO*. Pat Dawson's home state. Where Dion waited. Where I'm from. Why did you burn up the identity you'd clung to through everything else?

Walking back toward the kitchen, he pushed the bathroom door all the way open.

What had been a white room seemed rust splattered.

What had been a white bathtub was a darkly smeared trough. A filthy ax leaned against the cold tub. A machete lay balanced across the curved sides of the tub. Rusted gardening shears waited on a dark-splattered floor, beside a chainsaw and a plastic jug labeled GAS.

The tub was empty of everything but *damp brownish crusts*, lumps of . . .

Flies, flies buzzing everywhere.

An aluminum tub sat near the bolted-to-the-floor bathtub, the kind of portable carryall filled with potatoes or sweet white corn at roadside stands on the road back to Washington from Maryland's Eastern Shore ocean resorts. That aluminum tub was smeared brown; its handles dangled above scars on the bathroom linoleum, lines pulled through maroon stains like tattoos on a Martian's skin.

The drag lines on the bathroom floor led to the hall, down that gouged wood to the kitchen. Patchwork, overlapping, multiple trip scars zigzagging across the kitchen floor to the sink above the yawning-open cupboard doors. Tools on the floor where someone had been working on the garbage disposal.

Flies, stench of sour meat—and a burned-out electric motor.

Kitchen sink. Clean aluminum, centered by its black hole drain.

Some rope or thread fibers curled from the sink down into that black hole, something that hadn't quite cycled through before the disposal motor worked so hard it burned up.

With his fingers, Quinn tugged on the thin, matted fibers.

He pulled hard. Out of the black hole came a long mat of ebony hair rooted in a flap of flesh that Quinn's whole being knew was the last of Pat Dawson.

Quinn screamed. Dropped the hair and scalp, his hand shaking like it was on fire. He staggered, bumped the rickety table and stumbled, slid along the wall to the corner, trapped in the corner, and he threw up.

Flies buzzed everywhere.

Wheezing, gasping, frantically rubbing his hand that had touched horror on his shirt. His vision cleared. On the table he saw the crumpled cigarette pack—Pall Malls.

The Silver Mirror bar, blue light dropping a cone through smoke to a table, a man with glasses and a drink, a cigarette ember glowing in one shadow-obscured hand, a crumpled pack of Pall Malls in front of him and a rasping cough.

Quinn drew his revolver and swung the world past its gun sight.

Pistol held two-handed rigid in front of him, whirl to face the back door—*lock it!*

Back, down the hall, the bathroom—clear!

Bedroom—

Closet door—he hadn't checked the closet!

Cock the hammer, throw the closet door open—

Six slot machines huddled inside the closet.

Slot machines? In '63, JFK goes down and Joe Nezneck is busted in suburban Maryland for illegal gambling, his case stetted to nevermind; '65, he gets a mistrial in another Maryland case for possession of illegal gambling equipment.

Living room—the fireplace, plastic-globbed *OHI*. On the card table, Quinn spotted another crumpled Pall Mall pack.

Crime scene, this is a crime scene! Fingerprints, somewhere, probably everywhere, his, too, but OK, OK, he'd find some way to make that OK, get back here with help, with the law. He was the law! He had the law!

All he had to do was get it, and get it *right*.

Probable cause: that's all he needed.

And he had it, he could do it! Hell, probable cause led him here in the first place! Probable cause, cross-jurisdictional assistance on an active missing person's case, search warrant from a neighboring jurisdiction's judge— Sergeant Madison, he'd paper his part! Get Alvin! Get a confidential informant statement from him. Maybe Alvin had searched Pat Dawson's Camaro, found something he could swear was a woman's; he might—he could *remember* the registration slip! Buck would know how to play it!

Phone: a black dial clunker sat on the living room floor.

No: can't risk leaving any record, making a poisoned tree, screwing up the case. *"Make sure your paperwork says what it's supposed to say."* Quinn glared at the crushed cigarette pack: Got you! Nothing else, at least, you fuck, I got you!

If I can go light-speed fast.

He went out a window so he could leave the doors locked.

Quinn checked his watch as he roared toward the Beltway: 2:33. Scoop up Alvin, call him out and hell, cuff him and make him come along. Get to Alvin fast, get him to Buck and then the law ball's rolling, he thought as he raced back to the city.

Lightning crackled the sky.

From a gas station pay phone, he dialed up Alvin's code. A woman interrupted the first cycle of rings by answering. Quinn hung up. Got back on his bike and rode. Next exit on the Beltway, he pulled off and called Alvin's number again. First ring and a woman grabbed the phone before Quinn could hang up: "He ain't here so quit playing this fucking phone game!"

She slammed the phone down.

Alvin had said he was going back to bed.

Unless he hadn't.

Unless he'd gotten a call.

Unless he'd made a call.

Storm clouds churned the air. Quinn roared past cars and trucks. He charged the Harley straight up Fort Stevens's long apron of green to the grassy knoll—no kids around, nobody outside, a spring day that had turned cold and gray with threats of a cloudburst.

Alvin slumped against the trough's earthen battleworks, his palms up to catch heaven's tears. His Hawaiian shirt was a smear of red mush from the blast of a sawed-off shotgun.

Probable cause, slack-jawed, glassy-eyed and gone.

What came to Quinn first was: *How bold!*

Broad daylight. A shotgun blast—citizens would have wanted it to be thunder, kids weren't around and standing just so, Alvin screened from the roads and housing complexes, but . . .

Who had that kind of balls?

Who had such a need for a no-time, high-risk, no-nonsense hit? What was worth that?

Who could walk into a national monument with a sawed-off shotgun? Who could lay his hands on a ballistically smart terror weapon like that on a short notice? Who could stroll up that hill, Alvin there, waiting, seeing who had summoned him—or who he had summoned?

Cop.

Quinn ran off the hill. From a gas station wall phone he called the locker room at the precinct.

"You gonna be late for roll call!" hissed Buck. "I can cover your ass for—"

"They killed Alvin! Shotgunned him at the fort!"

"What?"

"You gotta get up there. Nezneck butchered her. Madison knows. Alvin, he helped me!"

"Butchered who? John, what the hell are you talking about?"

"I gotta go! All I got left is the crime scene! Gotta get there and preserve the crime scene! You gotta cover Alvin, you can't wait because a cop pulled the trigger for Nezneck!"

"Preserve the—Nez—where are—"

Buck realized he was holding a dead line. He stared at the locker room full of fellow cops, at the high window to the world outside, where it looked like rain.

CHAPTER 6

An inferno engulfed the house in the woods. Heat and spinning red blaps of light from the fire trucks beat against Quinn as he stood in the smoky rain.

"Who are you?" yelled a fireman.

Flames lit Quinn's eyes. His hand held up his badge.

A fireball blew through the roof of the house.

"Gotta be propellants!" yelled the fireman. "Can you smell it? Probably gas."

The burning house collapsed into its roaring white center.

The fireman said, "Place is a blast furnace. Melts the metal in—Where you going?"

On the road, the slick highway was jammed with homebound commuters who barely noticed the rabid biker in wraparound shades and rain-soaked leather jacket hydroplaning past their cars.

New Mexico Avenue, the expensive high-rise, where the front desk attendant swore to the cop dripping water on the carpet that nobody was home in Mr. Nezneck's apartment. *OK, yes, come with me, check the underground garage! See: his car isn't here!*

Quinn ran back to his chopper. Raindrops hissed on his hot muffler. Under his lead-heavy wet leather jacket, the .38 rode his hip. He sped over rain-slick streets to The Silver Mirror, where Nezneck smoked his Pall Malls and hid his bloody hands in the blue shadows.

The bartender didn't spot Quinn until he'd been there a minute, maybe more, stalking through the dark haze, ignoring catcalls as he passed between customers and the woman on the stage who'd gotten down to her G-string and white go-go boots.

Not here. Nezneck's gold Caddy wasn't parked outside either.

Once a creep, always a creep. Go where the creeps go.

Quinn throttled the Harley down Fourteenth Street; past the bookstores selling *Fabulous Fannies* and *Jugs,* past the topless bar with a ten-foot yellow-bulbed sign flashing *THIS IS IT!* Quinn didn't see the police cruiser appear in his mirrors as he turned off Fourteenth Street; he didn't have a police radio over which he could have heard "Spotted him, go to Tac Channel Two."

Quinn rode the night and the rain to the bus station zone of strip clubs where the "normal" whores shared the turf with male hookers whose voices had yet to change. Quinn cruised the bus zone turf, saw no gold Caddy, and gunned the Harley away.

The rain stopped. The streets stayed slick, black mirrors.

Quinn found the gold Caddy stashed in a lot on a neon street near where Uncle Sam would build J. Edgar Hoover's new FBI headquarters. The parking lot served a burlesque palace where vaudeville artists had been replaced by ecdysiasts with silicone breasts. The midget barker out front of the palace said, "Hey, that's right, come on in, soldier, no cover tonight!"

Rows of torn seats sloped down to a stage where a woman in the white spotlight swayed and pranced on high heels, an unzipped sequinned red evening dress clinging to her shoulders.

Forget about the guys scattered in the audience, the saxophone, drum and piano player thumping out the background music. Nezneck's not in the crowd. He's not here for the show.

Quinn pushed open a side door marked PRIVATE as the stripper's red dress slid to the stage. He shut the door behind him, muffled the music in that narrow and close darkness rouged with red bulbs. A staircase led up to a dimly lit hall.

The outline of a man loomed at the top of the stairs.

"Well, what the hell," said David Strait. "Officer John fuck-you Quinn."

Strait sauntered down the stairs Quinn climbed. The black man said, "Man, before you was just wet behind the ears! Now look, here you are, wet all over."

Quinn's left hand grabbed Strait's crotch.

Strait yelled as Quinn slammed him against the wall. Strait's hand dove inside his sports jacket. Quinn jabbed the muzzle of his .38 against the black man's temple.

"Were you there with him?" hissed Quinn. "Did you drive him? Did you help?"

"Fuck you, dead man!" gasped Strait.

Quinn's .38 pinned Strait's face against the wall. He took a gun out of Strait's shoulder holster. Quinn threw Strait to his hands and knees on the stairs.

"Get up! You go first!"

"You're going to die, asshole! Get it? You're going to—"

Quinn cocked his revolver.

Strait eased to his feet. Hatred glared from his face. He tramped up the stairs.

They heard the muted wail of the saxophone.

The hall stank of dust and cigars and disinfectant. A red Fire Exit sign glowed at the corridor's end. Four doors, two on each side of the corridor, all closed. Only one door, the second one on the left, had light escaping beneath it. Quinn filled his left hand with Strait's snub-nosed .44. Two guns now trained on Strait, Quinn marched him to that door, said, "Open it!"

As the doorknob turned, Quinn shoved Strait into the room.

A heartbeat—no bullets or club or knife thrust hit the first man through the door. Strait crashed against the far wall. Quinn leapt inside.

Left gun, keep it locked on Strait—
Right gun, look—

A blonde in a black plastic raincoat stood beside the desk, with a drink in her hand and a stunned look on her pink-lipsticked face. *The bar picture! She's in the picture sitting in a bar with Pat . . .*

Joseph R. Nezneck presided behind a desk covered with receipts and cash. His thick hands held a Pall Mall pack and a gold lighter. He wore a sport jacket over a golfer's shirt. Bright black eyes stroked the rain-drenched cop.

Nezneck lit a cigarette. Blew a smoke ring. "Call pest control, honey. We got us a drowned rat."

Quinn zeroed his police pistol on the man behind the desk. Keeping the other gun on Strait meant Quinn's guns aimed at a 90-degree spread. He shot words at Nezneck: "Why'd you kill her?"

The blonde stood like a rock.

Strait eased himself around to face a wild man whose eyes darted from gun sight to gun sight.

"You're a lousy cop," said Nezneck. "You got no idea what you're doing and nowhere to go."

"You killed Alvin, too!"

"Who's he? The chipmunk in that damn kids' song?"

Strait laughed. The blonde cracked a scared smile.

"I got—"

"You got shit for brains and a lot of it. Poking around where you got no business and no clout. Busting in here. What you going to do now?"

Strait laughed again.

"You're holding my guy's shoulder-holster piece. You get his other one? The pearl-handled tucked down along his backbone?"

A chill brushed Quinn.

Strait smiled. Kept his hands at his sides as Quinn's eyes darted from him to Nezneck, back and forth, back and forth.

"You missed that one, didn't you?"

"You're under—" Quinn ran out of words.

"Under arrest?" Nezneck laughed. He flicked his cigarette at Quinn.

The burning tube bounced off Quinn's chest and Quinn jumped back; his guns waved, locked tight, then his arms thrust out like he was squeezing triggers as the room roared with electricity and Strait flinched. The blonde cried out.

"You're lucky you didn't get burned. Stick around, I'll

give you another chance. Normally, I'd let the hired help take care of fucks like you and other people who get out of line, but . . ." A leer twisted Nezneck's face: "But even when you get to be a big-shot executive, there's things a man enjoys doing with his own hands."

Then he laughed. "You ain't arresting me."

Quinn staggered, his eyes flicking from the man who mocked him to the gunman who might have a pearl-handled pistol by his spine.

"You ain't ever arresting me. You ain't getting one over on me. Nobody gets over on me. So fuck you. So what you going to do? You think you got a beef with me? I ain't got no beef with you. You ain't worth having a beef with. You got a pissant badge and no stones. You're shit under my shoes. You think you're tough? You think you're smart? You think you got angels riding on your shoulders, gonna carry you through this shit life you're fuckin' up?

"So go on. Do what you came here to do. Be a man. Fuckin' pull the trigger."

The triggers' steel bands pressed against Quinn's forefingers.

"Come on, *lawman*. I ain't got all night to die."

And in that moment, with that *lawman* word Nezneck spit, Quinn felt the inferno in the woods flow from his blood. A coolness spread through him, and he knew he couldn't simply squeeze the bands of steel and go home. When he knew he couldn't just *do that*, he saw that Nezneck had gambled on such a truth all along, and now knew it for sure.

Knew, as did Quinn, that it was the man holding the guns who was trapped in this office.

The voice behind Quinn said, "Easy, John. We got it all under control here."

Buck Jones, uniform pressed, shoes shined and pistol unsnapped in its holster, stood in the doorway of the room where his partner trembled, two guns primed for death.

"Ease on back with me," said Buck. "We're covered here."

Nezneck stared at his hired gun. "You know your brother in blue?"

"I will," said Strait.

"That street's got two sides . . . *brother*," said Buck. "It's OK, John, you're OK. We're gone from here, just gotta get the going."

"You think this is that simple, nigger?" said Nezneck.

"I *know* that's how you want it, asshole!" snapped Buck. "We're about equal witnessed out here, if'n you call lawyers or headquarters dogs. We got the same equation if we haul your ass in. You wanna play this all the way, hell, homicides are the easiest mess for cops to clean up."

Nezneck lit another cigarette. "So your play is zero. You both got monkey balls."

"We're gone now." Buck eased John out of that musty office, eased him down the stairs.

Back to the street where cops had scoured the city for a fellow officer floundering in the shit, coordinating over their radios in double-talk so the rookie wouldn't get jammed up with the bosses.

To the street, where Patrolman John Quinn was shown on the books as absent from roll call on detail per request of Sergeant Madison, assisting the search for two lost girls, a search that would crest the next morning when a citizen found one girl raped and strangled and stuffed into a Dumpster; her still-missing best friend sunk into the dark nevermore.

To the street, where a homicide team chased leads to nowhere on the shotgun murder of a car thief at a historic park.

To the street, where spring rain no longer fell and the pavement was cool and clean and reflected Buck's cruiser, its red lights whirling where it sat parked next to Quinn's Harley.

To the street, where John told Buck everything: Strait and Nezneck and their laughing detectives, Alvin and beautiful violet-eyes lost Pat Dawson and promises to Dion, a garbage disposal, a gotta-be-propellants inferno.

To the street, where Buck followed John to his locker with its sheared-off padlock and its Nezneck file gone, then to John's apartment, where the photocopy of that file he'd kept on a bookcase was gone, too, where a thorough search by Buck found no drugs or contraband hidden for IAD to uncover.

"You got nothing on nothing," said Buck.

"And I'm nailed to it," answered Quinn.

"You can rot there. Or you can pick up your cross and keep going."

Quinn went back to the street.

CHAPTER 7

Surveillance film shot five months later at 7:33 P.M. on Wednesday, November 12, 1969 showed John Quinn park a Harley-Davidson motorcycle in front of the Little Red Bookstore near Washington, D.C.'s Dupont Circle. An IBM typewriter was chained to the seat behind him. Quinn wore boots, blue jeans, a beat-up leather jacket. A beard covered his face. Thick hair hung down his forehead to eyes that blazed.

A skinny seventeen-year-old boy wearing Coke-bottle glasses and a Mao button on a T-shirt turned inside out to hide the logo of the Sidwell Friends Preparatory School yelled, "Hi, Quarell!"

Call the man in the surveillance movie John Quinn. Call him John Quarell. Call him Q.

Q paused in front of the Little Red Bookstore's picture window. Color eight-by-eleven portraits of the Beatles from their *White Album* filled the window's corners. In the fall of 1969, Q saw his own reflection in the window glass, shook his head in wonder.

Surveillance footage shot inside the store showed Q walking past shelves stocked with used paperbacks and bins of secondhand record albums. The hidden camera filmed hundreds of shoplifters, none of whom were prosecuted.

The woman working the cash register had been a juvenile officer before she let her hair grow. Q smiled her away from two college boys who just knew she was digging them. "Mark in back?"

"Sure," she said, lifting the countertop so Q could pass by.

Q entered the cramped office, where four men and a woman watched a shaggy-haired former bunco cop known as Mark type their words onto a mimeograph sheet.

"If we say, 'Confront the Establishment Pigs!' " argued one of the men, "that's enough!"

The woman snapped, "The headline has to read, 'Establishment *Sexist* Pigs'!"

"Hey, Mark!" said Q.

The typist grinned at Q. A balding grad student asked, "Did you get it?"

Q winked, nodded.

"Right on!" snapped the grad student. "Up until now, the only electric typewriter in the whole Movement is this one Mark lets us use in the store."

"Did you call the house?" said Q. "Let them know I'd be stopping by?"

"Well, yeah, but it's not like this is the fucking Pentagon and we need to, like, 'clear' you."

"It's better to be expected when you show up." Q looked at Mark: "Need anything?"

The man who typed everything from secret protest plans to letters to newspaper editors to flyers for distribution at demonstrations smiled. "I think we're cool."

Q wore wrap-around sunglasses as he roared off on his motorcycle. A few months ago, the world knew who I was, he thought. Now, because I'm the right age and a "loyal" rebel, I'm spying on kids whom I could have been. He swung his bike around Dupont Circle, where a dozen guys with long hair milled around, waiting for something to happen.

Not tonight, he thought. At least, not so far as we know.

He throttled the Harley down as he rolled past the Institute for Policy Studies, the premier anti–Vietnam War, left-wing think tank. Lights glowed in the IPS building, scholars and activists working late. They'd be gone by 3 A.M. No one would notice an IPS cleaning woman open a door for the cop who'd gotten her burglar son transferred out of Lorton's prison walls to the safer minimum-security farm. The cleaning woman fished documents from IPS garbage and was blind to the electronic bugs Q hid.

Q parked his motorcycle in front of a townhouse north of Dupont Circle's tear-gas zone. A banner draped across the front of the townhouse read:

NATIONAL COMMITTEE TO END THE WAR IN VIETNAM

Q lugged the forty-pound IBM Selectric typewriter up the front stairs. Two college kids opened the door and he was inside.

What had been a dining room now hosted an assembly line. Volunteers ranging in age from couldn't-legally-drive-here to had-grandkids-in-high-school stuffed envelopes with a "Come to D.C. for the November Moratorium" flyer, plus instruction mimeoed via the Little Red Bookstore's typewriter. A "marshal coordinator" named Donna who'd left a Midwestern university for a more important life had a phone pressed to her ear.

Q glanced into the neighboring room. A dozen people sprawled in a marijuana haze around a couch and chairs as a record played. *Ca-thunking* bass guitar, drums: "All Along the Watchtower" tore out of the stereo, a ballad written by a Jewish Minnesotan self-named Bob Dylan (who, FBI reports informed Q, had polished his musical vision on a communist sympathizer's Depression-era hobo odes), a song rearranged through acid-rock fury by Jimi Hendrix, a Seattle black guitar star (who, his FBI file noted, had been a paratrooper in the 101st Airborne). Their lyrics screamed of confusion, escape, rage.

Donna braced Q in the hall: "What do you want?"

"Peace, OK?" Q hefted the typewriter. "I come bearing gifts."

"So did the Greeks." She softened. "I saw you at the October march. In the rain. People with placards around their necks, the names of our dead boys. Candles. I saw tears on your cheeks."

"Must have been the rain."

"Must have," she said. "A tough guy like you."

"Hey!" said a shaggy-haired man. "Quarell's cool. Why do you got a stick up your ass?"

Q saw Donna swallow a retort that might crack the fragile egos holding the house together.

"Look," she said, "Quarell, maybe it's me, but I think you're a blink away from being somebody else. The moms and dads we've got to convince we're right about the war, when they picture whoever did those 'helter-skelter' murders of that actress, they see somebody like you. Not your hair and beard like everybody has. Your eyes. They give you a look that hurts the cause."

"If that's what you see, one of us should change how we look."

Shaggy hair said, "You know what would be cool? Like, what if Quarell was a cop?"

Q kept his grin. Passed the IBM to the shaggy-haired man. Ducked into the smoky living room, popped back out, raising a cupped hand to his face: "If I were a cop, I wouldn't do this."

Q revealed the smoldering marijuana joint, took a deep drag.

Donna shook her head, left them in the hall.

Q traded the joint to the shaggy-haired man for the IBM. Q followed him into the living room. Faces he tried to memorize smiled up at him through the smoke. His buddy started introductions, forgot where he was, mumbled off into monosyllables, then laughed at his own failure. He held a joint to Q's lips so the bro could take a deep drag.

An earnest boy leaning against a couch poured words into a girl's glazed stare: ". . . like everything is suddenly in motion! Plus, we're the first generation born under the bomb, grew up expecting the world to end in fifteen minutes, stick your head under your school desk and *Blammo!*"

The girl flinched.

"Grew up with Auschwitz, TV, the Pill, King and the Kennedys murdered, and we know that working for twenty and a watch's not the way it should be, and the whales are dying!"

"Wow."

"The whole world is changing. Not going to be the same old war and famine and racism and pollution and killers. Hell, *we're* here! *We're* different! How could the shit stay the same?

"Right?" he said, suddenly talking to Q, who hadn't dared refuse two more hits off a joint.

"I think you're all really stoned," said Q.

Everybody laughed.

Hendrix's song cut through their mirth, a cry for escape in the smoke.

Q climbed the stairs.

She met him there, kissed his cheek: "Hey! How are you?"

"Great," he said, leaning the typewriter on the railing.

"You remember, I'm—"

"Cheryl. Give me a break. You think I'd forget?"

She shrugged, not knowing the gonorrhea she'd passed along helped Q tie the Washington, D.C., law enforcement community's record for most on-the-job injuries of a sexually transmitted nature. He remembered her riding above him in John Quarell's apartment, a basement on Capitol Hill furnished with a waterbed, Day-Glo posters, college textbooks, paperback Herman Hesse, Richard Brautigan and Kurt Vonnegut novels, a memoir penned by a black ex-con/radical who claimed enlightenment through raping women, a stereo and used records from the Little Red Bookstore. Quarell paid that rent in cash that Quinn got from men in Ivy League suits.

"Where'd you get that typewriter? Smells like smoke."

"I liberated it from a cop."

"Cool." Her smile was shy. "So . . . what are you doing later?"

Using abuse of discretionary police power as blackmail in furtherance of unlawful entry, illegal eavesdropping and larceny with a degree of success that will receive commendations from the D.C. Police Department and federal law enforcement agencies.

Q lied twice. "Not much. Maybe we can get together."

"Sure," said Cheryl, absolutely sincere for the entire moment in which she spoke the word. She left it on the stairs with Q as she walked down to wherever it was she would go.

Arms heavy with the IBM, Q climbed to the second floor, opened a bedroom door: Two bushy-haired lawyers argued a mock brief countering denial of a parade permit. They waved him away. Q was glad to go: anything in open court would be in open court.

Door two on the second floor: straining, barely able to turn the doorknob without dropping the typewriter that was his ticket to wherever he was, getting the door open . . .

The black man in the beret and black leather hip-length coat stabbed his long finger at a nervous audience of rapt white faces: ". . . is why in this or any action the black man must not, cannot, will not submit to some oppressive white-power-structure so-called leader or—"

Q eased the door shut: no way could he glide in, absorb what was going on in that room. He set the typewriter on the floor where he could quickly point to it. Swung open a third door.

Couldn't see her face. She was bent across the bed red sweater shoved up jeans shoved down and he was standing behind her thrusting his hips into hers/*ass so white, quivering*/she was moaning, squeaking bed, he had long hair and was turning to face the open—

Q shut the door. Picked up the typewriter. Bent over, stood up *way* too fast! Stars, dizzy. Gotta keep on keeping on, rubber legs gotta go up those stairs, man, they stretched up to like forever, all steep and gliding down at him like an escalator.

Oh-oh.

Q realized he was stoned.

Really, *really* stoned.

Oh, shit! Not now! Maintain. Get through this. Get out without blowing your cover. Don't talk, start *babbling*, say something too *street* for a Movement man or too *straight* or too . . . out there helter-skelter like Donna, she was what all this should be about, scare 'em off 'n' blow your cover.

Q climbed the long, *long* stairs to the third floor.

The master bedroom door was closed. Q heard the murmur of low voices. You belong here, he told himself. You got the typewriter. He hefted his burden, threw the door open—

Faces spun in front of him, a woman flew out of a chair, her hand dove inside her coat—

"Whoa!" yelled Q. "This damn thing is heavy!"

"Who the hell are you?" The woman had thick hair and big eyes, a swell of breasts under the gray clothes of a laborer. The two men with her also wore gray clothes and heavy work boots, *cool*, expensive aviator sunglasses. Seated on the other side of the room were four leaders of the Movement—three men, one woman, all in their late twenties, all white. They wore blue jeans and more colors than their three visitors. The gray woman kept her hand under her jacket. Q saw the glint of a chrome gun, hunger on her sensuous lips.

"I was told to bring this here and set this up." *Stand straight! Don't fall into those big eyes gun*—Shit, gun!—*but don't look away!* "They called from the bookstore."

"They didn't call me," said Gunwoman.

"It's not your place," said one of the Movement leaders.

"I thought this place was all of ours," she replied.

"When that's convenient for you," muttered a Movement woman.

"This is too heavy to fuck around with." Q lugged the typewriter over to the first clear table space he saw, prayed that there'd be an outlet near it on the wall, and for once had his prayers granted. When he turned around, they were all facing him. Waiting.

"What's that in your pocket?" Gunwoman flowed to him— *Maintain! Maintain!*—and let her hand float inside his open leather jacket. "Why do you have a little bitty screwdriver?"

"For the machine," said Q. "It's not quite put together."

Because I took it apart! He wanted to scream at her fucking Gunwoman orthodontist's-dream face. Took it apart so I'd have to stay around to put it together. Jesus, her eyes, no bra/*Pat Dawson more beautiful than*/why with a gun so damn close, her hands floating on me, finding no wire or gun or badge. Took it apart, sawed where repairman taught me, and about forty typed pages from now *snapareeno!* goes that cable and one smoky IBM becomes a slab of useless steel that lasted just long enough so the money that was going to be spent to buy the Movement a machine is gone and they gotta go back to depending on the Little Red Bookstore.

She leaned close. Sniffed. "You're wasted."

"No, that's one of the other seven dwarfs."

Everyone else laughed.

That bothers you, doesn't it, Gunwoman? thought Q. 'Cause now they're all looking at me.

"Go do your thing." Gunwoman sat in a folding chair beside her comrades, toed the table and tilted back like a gangster in a movie. "You must have read about us. We made all the papers."

The Movement people nodded as Q lifted off the lid of the IBM, found the screws he'd taped inside, tried to hear everything and not fall into the machine's smoke-and-ink-smeared maw.

"We sent seventy-five cops to the hospital," said one of her gray-uniformed comrades. "They busted some of us, but we got 'em for the convention. Chicago pigs ain't gonna forget the Days of Rage."

"That's not what we're about," said the Movement woman.

Gunwoman laughed. "It's not about your Vietnam War anymore! It's about our revolution."

"Not for us."

"It will be," said one of the gray men.

"Look, we're getting ready for the biggest anti-war demonstration this country has ever seen. In three days, we're
going to get a couple hundred thousand people here to—"

"All that marching and singing. Cute, but it's not how
we'd do it."

Q tossed a screw so he had to crawl under the table to
look for it; no one noticed him.

"Why are you here, Bernice?" said a Movement leader.

Gunwoman laughed. "There's no 'Bernice' here."

*Bernice, Bernice, Bernice! Get the screw! Remember
Bernice!*

"You've done big time with all this," said Gunwoman.
"When I walked out, didn't think you'd keep it together.
Must be getting a lot of 'buy peace instead of dope' change
from the crowds, from Mommy and Daddy's trust funds."

"Like yours, *Bernice*?" snapped her Movement sister.

"The point is, you have an opportunity to contribute to our
legal defense fund."

"You're crazy! We need that money—"

"You need a trouble-free, no-violence-in-streets, fucking
peace march mor-a-torium!"

Fuck the screw! Q froze on his hands and knees.

"You're shaking us down! If we don't 'contribute,' you'll
pull a Days of Rage at the mora—"

"I'm—we're showing you an opportunity to serve the people's just cause."

"And keep your ass out of jail."

Gunwoman shrugged. "Same thing."

"Riot, blackmail us . . . What are you gonna do next? Rob
a bank?"

Q screwed the lid to the typewriter, working the screws
long after they were tight.

"Forget it," said a Movement leader. "We're through here.
Don't fuck with us."

"But that's so *easy*! You're *nonviolent*!" Gunwoman
laughed. "What are you going to do? Call Daddy? Call

Nixon? Call the cops? Oh yeah, the pigs are just lining up to help you."

"No," said the Movement woman, "we'll announce it from the podiums. Doesn't matter if the police believe us or not. Nobody on our side will ever believe you again."

Q watched his second hand spin twice around the watch dial.

"I knew you guys were lame." Gunwoman took her time putting on her sunglasses. "I didn't know you were lying about wanting to change the world."

Then she led her comrades out.

"Aren't you done with that damned typewriter? Are you too stoned to . . . Look, I'm sorry," said the Movement leader. "I just—could we be alone for—"

"Hey," said Q, leaving. "It's like I was never here."

CHAPTER 8

Tuesday morning, May 5, 1970, Quinn and Buck sat across from each other in a booth at the Florida Avenue Grill. "We don't have much time," Quinn said.

Sausage patties shotgunned with pepper, unblinking fried eggs and onion-laced home fries ladened their table. The grill fed predictable patrons: a floorwalker from a department store, cabbies, telephone linemen, a matron's maid sipping tea and nobody from the Movement.

Buck wore a windbreaker. "Don't worry about time. I'm off for two days."

"No, you aren't. There'll be a callback for everybody." Quinn held up *The Washington Post*. A wire photo showed a young woman kneeling and screaming, her arms thrown wide above the body of a college boy facedown on the concrete. The banner headline read:

OHIO GUARDSMEN KILL 4 STUDENTS

"Ain't that some shit," said Buck.

"Wasn't supposed to happen," said Quinn. "Those Week-end Warriors sent to Kent State had just come off policing a Teamsters strike, so they were jumpy and ragged. Our man in the crowd—"

"*Our* man?"

Quinn whispered, "We had a D.C. cop undercover out there. The feds almost sent me, but since I'm from Ohio, we figured I might get recognized by somebody who knows I'm a cop."

"What the hell—No, don't tell me. I don't want to know."

"You can't believe what they got me doing! I've been schooled: safe houses in the 'burbs. Lock picking. Burglary. Bugs. Cameras. 'Active measures' shit."

" 'Shit' is right. Look at you: all hippied up, hair over your ears, wild beard. Who are you these days?"

Quinn peered through his coffee steam. "I started out knowing what was what. What I know now is there are secrets inside the way things are. Lies inside the truth. Rules inside of rules."

"You're smoking too much of that hippie shit."

"Or not enough." Quinn rubbed his brow. "I'm the sane man running with crazies. Lawmen in love with their handcuffs. Psychos playing TV star revolutionary. Starry-eyed kids who just want us out of Vietnam—or now, fucking *Cambodia*! Last week we fucking pushed the war into Cambodia to wind down the war in Vietnam, and Vice President Agnew says thinking that's weird means you're an 'elitist undermining optimism'!"

"Politics make a man crazy, John. Just be a good cop."

"That's why we're having breakfast." Quinn leaned closer. "I've played it cool. Half the time I don't know the suits running me—and they don't know where I'm running. Now, while I'm Officer Invisible, while I got more punch than most cops can imagine, now's when we nail Nezneck."

Buck put his fork down. Took a pull from his tan coffee mug.

"You know I'm right, Buck. He butchered Pat Dawson! Alvin! Put two cops in his pocket! And nobody cares but you and me."

"You hot on this for the job? Or is this a personal hard-on?"

"I take killers personally. Thought you did, too."

"Like I said: Is this about the badge, or is it about you? I mean, murder is murder is murder, right? But this Pat Dawson: we figure she'd turned herself out as a party child before she ended up on Nezneck's chain as a call girl. High class, dreamin' about being *good*, but a whore's a whore."

Buck leaned closer. "Don't look at me like I ain't got a heart. I know it's rough."

Quinn nodded to his mentor's gaze.

"You said you told Gramma that the girl is long gone, MIA forever. That she added up what you wouldn't say. Whatever the old lady told the kid about his mom—"

"His name is *Dion*. Her name was *Pat*."

"No way could you have saved her. And you did all you could for them."

"This isn't about her," said Quinn. "I'm not out to avenge some angel. I want to nail a devil. This is about Nezneck."

"Ambition like that ain't gonna get you rank."

"Maybe no, maybe yes."

Buck shook his head. "Shit, what fool was your training officer?"

"Y'all want some more coffee?" The waitress's salt-and-pepper customers let her pour and walk away without saying a word she heard.

Buck sighed. "When a man thinks that just 'cause he's got a badge, whatever he wants is the right thing, then he's gonna make a world of hurt."

"So what am I supposed to do? Pretend I don't know what I know? Go along to get along?"

Buck said nothing.

"What about honor?"

"What about being smart?"

"Being smart isn't enough," said Quinn.

The police sergeant sat like a hunk of granite.

"Come on, Buck. Nezneck fucked with you, too. He hasn't forgotten us. How smart is it to forget him?"

Granite cracked. "Well, shit. My brother's got rank on Congress's force up on Capitol Hill. I can trade badges, become a cop up there. Direct tourists. Escort drunk senators to their cars.

"Only thing is," said Buck, "something like this, we gotta remember we're supposed to be the good guys. Being a black cop in a world of white, I got practice on that. But you ... hard enough you keeping your head straight playing street spy for the bosses and the feds. You start weaving the 'gotta get my personal bad guy' into your play, you could get twisted and tangled up in your own rope, all the time thinking you're playing it loose and straight. You gotta watch that."

"Sure," said Quinn, said Quarell, said Q. "Sure."

"So, Officer Quinn, we just gonna strap down and siren right up Citizen Nezneck's ass?"

"These days his ass isn't there to hit. Near as I can tell, he's way off our streets."

"You gotta catch a guy like Nezneck law-breaking on the street, otherwise you won't catch him *period*."

"Don't worry. He'll be back on our pavement. I know that in my bones. If not ... I'll pull him out there. I'm not waiting for him. Can't let him set the clock."

"So how you plan on nailing him?"

"One stroke at a time."

But by noon Quinn and Buck had been sucked into the vortex of the Kent State strike as thousands of war protesters streamed into Washington and shut down 448 colleges across America.

Thursday found Quinn slumped in a security command post near the White House. The room was packed: cops from a dozen jurisdictions, soldiers, FBI agents and suits who didn't say they were from across the river at the CIA. Quinn and another D.C. cop sat at a table covered with aerial photographs of the crowds. Phones rang. Radios squawked. Men yelled orders.

Eyes crawled up Quinn's back.

Heart pounding, face calm, Quinn let his gaze brush across the faces swirling. Across the room, using the reflective glass door like a spotting mirror: a wire-thin man. The thin man wore a suit and black wingtip shoes. He smiled at Quinn.

"You know that guy?" Quinn whispered to his fellow D.C. cop.

"Mr. Blond Hair Over His Collar, jawing with the other big shots? Dean something—no, something Dean, lawyer hotshot with Justice. Does something with intel and—"

"Not him. The long skinny wire guy."

"He's FBI. I heard him asking about you."

"Asking what?"

"This and that, nothing big."

"What do you know about him? What's his name?"

"Hey: he's FBI. What more do you need to know?"

The thin man vanished in cascading crises.

By the next Tuesday, most of the protesters had gone home.

Thursday, Quinn and Buck blitzed Jake the Jar.

"What the hell!" yelled Jake as the wild cops herded him and Elma onto their living room couch. "What you guys doing?"

Buck flashed prison mug shots to Elma and Jake. "You know these guys?"

"You know I do! I helped you send that Larry to the joint!"

"What about these guys?" Buck showed him an FBI surveillance photo of two black men sitting in a van parked across from a bank.

"Yeah. I don't know the driver, but the shotgun is Marvin Fulsome. He did some time once, but ain't been round here lately."

Buck held picture number three right under Elma's doe

eyes: four black males, a grainy black-and-white surveillance shot from across a D.C. street.

"These four dudes," snapped Buck. "You know all them, too?"

"Them? I—no. Don't know them."

Got you lying, thought Quinn. So we'll play it that way.

"You sure 'bout that?" said Buck. "How 'bout you, Elma? You know these brothers?"

"She don't know nothing!" said Jake.

Elma nodded yes, shook no, shrugged I don't know.

Buck cursed. "Well, you better know something! They got me and White Bread here flat out hard after four Black Panthers who shot up a cop in Jersey and come down here to—"

"*Black Panthers*? Shit, not those—I mean, they don't look like they into no political shit!"

"Appearances can be deceiving," said Quinn.

Buck shot Quinn a *Don't make me laugh!* glance. Told Jake: "Just be sure you two don't go lying to us!"

Jake waved his hammy arm. "I knows the Panthers round here—"

Bullshit, thought Q.

"—and those guys, they ain't into that Black warrior rap. I bet they just four brothers strollin' 'long. Probably don't know jack shit about each other."

You don't know how right you are, thought Quinn.

The day before, he and Buck snapped a photo of a trio of stickup artists whom Buck couldn't prove guilty. The fourth man in picture number three wore an expensive blazer and a thin mustache. Quinn had taken his photo months earlier. With dark room magic and scissors, Quinn created picture number three, which put the mustached man together with the stickup trio.

The mustached man was David Strait, Joe Nezneck's driver.

Buck waved more photos in front of Jake, but like the first two sets of pictures, they were just for show.

Two days later, Quinn and Buck sat in an unmarked police car near a corner grocery store.

"You got a real girlfriend yet?" said Buck.

"How is a guy doing what I do going to meet a real girl? Hard enough for normal cops to get a good woman."

"Gettin' 'em's easy." Buck kept his eyes on the store. "Stickin' together, that's hard."

"Thought you patched it up at home."

"We got patches on patches." Buck sighed. "I wish I knew how you can be hellfire, door-slamming pissed off at someone *and* can't-leave, keep-coming-back-to-'em at the same damn time."

Quinn watched the street: *Not yet.* "How'd you end up with your wife, anyway?"

"Way down in the bone, I'll be damned if I know. And that's where it happens when it really happens: a jolt way down in the bone."

"The ones that are worth it have to be in the bone, right?"

"When you find out, let me know." Buck lit a cigarette. "Least me and the missus got somethin'. You oughta get you a regular girl."

"No regular girl would have me. I don't want one anyway. I want a *woman*."

A squat black woman trudged out of the corner store, a canvas shopping bag clutched on one shoulder, a purse in her hand.

"How 'bout her?" said Buck.

"You take what you can get."

"Which bus stop she headed for? Going out or going back?"

The woman crossed the street to the white-poled bus stop.

"She's going back." Buck tossed his cigarette out of the cruiser as he whipped the police car away from the curb and braked to a stop in front of the bus pole.

Quinn lowered his window. "Get in, Elma. We're your ride now."

She wanted to run. She wanted to not be there. But obedience was the only hope she knew.

Elma got in the backseat. The cops whisked her away. They parked under a freeway overpass by the football stadium. The only other living things around were seagulls skimming the asphalt for trash; those citywise birds wouldn't flinch at the sound of a gunshot or the sight of a body tossed in a Dumpster.

"Elma, you're in deep and painful trouble," said Buck.

"I just doing my shopping!" Elma cowered in the backseat.

"So far today, you been to eight corner stores. Let's see what you got. Pass your bag up here, your purse, too."

"Do I . . . I don't . . . Do I hafs to?"

"What the hell do you think?" growled Buck, trying to keep his search voluntary and legal.

Quinn took the worn canvas shopping bag from her hands. Dumped it. Bundles of paper slips and worn money covered the front seat between the two cops.

"Shit, Elma!" said Buck. "You just done iced the cake!"

She sobbed.

"Woman hands over a bag of number slips and cash she can't say is nothing but illegal gambling money. Gonna take a bust on that."

Buck emptied her black purse on the seat. "Look at that! You packin' all that gamblin' green in your purse, but you riding the town on a damn jingle-jangle pile of bus tokens!"

"Whoa-ho!" Buck picked a home-rolled cigarette out of a pack of factory-made cancer sticks, smelled the marijuana with closed eyes and an appreciative smile. "This is good shit! We got you with felonious gambling paraphernalia. We got cash to confiscate—maybe we should call the tax man! Now we got evil narcotics to staple to your jacket. Icing on top of icing!"

Tears streamed down the woman's cheeks.

Good, thought Quinn, at least she's still able to cry.

"Elma," he said, "time to think real hard. We had you before, now we got you on this. What are you going to do?"

"I ain't no thinker! Honest!" Sobs overcame her.

"Jail's not your only problem," said Buck. "What's Jake gonna do when he finds out you lost his slips and cash to the law?"

"He gonna do what he always do, but this time he gonna—" She broke off in a wail.

"Here's the way it lays out," said Quinn. "We came at you today because we know you lied when we dropped by the other day."

"I didn't say nothing!"

"Sayin' nothing's the worst damn lie!" yelled Buck.

"That picture of four dudes?" said Quinn. "The guys Jake said he didn't know? The one you 'didn't say nothing' about? One guy was his cousin Leroy, lived with Jake, been seen dropping by the house since you been there, so we got you on lying to the police! Interfering in an investigation! Conspiracy! Those dudes being Panthers and killing a Jersey cop make you and Jake just as murdering guilty as them, plus you giving us the icing on—"

Elma cried out for Jesus.

"He can't hear you down here," said Buck.

"Oh please, oh God, oh mister sir, you gots to help me!"

"Maybe," said Quinn, "if you help us out with the Panther-hunting feds, maybe you can sneak back into what was, not what is."

"Oh Jesus, mister! I do whatever I gots to do!"

Quinn held up picture number three.

Elma's finger flew to touch each of the three stickup artists. She gave them names that the cops already knew.

"And they ain't no Jersey cop-killing Panther guys! They just regular thieves! Cousin Leroy . . . Jake just coverin' his kin!"

Quinn said: "The other guy. Is he—"

"Dave Strait ain't no Panther! He likes his money, and he—"

"If he's no Panther," said Buck, "why is he with the other three?"

"He don't got no business with them! I don't know why he's there! He does the business with Jake takin' the cut to the man!"

"What man?"

"Some white man. I don't know no white men but you."

Quinn gambled: "This Strait's got to have more than an errand boy business."

"But no crazy, murderin' Panther shit! He just moving powder!"

"What powder?"

"You know. Just smack. Don't got no habit myself, shit, that stuff will make you stupid, but Strait, he's too slick to be some Panther murder man."

"So he works heroin deals with Jake."

"Jake, he sell his jars, loans the money and runs some numbers for the white man he 'n Strait says yes to. But Jake too lazy to run powder, I swear!"

"Strait doesn't move any powder through Jake?"

"No, he gets it from some New York bloods."

"And they're—"

"They ain't no Panthers! Why you keep pushin' that? It ain't true! I be always around, makin' sure Jake get what he wants, he don't even fetch his own drinking beer, and I be hearing his business with you, Strait, too, how the Harlem bloods got the nod to come down the highway Thursdays to bring powder to D.C., shit like that. So you can't bust none of those people for politics shit, then tie that can to Jake and me! *We innocent!*"

She leaned back, her eyes full of righteousness.

Quinn shrugged. "Maybe we can convince the feds that their Panther stuff is off."

"Oh, yes, sir, way, way—"

"But we still got all the stuff in the front seat."

Elma wailed. "Why don't you just take it and leave me be? Jake understands that cop game!"

"Ripping you off ain't our play," said Buck. "We can make today go away only if we know what we got, like how your numbers action works."

Words tumbled out of her: "Just like supposed to, guys workin' the *Post* delivery trucks does the slip pickups and drops at the corner stores and Saturdays I comes by and picks up the cash and countins and takes it to my sister, she older 'n me, down at the wig shop. Then I goes home, mister, I gots to go home to Jake 'fore he whumps up on me more 'cause I got nowhere else to go."

She deflated like a wrinkled balloon.

Quinn had to know. "What wig shop?"

"The one downtown. Freedom Wig."

On fire, Quinn stepped out to warm spring air. He heard Buck growl: "Get up here and get your shit together."

Quinn knew she'd hold her tongue and not tell Jake that she, his loyal dog, had betrayed him. Quinn knew she'd bought this roust as cops being stupid about political nonsense—a dose of pain to be chalked up as the way things are and forgotten.

He burned with memory.

Freedom Wig and Beauty Shop, Inc. in downtown Washington, D.C.

And in Pat Dawson's pink address book.

CHAPTER 9

Marine Captain Nathan Holloway followed orders. At zero dark thirty, September 5, 1970, he left his uniform hanging in the bachelor officers' quarters closet at Quantico, Virginia, tracked the North Star on Interstate 95 to circle the Beltway around the city where one day he'd face the death hole of Quinn's gun, and drove to a suburban Maryland pancake restaurant. He fed coins to a newspaper box for a *Washington Post*, then claimed a corner booth.

Into the pancake house walked a man in his twenties with close-cropped hair, civilian slacks, an unzipped windbreaker. He took a booth and never once looked at Holloway.

Good morning, thought Nathan.

His *Post* said a Marxist named Allende's victory in Chile's presidential election was the first free election of a communist head of state in the history of the world. The Vietnam War's box score said that only 623 GI coffins had flown home to America since the U.S. troop pullout from a two-month "incursion" of Cambodia. Seven new divisions of North Vietnamese troops were working their way down the Ho Chi Minh trail, headed toward 396,000 American soldiers who were sweating out their tours of duty in South Vietnam.

Get some, whispered a voice deep inside Holloway. He forced that voice to silence.

A puffy-eyed woman with last night's camouflage smudged on her face slumped alone into a booth across the room from Holloway. She could have been some soldier's mother.

Holloway turned to the *Post*: "President Nixon's national security adviser, Henry A. Kissinger, is making like a movie star . . ."

A second cropped-haired man entered the restaurant. He chose a table, glanced at Holloway, but not at Mr. Crew Cut.

The portly man in his late fifties walked to Holloway's booth on time at 0700. He wore civilian clothes. His gesture told Holloway not to stand as they shook hands.

"You're looking good, Nathan." The old man squeezed into the booth. "Still damn tan.

"No, thanks, dear," he told the waitress when she offered him a menu. He patted his stomach. "I can't have everything I want anymore. You eat, son: you need your strength."

Holloway ordered.

"Thanks for coming, Nate."

"No problem, Admiral."

"Here, I'm Burt. How's your father?"

"You know better than me."

"He's doing a damn fine job at NATO."

"Yes. I suppose he is."

"You didn't tell him about this, did you?"

"I followed your orders. Told no one anything."

"Good." The Admiral frowned. "Why'd you put in for a third tour after intel school? Your ticket's punched and then some."

"I'm a Marine officer. In-country is where the job is."

"Did you like it over there?"

"I like being a Marine."

"That still rankles your old man. I saw him at our reunion in Annapolis. He pointed to you on the wall with your class and still can't figure why you'd choose the Corps over our Navy."

"The suit fits me better," said Nathan.

"Todd's there. Brown-water Navy." The Admiral dropped his voice. "How bad is it?"

"Todd'll be OK. You know him. He's golden. Lucky."

"Yeah. Sure. Sure, he is. I remember the two of you playing baseball when we were all stationed in the Philippines. Two boys in all that sun . . .

"Why'd you ask to go back?" repeated the Admiral.

Nathan blinked. "I know how to do that."

In the steel valley of his teaspoon, a ceiling fan spun like the rotors of a helicopter.

"What's the worst thing you saw?" asked the Admiral.

"Begging your pardon . . . *Burt,* but I never figured you for that kind of guy."

"You're not here to amuse me, Captain." Wrinkles flattened in the Admiral's napkin.

"Sorry, sir, I just . . . Guys who've been there, we get a lot of shit here in the world."

Nathan took a breath. "Worst I saw? The look from a nineteen-year-old who'd counted on me to bring him home with legs and testicles. A napalmed baby. Hue, after Tet, when we liberated it and found the five thousand mass execution graves. In the jungle, I saw three Army Special Forces guys—saw their heads on stakes."

The Marine raised a fork of scrambled eggs with a steady hand.

"I have to ask," said the Admiral. "I need what isn't in your file. Your answer never leaves this table: What's the worst thing you did?"

Nathan felt himself swept up by the beat of the pancake house's whirling ceiling fans. He showed a face of stone to

the Admiral, who thought he knew him, who thought they
were just two men sharing secrets in a pancake house. The
ceiling fans whirled; Nathan's heart raced and rode the Admiral's bull's-eye question to another time, another place, a
parallel reality where he experienced himself in a world that
had been, in a world that was.

*Emerald-sea morning at the firebase, Choctaw work-
horse chopper whumping up red dust. First sergeant
sees me walking toward his squad with my pack, bush
hat, M16 with its sling mounts taped so they won't
rattle, says: "Shit, Captain, you taking us out, we must
be some kind of special today." Laugh, tell him: "I
want to ride with the best."*

Pancake house. With the man who'd gotten old. Holloway
thought, Tell him the truth. "Worst thing I did? I don't
know."

"OK," said the Admiral. "Never mind. We've got a job.
A mission. Classified beyond what you can imagine. Here,
the worst thing you can do is tell anybody anything. Do that,
you won't need to worry about a court-martial."

Nathan kept his hands flat on the table.

"We need someone who's service all the way, someone
we can count on. Someone with guts, who can operate alone
and won't flinch. You'll never speak of this to anyone—
including your father. And while this will help your career,
you'll get no official credit for it. There is no 'it.' "

"Understood."

"Will you do it, Nate? Can I trust you?"

"That's why I'm here, sir."

"As of now," said Admiral Burt Petersen, "you belong to
us, to this thing. Not the Corps—us. Your commanders."

"Who are—?"

"You don't need to know, but it's joint-chiefs level. I'll
set you up. Then you're on your own. You may not even
deal with me again, that's a developing contingency."

"When do I go in-country, sir?"

"Hell, son, you're already there."

"Sir?"

"Expand your mind, Nate. Open your eyes. Vietnam is a battle, not the war."

Holloway blinked.

"The war's been going on since . . ." The Admiral shrugged. "Some would say since Lenin rode the sealed train to Moscow. But it's not just about communism, not just about saving us from the damn Soviets and Chinese. It's about surviving, keeping the whole thing called America going. You're on a deep-cover, intelligence/counterintelligence operation. Solo. And your rules of engagement are total compartmentalized secrecy, with loyal obedience, which means you can never, I say again, *never* ask why."

"I'm a Marine . . . Burt. My life is about *how,* not why. But I've got a question."

"Don't make it a wrong one."

"Those two buzz cuts pretending we're not here. Are they with us?"

The Admiral smiled. "You *are* the right man for this. They're ours. But the next gun you spot might not be. So be smart. You're in-country, and it's a land-mined jungle."

"Admiral, I need to know my objective."

The man Nathan had known since boyhood shrugged. "You don't have an 'objective,' son. You got a process. You got a target."

The Admiral leaned close to whisper, "The White House."

CHAPTER 10

"I know what you're thinking," said the National Security Council aide named Boyd as he led civilian-suited Holloway through the White House, 0800 on Monday, September 18, 1970. "The first day, everybody thinks the same thing: 'This place is so damn small!' These walls can close in on a guy. Like a prison. Or a coffin."

Boyd walked him past a Marine sergeant posted at a desk in the hall, down two blue-carpeted stairs. Boyd punched a code into a keypad on the yellow wall that unlocked a set of double doors: "Welcome to the White House Situation Room."

Cigarette smoke drifted like a cloud through a narrow corridor of closed doors and secretarial stations. A *phonk* sound like a mortar firing shot through the haze.

"Pneumatic tubes," said Boyd. "The message capsules whoosh between here and our NSC offices on the third floor of the Executive Office Building next door, where most of us work."

Holloway followed his guide up a second set of stairs to a cubicle outside a closed door.

"This is your spot. Primo turf. Actual White House space, just outside Herr Doctor's door. What is it that you're supposed to be doing again anyway?"

"I'm special assistant to the National Security Council advisor," said Holloway.

"But you've never met him."

"No."

"Un-huh. And why you?"

"My official job is ground-forces advice and make-it-happen bureaucrat, a gofer with the highest security clearances. Plus I've seen our war. The way I understand it is that somebody's got to make sure you pros get what you need."

"Whose bullshit is that? Yours or theirs?"

"Who's *they?*"

"Could be the Berlin Wall—Haldeman and Ehrlichman, Nixon's two top guard dogs, the German shepherds. Could be their Henry Handling Committee. Could be R. N. himself—the President wants to be his own action officer. Could be Laird, he's the smartest of the political pros, over there running the Pentagon. Could be anybody but Rogers, he's just secretary of state and the last to know anything. So who are you—*really*?"

"I'm nine weeks out of the jungle," said Holloway. "Somebody here asked for a body to keep your wheels greased; somebody pulled me out of a Pentagon hat."

"You think you left the jungle?"

You don't trust me, thought Holloway. But you want to. "So what should I do?"

"Just tell me what's going on." He laughed like it was a joke.

"My files are locked," said Holloway. "Why?"

"*That* I do know. You inherited the MENU books—the real ones, plus duplicates of the doctored ones we reported to Congress, the Secretary of the Air Force, the State Department."

"MENU? I'm still catching up, and all the code names blend into one."

"Maybe that's the ultimate truth. MENU is—was—the B-52 strikes in Cambodia. We ran them out of the basement here for more than a year, stopped them in May. More than three thousand missions, dropped maybe one-hundred thousand tons of bombs. It never happened."

"But the Cambodians know! The commie Khmer Rouge and Viet Cong we bombed know! Hanoi knows, and they'd have told the Russians and Chinese, who probably saw it all on radar anyway. Who are we keeping it secret from?"

A door opened and out came the pudgy, bespectacled man Holloway had seen on TV and in newspaper photos. The first thing he noticed was the man's compressed intensity; the second was the egg stain on his tie.

"Dr. Kissinger," said Boyd. He introduced the Marine in a civilian suit.

Why am I suddenly like a ten-year-old kid? thought Holloway.

"Don't worry about a crisis this week," Kissinger joked. "My schedule is full."

Aides appeared out of the woodwork. Even as Kissinger shook Holloway's hand, someone read the ex-professor's schedule: first a meeting with the Yugoslavian ambassador about President Nixon's meeting in Belgrade with Marshall Tito, the head of that communist state, then a meeting with the Spanish ambassador about Nixon's meeting with Spain's fascist dictator.

"From one political extreme to the other," said someone.

Kissinger smiled.

So everyone laughed.

Kissinger learned that Russian-built MiG fighters chased a CIA U2 spy plane out of Cuba's skies before a U.S. bird could snap recon photos of a Cuban navy base in the Bay of Cienfuegos. Holloway was still trying to picture the area when Kissinger said to order the CIA to try again.

Then Kissinger was hurrying down the corridor as Boyd yelled, "Don't forget your lunch with Attorney General Mitchell! His friends on Wall Street are upset about Chile!"

As Boyd chased after Kissinger, he told Holloway, "Welcome to the war for the world."

I'm the fly on the wall, thought Holloway that afternoon as he sat behind "the principals" of the 40 Committee, the secret group at the long conference table who officially ran what Holloway learned to call "the intelligence community"—everybody from the Central Intelligence Agency to the National Security Council to who knew what other groups.

But not mine, thought Holloway: Not "our" thing.

As the 40 Committee authorized spending a quarter of a million dollars to bribe Chilean congressmen to oppose President-elect Allende, Holloway saw a man sitting across the room wink.

What?

The committee ordered the CIA to arrange for twenty journalists to fly to Chile and produce anti-Allende news stories.

"Too bad we can't do that here," said someone.

Nobody laughed. The meeting ended. Holloway knew that some of the post-meeting whispers were about him: Who is he? Who is he *really*? He kept his expression somber but warm, peered through the shifting suits for a good look at the man who winked.

Spotted him: a fragile man whose suit looked too big. Pleasant not handsome, with a horseshoe beard that like his thinning hair was turning from gray to white. His hands were delicate, his skin almost translucent. His movements were quick. Precise. Like a bird's.

Someone shook Holloway's hand as the secret team gathered their briefcases. Birdman brushed past a CIA deputy director and slid out the door.

Holloway lost twenty seconds before he could follow him. In the hall, he saw only Boyd, who'd been compartmentalized out of the 40 Committee meeting.

"Congratulations," said Boyd. "You caught on fast."

"That guy who just came out? Skinny guy, like a bird with a beard. Who was he?"

"Him?" Boyd smiled. "He wasn't here."

Then Holloway found himself helping the newly appointed chairman of the Joint Chiefs of Staff, Admiral Thomas Moorer, deploy the Sixth Fleet to the Middle East, where Palestinian guerrillas/terrorists in Jordan were holding hostages from four hijacked airplanes.

September swept Holloway into tumult.

Tuesday, he knew that Kissinger, CIA Director Helms and Attorney General Mitchell met with President Nixon in the Oval Office, but no one on the NSC staff knew why. Holloway sat through a late-afternoon Senior Review Group meeting where Kissinger let his aides argue over offering Hanoi a cease-fire. Kissinger went to the Oval Office to brief Nixon, and Holloway stole a scrap of paper from Kissinger's trash that hadn't been there before the Oval Office meeting. Holloway held it up to his desk lamp, found the words *scream* and *Track II* beneath the doodles.

That night as he walked out the White House's side door, a helicopter landed on the south lawn. Men in tuxedoes scurried into the White House like penguins to an ice floe—Kissinger, CIA Director Helms, JCS Chairman Moorer, choppered back from an award ceremony for Secretary of

Defense Laird to an emergency meeting of the Special Action Group: King Hussein in Jordan had militarized his government to throw the Palestine Liberation Organization out of his country.

Thursday, combat broke out in Jordan between the army and the PLO. Holloway analyzed satellite photos of Syria moving tanks to its border. Israel went on alert. Kissinger had the Pentagon send a third aircraft carrier to the Mediterranean and called Nixon in Chicago.

"Nothing better than a little confrontation now and then, a little excitement," the President told Kissinger. Nixon ordered that the military's moves be publically announced.

Kissinger ignored Nixon's order.

Shit, thought Holloway. Who's the Commander In Chief?

The CIA's U2 pictures of Cuba hit the White House on Friday: Castro's navy base was being expanded to service submarines. Analysts decided a new soccer field had to be for the recreational use of Soviet personnel, because Cubans favored baseball, not soccer. If the Soviets succeeded in building a submarine base in Cuba, the time they needed to nuke the U.S. mainland could be cut by one third. New York could melt in a hydrogen fireball while the President was still opening the locked briefcase with the nuclear war response codes.

Holloway spent hours refereeing arguments among the NSC staff: the State Department loyalists wanted to follow Secretary Rogers and avoid tension over Cuba; Kissinger loyalists lobbied for his hawkish, confrontational approach.

Saturday, Holloway carried a newspaper to work before dawn. Over coffee from the White House vending machines the NSC staff were forced to use because Kissinger did not want them frequenting the White House mess, where they might meet Nixon team members without him knowing, Holloway spotted an article in the *Post*: a rock star named Jimi Hendrix had died in London from an overdose of drugs.

Hendrix, thought Holloway: Was he the one . . .

Chopper whumping up red dust, a ground crew radio blares Jimi Hendrix's "Purple Haze." Sergeant checks

*our men—Cole, Mizell, Waters, they give me the
"know you" look. Black guy named Big—short for
Big Easy. Mardigian and O'Brien. One grunt wears
his helmet and Fucking New Guy tattooed across his
sunburned face. Dalton jokes: "Captain, us being thirteen is bad mojo, so I volunteer to stand down." Sergeant says: "Volunteer? For point? You got it." My
hands distribute the tape measures. They listen close,
good Marines, no older than twenty-two or younger
than forever. Wide-eyed Mizell: "Field test the new
M79 grenades? Like, the laws of physics and geology
are different in 'actual combat conditions'?" Sergeant
sighs. "Captain, say the real plan for this patrol ain't
to get us into the shit and then measure the holes we
make! That is zero good." Give him the command
voice and the lecture drummed in since boot camp:
"In the course of events, the mission is always the
greater good." Give him the man-to-man smile:
"Don't sweat the small stuff. Remember, we're here to
win the hearts and minds of the people." Sergeant
spits: "Shit, radio Hendrix there's got it all, the brass
don't know which way is up or down. They going to
break my heart and fuck my mind."*

That Saturday in Washington, Holloway worked until midnight, ninety minutes after his "principal," Kissinger, went
home. Holloway made sure Kissinger had a copy of the latest
Vietnam body counts: that week, only fifty-two Americans
were listed Killed in Action. Another 3,200 GIs had flown
home under America's program to give the Vietnam War
back to the Vietnamese.

At 4 A.M. Sunday, Holloway's phone rang: Syrian tanks
were invading Jordan.

As church bells tolled for morning services across Lafayette Park from the White House, Holloway sat at his desk,
full of visions of invading Syrian tanks with Viet Cong flags
racing through the D.C. streets. Somewhere beyond the ringing phones and shouted orders, he heard Hendrix's guitar

screaming "Purple Haze" as Marines from the sorry-your-son-died letters he'd had to write boarded airliners hijacked by PLO terrorists to mushroom-clouded Cuba, where welcoming blondes in bikinis held up pictures of Marxist Allende; in the crowd, watching, stood a portly admiral.

"So do you miss Saigon yet?" said Boyd.

"Is it always like this?" asked Holloway.

"No. Sometimes we actually think we're in control."

At nine-thirty that night, Holloway took notes as the Special Action Group argued its recommendations: Encourage Israeli air strikes against Syria's invading tanks. Launch a reconnaissance plane from an American carrier, making sure that the U.S. plane flew so that Soviet radar would detect it. Put the 82nd Airborne Division on alert, and make sure that news of that alert leaked so the Soviets, Syrians, Israelis, PLO and Jordanians knew the U.S. was serious about the crisis.

Holloway carried briefing books for Kissinger and a State Department prince as they searched the White House for Nixon to present recommendations about how to lead the country along the brink of global war. They couldn't find him. Finally, the Secret Service informed them that "Searchlight" was in the secret Presidential bowling alley. Nixon approved the recommendations while holding a bowling ball.

By Thursday, the strife in Jordan had wound down from a crisis to a situation, with the Soviets pressuring Syria to back off and the U.S. keeping Israel in check. Late Thursday, Holloway sat in on a 40 Committee discussion on how to nudge the Chilean military to a coup against Allende.

Friday, in part through leaks by Kissinger, the Soviet soccer field in Cuba story hit the world press. The Soviet ambassador came to the White House to talk about a summit conference. And Holloway helped pack Kissinger's briefcases for secret negotiations in Paris with the North Vietnamese and Viet Cong diplomats.

"But first he's got to do a snow job," Boyd told Holloway as the White House car drove them to Andrews Air Force Base with briefcases for Kissinger's plane. "Vice President

Ky of South Vietnam wants to come to the States to talk about the war we got ripping up his country. But that would piss off the North Vietnamese, screw up the Doctor's negotiations. Ky's in Paris, and Henry's got to make sure that he stays away from us."

"We got our men dying to protect Ky's government in Vietnam," said Holloway. "And we won't let him come here?"

"Geopolitics," said Boyd as a D.C. ghetto streamed past their car. "Hell of a game."

CHAPTER 11

Quinn watched the federal narc peer through binoculars toward the curb across the street from their second-story townhouse filled only with dust, empty coffee cups and lawmen.

"You better be right this time!" The narc's breath made clouds in the November air. "Last three times, you just wasted ours."

"My partner and I have worked this since spring," said Quinn. "You got zip to complain about."

Quinn and the narc at the window wore scruffy clothes. So did the other two agents from the federal Bureau of Narcotics and Dangerous Drugs waiting beside them.

"Why are you so good to us?" said the narc.

"What do you care? You get the bust. All I want is him."

Outside, on the '68 riot–scarred street of mom-and-pop stores, laundromats, burned-out and boarded-up buildings, shuffled David Strait, Nezneck's driver, now seconded by a chauffeur of his own, a huge, ebony-skinned rent-a-beast known in the streets as Manster.

The radio crackled: lone federal agents were parked a

block away in both directions from Strait. "We got two cars, New York tags cruising closer to—"

"Two!" yelled the narc. "The six of us can't take down an army."

"No!" crackled the radio. "Make that three New York cars!"

Three Big Apple machines glided to the curb by Strait's Caddy. Black men poured out of each car, moving slow, moving cool, eyes hard and hungry.

Radio: "One of the 'Yorkers got a blue gym bag!"

"Hold positions!" radioed the narc beside Quinn. "Let it ride!"

"They're gonna do it right in front of us!"

"They got us two to one! I ain't—Quinn, where you running to?"

Down the inside stairs, along the musty hall. Quinn snatched a wine bottle off the floor, ripped the tear in his blue jeans to an eye-catching flap, flipped the hood on his Army surplus parka over his collar-length hair. Two years of uncut beard flared out from a street veteran's face, far different from the rookie white-boy cop Strait knew. Quinn charged outside with a stagger to match the wine bottle just as Manster opened the trunk of a Caddy to fetch a briefcase.

Not going to lose it now! Not gonna lose!

Strait flashed the briefcase to the New York crew boss.

A metrobus roared toward a wino staggering across the road. Strait gave the briefcase to Big Apple hands and got the blue gym bag as the wino careened out of the bus's path, bounced between two cars and bumped through the grasp of two New York businessmen.

"Watch what the hell you're—"

Quinn grabbed the blue gym bag, yelled, "Police!"

And ran.

Strait stumbled into a New Yorker. The briefcase popped open. A blizzard of green paper filled the air.

Quinn ran toward the corner, heard Strait four, maybe five steps behind him, cursing, running. Thirty feet ahead of Quinn, two New Yorkers loomed like linebackers.

A siren blared from an unmarked car. "Federal officers! Everybody freeze!"

Underneath the cacophony—screaming narcs, sirens, shouts, running feet and his own pounding heart—Quinn heard the *snick* of a switchblade.

He dodged right, tripped up concrete stairs and crashed through plywood dangling across the portal of an abandoned building. Stumbling inside, running—*stairs ahead are*—

Hard fire poked Quinn's back.

He whirled, hit Strait with the blue gym bag. Strait grabbed the bag and Quinn let him have it, drew his .38.

Strait batted the revolver away. The gun skidded into the shadows. Quinn bent Strait's knife, thrust it back on itself. The knife plunged into the blue gym bag, flicked out with a dusting of white powder. Quinn punched.

The blow knocked the two men apart. Blood splattered from Strait's nose. He ran up the nearby stairs. Quinn charged after him—tripped, slid down the stairs, looked up—

Gone, Strait was—

A line of blood drops led up the stairs.

Gun lost somewhere—No time: Go!

Up two flights, drops still . . . *Breath, out of . . . Go!* Four flights. Quinn threw open a dead-end door, ran outside to the roof.

Flat empty black tar, parapet, fire escape, autumn-skied D.C. horizon, Capitol dome.

Quinn whirled and caught/pulled the matador-thrusting wrist of the man attacking him. Strait spun past Quinn like a marionette whose strings had been cut. The switchblade flew from his fist. He would have lost the blue gym bag, but he'd thrust his other hand through the handles' narrow loop so the bag clung to him like a bracelet. Strait flew across the tarred roof, hit the knee-high parapet by the fire escape and flipped over the edge.

"No!"

Quinn raced to the fire escape: the stairs were gone after the first steel grate platform that Strait clung to with both hands. He dangled forty feet above the concrete alley. The gym bag circled his left arm. Quinn sprawled flat on the fire escape platform and grabbed Strait's wrists.

"Pull me up! Pull me up!"

"Why?"

The dangling man stared at Quinn. "Fuck you. I got a better chance on that concrete."

"Give up Nezneck on the heroin, you can cut—"

"Cut you . . . Shit. Wouldn't give you that even if it was true!"

"Give me something or you got no chance."

Sirens died in front of the building. Strait swayed in the wind.

"Nez's got no time for no black-hippie dope trade. He's got bigger things happening."

"Gambling? Women?"

"You couldn't believe what you ain't never gonna find out."

"Tell me!"

"Let me fall or pull me up. I ain't your chump."

Quinn let go.

Handcuffed Strait's left wrist to the fire escape. Even if Strait found the strength to hang from his left hand and used his right to dump the heroin, the switchblade had torn the load open: there'd be residue in the gym bag Strait couldn't separate from his person. Quinn left the dangling man, went to find the feds who'd imprison Strait for narcotics possession, and to find his own gun.

SILENT NIGHT, HOLY *night* . . . The radio carol followed Quinn down the hall of an apartment building in Southwest D.C. The scent of pine wreaths filled the air. A sprig of holly and a brave red bow adorned door 624. Quinn's knock made the ornament tremble.

The door opened a crack. "*Aaa!* Go away! Go away!"

Quinn pushed his way inside.

"Go away!" cried the voice in the kitchen nook. "You're never, never supposed to come here!"

A white sofa and chair ensemble surrounded a coffee table. Quinn chose a chair. "I need to talk to you off the street."

"No!"

"Madeline," said Quinn. "Come here."

A barefoot figure huddled in a white robe slunk to the couch. Tears streaked the powder over freshly shaved café noir cheeks.

"How could you . . . how could you see me like this!"

"You look fine."

"You're not as good a liar as you think." A sniffle, a tissue dabbed at eyes that avoided Quinn. "Do you savage all your friends?"

"I've got no choice. I need to know how it works with prostitutes, call—"

"You get what you can afford. That's how everything works."

"I know what I find on the street. But high-end trade, call girls: there's a hink on the morals squad, so I can't go through my department to find out what's what."

" 'What's what.' 'Call girls.' Is that what gets you off?"

Quinn said nothing.

"If I talk, will you go away? Never come back? No, don't hurt me with another bad lie." Madeline's eyes closed. "Us girls gossip about big-money women. How beautiful, how lucky."

"Are they connected to somebody?"

"Everyone needs someone to watch over them in this town. I should know, I'm all alone."

"For that high-end business, who's—"

"I know gossip. Know 'bout your 'hink.' Some detective who runs a couple street women; poor things, he's supposed to—"

"The cop: What's his name?"

"Something precious, like—Bruce, or something Bruce."

"Billy Bruce?" Memories of leather aftershave, The Silver Mirror strip bar, Nezneck's cigarette smoke.

"If you say so."

"How can I find out about call girls?"

"Make a lot more money." Moist eyes stared at him. "You used to be a real person."

"A name. Somebody who'd know."

"When some *she* gets busted, a hassle, there's a lawyer they call. He likes that trade. Gets off on the action, those parties, being a manly man in a manly business."

"Is he more than just a lawyer?"

"His business makes him a whore's whore, doesn't it? They say he just takes his bite and gets his kicks. They say he's not as smart as he thinks he is, but neither are you."

"His name?"

"Will or something."

"Can you find out—"

"Go to hell. I'm a whore, that's a crime. I'm *me,* that's a crime. But I had privacy. You bullied that away. Are you happy?"

Quinn left to the radio sounds of "White Christmas."

CHAPTER 12

Holloway jerked awake in the dark of his anonymous D.C. apartment. He lay still until his heart stopped pounding. Monday, Christmastime 1970, 5:10 A.M.: enough time to boil water for coffee. He was watching blue flames heat the kettle when a thump landed in the outer hall.

The green-carpeted hall was deserted. Newspapers lay in front of all but one of the other eight blue apartment doors.

Maybe I should ambush the deliveryman, thought Holloway as he picked up his *Post.*

Maybe I should go to my window and jump.

He shook the newspaper over his kitchen table—out fell the envelope.

Clusters of numbers covered the sheet of paper inside the envelope. Holloway checked the date, wrote a key down the left-hand side of a notepad and decoded the admirals' communiqué:

MESSAGE 7 RECEIVED

That envelope Holloway had taped in the paper towel dispenser of the men's room in an all-night restaurant contained a photocopy of a note from Henry Kissinger to Chou En-lai, the premier of communist China, a blank hole on America's diplomatic maps, an officially unrecognized reality of a billion people. Kissinger's note to the Red Chinese leader had been typed on plain paper, handed to the Pakistani ambassador as a response to a Chou En-lai message. Holloway had been unable to steal Chou En-lai's note, but he knew that he'd kept his commanders one step ahead of Secretary of State Rogers and his professional diplomats, who knew nothing of either message. Kissinger's response said an American envoy would be willing to come to China.

INSERTION APPARENTLY ACCEPTED

No shit, thought Holloway. The White House keeps me so busy I barely have time to spy.

CONTACT REFUSED. MISSION CONSIDERATIONS. INCREASE PENETRATION

Holloway carried his coffee to the window, stared out at the falling snow.

In the jungle sky, 'coptering over a country that's so damn small on a map, so damn big one step at a time. Everywhere else existed a dream called the world. This

*sky ruled a separate place. Stench of machine grease
and sweat, the roar of rotors. Drop from the blue,
roller-coaster guts as we skim clearings with two false
insertions. Third time—Go! Out the door! Run to the
treeline, sergeant panting behind, sun bouncing in the
cobweb of tree branches. "Get down! Get down!"
Thick air swirling then the chopper's gone. Quiet.
Ants crawl over the hand gripping my M16. Jungle rot
itches my groin. A strip of trees. Patchwork clearings.
Bomb craters. A crane cuts the overhead blue. Com-
pass says we tumbled out the wrong direction. Radio
checks: seventeen months in-country, this is my only
patrol with Flash Priority. Somewhere down air-
conditioned Saigon way there's a room full of staff
officers and civilians, notepads at the ready. Sergeant
says: "Battalion got chewed up around here last
week." Single file. Keep them strung out so one burst
can't get everybody. Southwest, toward shimmers of
light the map says are rice paddies. Cole works his
mojo at long point. Mardigian—Idaho horseboy—
he's near point. Mizell won't fuck up: give him rear
guard. Remember everything. See everything. Hear
everything. Walk. Time's chains dissolve. Here is the
thick heat intensity of now, the grafted tonnage of a
pack and twelve other men. Each footfall on the red
dirt above no-land-mine-yet is a feeling of been-here
a thousand years ago, a thousand years yet to come.
Ghosts tramp with us. This is clear. Real. Me. Certainty frees a smile as we hump toward the shimmer
of sun and water and a wall of jungle where men just
like us are waiting.*

That snowy Monday in Washington, Holloway marched
upstairs in the White House to lie to a State Department
staffer, convince him his turf wasn't being threatened so he'd
return the phone calls from the Pentagon's arms control representative and begin slaving away on the latest National
Security Study memoranda Kissinger assigned to the bu-

reaucracies to neutralize them with overwork. *If they knew half of what I knew,* he thought.

Then he saw Elvis Presley.

"Can you believe it?" whispered a uniformed Secret Service guard. "Elvis just . . . shows up. Expects to see the President. For a while, the guys on the gate thought he was a fake."

"Who knows about this?" said Holloway, staring at that cultural icon dressed in a dark operatic suit and an open-collared white shirt.

"Nobody, or there'd be a mob hanging around up here."

Holloway hurried back to the basement.

Kissinger's regular secretary was sick. A substitute presided in his private office, a woman who'd relayed to Holloway dozens of magazine details about the celebrities "Dr. Kissinger" dated. Holloway checked his watch: twelve-twenty. Kissinger was out of the building. He threw open the door to Kissinger's office, told the woman who he'd just seen.

"Oh my God!" Her eyes darted to the door.

"Go ahead," said Holloway. "I'll watch the shop."

She scurried away. He closed the door behind her.

Where to start—no time! Briefing books—forget them, I can see most of them outside, hell, I helped organize most of them. Locked file cabinets. Top drawer of the second one is dented.

Holloway's Swiss Army knife sprang the file cabinet's government low-bid lock.

Jumble of manila file folders, FBI seals . . .

SUMMARY OF TELEPHONIC INTERCEPTS
RESIDENCE LINES, NSC STAFF

Other envelopes, FBI wiretaps on reporters—

The outer door flew open. Holloway saw Birdman looking at him—catching him, jackknife and secret files in his hands, the file drawer gaping.

Birdman said, "Hurry! Close it up! She's coming back!"

No better choice. Holloway plopped into the secretary's chair as she returned.

"So if he's not here," said Birdman to Holloway, as if the secretary had walked in on an innocent conversation, "we'll do it the other way."

"Ah . . . Yes. I guess so."

"Did I miss anything?" she said as she reclaimed her chair.

"Just the usual nonsense." Birdman stroked his beard. "And enough of all that for me. I'm going to go out and get lunch, do some Christmas shopping. Stroll around Lafayette Square."

"It's pretty cold out there," she said.

"The trick is to keep walking." Then he was gone.

Holloway found him twenty minutes later in the park across the street from the White House. Christmas carols wafted over them from a Salvation Army bell ringer's post. Birdman held out his gloved hand: "Penzler, Bill Penzler."

"You already know my name," said Holloway as he felt Penzler's bony grip.

Penzler smiled. "Come. If anyone sees us, we're just taking a walk in the park."

The two men in overcoats circled the scruffy block of snow-patched lawn, bare trees and winter-wrapped protesters. Penzler's words floated around them like clouds.

"We could stay by the bell ringer, his radio, but I don't think anybody has a parabolic mike on us. Not here. Not now." He shrugged. "You're one of the chiefs' men, the admirals'."

Holloway noted the plural *men*. Said, "Who are you?"

"You can call me Bill, but nobody does. I'm one of those people doomed to be known by his last name even to his intimate friends." Penzler hushed his already low voice. "I'm your counterpart from across the river. The export-import bank."

"The CIA."

"Like you, a compartmentalized force tasked away from the bureaucracy. My ID says liaison duties with the White

House via our Office of Security, but don't look for me there."

"What, you hang out in this park?"

"Lucky for you I don't, or right now you'd be slammed down in front of FBI agents, Secret Service, them yelling questions you wouldn't dare answer. Your bosses would throw you away. Probably without a trial—at least, not for espionage, not for rifling Colonel Boar's files. They'd bust you out of the Corps, 'let you' plead to some fantasy charge—say a bar fight. Give you the brig to sweat you more and keep everything quiet."

"Who's Colonel Boar?"

Penzler shook his head. "So that's the way they played you. Probably just as well. Clean eyes on the target."

"What target?"

"Did they teach you about MICE in intelligence school? Sums everything up—not just why people become spies, but why they do what they do and how to get them to do it: *M*oney, *I*deology, *C*ompromise, *E*go. Those are true four horsemen of the Apocalypse. Money's easy to understand— wealth is the great American promise. And if it isn't, then ideology provides the rest. Nothing like a true believer on the battlefield—huh, Captain? Compromise, that's my specialty. Get a powerful married man on film with a girl—or boy. Get a Moscow diplomat to break the KGB rules, develop a taste for surfer blondes or jazz-club blacks, and when he sees the pictures, he'll know what Ivan in the Lubyanka will do to him and his children. Ego creates all other motivations—just as it creates Einsteins and DaVincis. A spy or mole acting out of pure ego would be . . . sublime. Almost impossible to detect because his values are not ours. If that's the ego we're facing, we have to break our mirrors to see it."

"Who's Colonel Boar?"

"*Good:* determined, aggressive. I see why they chose you." They reached the corner that would take them past the front of the White House. Penzler turned around and retraced their steps. "I don't think there is a Colonel Boar. Colonel

Boar is what a Soviet defector claims our Dr. Kissinger is—a Soviet mole sent over here, nurtured, positioned to be right where he is now."

"Kissinger is a spy?"

"Personally, I don't think so. The in crowd even joke about it with Herr Doctor. But some of the stars and bars at the Joint Chiefs wonder. Some of the smarter men at the agency worry about it, too. That's one of the reasons for you and me."

"He's passed the most rigorous-security screenings!"

"So did Kim Philby. He was in line to be head of British Intelligence. Nobody believed the rumors about him, either—until he fled to Moscow. As for Kissinger, the only compromising thing in his security file is his relationship with Jill St. John, the actress. She worked for Senator Gene McCarthy's anti–Vietnam War campaign back in 1968."

"You said this mole bullshit is *one* of the reasons we're here."

"And you want to know the others." Penzler shrugged. "So do I. My masters probably told me less than yours told you. My sense is that they're afraid the clowns in this administration will take over the circus. And when the other side is waiting to nuke you or bleed you in little wars or incite revolution in your own streets, you can't have the clowns in charge."

They'd reached the other corner of the park.

"So where does that leave us?" said Holloway.

"I don't know about you, but when I'm not feeling overrun by our official work, trapped in the jungles of Southeast Asia or having nightmares about atomic fireballs—in those moments, when I'm alone with my secret mission, I feel lost. And like an all-alone sitting duck."

"That's why you saved my ass."

"If one of us gets caught, the other one won't be able to hide from the resulting witch hunt. There'll be no support. No rescue. They must have told you the rules about that. If you get caught, you take the bullet and you take it alone."

Holloway let his silence confirm Penzler.

A laughing couple hurried past them. The husband carried a shiny Christmas toy fire truck.

Penzler said, "I tumbled to you when you showed too much curiosity about the Chile stuff. Tell your bosses Nixon and Kissinger have a secret two-track system going there, one covert CIA destabilization program hidden from State, plus another track of dirtier tricks hidden from State and most of the CIA. Your admirals may know that, may not, but either way, you'll score for finding out, and they won't know you've been exposed. See, I never reported your existence to my people."

"Why?"

"I knew you were a good guy. No offense, but you reek of virtue."

"You'd be surprised."

"Really? Good for you. Your innocence is only half of it. When you're sent into a wilderness like ours, you need an ally you can trust. I've been watching you, and today you gave me a chance to try my luck." He laughed. "Thank God for Elvis!

"So now pay me back for saving you," said Penzler. "If you report me, I'll have to report you to cover my ass. The ironic thing is, both our teams are on the same side and probably both know about each of us, but don't care how much we have to sweat it out just to stay sane."

"How do I know that smell coming off you is innocence?"

"That's the last thing I am," said Penzler. "But on the list of sins after my name, I'm willing to jot down a deal with you."

"You don't report about me, I don't report about you."

"Yes. But there's no need to draw the bottom line there."

Penzler adjusted the lapels of his overcoat, then his hands returned to his side. No one saw Penzler's glove slide a tight fold of paper into the Marine's pocket.

"That's a copy of a July memo to Haldeman. Part of it is how they're trying to get the Internal Revenue Service to go after the anti-war movement. The tax man as a political attack dog. Talk about 'playing the game tough,' something about previous suggestions to 'go into' the Brookings think tank after classified material—although I can't understand why a private group would have classified material from our government that Nixon's men couldn't snap their fingers and get through channels. As bizarre as the memo is, your bosses should know about it."

A chunk of lava weighed down Holloway's pocket.

"You have to expand your recon beyond the NSC stuff in the basement if you're going to do your job right," said Penzler.

"I hear you."

"Be careful if you wander around the White House at night. Our President has a tendency to fight the darkness with martinis or scotch and go a-wandering. If you catch him stumbling around—and he remembers—his paranoia and pride will boot you out of the White House, your mission will be neutralized and you'll be no good to anybody."

"And you want us to be good to each other. Share our take."

"You're smart, tough. Plain talking. We don't see that enough in this damn town. You don't have to like me; I can understand that. I don't know if I like myself anymore."

Holloway looked toward the gray horizon.

"But we are in this town," said Penzler. "Here, alliances of necessity and convenience make things possible. I'll give you what I can—help, intel take, a heads-up if-and-when. In return . . . you do what you think is right."

Nathan looked at the man he still thought resembled some sort of bird. In those palest of blue eyes, Nathan saw his reflection, saw himself nod *yes*.

CHAPTER 13

CIA-issue lockpicks weighed down Quinn's right coat pocket as he stood in the silent hall outside a sixth-floor office on K Street, Washington's canyon of lawyers and lobbyists. Four A.M., Thursday, January 28, 1971. Quinn had hidden in the basement parking garage until the cleaning crews finished, peeked at the security guard dozing behind the desk in the lobby, followed the stairwell up to *that* office. Quinn's badge smoldered in his left pocket.

This is the right thing to do, he told himself as he stared at the wooden door bearing the sign: MELVIN C. KLISE. This is the smart choice, the best choice, the gotta-do-it choice.

Plus, no way would he ever get caught.

Quinn kicked in the locked door, caught it with his black-gloved hand as it bounced back toward the splintered jamb. He turned on the lights: plenty of paper pushers pulled all-nighters in the offices along K Street. A glow in one more power canyon suite wouldn't be noticed, but a bobbing flashlight beam might catch the eye of some brief-writing caged lawyer.

Mel Klise's secretary had a lone rose in a crystal vase on her desk. Her two file cabinets first: Quinn found folders for a cola company, a defense contractor, a grocery store chain, two oil companies, half a dozen other multinational firms, a professional football team. Panama had a file. So did Uruguay, an export-import business in Saigon, the Teamsters union. Three files bulged with documents concerning Las Vegas casinos.

But the cabinets held no file labeled American Association for Justice, the organization a feature story in Quinn's slow-news-day New Year's Eve newspaper had said that Joseph

Nezneck, "an old-time D.C. gambler," had recently returned from Yugoslavia to "work with." The newspaper identified the association as "a private prison reform group."

According to the paper, Nezneck "has been left behind by time," a washed-up crapshooter who said: "The only dice in Washington now is in Monopoly games. I went out the other night to some of the old places. I didn't know no one. There was no craps, nothing. They all got long hair."

The demise of illegal crap games had driven Nezneck out of Washington for more than a year, the paper said, compelling him to run a hotel casino in Yugoslavia.

"I was mistreated by their bureaucracy," Nezneck told his hometown rag. "One person can't decide nothing. They gotta have a meeting of 10 guys in cheap suits for every yes, no or maybe. I showed them American know-how, and they couldn't handle it."

Since the communist regime in Yugoslavia prohibited its citizens from gambling, Italian tourists were imported for the casino, said the newspaper. Since no Yugoslavians knew how to deal blackjack or run dice tables, Nezneck set up a training school.

"I had good intentions. I tried to promote gambling."

Nezneck's "shady" past appeared toward the end of the story: minor arrests as a kid in the bootlegging business, his acquittal of the "murder of a reputed underworld finger man." Nezneck insisted he "never knew nothing" about narcotics dealing. "You're asking about the devil."

Although the paper said Nezneck was "popular" with policemen, he complained about harassment by police and federal authorities, citing how the Securities and Exchange Commission forbid him to sell $300,000 worth of stock in his downtown wig store because he failed to disclose his criminal record when he advertised the stock issue.

The newspaper said he wore a monogrammed shirt and necktie, diamond cuff links, a black pinstriped suit, and used a gold lighter to ignite his Pall Malls. The reporter noted that fifty-six-year-old Nezneck lived in a high-rise condo with a twenty-five-year-old girlfriend.

Nezneck said he liked President Nixon, disapproved of violence on TV. What brought out Nezneck's passion, said the paper, was abuse of men like himself who'd once run afoul of the justice system: "Ex-cons are the most mistreated group in the U.S. of A."

Which is why, the newspaper reported, since returning from Yugoslavia, Nezneck had been working with the national association. The story ended with Nezneck saying, "What's happened to justice in America?"

Quinn threw his newspaper across the kitchen.

Then calmed down. Checked Pat Dawson's pink address book, where next to the name "Mel" she'd drawn a star and written two numbers, the first registered to a K Street office of one Melvin C. Klise, the second registered at the same address to the American Association for Justice.

So here I am, thought Q. On the scene of my crime. But it's the right thing to do.

Mel Klise's inner office held an ornate desk, tasteful chairs. Five paintings adorned the walls: a Currier and Ives fox hunt scene, a museum quality Impressionist, a soothing abstract, a print of dogs wearing sunglasses and playing pool, and an oil portrait of a treasured wife, who also smiled from a gold-framed photograph on the desk next to three metal Rolodexes and two telephones.

Quinn leafed through Mel's appointment calendar; found nothing that meant anything to him.

The desk's in box held a file labeled AM. ASS. F. JUSTICE. The folder was empty.

Why is it out? Empty?

The Rolodexes held thousands of names, phone numbers and business cards: senators, Congressmen, Capitol Hill aides, lawyers, executives of multinational corporations, reporters, union officials, a Chinese carry-out restaurant, embassies. Quinn found a card marked "Joe N." with one phone number Quinn knew was Nezneck's and other numbers he wasn't sure of. Quinn used the spy camera from one of his suit-and-tie handlers, shot a few frames of the "Joe N." card, and the

card for the American Association for Justice. He found no
phone card for Pat Dawson.

A cabinet held two fresh shirts and a bottle of mouthwash.

Quinn sat on the table's desk blotter and stared at the
painting of the dogs playing pool.

Do it. Ignore the queasiness. He put the framed photograph
of Mel's wife facedown on the desk (no need to be barbaric),
knocked the pen set and one Rolodex to the carpeted floor.

Saw the desk blotter shifted crooked out of place.

Saw the white sheet of paper poking out from under the
blotter: a photocopy of a letter dated two days earlier, January 26, 1971:

> *Dear President Dick*
>   *Al Dorfman of the Teamsters described for me the*
> *history of the personal vendetta that Bobby Kennedy*
> *had against Hoffa. Jim is a victim of Kennedy's revenge,*
> *continues to be a political prisoner . . . Add my support*
> *to those requesting executive intervention so that he can*
> *be released.*

Quinn didn't recognize the name of the man who signed
this letter to the President of the United States. Jim Hoffa
was the Teamsters boss who'd been sent to prison after years
of federal investigations and charges of union violence,
money scams and racketeering.

Clock is ticking. Quinn photographed the letter and rolled
it up in his coat.

*No leg space under the big desk . . . because there's a hid-
den drawer.* Quinn huddled in the desk well, held the penlight in his mouth while he used the CIA lockpicks to open
the lock on the drawer a real burglar might have missed and
probably wouldn't have had the tools to crack. The drawer
swung open.

Two shelves. The top one held an expensive wristwatch,
two stacks of rubber-banded money that a quick flip-through
tallied as equal to Quinn's annual salary. The bottom shelf
held a crumpled grocery sack; stuck to that wrinkled brown

paper bag was a yellow Post-it note with a handwritten scrawl: "May 27 lnchtime 17th & Penn."

The brown paper bag held twenty-, fifty-, and hundred-dollar bills: $70,000.

Why three groups of cash? One top-shelf rubber-banded bundle for Mel's "personal" needs, the other for "business" expenses, but the paper bag of $70,000. . . "May 27 lnchtime, 17th & Penn."

Quinn photographed the Post-it note, the bag, the cash, then put everything back as he'd found it, relocked the secret drawer. He tossed files helter-skelter through the office, pocketed an envelope of "official" petty cash from the secretary's desk to drop in a charity box later. Quinn unplugged the secretary's IBM typewriter, lugged it out to the hall and left it overturned on the floor. He left the lights on, the splintered door ajar. His watch read 4:57 A.M.

The sleeping lobby guard screamed when Quinn touched his shoulder.

"Police," said Quinn, badging the groggy man. "I spooked some guys running out of your parking garage. I think they were burglars. Pick up your phone, call it in."

By the time the scout car arrived, Quinn had the security guard covering his own dereliction by claiming that "Yeah, I thought I saw a couple guys sneakin' down the stairwell."

TAC Squad officer John Quinn helped two patrolmen check the building; together, they found a burglary on the sixth floor. The security guard now remembered he'd scared "two, maybe three" guys out of the stairwell. Quinn volunteered to wait for the burgled tenant to show up in response to the guard's call. The uniformed cops hurried to cruise the neighborhood for suspicious citizens. Quinn sat behind the desk and watched the dogs in the painting play pool.

Mel Klise beat dawn to his office, a spry entrance, his topcoat draped over the sleeve of his natty suit, his wispy white hair combed back from a gnomish face. "Holy cow! What the—and holy cow: you're *the cop*?"

"Nice to meet you, Mr.—"

"Call me Mel, everybody does. Oh my gosh!" Mel hurried

to his desk, righted the unbroken photograph. "I feel so . . . violated."

The spry man peeked under the blotter—and into the well of his desk.

"Looking for something?" asked Quinn.

"I—Who did this?"

"Burglars. They got spooked, ran before they could take much."

"*Mimi!* Gotta call Mimi, she was so worried when the guard called—" Mel frowned. "Sure it's just burglars?"

"What else could it be?"

"Come on!" Mel led him to the hall. "See down there? You know whose office that is?"

Quinn shook his head no.

"That's Jack Anderson's office. You want to meet him? I know him! Personally."

"Jack Anderson the—"

"The columnist! The guy *The Washington Post* stuck on the funny pages—dumb move. Everybody reads 'Peanuts' so they see Jack, too! That's the office for him and his legmen! They do stories on government boondoggles, J. Edgar Hoover and the Kennedys when they get extreme, congressmen. Muckrakers, that's what they call them. I think Jack goes too far, but—"

"I'm lost," said Quinn.

"The guys who did this to me, they could have been after Jack's office, break in there, plant bugs, see what they could find! He's got a lot of enemies and a lot of people scared." Mel whispered, "That's never a safe combination."

"Why would someone burgle you if they were after Anderson?"

"People do the damnedest things. Maybe they just plain got the wrong door."

"Your name is on yours," said Quinn. "What do you do?"

"Me?" Mel laughed. "Me?" He gave Quinn a business card that listed his address and phone number. Bold letters in the middle read: ARRANGER.

"What the hell is that?"

"What do you got?" Mel led him back into the trashed office. "What do you got, what do you want. Let me arrange it!"

"Wish it was that easy."

"If life was easy, I'd be out of a job! Hell, Washington is made for guys like me! This city is about guys who know guys who can make things happen, who can give 'em an edge, help find a better possibility, cool down somebody's not-so-bright idea. Guys who know how to count the potatoes. Always been that way, always will. Somebody's gotta arrange the this and the that."

"In all this mess, I spotted a file folder for some justice association. What's that about?"

"About doing good. You'd like it. I bet you've locked up some bad people, but the association is out to be sure everybody, even convicts, gets a fair shake.

"Tell me the truth," said Mel. "If a guy does a day of crime, does it make him bad forever?"

"I hope not," said Quinn.

"See? I already *arranged* you and me agreeing!"

"Oh, shit!" Quinn pulled the rolled-up photocopy from his jacket. Mel's eyes widened. "Damn near forgot! I almost stepped on this. Figured I better keep this safe until you showed up.

"This is yours," said Quinn, holding the paper out. "Isn't it?"

"Thank God you found it!" Mel pressed his free hand over his heart. Winked. "I'm not supposed to tell anybody I got leaked a copy of this. I always say, this town doesn't leak, it pours.

"Did you read it?" said Mel.

"Couldn't help myself."

"Can't blame you! Couldn't have trusted you if you said you didn't. But you won't say anything about it, will you? Doesn't need to be in the burglary report?"

"Not unless you want me to—"

"No need for that!"

"Hell, I'll stay out of everything, too."

"Good idea. And you won't . . ."

"I got nobody to tell who gives a shit," said Quinn. "I recognized the President's name, of course, and Mr. Hoffa—"

"A man unjustly punished! That's what the American Association for Justice is all about, helping out him and guys like him who got the short end of the stick."

"—but I can't place the guy who signed the letter."

"He was governor of Nevada, now he's a very important lawyer," Mel whispered. "He's got Howard Hughes for a client."

The two uniformed cops walked into Mel's office. The senior officer shook his head: they'd found no suspects. Quinn knew detectives would soon show up with notebooks and questions.

"Gotta go," he told Mel. "These officers have you covered."

"Thanks for everything," said Mel as he shook Quinn's hand. "And you need anything, you call. You got my card."

"Yes, I do."

"So go on, do your thing like the kids say. Don't worry about this little third-rate deal."

THE BOMB BLEW apart the Senate barbershop in the basement of the Capitol in the dark hours of March 1, 1971. By 9 A.M. that Monday morning, a horde of FBI agents were working the Senate offices, interviewing every staffer who'd signed into the congressional complex over the weekend and showing them four grainy surveillance photos of members of an anarchical left-wing terrorist group called the Weathermen. Every intelligence and counterterrorist cop within fifty miles of the Capitol dome got hot-buttoned, including Quinn, whose commander sicced him to a briefing at the Justice Department.

The thin FBI agent who'd hawked him before stepped out of that crowd of armed men.

"Hey, John!" said the whisker-thin man. "You're assigned with me."

"I don't know you from shit."

"I'm the only guy who can get you out of the shit you've stepped in." The thin man held up a set of car keys. "Come on. It's not like I'm taking you for the long ride."

The thin man shook Quinn's hand with a grip of steel. "Gary Harmon. Call me Gary."

The FBI agent piloted the unmarked sedan toward New York Avenue's seedy strip. "You and me will cruise motels, log the license plates and scope out interesting tourists. While I drive, check out that manila envelope in the glove compartment."

The manila envelope held two spools of eight-millimeter film and a half dozen photos: one showed Mel Klise standing in an office building hall beside an overturned typewriter and whispering to Quinn, another showed Quinn kicking in Mel's office door.

"So what do you think?" asked Gary.

"Looks like illegal electronic surveillance that is inadmissible in a court of law."

"Corridors of multiple-use buildings constitute *public* space, and therefore any law enforcement record of a crime committed in that space—say breaking and entering—is admissible. Of course, no one will use the evidence against you formally, because that would blow the surveillance, so your biggest problem is not what goes to court."

Gary pulled the cruiser to the curb of a seedy rooming house, wrote the license plate numbers of two cars parked in the lot in his notebook.

"What is my biggest problem?"

"That wasn't our surveillance that caught you. Bureau techs service the unit—cool little motion-sensitive auto-trip machine in the hall heating duct—but the intel take goes to the Ivy League boys across the river."

"So how come you got this?" said Quinn as they drove to the next lodging.

"I'm Washington field office. That means it's my job to

be sure Mr. Hoover is not embarrassed by activities of other agencies. When the techs pulled something . . . unusual out of the take, I got a call."

"Is this batch the only copies?"

"Wish I knew. That's everything I could get my hands on."

"So what's my problem?"

Gary parked their car in the parking lot of the Diplomat Motel. He shut off the engine.

"Your problem is, if those boys know you, they own you."

A scream shook their car. A motel room door flew open and a woman wearing only a red bra and a leather skirt ran out into the cold morning air. A hefty man in a suit charged after her, swinging a coat hanger, yelling, "I told you, always get the fucking money first!"

The red bra woman ran past the cruiser as the two lawmen jumped out. Skinny FBI Agent Gary Harmon thrust his palm toward the hanger-swinging man: "Hold it!"

The pimp swung at the FBI agent.

Gary flipped the pimp over his shoulder, shrugged to Quinn: "Marine Corps judo team."

Red bra woman ran and never looked back.

"FBI," Gary told the man he'd thrown to the ground. "I was wondering if I could ask you a few questions, sir. Have you seen any other patrons of this fine establishment with long hair or scraggly beards like my companion here?"

"F.f.f.fff . . . N-n-n-no, man! Just johns 'n' bitches!"

"Ahh. Well, in that case, I couldn't help but notice your discussion with that woman."

"Bitch Aleesh—*ow!*"

Gary grabbed the pimp's ear and dug his thumb into the flesh by the hinge of the pimp's jaw.

"I was wondering if you realized that ripping someone's ear clean off their head or hitting them with a coat hanger is not an appropriate conversational technique. Nor is slapping, punching, pistol-whipping, or other techniques I'd be happy to demonstrate."

"No, man!"

"Well, if you ever need another lesson in communication skills, I'll be glad to oblige." Gary released the pimp. "Thanks for your cooperation. Have a nice day."

The pimp fled in his Cadillac. Gary let him see the FBI log his license plate in a notebook. Gary recorded the rest of the plates in the parking lot, told Quinn, "I could use a cup of coffee."

Everyone in the McDonald's sat far away from the obvious cops.

"Why are you being so good to me?" Quinn asked the FBI agent.

Gary dumped two packs of sugar into his two-creamed cup. "Could be I'm not totally enamored of the Ivy boys. Could be I just like your style. Could be we got common interests."

"How would you know that?"

"A long while back, you pulled some records, and a guy in your system who keeps an eye on stuff for me let me know."

"Nezneck!"

"Took me a long time to be sure you weren't covering a trail, you were following it. This and that happened, you got detailed to Red Squad work, me, too. Kept my eyes on you. Here we are."

"The film the CIA's got: I don't give a shit. Nobody owns me."

"Keep that attitude and your ass clean, and you got a chance."

"Why are they set up on Mel Klise?"

"They aren't."

Quinn took a minute. "The columnist Jack Anderson. They're on him."

"They're all over him," said Gary. "You just got in the way."

"You weren't checking the surveillance just to keep tabs on the CIA. You got your eye on Mel Klise, too."

"You're up, Quinn. I put my trust in your hands giving

you that film. Now it's your turn: tell me about you and Nezneck."

"Why should I?"

"Aren't you lonely, too?"

No shit. Risk it.

Quinn told him everything, from burglarizing Mel Klise to Pat Dawson's murder to the guns-out standoff with Nezneck and the secret war he and Buck waged. Their coffee vanished.

"I figure Mel's cash is politics," said Quinn. "I'd like to know for sure, but for us, for lawmen, it's tainted evidentiary knowledge and no good."

"The evidence might be tainted, but the cash—Who knows? This town runs on bucks and bullshit."

"That means it's your turn to give all this up to me—and no bullshit."

"For me it started because I hate wearing blinders," said Gary. "See, there is no organized crime in Washington, D.C. We at the Bureau barely admit that it exists anywhere, probably still wouldn't except Bobby Kennedy used the BNDD's intel records to embarrass our director in public. So now there's a mob, a mafia, and sources agents have been working for years get to be on the books. But one thing can never be true, and that's that there is any kind of mafia or mob activity in Washington, D.C., the Bureau's backyard. Ask anybody. Ask your department. Ask the Bureau. Ask *The Washington Post.*"

"So?"

"So there's *especially* no mob in Washington headed by anybody named Joe Nezneck. A special agent in charge told me Nezneck couldn't be a mobster, because he's a Jew. But he's not. Besides, being a Jew means shit. Ask Meyer Lansky; everybody knows he's the mob's business whiz and a Jew. We got twenty-nine mob families in twenty-five cities, and those racket boys got a dozen ways to do crime biz with guys who aren't Italian or Sicilian. They got all sorts of hooked-up crews. Their big genius is Meyer, and the Bureau's got Meyer on tape saying Joe Nezneck is one of his protégés."

"Figured that," said Quinn. "Nezneck runs D.C. for the mob."

"Not that simple," said Harmon. "The mob's not like you see on TV, plus D.C. is special. There are three 'open' cities: Las Vegas, Miami . . . and Washington, D.C.

"Everybody thinks the New York families are the big muscle, but Santo Trafficante in Florida and Carlos Marcello in New Orleans look up to no one, even though Marcello's doing time. Those guys, Giancana in Chicago, they don't bow to the Big Apple."

"So Nezneck fits in where?"

"That's the big question. I know he goes back to the days when the mob was taking over Cuba. He worked in a mob casino in Havana, got out the day before Castro took over. New York field office has an informant that says Nezneck is a capo in the Genovese family. Maybe, but New York doesn't own him. I've got him working with Marcello and Trafficante and Bonanno, with Russell Bufalino out of Wilkes-Barre and "Pay Me" Raymie Patriarca up in New England. Nezneck is a Lansky clone: that makes him a wolf. Runs with this pack, that pack, but runs loose. He's the perfect big man for an open city. His past is vice rackets: booze, gambling, women. But he's a Meyer wanna-be, that means his present and future are all about process, power."

"So are we going to get him?"

"You, me, and your buddy Buck?"

"Sure," said Quinn. "Why not?"

They both laughed.

"Know what I don't get?" said Gary. "What's so important that Nezneck ran that woman through a garbage disposal, then had a car thief shotgunned to keep the cover sealed tight on a case nobody can ever make?"

Quinn shrugged. "What I don't get is how does a full-blown American free-enterprise capitalist pig get to run gambling casinos behind the communist Iron Curtain."

CHAPTER 14

That May of 1971, mass arrests of anti-war protesters forced the D.C. police to use the RFK professional football stadium as a temporary prison to hold many of the demonstrators. Q huddled on the football field with thousands of his unknowing peers. Cops still patrolled D.C.'s streets with riot gear in their cruisers the afternoon that Holloway spotted the blond woman silently crying on the marble balcony overlooking the south lawn of the White House.

She should never have to cry, thought Nathan. Especially on a beautiful May day. She pulled at him like a magnet with the way she refused to lean on a marble column for support as gravity stole her tears, with the way she kept her pain silent so she wouldn't disturb a workplace more important than her troubles, with the nylon-sheathed smoothness of her legs.

"It's OK," he said as he closed the French door out to the balcony behind him and she redrew her expression with apology. "Whatever I can do to help you . . ."

She glanced at the staff ID clipped to his civilian suit; hers dangled on a chain around her neck. Her moist eyes were green. "You're one of the military aides, aren't you?"

"Nathan Holloway, captain, Marine Corps. I work in the basement, the NSC."

"Back home they call me Sandy. Never liked that, but Sandra Bennet seemed too . . ."

"Cold."

"Grown-up. Formal. But I always was. So you'd think I'd know better than to cry."

On the other side of the French doors, a White House aide gave a special tour to VIPs.

"Were you in Vietnam?" she asked.

Brace for the gung-ho war rhetoric. At least a Nixon staffer won't toss out "Baby killer!" or spit. "Yes."

"I'm glad you're here," she said. "Billy Fallon, boy I knew in high school. Talked to my mother. He just got killed over there. In the Army."

"I'm sorry. Was he your—was he a—"

"He was just a guy I knew. We weren't friends, not really. He was quiet. There was this ordinary, usual, OK life waiting for him. He was drafted, and . . . I know that just going there doesn't make you noble or a hero, but . . . Now he's gone. No more for forever.

"Look at me," she said, wiping her cheeks. "I'm a press aide. If a reporter sees this, I'll be a headline: 'Nixon Aide Mourns War.' Every jerk will find some twist for that."

"If a newshawk targets you, tell him I'm a bastard and I broke your heart."

"Nobody'd believe that," she said, "any of it."

They stood in the afternoon light. Not touching.

"This is the wrong time, wrong place," said Nathan. "I want to see you again. There are a hundred reasons why you don't—"

"OK."

Wipe off your stupid grin! "I'll call—what should I call you?"

"Let me hear you try."

"Sandra," he said. "Sandy."

"The unformal sounds . . . OK. From you."

He watched her walk away, then floated to the Oval Office, where a secretary responding to his glow revealed that President Nixon huddled behind those closed doors with top aides Haldeman and Ehrlichman. As she shifted in her chair, happily married yet appreciative of the flirtatious aura of the handsome young officer grinning beside her desk, a white-coated Navy steward carrying a tray with a coffee flask and cups walked past them, rapped on then opened the Oval Office door.

President Nixon's distinctive grumble slid out of the open

door as the steward entered the Oval Office: "—be sure he's a ruthless son of a bitch! That he'll do what he's told. That every income tax return I want to see, I see. That he'll go after our enemies and not go after—"

The door closed.

Make up something quick! the Marine ordered himself. Ask about . . . movies. Had she seen any movies that maybe a guy like him who had a date with a smart wo—

The Oval Office door swung open and Holloway heard Chief of Staff Haldeman's voice inside the Presidential lair: "—it's using the law to its full art."

Nixon said, "Art. That's it. Over in the corners."

The door closed; Holloway ran out of excuses and floated back down to his NSC desk to make coded notes on what he'd heard to dead-drop to the admiral.

After that day's sunset, Sandy and Nathan sat in the corner of a beer and hamburgers bar, a place they'd chosen because of its lack of White House staff customers.

"So is it turning out like you expected it to?" she asked.

"What, life?"

"I was thinking more of the White House, but, OK, life."

"Life is strange enough. And the White House . . . it's like no place I imagined."

"I try not to imagine anything anymore," she said. "Getting through the day is hard enough."

"Bullshit." Anger flared in her eyes, but he kept going, all or nothing: "Yes, this life you and I are doing is strange, hard, but . . . you're not the kind of person who plods along, suffering it as it comes. You're looking to find something bigger than yourself that's worth all this life."

"Is that me? Or you?" She smiled. Ordered another beer.

At her rented townhouse door, she let Nathan cup her face, kiss her oh so softly.

Her forehead pressed against his chest. "Go home, Marine."

Sandy smiled, went inside and locked her door. Nathan sailed back to his apartment.

Friday Nathan worked until eleven-thirty at night, sifting

through battlefield intelligence reports to help Boyd prepare a reality check to contrast with the latest hints from North Vietnamese negotiators in the secret Paris peace talks. He didn't begrudge devoting all his time to work, because when he'd called her at her White House desk earlier in the day, Sandy had told him she'd agreed to "volunteer" to work that night, helping with the start-up of Nixon's re-election organization, something called the Committee to Re-Elect the President.

"Professionally speaking," she said, "I'd have called it something else; the acronym CREEP is not going to help win the hearts and minds of the voters."

On Saturday the threat of nuclear war was officially only in the medium range, Middle East/Israel versus Anybody crises seemed likely to stay in the back alleys, no major offenses were shaking Vietnam (though Americans were still sliding into body bags), and whatever was happening in Chile seemed beyond his covert reach, so Nathan justified taking the night off to go to the movies with Sandy. She held his hand as *The Summer of '42* flickered on the screen. Sunday he took her to dinner. When he walked her to her door, she put her arms around him, whispered, "OK, Captain, I surrender."

"Me, too," he said as he kissed her hair. "Me, too."

She was soft and true blond, breasts that hid in his palm, and she felt the terror raging in him before she reached down and found he was limp.

"OK," she whispered, kissed him softly. "It happens. It's OK."

"No, it's not. Not with you, not you, not—I'm—"

"Don't say you're sorry."

"I have to, I don't want any lies with us."

She kissed him. "Do you think that there would be?"

"No, I, it's just . . ."

"Hard to trust?"

"So to speak."

"At least you haven't lost your sense of humor. What is it that's hard to trust? Me? You? Us?" She felt him shrug;

said, "Don't worry. Trust will come. And I'm not going anywhere—after all, it is my house."

Sandy lay across his chest but her weight was nothing and
he felt her sigh into comfortable, felt her want to be *here*.
He surrendered to exhaustion he'd fought off since his pancake house meeting with the Admiral, smelled her sunshine
hair and the cool sheets and half-asleep her hand brushed
across/found him hard—before he could think, she'd straddled him and he didn't have to stop.

Holding her, calling her name. Tears on her cheek, his,
too. Kissing, he couldn't stop kissing her. After tenderness
came hunger, her long nipples electrifying his tongue. When
he mounted her she pulled her knees up along his arms,
rocked and moaned, going so long, she screamed *Yesss*.

Tuesday was beautiful. Robins, crisp air but a warm sun.
Nathan and Sandy snuck away from the White House for a
carry-out sandwich lunch in Farragut Park, four blocks from
the White House, the turf of ordinary Washingtonians, lawyers and secretaries from the K Street corridor, lobbyists,
bicycle messengers, whoever, Nathan didn't care as they sat
on a bench, ate and laughed and told each other secrets about
everything except politics and government and war. He
couldn't keep his hands off her thighs where her skirt ended,
and she let him. They stole one last kiss. She disappeared in
the crowd to follow the plan and appear at the White House
five minutes earlier than he. Nathan crumpled their brown
paper bag into a ball, spotted a trash container—set, pump,
shoot . . . two! He grinned, turned to walk out of the park
and there, smiling at him, stood Penzler.

"Tell me," said Penzler. "Is that business or pleasure?"

"That's personal."

The two men fell in step, crossed to the least crowded side
of the street and walked.

"Really. Congratulations. Press office, isn't she? Not much
access worth having there. She could make something of it,
I suppose, but probably not us. Reported about her yet?"

Holloway kept walking.

"Smart," said Penzler. "Don't let them muck about in your

private life. Not that we're supposed to have one, but every-one does. Corners here and there. Secrets. It's OK, I under-stand. Me, too. We're both safe there—as far as I know."

"Were you looking for me?"

"Always looking. Maximize every opportunity in every creative fashion possible. Like for instance—Sandra? Is that her name? She affords you a chance to be in step with the times, maximize your pleasure, and creatively increase your abilities in our business."

"What are you talking about?"

"Just because we live in the free love era doesn't mean that love can't pay." Penzler's bony fingers cupped Nathan's elbow as they walked. "There's an informal group. Couples only. We pick a night, a house, get together . . . What hap-pens is totally voluntary for everybody. But even a wispy guy like me has no trouble pairing off—especially since you and your date can make it a rule that if a man wants her, then you have equal access to somebody. Given a young stud like you and a blonde like her, you two should have your pick. And besides some wonderful personal experiences, pro-fessionally you'll get to meet people you should be close to anyway: Pentagon types, lawyers, *Post* reporters—you'd be surprised."

"I already am. Does your . . . wife enjoy these swapping parties or whatever you call them?"

"I call them pleasure *and* business. My wife died when we—I—was stationed in Pakistan. Snake bite." Penzler sighed. "But one must go on. And though I don't have a lover, I know a number of fascinating, adventurous women. I can swallow my insecurities and introduce you to—"

"Leave my life alone. Leave S—my friend alone, too."

"You're probably right, we shouldn't shit where we eat." As Nathan reeled from that crudity, Penzler said, "Besides, we have enough trouble to worry about."

"What are you—"

They'd reached the State Department neighborhood known as Foggy Bottom. Rows of townhouses stretched toward the new Watergate office-hotel-apartments complex by the river.

"I hear trees rustling," said Penzler. "Rumors of movements. I think somebody's been activated, and we're the target."

"I don't like walking around with a crosshairs on my back."

Quinn's senses tingled, but he saw only the innocent city, heard only their footfalls.

"I've got no proof," said Penzler. "Just a feeling. Instincts. But spooks like us live or die by instincts. And logic. It's logical to assume that somebody should be on guard and watching out for us—Hoover's boys, Nixon's people . . . *somebody*. But nobody is there to be seen. Like the dog who didn't bark, but should have."

"Paranoia creates its own trap."

"Better for us to get caught in our own trap than someone else's." Penzler shrugged. "Doesn't matter if I'm wrong, it matters if I'm right. So let's assume I'm right, and start hunting whoever might be hunting us."

Three cruising blue-jeaned college boys snickered at the two men trapped in cinched-down ties. Penzler waited until their footsteps couldn't be heard, then gave an envelope to Holloway.

"Whoever's after us will find a way into the White House," said Penzler. "You can't stab a man in the back from across town—well, you can, but . . . That's a master key for the locked files in the Secret Service's White House Personnel Clearance Unit. No plausible way I can get in there, but you . . . Get assigned to the Security Council's vetting duties. That gets you file room access whenever you want—you're far too busy to work regular hours. The security officer gives you the file you request, relocks the cabinets, leaves you alone. That key lets you check everybody's files, not just what's logged out to you."

"What am I looking for? Who?"

"Someone who can roam like we do, hunt like we do. Someone who's got holes or something—odd in their file."

"I could spend a lifetime on this, plus my mission for . . . and my real job."

They reached a scruffy lot near the Parkway separating the city from the river.

"A lifetime is all we have," said Penzler. "Let's not waste it. I know you've got a lot going and that this is a long shot, but if it works, we'll all be safer."

A mosquito crouched on the back of Penzler's blue-ribboned hand. The mosquito's table stayed as still as a rock. Second after second ticked by. Nathan watched the mosquito bloat. Penzler's slap came as blur. The mosquito was crushed in a smear of blood.

"The trick is to realize that the hunter is there, let him think he's getting what he wants, then . . ." Penzler smiled: "Give it a try. See what you can do."

Mosquitoes swarm off rice paddy pools thick with the dung of absent water buffalos and farmers. A blasted hooch sags by the paddies. Good place to rig booby traps. Watch the treeline, one hundred meters, closer, cl—FLASH far right/BRDING! A slug dents FNG's helmet! Slam to the ground! O'Brien rips a burst! Sergeant yells: "Two! Hard right! Two!" M16s chatter! Wriggle to the radio operator: "Laptop! This is Sandman! Contact, say again, contact!" "Sandman this is Laptop. What are your readings?" "Taking fire, coordinates—" "Sandman, have you effected mission data?" Cole and Mardigian run for the treeline, Sergeant yells, "Motherfucking new guy fucking fire! Cover fire!" "Negative, Laptop, securing—" "Sandman, proceed mission." Cole and Mardigian make it into the trees. Nobody shooting at us—now. Leapfrogging, half of us run while half sprawl and watch the jungle beyond our rifle sights. Treeline, last in is Mizell. Sergeant spotted where the flashes came from— maybe. Cole unslings a blunderbusslike M79 grenade launcher, pops one of the new rounds toward "maybe." The explosion mists green the jungle Cole shot.

Silence. Cole says, "Now we call our taxi?" Reply: "You want to go measure your hole?" "How the hell do you measure shredded trees—sir?" Sergeant figures two VC, sniper team. Gone now. Probably. The fucking new guy moans to Big about how smart he was to wear his steel pot, how lucky: "Gonna never fucking take this thing off! Gonna get married in this fucking beautiful thing!" Tell Sergeant: "We're men with a mission." Form up. Into the jungle. Gonna fucking get married in that beautiful thing.

Nathan ordered himself not to think about marriage during May of 1971. He saw Sandy whenever he could, though after that first night, he never again risked sleeping at her apartment: every morning he had to check his *Washington Post*. She bought his argument that his D.C. pad was closer to the White House than her Virginia townhouse, and thus the best place to sleep for an NSC aide who might have to race back to work in the dead of night. They vowed to keep their affair quiet: who could guess the consequences of an office romance in the buttoned-down atmosphere of the Nixon White House? Sexual adventures were the prerogative of National Security Advisor Henry Kissinger.

Colonel Boar, thought Holloway: still don't believe it. Know you wiretap people who work for you, flatter Nixon as a genius to his face and make fun of him behind his back (like your aides do to you), take it when the President baits you with "Jew boy" talk, change masks from heartbeat to heartbeat and phone call to phone call, whisper to reporters all over town and rail against "leaks" in the White House, suck up to old-money bluebloods and Rockefeller cronies and Hollywood actors. But a Soviet mole . . . That can't be true! *MICE*—Money, Ideology, Compromise, Ego. None of them are big enough for you or in you for *that*.

Holloway let the overworked NSC aide in charge of reviewing White House–cleared personnel-security reports beg him to take that load off his back. Holloway waited until all eyes in the White House were busy making sure nothing went wrong with the state dinner for Anastasio Samoza, the bloated military dictator of Nicaragua. While gowns, tuxedoes and dress uniforms glamorized the White House State Dining Room, in the gray-columned Old Executive Office Building next door, Holloway sat in a locked room full of government file cabinets, a stack of FBI, Secret Service and other agency personnel-security reports at his fingertips.

Where are you? he thought as he searched dossiers for a secret hunter. Do you even exist?

Two files burned in his hands: Liddy, G. Gordon. Ex-FBI agent. Former prosecutor. Treasury Department assistant. Firearms expert. Detailed to White House domestic operations. A gunner, but who was he looking to put in his sights? And for who?

Simon, Jud. A scant five months earlier, Jud Simon had been in the Army. U.S. Special Forces, the Army's elite Green Berets counterinsurgency warfare unit all but under the command of the CIA. His two-page service record claimed the closest he'd gotten to Vietnam was the Philippines. Some time in Iran. Weapons, intelligence, "counter-intrusion tactics" and medic expertise. His records called him a "beyond outstanding" soldier—but officially, he did nothing interesting during his three-plus-years hitch in Special Forces. Then in a blur, he went from being an Army sergeant to a rookie Secret Service uniformed branch trainee to elite White House duty.

Holloway photocopied those two files, used his Swiss Army knife to unscrew the plastic front of the copy machine, and rolled the copy counter dial back to where it had been.

Could read Sandy's file, see the wonder of her school transcripts, see how beloved she was by her friends and family, who the FBI would have interviewed for her clearance.

Can't do that to her.

Kissinger's file was as thick as a fist. Data back to World War II.

Holloway glanced at his watch: *Hurry!* A random report caught his eye: a Secret Service alert. The alert said that Kissinger's "social friend" actress Jill St. John was a long-

time companion and former business partner of Sidney
Korshak, a Los Angeles attorney "affiliated with organized
crime." Korshak and the actress had been roughed up by the
Securities and Exchange Commission over a murky deal involving a Las Vegas casino.

Penzler'd mentioned the beautiful James Bond movie her-
oine, thought Holloway. Took a shot at her for legitimate
though leftish political activity as a security risk—but never
mentioned any mob ties to her and Kissinger. Maybe he
didn't know.

Holloway locked Kissinger's file back in its cabinet.

Cruising through the White House, the clatter of the state
dinner echoing down the halls, Holloway spied a watch commander for the uniformed branch of the Secret Service: *How
can I bring up Jud Simon?*

The watch commander drew Holloway close. "What's going on?"

"What do you mean?"

"Your boss Kissinger just pulled Searchlight out of the
state dinner! The protocol boys are having a fit! If we got
another crisis, gonna get demonstrators. I gotta scramble!"

"I'll see what I can tell you," said Holloway.

The watch commander said Nixon and Kissinger were
huddled in the Lincoln Sitting Room.

Where I've got no business going, thought Holloway.

Risk it. No one challenged him, but when he got to the
Lincoln Sitting Room, the door was open and the room
empty, except for two glass snifters that smelled of brandy.
In the Situation Room, all he could learn was that a secret
cable had come for Kissinger, who then raced upstairs. "Why
do you want to know?" asked someone. Holloway yawned:
"Just want to be sure it's safe to go home." Before he birthed
any more curiosity, that's what he did.

Penzler met him during lunch hour the next day at the
National Gallery of Art.

"Don't worry about Gordon Liddy," said Penzler, "I'll
take him. But this Jud Simon. You've got the best crack at

him: you both wore uniforms, he's your age. And he reeks of intrigue."

They strolled over marble to a room of American scenes painted with such intense realism that they seemed more surreal than the swirling blue Picassos in another gallery.

"What else?" asked Penzler.

"Something with Kissinger and Nixon, something they're excited about. Really excited."

"So I've seen," said Penzler. "Any ideas?"

"Nothing I'm sure of."

"Let me know when you can."

"*If* I can."

"Yes," said Penzler. "*If*. Don't you think that's our most *fascinating* word?"

"I'm more of an *is* man myself."

"Pity." Penzler swept his examination from the paintings to the room's shimmers of light. "We have to go now before we're seen. I'll watch out for you, and I'm sure you'll watch out for me. After all, if you can't trust a Marine, who can you trust?"

CHAPTER 15

Quinn willed himself to merge with the wall of an office building on K Street. He wore sunglasses, an Army surplus shirt over colored T-shirts, jeans. Even though it was a sunny May 27, the breeze made him shiver as he sought invisibility in the passing stream of men in business suits, women in office clothes, construction workers with American flag decals glued to their hard hats. Quinn checked his watch: two more hours before the end of "lnchtime."

Don't think about the people walking past and they won't see you. Don't tense up, telepath your presence. Don't lock on the building across the street that you're watching or all you see is the doors, not who comes out of them.

If he's got a car, I'm fucked. If he hails a cab, got a chance. He shouldn't use a car: "17th & Penn." Only four blocks away. Nice day—

A delivery truck clattered across Quinn's view, then he saw across the busy four-lane street to where a black woman stepped past a glass door being gallantly held open by Mel Klise.

Don't move, catch his eye and make him look!

Mel wore a blue suit. When he walked west on K Street, Quinn spotted the brown paper bag in Mel's right hand. A brown bag. Like lunch; *lnchtime.*

Quinn flowed west on the sidewalk across the street and parallel to Mel.

Mel turned left at the corner. Quinn dodged through K Street's raceway traffic with another jaywalker to keep controlled distance between him and his quarry. All it would take was five unseen seconds, a couple of steps, and Quinn could lose him in an alleyway or—

"Watch where the fuck you're going!"

Bounce off that guy! Quinn hid in the wake of a lumbering fat man in the lawyer suit.

Mel walked on without a backward glance—and with the brown bag of $70,000 in cash.

Quinn followed him past the Army-Navy Club, past Mc-Pherson Square, an urban greenery with trees and benches and office workers out to lunch with brown bags just like the one Mel carried; pigeons pecked the sidewalk by their shoes. Mel headed through Lafayette Square, across from the White House.

"Hey, man, spare some change?" Quinn ignored the college-dropout beggar.

Mel entered an office building up the street from the White House.

Run! Risk it! Get there before—

Revolving doors spun Quinn into a tiled lobby where he was alone and ran to the elevators. The brass bar above the doors was solid, no backlit floor numbers. His hand pressed against the elevator's doors felt the hum of machinery.

Up there. He's somewhere up there! And I don't know where!

Quinn scanned the building directory: law firm–sounding places, something called CREEP.

Sunlight spiraled as the revolving glass door spun. Quinn raced to its turnstile, averted his face from the business-suited men pushing their way in, spun out to the breezy May day.

Son of a bitch! Quinn stomped into Lafayette Square. *But I know generally where the Arranger went. I can narrow the possibilities down to who might have gotten the $70,000.*

Gasoline: Quinn caught the scent of gasoline. Not car engine fumes—raw gasoline.

Ten steps ahead of Quinn, a man wearing a rucksack shuffled toward the sidewalk bordering the park and Pennsylvania Avenue, toward the black iron fence surrounding the White House.

Gasoline . . . Molotov cocktail . . . bomb.

"Hey!" Quinn ran after the rucksack man. He wore a high school graduation suit, reeked of gas. His eyes were dead. Quinn jumped between the rucksack man and the White House. "Hey, we know each other. What's going on with you?"

Never seen him before. Hair is home-cut short. Imagine him with long hair, freak clothes.

"You remember me, don't you? John Quarell?"

"No." *Nothing. No emotion. Just a bomb of gasoline on his back.*

"Sure you do. We're bros."

Dead eyes drifted past Quinn, drifted toward the oh-so-close White House.

"Are you stoned?" *Nothing.* "What are you doing?" *He's holding an envelope. Is he strapped up with dynamite? Where's the detonator?* "I can help."

The dead eyes drifted back to Quinn.

"That's right, I can help. I'm your friend, remember? You're—"

"Too late."

"I bet there's something I can do." Has the Secret Service spotted us? Can't let them bust us together, or he'll pass the word that I was there, and when I don't get arraigned for attempted bombing of the White House, my cover will be—

"No, man! Don't walk away—"

"Don't touch me!"

If he blows now, the blast will shred a dozen innocent bystanders. Kill me.

"Hey, whatever you want." Punch his throat and while he's gasping find the detonator, fuck my cover, he could kill ten, twenty pe—

"I'm standing here, still as a rock. Bet you can, too."

The man with the rucksack froze on the grass in front of Quinn.

Oh, *shit*! If the Secret Service spots us, if they react to bomber threat, they'll green-light the snipers on the White House roof, clean shot, they'll hit the gas.

Quinn said, "How about I look at the envelope? I'll give it right back."

The pale hand holding the envelope floated up, dropped after Quinn took its burden.

Quinn's gun rubbed against his spine. If he's that slow, that disconnected, I can clear leather and blast one smack through his forehead so he'd drop like a sack of cement.

And "Gunshot!" would pull every Secret Service spotter straight to me. They'd see a long-haired freak with a pistol, a suit-and-tie victim falling to the grass. Hell with a green-light authorization, the sharpshooters'd drop me dead on the grass, and maybe set off the bomb, too.

"Is this your name and Soc' number printed on here?" asked Quinn. "Steven Pettigrew?"

"Better this way. Now I know somebody's got it. Knows what to do."

"But, Steve, I don't know. You gotta tell me. What's in the envelope?"

A mother pushed a baby stroller past them; she wrinkled her nose at the gasoline smell. Mom and stroller stopped to bask in the park's warm sun. Out of earshot. Still in the blast zone.

"Steve: what's in the—"

"Everything. The . . . how they arrested me."

"For the May Day demonstration? Cool, I was arrested, too!"

"Did they . . . did they put you in the jail?"

"No, man, the stadium, about a thousand—"

"Put me in the D.C. jail. They were supposed to. That's the deal. Civil disobedience. We break the law, they arrest us. The jail is the just punishment for doing what's right. But they . . . I have to go now. It's all in the envelope."

"No! Wait!" Let me get closer. "You need to tell me. So I know it's true."

A tear rolled down Steve's scrubbed raw cheek. "They didn't lock the doors."

"Who? What doors?"

"Cell doors. The guards went away. And they came in. Grabbed my hair. Called me hippie bitch. Tried to fight. They were so strong, five or six of . . . They held me down and they . . . and they . . . Over and over again. I screamed and they laughed and said I was a faggot hippie, that now I was in their 'care and custody,' and they . . ."

"Oh God, Steve, the police. Cops don't mean that to—"

"They dragged me down to another cell. A line. Kept counting off numbers. 'For your scrapbook.' After nineteen, I . . . Next morning, guards hosed me down. Said the moratorium fund had paid my fifty-dollar fine for disturbing the peace. Put me outside."

"It's OK. It's over. Come with me. We'll find somebody who—"

"Who can do what? Make it not real? Give me back . . ."

"We can go to the police, have the guys who did this to you—"

"They're already in jail. The cops don't care."

"Yes, they do! Honest, yes, they do! Some cops care! They can—"

"They put me there. They had to know. The deal was to

put me in jail, I earned jail, deserved jail. Not . . . But they wanted their law."

"Doctors, we'll find—"

"What's the cure for that? For me?"

"Your family, friends—"

"How can they look at me? Wendy, she . . . If I tell her . . ."

"She'll understand! So will—"

"Can't ever be a man, do a man's thing like they . . . All that's dead. Can't fix what's dead. Can only make people see. Force them to know."

Quinn saw it in his mind. Buddhist monk sitting ablaze in a Saigon street. Quinn knew that dead-eyed Steve standing before him lived in that vision. "The gas is just for you."

"It'll stop everything for me. And for a moment, just one lousy moment, it'll force everyone to see, to know. Maybe stop someone else from . . . to see. They'll have to see."

No detonator, no bomb, just a can of gas. Can tackle him, muscle him down. Secret Service will come running, bust us. Probably ship him to St. Elizabeth's nuthouse, shoot him full of drugs.

Put in a death place by cops with badges just like mine.

"No," said Quinn.

"It's the only way left."

Grab him, get the gas, get him to . . . No, he's got to want to walk away.

"Won't work," said Quinn. "You sit in front of the White House, pour the gas over yourself, flick a lighter, won't stop the war that made you do what . . . that put you . . . That won't stop nothing."

"It'll stop me. At least I can do that one thing."

"Yeah, but they'll laugh at you."

Steve blinked.

Quinn's river of words floated him closer, ever closer to Steve.

"Yeah, I got the envelope, but even if I get it on the front page of every newspaper, they'll laugh at you. They'll know you're a punk who they got over on, who they won from,

Nixon and the war guys and psychos in the jail. If you burn yourself up, they'll know they won. Wendy, your folks, your friends—all they'll feel is pity. Plus pissed off that you didn't let them try."

I hit something in those vacant eyes! Quinn stood nose to nose with the man in the high school graduation suit. The stench of gas swirled around them.

Quinn slid the rucksack off Steve's shoulders.

"If you don't let the good guys try, you let the bad guys win. You don't want to do that. Maybe we can't help you, but you have to let us try. Hell, you can always come back here."

Quinn backed out of the park, away from the White House and its army of badges. The heavy rucksack swayed at his side. His eyes never left the man who followed him like a child. The stench of gas and his own sweat swirled around Quinn like a toxic cloud.

Get him away from here. Get him to somebody who . . . "All your stuff is in the envelope, right? Who to contact, your folks, Wendy, where they are."

Each step Steve took after Quinn seemed stronger.

Got to put distance between him and the rucksack. "You know the Little Red Bookstore? I gotta go stop some guys from doing more bad like happened to you. I'll take the gas, you go there."

Quinn stiff-armed Steve's chest. "Go there now. You'll be safe. The Little Red Bookstore. Ask for me, John Quarell. Remember that. I'll take care of what you want me to take care of, I'll find you, we'll do this right, you'll be OK. Here—that's ten bucks I stuffed in your pocket. Catch a cab to the bookstore. Tell them you're waiting for me, for John Quinn."

"Said your name was Quarell."

"Just ask for John. Go now."

The dead-eyed man shuffled away on the sidewalk. At the corner, he looked back.

"Don't worry!" yelled Quinn. "It'll be OK. I won't let anyone laugh at you. I promise."

Quinn saw the traffic light at the far end of the block turn green. Saw Steve raise his hand as if to flag down a taxi. Saw that hand become a fist and the fist soften to the two-fingered V salute that meant "victory" for their parents and "peace" for them. Quinn raised his hand to return the salute.

Steve Pettigrew stepped into the path of an accelerating bus. Brakes screamed. A horn blared. The bus smacked him spinning through the air to crash on the blacktop. Pedestrians screamed. Quinn watched, his hand full of a half-finished gesture.

In the blur of time that followed, Quinn swore to his police superiors what he wanted to believe, that a citizen had died in a senseless accident. Quinn burned the envelope, let parents and a girl named Wendy grieve over an ordinary death. He filed a report alerting D.C. jail authorities to their risk from civil suits because of lax inmate protection as confided to him by "confidential police sources." Quinn knew the report would do little good; knew it was all he could do. Most of all, Quinn tried to forget everything about that day except that it wasn't his fault, he'd done his best, he kept his promise: no one laughed at the young man who died broken on the street.

CHAPTER 16

Sandy discovered Nathan lying awake beside her in their bed at four in the morning.

"Can you talk to me about it?" she said.

"I wish."

"Whatever's eating you up, you have to talk to somebody. Or you'll disappear into your silence, and I couldn't bear that."

"I'll try," he promised.

She held him until he let go of the world and slid inside her.

Holloway arrived two hours early for the rendezvous on the city docks of the Potomac that Saturday while Sandy "volunteered" at CREEP. "You can't believe the cash that's coming in," she'd told Nathan. "I feel like a bank teller." He loitered in the open-air fish market, spotted no hunters' eyes. An hour passed. The *Spirit of Washington* tour ship deposited its morning group. Holloway tipped the burser to let him board early with the cleaning crew. Holloway climbed to the upper deck, stood at the rail so he could see the parking lot and nearby streets. The spring afternoon was crisp and beautiful.

Taxis, tour buses and private cars began to discharge passengers—tourists in bright-colored pants, a pack of high schoolers charging out of a bus from Missouri.

A gray-haired woman in red pants and a white golf jacket chattered her way up the ladder's metal stairs to the top deck. The beefy man in the yellow windbreaker trailing her fussed with the two cameras slung around his neck, with the camera bag slung over his shoulder.

They moved to the side rail to get the best view as Holloway watched a white station wagon park in the lot. Admiral Burt Petersen climbed out of the station wagon. He wore civilian clothes, locked his car door, and hurried to the gangplank.

Holloway swept the shore with his eyes: no one seemed focused on the Admiral.

The gangplank slid aboard. The ship's horn blared. Engines rumbled and the *Spirit of Washington* chugged away from the Potomac's shore, the city skyline slipping into its wake.

A pack of teenagers charged toward stairs just as the Admiral reached the top deck. A boy yelled, "Hold it!" His companions mugged at his camera. The Admiral turned his back to the camera's flash. The loudspeaker announced that the buffet and beverage bars were now open. Most passengers hurried into the covered decks, leaving Holloway and the Admiral standing alone at the upper rail amid the cold wind off the river.

"Where are your watchdogs?" asked Holloway.

"Not here to see a mistake I didn't want on the log."

A frail widow raised a camera. The Admiral lowered his face into his hands until after the widow's click. Holloway and the Admiral stood so no one could hear their whispers.

The Admiral said, "I'd hoped you'd forgotten that putting a flower pot on your window ledge is a signal for a meeting. We shouldn't ever meet. You've got your mission."

"You need to give me more," said Holloway.

"I gave you orders, that's all a Marine needs."

"And I'll keep following them. But I'm shaky about *why* I'm doing *what* I'm doing. You've got to help me, you're my commanding officer, that's your job."

"No junior officer lectures me on my job!"

"Best lesson I've learned is to listen to my men in the field. For you, that's me." The river flowed beneath their boat. Holloway stared at the man he'd known forever. "Is Kissinger a mole?"

"That doesn't matter."

"Are you crazy!"

"No, I'm an officer of a ship in a typhoon. A ship captained by a mad genius juggling nuclear bombs who gets drunk every other night but who was chosen for his post by a system I've pledged my life to defend.

"Kissinger—that two-faced Harvard bastard pisses me off. Maybe some of the joint chiefs are right, maybe he is a Soviet agent. Half the time, with the 'negotiations' he does, he qualifies as an inadvertent agent. The other half of the time, he's superhawk: bombing runs, covert stuff you don't want to know about. We can't prove anything against him. We can't just take him out. He's got powerful allies. Even if his ultimate loyalty is to himself, he's brilliant. Maybe we're lucky if he is a Soviet spy: Moscow's full of trigger-happy fanatics. If Herr Doctor is whispering what we're *really* doing, that we're not about to launch an attack at them, that we're militarily strong enough so that our strategy of

Mutual Assured Destruction works, maybe we're all a little safer then.

"Besides, Kissinger and Nixon have their secrets from us, their games. Well, we've got our secrets, too. Secrets like you."

"They're all excited about something."

"Kissinger's sneaking into Red China, gonna open that door in time for Nixon to be a visionary statesman before the elections."

"You've got other people on them, too," whispered Holloway.

"That's not a mission concern of yours."

"Why are we doing this? Even if I buy your who-cares-if-Kissinger-is-a-mole crap, it's not just me: you've got a whole team targeted at our Commander In Chief. Why?"

"You don't have a need to know."

"I'm running in the middle of it! Technically, I'm spying on my government! I'm a traitor!"

"The hell we are!"

"Then tell me why."

"Forget it, Captain. You've got your orders. Follow them."

"Or what?"

The Admiral stared at him. "Don't make me think of that answer, Nathan."

The boat shuddered beneath their feet. Engines revved. The *Spirit of Washington* slowly turned in the current as the loudspeaker directed passengers to the fine view of Mount Vernon.

"Wait one." Holloway nodded toward the door labeled "Men."

"Don't tell me you don't have your sea legs." The Admiral frowned as the Marine entered the head. The old sailor watched water rippling off the bow. The rhythm of the waves and the swaying of the ship transported him to other times, better vessels.

Suddenly, Holloway's arm draped around the Admiral's shoulders; he turned—

"Smile!"

St. Paul Bob's camera flashed at the young man with his arm around his father.

Admiral Petersen tried to break away but the steel grip of a young Marine trapped him, facing him straight into the camera's second flash.

"I know how you feel," Recie told the "father," about her age. "Your son said if we didn't surprise you, you'd be too shy to make a memory."

Holloway handed a twenty dollar bill to Recie as Bob wound the roll of film, dropped the yellow cylinder into the young man's hand. Recie smiled at the father, who was handsome even when he was angry. She led Bob away so that the family could have a private cruise back to the city.

"What the hell are you doing?"

"If I have to go to my Commander In Chief and confess treason against him," said Holloway, "it'll help to have proof of our relationship in the evidence pile."

"I can have you shot for this!"

"Not in time to save your ass or your op. My White House pass is in my pocket, your team is out of position, and once I get to Nixon's base camp, I can set up something so that my future incoming will get through."

"Last time I looked, blackmail wasn't in the Marine Corps manual!"

"Neither am I, not after all you've had me do here, not after what I did in . . ." Holloway trailed off. "Now tell me why you're all over the White House and Nixon's people."

The boat engine throbbed.

"We have to be on them," said the Admiral. "Our men's lives are at stake."

With a blink, the Admiral seemed old to Holloway; not just older, but old.

"In sixty-eight, LBJ had J. Edgar Hoover bug Nixon after he got the Republican nomination for President. They found out that Nixon was secretly working with Saigon to sabotage Johnson's peace moves with Hanoi and the Viet Cong. If LBJ could have pulled off any success toward ending the war, Vice President Humphrey would have beaten Nixon out of the presidency. Nixon needed the war going until after the election. In November, before the vote, LBJ told Humphrey. Gave him tapes, photos, other evidence, but Humphrey wouldn't use it, was afraid it'd look like a desperate cheap shot. LBJ figured it was worse to let a politician win who would let our boys die just so he could be President. Nixon won. Hoover told him about the bugging. Hoover gets to be FBI czar for life. We knew because . . . well, we found out. Now you know. And now Nixon is Commander In Chief, and if he's playing those games, we have to know what he's really doing, not just what he's telling us."

The boat churned river water.

Holloway said, "This isn't my jungle. Pull me out."

"But you're doing a great job—for the NSC *and* for us. We can't pull you out. Not for a long time. Too many questions, too much attention. You got to hang in."

"I lie, steal, manipulate, betray, con. Make allies with people who make my skin crawl."

"I don't want to know what you do. I don't need to know. Just effect your mission."

"What about its effect on me?"

"You're a Marine."

"Vietnam, they're bending the hardline. They talk tough about POWs, but—"

"Forget about the POWs."

"Those are our—"

"I know who they are! I got a son over there! We'll get who's there back, or I'll nuke Kissinger myself. Did you think we were incompetent? Coldhearted? You don't know this; no more than a handful of people do. We didn't even tell Nixon. Christ, if he got drunk or Machiavellian and shot off his mouth! Given it's a jungle war, and if you get lost you can get eaten by the brush without a trace. . . ."

Holloway said nothing.

"Except for guys like that, some flyers and commandos in Laos maybe grabbed up by the Pathet Lao, or by those Cambodian ragtags or some splinter Viet Cong unit or drug armies, we know every American Hanoi is holding, every POW."

"Jesus!"

"So forget about the 'issue' of POWs. That's just hawks playing with the public."

"But why don't we say that we know? The families and politicians and hucksters will keep the war going until they get answers that the Pentagon has!"

"If we tell what we know, we reveal that we've got a way to know it."

Holloway leaned his head on his hands holding the rail. Recie glanced over her shoulder; she wondered if the young man was seasick.

"Every week," Holloway told the Admiral, "I sit in the basement of the White House and write letters to families and say we don't know what happened to their boys. Every word of those letters rips my guts, and now you're saying every word is a lie."

"Welcome to the burden of command."

The boat pitched and yawed as it turned to go back up-river.

"I know it's crazy, Nate. That's why we need you there. Everybody is lying—us, too. But for us to keep the whole country and maybe the whole damn world from exploding, we need to know as much of what's really happening as we can."

"Can't you just . . . do something better?"

"Do what? I'm not the Commander In Chief, Nixon is. Kissinger is his right hand. The Constitution I swore to uphold orders me to obey them. Four years ago, 1967, McNamara and LBJ were pontificating about how well the war in Vietnam was going and paying for those lies with the lives of men who trusted commanders. The joint chiefs voted to resign en masse to protest that slaughterhouse. Then they realized that would be mutiny and that LBJ would just stick more compliant bodies in their chairs. So they decided to stay, fight it out, make the best of it and try and keep the whole damn thing from collapsing. And by God, that's what we're going to do!"

Loudspeaker: "Ladies and gentlemen, we'll be docking in approximately fifteen minutes."

"Don't do this again," said the Admiral. "Activate a meeting because you get queasy, like a wanna-be-a-virgin-again after the prom. Us meeting risks blowing our operation. You got any more problems, solve them. And one way or the other, take all of this to your grave."

The boat groaned as it reversed engines to slow the glide to the docks. Without taking his eyes from that action, the Admiral held out his open palm.

Holloway filled it with the film canister.

The Admiral tossed it into the churning foam, left Holloway alone, staring at the river.

ON A BEAUTIFUL Monday in June, Boyd grabbed Holloway in the White House basement corridor. "The shit's hitting the fan!"

But Holloway only half-heard the NSC aide. There, standing guard near the Sit Room, white-shirted uniform, Secret Service gold badge, sidearm: Jud Simon, a match for his file photo—handsome, lean face, thick through the shoulders and chest.

"You listening to me?" said Boyd.

"Sure."

"Henry's ballistic over The *New York Times* publishing those documents yesterday, the Pentagon Papers, history of the Vietnam War. Why do we give a shit? It's all stuff that happened before Nixon was President. Makes LBJ and Kennedy look bad. I don't get it."

The NSC aide shook his head as they entered the morning staff meeting. "What I do get is that Henry is cranked up and he's getting Nixon cranked up."

In the staff meeting, the ex-Harvard professor paced, waved his arms, raged about the leak of the Pentagon Papers.

"It will destroy our ability to conduct foreign policy in confidence!"

I get it, thought Holloway: a precedence of truthful disclosure means that tomorrow's revelation may condemn you. Especially if documents ever surface about Nixon and his people sabotaging LBJ's peace plans. He whispered to Boyd, "Who did it?"

"There are rumors about some guy named Ellsberg. Kissinger knows him."

Later that day, at a deli counter near the Treasury Department, Penzler whispered to Holloway, "He's right. Everybody's looking at Ellsberg."

"That Jud Simon is always around. Logs show him volunteering for extra shifts."

"Be careful with him," said Penzler. "Avoid contact, but keep him in your sights."

"What about your target, Gordon Liddy?"

"I don't think there's much there." Penzler paid for his tuna sandwich, walked away.

JULY UNFOLDED HOT and humid. On a good day, Holloway might glimpse Sandy in the White House. She used comp time to work at CREEP. She'd walk back across the sticky pavement of Pennsylvania Avenue, stroll through the White House. They'd run into each other, exchange discreet pleasantries. He'd watch a bead of sweat trickle down her neck. Most nights, she'd lay naked beside him in air-conditioned darkness. He was always up first to retrieve his *Post*. Never during that month did he need to hide from her any envelopes found in that paper. Sandy would call to him from the bedroom, he'd leave the *Post*, get the news he wanted from the rhythm she made as she rode him, the tremble of her breasts, the whisper of her lips.

On a bad day, American grunts in-country got mauled. Or a PLO-Israel clash threw sparks on the Middle East oil fields. Or the Soviets glitched strategic arms limitation negotiations that Kissinger kept secret from the Pentagon commanders (who knew about them from electronic interceptions and Holloway) and Secretary of State Rogers (who nobody told much of anything). Or the North Vietnamese negotiators in Paris vanished into silence. Or Nathan lost track of Jud Simon. Or CREEP/the White House kept Sandy away from his bed in the lonely darkness.

Walking down the black-and-white-tiled corridor of the Executive Office Building next to the White House one August afternoon, Holloway spotted a new sign taped to the door of Room 16: DAVID R. YOUNG/PLUMBER.

But the room's primo location near a staircase that spiraled up to a stained-glass skylight being scraped free of the World War II blackout paint and the high security lock on the room's door equaled more than an office devoted to clogged toilets.

"You're right about that," said Penzler when they met in a hotel bar one evening that week. "Nixon turns into a mad dog over the Pentagon Papers, so his boys end-run J. Edgar—who they don't trust—and create an antileak research unit to churn out memos, look busy but do nothing. Classic bureaucratic response."

"If they're concerned about leaks, we should be worried about them," said Holloway.

"Did you help Ellsberg leak the Pentagon Papers? No, me either. Don't worry about room sixteen and its 'plumbers.' The best they'll do is make a mess somebody will have to sweep up. We best keep well away from them, or we'll get swept up in their mess, too."

CHAPTER 17

Quiet! Holloway ordered himself as he stood in the deserted White House corridor at 1 A.M. on September 4, 1971. Nobody knows you're here. Even if they do, they think you belong.

As long as you're just in the hall.

The intrusion mechanism he'd gotten from Penzler clicked open the lock on H. R. "Bob" Haldeman's office door.

You go in, you're way over the line. Hell, who knows where those lines are anymore.

Holloway eased inside the dark office and shut the door.

Quiet, gotta stay quiet. Use a penlight. Safe, can't crack it. Need to be a pro to do that. Desk—locked, but CIA tools opened Haldeman's drawers. Notes, letters, memos. The camera jammed when he reached the last memo in a "Confidential" file. Risk it. Holloway hid the memo up his sleeve and walked through the White House corridors like an honest man.

The memo was from John Dean, a White House lawyer, to Haldeman and Ehrlichman, concerning "how we can use the available Federal machinery to screw our political enemies."

If Ehrlichman got a copy, too, it's in the system, reasoned Holloway. Which means that maybe Haldeman won't miss getting this one memo among the millions that cross his desk.

Or maybe those White House paranoids might conclude they were victims of a spy.

Unless the memo could have been . . . misrouted.

First he made three photocopies: one he dead-dropped for his commanders, the second he gave to Penzler when the

CIA spook next materialized, the third he stashed with his copies.

During lunch hour the next day, Holloway marched to the plumbers' Room 16. Knocked.

A White House face opened the door. "Who are you?"

"Security, NSC. Got something I think this office should handle."

"Wait one." The White House aide closed the door. One minute. Two. The door opened again and the aide motioned Holloway inside. Sheets hastily thrown over charts. Doors leading off the main room—desks, phones, phone chord for a scrambled phone. A photocopy machine. A shredder with a stack of documents awaiting its effort. "What do you want here?"

"Don't tell me what you're doing," said Holloway. "I'm not cleared to know.

"This," Holloway handed over the Dean memo, "turned up in the Sit Room. Looks like something that could leak. I hear you're an outfit to stop leaks. So I figure if this memo ends up here, you can handle it."

The aide smiled. "You don't want to see what happens to it."

Holloway smiled.

"Wait one."

When the aide disappeared into an inner sanctum, Nathan snatched a document from the shredder's pile, had it folded inside his suit before the aide came back.

"Well," said the aide, "whatever brought you here won't be a problem. You have an aptitude for doing the right thing. Think you could fit in an action kind of place? Like here?"

Holloway's mind surged; he followed his guts. "I'm happy with the pension where I am."

The aide shrugged, let him return to the hall.

Whatever happens, at least I got a cover story. The document he'd stolen from Room 16 burned in his pocket until midafternoon, when he sat in a closed bathroom stall and read it.

The document was a memo on White House stationery

from the Special Investigations Unit—the official name of the "plumbers" in Room 16—and concerned a meeting at CIA headquarters on August 9 between the plumbers and CIA personnel, summarized a fourteen-point CIA analysis on leaks and the ongoing relationship between Agency personnel and the plumbers.

The memo identified a key CIA player in this operation as "Mr. William Penzler."

"We better keep well away from them, or we'll get swept up in their mess, too."

All the colors of autumn dotted the green of the trees in the Virginia park where Penzler and Holloway met for a walk that Sunday afternoon.

"Have you been minding the store while I was away?" said Penzler.

"Where you been?"

"Here. There. Sailing. Do we have anything?"

"Only this," lied Holloway, passing him a photocopy of notes from Ehrlichman's White House desk that said "let the CIA take a whipping on" the violent death of former South Vietnamese President Diem in a coup during the Kennedy administration.

"They are smart, aren't they?" said Penzler. "Folds into the Pentagon Papers, spins the truth. Distract public criticism of their current Vietnam policy by hinting at a murderous scandal during the watch of the sacred Kennedy team. Control the past to manipulate the present."

"Is this what those plumbers are doing?"

"My sources tell me they're bunglers buried in paperwork."

"So there's no action there."

"Not for us. I think we should focus on the 'Berlin Wall.' Haldeman, Ehrlichman."

"What is it you think we're going to find?"

"Whatever is there. We're on patrol. You remember what that's like, don't you, Captain?"

Flickering patches of clarity, gaps in the vines and branches show Mardigian's shifting pack as we creep through the jungle. A billion greens dancing in the afternoon light create speckled thickness ten feet every direction except down. The air is thick with wet rotting wood and flowers having sex. O'Brien's footsteps whisper behind me. Faith means everyone is still there. Have to make camp, ring Claymore mines, cold rations, two hours on, two hours fitful don't-call-it-sleep. Two of seven canteens empty. Ahead is the aromatic promise/threat of a stream. Mardigian smells like cherries, should smell like horses. Cole smells like charcoal. Don't know the fucking new guy's scent. Inhale: cherries and charcoal, no VC rations' fish sauce or Vietnamese cigarettes or fresh human shit. Brush thinning. Can see all the way back to—blur-flying and thwonk *steel hits a tree twenty feet up. Dive with everybody but FNG as the grenade airburst explodes.* "Hit! I'm hit!" *Big's scream, FNG still standing, gunfire flashes ahead and along our right flank.* "Ohshi-tohshit I'm hit!"

"I remember," said Holloway.

"Well, on this march, don't worry: I'm right beside you." Penzler left him alone in the autumnal swirl.

Holloway waited three nights before he targeted Haldeman's office again. No crises were brewing, so most of the White House staff went home long before Nathan made his move. The CIA lockpicking device let him inside the moonlit office. He stepped toward the desk—

Grabbed by the shoulders! Break hold/spin ground!

Two warriors fought in the shadowed White House office. Nathan's punch deflected past the dark phantom. One hand cupped his elbow, a second bent his wrist. His feet swept out from under him. He crashed to the carpet—*didn't yell, can't yell, can't let Charlie know*—the phantom fell on top of him and knocked out his breath. Holloway's shin banged the desk. A vise clamped Nathan's windpipe. The Marine rocketed up from the carpet. The phantom slid off the Marine, banged into the desk, rattled a lamp, but kept his vise grip on Holloway's throat.

Burning black can't breathe!

Up! Standing—Holloway chopped the hand off his throat. The phantom spun along Holloway's side, drove his elbow into the Marine's spine—*redfire electric jolt!* The phantom judo threw the Marine to the carpet, wrapped his legs around Nathan's hips and locked his heels above his groin. An arm yoked under Holloway's armpit to weld the vise grip back on Nathan's throat. A voice hissed in his ear: "Be quiet or they'll catch us both!"

Heart slamming—

A key turned the door's lock.

Dragging, heels digging into my groin, not losing grip on any throat, free hand pulling on the credenza, using his body like a sled to drag us across the carpet back toward the wall behind desk—

The door swung open. A shaft of light shot across the carpet, Haldeman's desk. From behind the desk where he lay trapped with legs scissored around his hips and a hand vise-gripped on his throat, Holloway watched a flashlight beam snap on: someone standing in the door swung the flashlight beam across the desk, along the windows shut to the White House lawn.

The flashlight beam died. The door closed. Locked.

A voice in Nathan's ear whispered, "If you fight when I let go, you'll lose, and we'll both get caught. Whatever you do, don't touch the top of the desk!"

They stood, two shapes facing each other in the darkness.

"You're Jud Simon."

"No shit. We work for the same people."

"How do I know that's true?"

"*Know?* You can't *know* in this world. Live or die on information, instincts. Watch."

Jud flicked on a glowless flashlight: purple dust glistened all over Haldeman's desk, his stack of legal pads, his phone.

"CIA powder. Can't feel it, only see it with ultraviolet light. Takes days to wash off."

"How did you know?"

"Nothing moves in the White House that somebody in the Secret Service doesn't know about. I hide behind their badge, keep my ears open. The President's men have been spooked for weeks. Stuff not right on their desks, missing."

"And you show up here? Tonight?"

"Here for the last five nights! Took vacation. Been sliding in off the books. Knew you were walking the walk. Gambled that Nixon's top guy would be your priority. Figured you're smart enough to hit the target between midnight and dawn—if you'd have waited two more days, I couldn't have been here to save you."

"You mean ambush me. You could have just warned me."

"Oh, you'd have believed me? Owned up to what's what? Not tried to burn me?"

"You could be—"

"I could be *anything*. I'm Joe Shit, the ragpicker. A figment of your imagination. Your worst nightmare. Part of your team. I'm a guy who doesn't want us burned. You torching up would light up my life, and that can *not* happen! But don't just believe me. Lay low. See for yourself."

Jud moved to the door. "When you figure out who's on your side, see me then."

The opening door flashed light on a man in a White House uniform, then he was gone.

Three days later, all White House employees had to pass their hands under an ultraviolet light when they checked in: Nathan's hands showed up clean. Eight executive branch employees showed purple hands under the light; they confessed to "casual" contact with Nixon executives' desks in search of souvenirs. Those employees were rotated out of White House duty with no mention of the incident to the press.

Penzler and Jud Simon, thought Holloway: both ambushers. Can I trust either of them?

Lay low: How long can I do that?

CHAPTER 18

Chugging roar of enemy AK47s! Lights flash out front and along our right flank—L-shape ambush! "Fuckers! Fuckers!" Mardigian screaming, M16 spitting brass. Radioman/bloody face scrambles beside me: "Laptop! Laptop!" Cole firing prone between two fallen logs—poof, he's facedown, left palm turned up to catch falling sky. "This is Sandman! Taking heavy fire! About half klic north of river! Request—" "Sandman, is mission effected? Report data!" "I say again, heavy fire! Marines down! Request air support soonest!" Flashes in the jungle. AKs roar. Asian screams. "Where the fuck are they?" A crimson stream spurts out of a black Marine. FNG full auto cuts a pattern in the brush. Bright winks of death. Anderson: "Where are you motherfuckers? Can't see them! Can't see them!" "Sandman! Report data!" Screams. Flashes. Mizell launching M79 grenades, O'Brien spacing the new '79 rounds along our flank. Sergeant drags Waters, who's clutching his leg— Sergeant ballet spins, both men clump down, but their packs wiggle behind a fallen tree. "Motherfuckers!" yells Anderson. "Where the fuck are you?" Muzzle bursts—

Can't get what command wants. That's crazy anyway and doing it will make my men die.

The greater good in the course of events.

Choose the men. Lie. Risk court-martial: "Laptop, this is Sandman! Brush blast approximately two feet bigger than the old rounds! Hole depth, jungle turf, ah, eleven inches! Diameter—diameter indefinite!

Team data collectible at base! Only at base!"
"Sandman, outstanding! Status?" "Extraction im-
mediate! Casualties! Heavy fire!" Radio the LZ co-
ordinates, a klic away, God no more please no more!
"Sandman, choppers on the way. Be advised, air cover
delay." Do the deathflashers know English? "Mardi-
gian! Mizell! Extract in LZ beyond stream! Mad min-
ute, everybody goes! On Charlie: Alpha, Beta—Jungle
explodes, all of us spraying full auto screaming. FNG
throws Big over his shoulder like a duffel bag. Ser-
geant and Waters, Siamese twins hobbling retreat.
O'Brien grabs Cole's body and some Marine grabs the
black guy who's clutching his neck. Mardigian, Mizell
and me, backing up burning through ammo mags,
screaming at who we can't see as we run the only
direction they'd left us to go.

"Nate!"
Shaking me, somebody's—
"Nathan! Wake up! It's OK! It's me." *Sandy. My bed,
Washington: 1971.*

"God, honey: look at you! December in here and you're
out of the covers, soaked in sweat!"

"Just a nightmare. Everything's OK. Just a 'mare." *Close
your eyes and wish it so.*

"You have rough nights," she says. "Last couple especially."

I'll tell her what's public. Won't tell her more than that,
but that's OK. "You read the comics pages Tuesday?"

"Busy as I am shuffling between CREEP and the White
House, I can barely read real news."

"Jack Anderson's column, the muckraker on the comics
page: if the *Post* and the establishment media took outsiders
like him seriously, we'd be in trouble. Somebody leaked him
cables about us moving a convoy into the Indian Ocean to
influence the India-Pakistan war. Earlier this month, he reported that Kissinger and Nixon secretly want to tilt toward
Pakistan."

"We get all the papers in the Press Office. They say the Pakistani soldiers are deliberately butchering, raping."

"It's not our war, OK? Pakistan is a good ally helping Kissinger get into China! . . . Sorry! I'm sorry! Didn't mean to snap but . . . Jesus, this job! What you end up defending! And why!"

"What about Anderson this Tuesday?"

"He's getting eyes-only stuff for people like Kissinger, JCS Chairman Moorer, the President. Anderson mentioned 'Tartar Sam,' thought it was a ship instead of a missile, but . . ."

"Leaks are a real problem for you guys."

"No shit."

"What's happening?"

"They're looking for someone to shoot," said Holloway.

She hugged him. "Don't worry. You're not swiping documents to give to Jack Anderson, so you're not in any trouble."

Holloway held her while she went back to sleep.

At two-thirty that afternoon, the phone rang on Nathan's White House desk. He was sifting through reports of a cease-fire in the India-Pakistan war and memos predicting the defeat in the Senate of an anti–Vietnam War amendment, so he paid little attention to the voice that said he needed to sign in a batch of security files in the Executive Office Building.

Jud Simon fell in step beside Holloway in the brick passageway between the Executive Office Building and the White House.

"Don't look at me!" whispered Jud. "Keep walking. That was me who called. Had to get you out here. We're under fire. Right now at the Pentagon they're polygraphing a Navy yeoman named Radford, Charles Radford. He's—"

"Like a secretary, an aide for Kissinger, and—"

"One of us. The brass goofed. Went ballistic about the Anderson leaks. Somebody suspected Radford of leaking to Anderson, too. So they fed him to the Pentagon sharks, the main line bureaucracy that doesn't know shit about . . . But now off-program gumshoes have him hooked up to a lie detector. One slip on his part, our whole thing could crack."

"If the Pentagon has him, our people can cover his ass, keep us secure."

"Don't you get it yet? There's 'our people' and then there's '*our people*.' "

"So who are you?"

"Precisely," said Jud before he drifted away. "Be sure you're clean."

When Holloway came to work the next morning, he found Boyd pacing outside the doors to the Situation Room.

"Come on," said Boyd. "The vending machine. I'm buying you coffee."

"Thanks, but—"

"I said, *come on!*" Boyd clung to the Marine's arm as he steered him away from the Sit Room. "FBI and Pentagon gumshoes are in there going through every military officer's desk, including yours! All I know is that sailor Radford confessed that he's been spying on our boss for some admiral! Now, all you military—"

"What admiral?"

Boyd stared at his friend. "Why does that matter?"

"Hey, I'm just as shocked as you! But if they're looking at all . . . What admiral?"

"Tell me you're not involved in this bullshit."

"Promise," said Holloway. "I'm bullshit free."

Boyd watched him for a long time. Then shook his head. "Stupid me. I forgot the rules and asked an honest question to get an honest answer, not an 'operative policy assessment.' "

"You can trust me, Boyd."

"Doesn't matter. Word is, Nixon wants a total secret seal on his dogs' investigation of renegade snoopers. Life goes on. And we're stuck in it together, right?"

"Sure," said Holloway. *Why haven't I been alerted by someone besides Jud?* "Right."

Holloway drifted through business as usual. Waiting.

Logic grabbed him two days before Christmas: *After they*

caught Radford, why didn't I get a warning or instructions in my morning paper? Or even a phone call?

"Think I'm sick," he told an NSC secretary. "Going home."

No ghosts trod behind him in the fading afternoon light. No cars slid on the December streets to follow him through turning-yellow traffic lights. No vans waited outside his apartment building, no strangers sat in cars where they could watch the building's front door.

Door to the apartment: looks OK. No scratches on the lock.

The orphan Christmas tree he'd bought with Sandy scented his apartment. He tore the place apart. Ninety minutes later, he found a bulky manila envelope taped under his kitchen sink. Incriminating photocopies of documents he'd purloined going back to the July memo when Nixon's aides proposed using the IRS taxman to go after antiwar groups—the first memo Penzler gave him.

Holloway disconnected the smoke detector. Filled a cake pan with the stolen secrets. He put the pan in his kitchen sink, dropped a match into the pan and stared into the blue flames.

They knocked on his door at eight that night.

"Captain Holloway?" said the tall, thin man leading the quintet of overcoats and grim faces. "I'm Special Agent Gary Harmon, FBI. Can we come in?"

"Unless this is routine for my job . . . Don't you need some kind of warrant?"

"None of us wants to have to get one."

"Jingle Bells" played softly from behind some neighbor's door. *No need to focus their eyes on me with this, too.* Holloway led the five men into his apartment.

"ID's everybody," he said.

FBI Agent Harmon showed him well-worn credentials. The man beside him had a similar set. The third man flashed a Defense Investigative Service badge. Holloway knew the fourth man, an NSC gumshoe. But the fifth . . .

Harmon sighed when Holloway asked for the fifth man's

credentials. "I'm empowered to say that this gentleman is from a related federal agency assisting us in our routine inquiry."

"Can he speak? Or is he dumb?"

"Look," said Harmon, "I'm an ex-Marine, and this Christmas, what I'd like under my tree is a chance to chase really bad guys, not run after leaks to newspapers. But I serve such duties as the President may require, and today, when the President is commuting the prison sentence of a thug like Hoffa, I'm sent to roust a fellow leatherneck."

"Gary!" snapped his partner. "For Chrissakes! You crazy?"

"What do you want?" said Holloway.

"We have a report that you photocopied classified documents and have given such documents to journalists. What we want is for you to consent to a search of your premises."

"What if I say no?"

"Then we have to do this another way."

"Knock yourselves out. But don't make a mess."

Agent Harmon baby-sat Holloway in the living room while the other four men searched the apartment. Twenty minutes after they'd knocked on his door, the fifth man looked under Holloway's sink, looked again and then *again*, and Nathan knew.

They found the .45 automatic in his closet.

"And you found the authorization for me to possess and carry said officially issued weapon," said Holloway when they confronted him. "Verify its serial number, put it back."

They did.

"We've got nothing," said Harmon's partner after an hour. The fifth man looked like a deer caught in headlights.

"So I'm innocent?" said Holloway.

"What else can we report?" said the thin FBI agent.

"That I'm royally pissed off. That I'm insulted. That with all due respect and all proper procedures, I'm going to go through channels and ream somebody a new asshole."

"I wouldn't blame you," said Harmon, "but all that would get us is bigger assholes."

The five gumshoes turned to leave. When the Pentagon cop had his hand on the door, Holloway yelled, "Hey!" They looked straight into the popping flashbulb of his Polaroid camera.

The fifth man yelled, "You can't do—"

As the camera whirred out its developing snapshot, Holloway said, "Merry Christmas."

The only other time Holloway had used the camera his uncle had sent him was to take a picture of Sandy as she stood in his bedroom, naked, her hands covering her eyes and hiding all of her face but the tip of her nose and her mouth saying, "You can still see all you really want a picture of." Now that picture too was ash, washed down his sink.

"You guys wait in the car," said Agent Harmon.

The fifth man said, "You're not supposed to—"

The door slammed in his face.

Harmon smiled at Holloway. "Mind if I have a cigarette?"

Thin as a coffin nail, thought Holloway as the FBI agent lifted a cigarette from his shirt pocket. The G-man wandered into the kitchen, smiling at the white refrigerator, the yellow walls. He turned to face Holloway, leaned against the gleaming aluminum sink. Stood directly under the blackish smoke smear on the kitchen ceiling.

"Got a match?" he asked. "Never mind. I got a lighter."

A click, a flame, white smoke circled up from his hand.

"If you are a security risk," said the FBI agent, "I'll find out and nail you to the penitentiary wall. If you're playing First Amendment games, maybe I'll find that out, let the guys in charge handle you. If you're a good Marine, sorry to bother you, but orders are orders."

"Were you really in the Corps?"

"*Semper fi.* Judo team, too." Agent Harmon held the burning cigarette between them. "Really should quit. Things like this . . . You gotta be careful when you play with fire."

He blew a smoke ring that he didn't watch float up to the dark stain on the yellow ceiling.

Holloway said, "Who sicced you on me?"

"I couldn't tell you that even if tracing anonymous calls

to another agency were within my job description."

"Guess somebody's shooting in the dark. Thanks for doing your job right."

"That's what they pay us for, isn't it?" Harmon dropped his Bureau business card on the counter. "Who knows when you might want to help the FBI? Or vice versa."

Then he left.

Twenty minutes later, Holloway wore his Corps field parka as he stared out his bathroom window at snow falling to the bricks on the floor of the airshaft five stories below. *They'll be watching all the doors and will know if I use them.* The airshaft dropped through the heart of his building, invisible to the outer world. He opened the window, climbed outside and sat on its ledge so his feet dangled in his tub. Snow whirled around him. His bare hands burned cold when he grabbed the metal drainpipe.

Never think about falling. Never happen.

Grab and—go!

Pulling up—hands don't slip, shoes scrambling on the wet bricks, like climbing a rope with just hands and burning shoulders—

The drainpipe popped away from the bricks. Gravity pulled at his burning arms, his hands slid down the metal pipe. He dangled, swaying in the night snow.

OK, OK, grip tight. Pipe's wet, melting snow. No: Pipe is slick with blood, my blood. Hands frostbitten or a metal snag or—

Climb! Shoulders aching, the creaking drainpipe straining against its bolts, Holloway climbed. His left arm hooked over the roof parapet, his left shoe stretched up to that edge—

A window opened below him: *Don't move! Don't—*

A man said, "You're stoned, babe! Nothing here. Even Santa wouldn't fly tonight!"

Holloway heard the window close. He pulled himself over the edge, flopped to the peaceful roof on his back. Falling snow kissed his face like a flight of angels.

*   *   *

AN HOUR LATER, the man in the overcoat and pre-JFK vintage hat who joined Holloway in a downtown hotel bar said, "You shouldn't have called me at home."

"Why not?" countered Holloway. "Nobody's tapping you who you can't control."

"That may be, but—"

"Why'd you do it?"

Penzler sat absolutely still in the chair across from Holloway. As the Marine watched, the image of a wispy, bearded, fragile sparrow melted away like the snow on the shoulders of Penzler's overcoat. The illusion melted off hunched wings of stone muscled onto a raptor with piercing ice eyes and gloved talons curled beside a shot of vodka.

"Why'd you sell me out?" said Holloway.

"Such are the wages of our profession."

"Nothing personal, right?"

"Everything is personal. That makes life interesting."

"Why did you target me?"

"You chose yourself. Nixon's people are chasing phantoms who are real but who are also figments of their paranoia. Their witch hunts make life uncomfortable for me, for my operations, so they must be appeased. Poor Yeoman Radford is like a chicken caught by a barnyard dog. Once the taste is acquired, the appetite must be sated. Or the dogs run amok. Like dogs, Presidential aides are fickle, with a short attention span. They've got Radford and an admiral—not your admiral, a self-sacrificer who fell on his sword and 'confessed' the whole 'spy ring' included only him and Radford. He and Radford will get slaps on the wrists, transfers out of our big picture. But the President's dogs are still panting. To tide them over until they forget about the blood in their mouths, they needed another bone. You had a chance to help me make Jud Simon that bone, but you didn't do your job. Thus, you volunteered to be the designated casualty."

"Designated by who?"

"By me."

"And who the hell are you?"

Penzler rose from the table like a wind whose whisper was audible only in another dimension, rose until he loomed above where gravity had trapped Holloway in a cheap wooden chair. Before he floated from the bar and vanished in the night, a smile curled like a flame on Penzler's stone face, and he said, "I'm whoever I want to be."

CHAPTER 19

"Let me go out on a limb with you," FBI Agent Harmon told Quinn one cold January 1972 night as they sat parked a block from the White House, two hours into an off-the-books surveillance of the porno movie theater just opened in D.C. by a capo from Joe Bonanno's New York family.

"What are friends for?"

"We'll see." Harmon snapped a lighter for his cigarette. "Federal prosecutors down here have a secret grand jury hunting crooked cops in your department."

"Just corruption, right?" asked Quinn.

"You and the other constitutional cowboys messing with the street rads aren't on the block. Hell, you guys will probably get medals and pardons from Nixon if you get in trouble."

"So why are you telling me?"

"You want to help?"

The prosecutor Harmon introduced Quinn to in a safehouse had lost all but a horseshoe of hair though he was just thirty. "Go easy with him," Harmon had said. "It's his first big case."

"Max Avrakotos," the balding man said. His handshake was firm and real. "Call me Max."

"I won't grand-jury, *Max*," said Quinn. "I won't run against my own guys. I won't wear a wire. And if all the other feds I work for are going to stay happy, I can't appear on any paper."

"Then what, really what the hell good are you?" said Max.

"I can tell you if you're headed wrong. I can help keep you from making a fool of yourself."

Max looked at Harmon. Got a nod, a smile. Gave them in turn to the city cop.

Quinn told the prosecutor about bald, hooded-eyed IAD Lieutenant Godsick. About Morals Detective Bruce. About a connected mobster named Nezneck who held their strings.

"There's more about Nezneck," said Q. "But if I give it to you before you got him nailed on something, it'll leak or backfire or disappear."

"You've got to trust us," said the federal prosecutor.

"Why?"

"Because we're going to clean your department from top to bottom."

"When I see it, I'll believe it, and then I'll come out front to go all the way with Nezneck."

"You're about as good as I'm going to get, aren't you?"

"Sorry about that," said Quinn. When the bald prosecutor sighed, the cop liked him. "Look, I gave you targets, direction. Crooks are vulnerable through their money, every good investigator knows that. Money leaves trails. 'Follah the dollah.' "

Five weeks later, the federal grand jury indicted sixteen Washington cops for providing protection to gambling and other rackets. The grand jury indicted no gangsters higher than mere numbers runners, didn't lay a glove on IAD Detective Lieutenant Cleveland Godsick or Morals Squad Detective Sergeant Billy Bruce. Nezneck stayed out of the light from their flares. Max apologized to Quinn: "We did our best. You got my marker."

SPRING BLOSSOMED IN Washington way ahead of schedule in March 1972—clear skies, no wind, sunshine that reached a freaky seventy-one degrees and scared environmentalists

with the specter of global warming. Quinn got his hair cut
to an over-the-ears shag and trimmed his beard. Q had been
too many places for too long: changing the werewolf's image
made it safer to obey the moon.

Eight o'clock that night, he sat at the bar of Rendezvous,
a mahogany and mirrored night spot in the heart of Georgetown. Every change in Presidential administrations divides
Washington nightlife, with the singles and socials from the
White House crowd anointing one set of night spots with
their patronage, while the bar-hopping crowd tied to the opposite party claims other turf.

Rendezvous belonged to the Nixon crowd—Republican
coats and ties, loud laughter and reverence for the man who
ran the White House and his team, macho derision of the
peacenick traitors and faggot hippies. The women wore hair-
dos, bras, makeup, perfume, but carried their birth control
pills in their purses just like their less cosmeticized sisters at
the opposition bars. Legal, all-American tobacco smoke filled
the air and hard drinks lined the tables and bar.

Quinn fit in at Rendezvous as badly as he did at the Democrat watering holes, where hair spray was seldom smelled,
makeup was subdued, bras were far from the rule and beers
fueled the camaraderie. But he'd haunted Rendezvous ever
since he realized that its back booth was probably where a
blonde smoking a cigarette and a smiling Pat Dawson sat for
the snapshot he'd stolen, the blonde who'd been with Nezneck the night Quinn hunted him and lost.

In all the months he'd been dropping by Rendezvous,
Quinn had never seen the blonde. Nor had his policeman's
eye ever seen any prostitution or call girls like Pat Dawson—
though who could be certain of that in 1972, when the worst
that could happen from consensual sex was an accidental
pregnancy easily and legally terminated or a social disease
curable by antibiotics? In Rendezvous and in its opposition-
party counterpart, Quinn watched as men and women met,
preened, then exited into the electric night.

Quinn always went home alone. What straight woman
could take him werewolf-naked? He fed his lust with cop

groupies from the Fraternal Order of Police's blue shack bar at the base of Capitol Hill, with Movement women for whom Q was another adventure on the road to liberation, or the grad student across the hall, until she announced she was moving to Arizona to teach and marry some guy she'd never mentioned.

That March night, he wore a dark turtleneck, a soft-as-butter smoke-black leather blazer Q'd bought from a fence he turned into an informant. Quinn's badge was in his back pocket and his .38 rode in a shoulder holster beside his heart.

A big man muscled himself onto the stool next to Quinn. He wore a lawyer's suit, a power tie. He'd begun to grow sideburns. TV talk show host Johnny Carson was letting his sideburns grow, so it was OK for other real men to grow their hair reasonably long like the faggot hippies who were getting all the media-touted free sex. The big man looked Quinn up and down.

"Double vodka, neat," he told the bartender. He smirked at Quinn's beer. " 'Fore you leave, remind me to buy you a real drink."

"I'll do that," Quinn told their reflection in the bar mirror.

"Guys like you love a free ride, don't you?"

Quinn sipped his beer, stared at the mirror.

The big man put his cigarette in an ashtray he pushed next to Quinn. Let the black-leather faggot breathe his smoke.

She swung into the place with a grim smile and sky eyes. Midnight hair brushed her shoulders.

The big man grabbed her arm. "You're looking for me."

She had to stop. "No, I'm not."

"Sure you are." He pulled her to the bar. "You just don't know it yet. You think I'm like all the other assholes in here."

"No," she said. "You're a special asshole. Let me go."

"Not without a drink. You look like a drinker."

Quinn felt the big man shift as the woman struggled with the hand gripping her arm.

"She said, let her go."

The big man whirled to the leather hippie without releasing her. His tie flopped onto the bar.

"When I want you to talk, I'll pull your chain." Then he faced the woman he trapped. "That's the kind of creep a fine-looking lady like you needs me to protect her from."

Quinn's knuckles knocked over the big man's double shot. Vodka soaked the man's tie and Quinn flicked the smoldering cigarette from the ashtray onto that synthetic striped blend.

Blue flame popped along the vodka stain.

"Shit!" The big man beat at his burning tie.

Quinn threw his beer on the man and drowned the blaze.

"Watch out!" Quinn swung open his leather blazer so the big man glimpsed the gun in the shoulder holster. Quinn drew a handkerchief, mopped the big man's brow, tucked the handkerchief in the big man's suddenly weak hand. "Gotta be careful not to play with fire."

The woman laughed.

"Are you OK?" he asked her.

"Relatively speaking. How about you?"

All he could do was grin and shrug.

"You need a new beer," she said. "Come on, I'll buy."

Neither of them looked back as she led him to a table, ordered his beer and her scotch. She said, "You don't belong here."

"I don't think you do, either." Quinn's heart slammed against his ribs.

"So you want to take me away from all this? Rescue me?" Her smile widened. "That's clearly not just a pickup line for you. In that beard and hair, you look more like Jesus than a white knight. My soul or my life: How you going to save me?"

"You'll do that yourself."

"Hope you're right." She clicked her scotch to his beer. "At least we can have a drink."

"Sure, but . . . You're like nobody I've ever seen for real before." He felt his face flush and knew she saw him lose all the easy, right words.

Before she could stop herself, she whispered, "What *are* you going to do?"

"Never forget you."

She swayed like he'd hit her. "You mean that?"

"Yes."

She shook her head. "I didn't come here for this."

"So tonight we both got lucky and got a chance."

She watched the scotch swirl in her glass. "In this town, this is usually where you tell me what you do for a living, show me how important you are so I'll swoon at your feet."

He put his badge and ID on the table so only she could see it.

"Jesus," she said.

"No. Just a cop."

"You're the absolutely last guy I was looking for."

"I hope." He shrugged. "This is usually where you tell me your name."

"Lorri. Lorri Larson."

He told her his name. "John Quarell" and "Q" rolled out of him, too. "You might hate cops, most people do."

She shrugged. "I never get to be 'most people.' "

"Me either." He swallowed. "Maybe I should have eased into telling you, but you'd find out real soon anyway, and I won't lie to you. If you're going to know me, you've got to know I'm a badge. I've done some weird things. Things I'm not too proud of. But being a cop . . . I love it."

"Lucky you. Got it all figured out, huh?"

"No."

And she laughed. "You figured out how to get me over here."

"No, *that* was luck. Down-the-bones luck."

"All you guys and you're 'getting lucky.' "

"You really think I'm one of those guys?"

Lorri looked at him for a long time. "No."

"I'm just trying to do this right."

She shook her head. "Have you done it like this before?"

"I never saw you before. And I don't think I've got the guts to step out there like this again."

She said, "Can we go now?"

Lorri swung up behind him on his motorcycle without a flinch, her skirt riding up her long legs. She held on tight to him as they roared through the cool night. Her breath warmed his cheek as she said, "Remember when you just knew it was all this simple?"

He took her home.

She was still there in the morning when he woke up.

The bed smelled sweet and salty and warm. He lay absolutely still so nothing would change. She stirred in the sheets beside him. Her eyes softened when she saw it was him.

"How did you sleep?" he asked.

"Great." She raised up on one elbow. "Did you stay awake all night watching over me?"

"Naw. Not *over* you. Just watching you. And not all night."

"Are you sure?"

"Pretty sure."

"Maybe you're right." Her leg slid up over his. "Apparently you're not . . . exhausted."

They laughed and the bed creaked and he dared to cup her small breast, kiss her neck as she wrapped her arms around him and whispered, "Oh, Johnny!"

Later, she sat curled in his living room chair, her black hair finger-brushed, the sleeves rolled up on his unbuttoned blue shirt, her bare legs tucked under her as she watched him mix cups of instant coffee. He wore MPD gym shorts and a grin he wished he could see.

"This beats room service," she said. "Are you this nice to all the girls?"

"Never."

"John . . . We can't . . . I'm not . . . This is too fast. Don't push me into this."

"I want you to want to come here, not be pushed."

"I want to, I do. But this isn't the time. I can't—"

"You don't want my high school class ring. You're not

ready to get married and work on a couple of kids and grow old."

"No."

"Me either," said John.

"You don't even know me."

"I've been waiting to know you all my life."

A tear ran down her cheek and hammered him to the floor.

"Me, too, John. But I'm just figuring out who I am. Right now, I can't give everything all the time to one person, even if it is you."

"Don't run away from me."

"Please don't make me. I don't think I could bear that."

The weight on him eased. Didn't vanish.

"You've got to promise me—"

"Anything," he said, meant it. "Anything."

"You won't chain me. You won't take away my being free to do what I have to do. You won't pry and mess that up. And the words, you've got to promise me you won't, *we won't* say the words.

"Not now," she said. "Not now."

"OK," he said.

"Yes," he said.

Her smile lit the room. Then she asked, "What time is it?"

He looked in the kitchen. "Ten-fifteen."

"I have to work this afternoon."

"I don't even know what you do."

"A temp job on the Hill. None of the bosses have gotten their nerve up to grab at me. Yet." She shrugged. "They grab, I walk out. I temp about a week or so a month. Mostly, I'm on call."

"On—"

"Stewardess. I'm so junior, I only get thirty hours a month. The airline likes that because it saves—Are you listening to me?"

"Every word."

"Oh Johnny, you are, aren't you?"

She flowed to him. Her hands held his cheeks so she could stare into his eyes.

"I'm falling and falling and falling," she whispered. "And for the first time in forever it feels OK and safe and great."

She led his fingers to where she was open and sticky and wet.

"Now, Johnny," she whispered, arching her hips to his touch. "Do it now!"

CHAPTER 20

All that spring Quinn and Lorri honored each other's secrets. That perfect arrangement gnawed his heart.

He couldn't tell anyone about the streets Q walked, about connections Quinn arranged with skill that would have made Mel Klise proud, the careful games he and Buck and Gary played beneath their official duties. Quinn didn't tell her about Nezneck. Quinn showed her the skeleton of truth, that he was a TAC Squad officer arresting muggers, rapists, regular patrol duties the department used to justify—and fill— Quinn's non-Q hours. Lorri laughed with him about Jimmy Duvell and held him when he told how he'd shot Cyrus Watson.

She told him about Nowhere, Nebraska, about her mother who smoked Winstons and stocked shelves at Kmart, her father who sold auto parts for the first man to pat Lorri's butt, her older brother who'd played guard for his high school basketball championship team, served a clerk's tour in Vietnam and now lived back home, awaiting his second baby and driving a cement truck. She told him about the married banker who'd offered her a job with an understanding. About the Methodist minister who sobbed confession to her one rose-lit Sunday evening in the church rectory after youth fellowship. Quinn froze as she told him about the ultra-cool disk jockey from Omaha who'd come to MC her senior class dance and married her the day after she wore a cap and gown. Six months later, the DJ couldn't take the pressure of watching her flower even more in Omaha, and bought their divorce with a semester at the university, where she felt kinship to no one: not to the sorority girls and their hollow pledges to suburban heaven, not to the stoned girls who talked about liberation from stifling marriages that they hadn't had, not to the middle-road women who no one noticed. She had no trouble finding college men and a professor eager to let her costar in their plans. Six months of that going nowhere and she signed up for stewardess school.

She always told Quinn when she couldn't see him, just as he always told her. Some nights she'd call him from far away. She'd mention people she knew. Stewardesses or friends of friends who'd laugh with her, mostly about how foolish men were, how it was to be a woman.

"Just like you and your crews," she'd say. "You and I, we're each other's best friend."

"More," he said, and she didn't blink.

Neither of them spoke the words.

They honored each other's secrets. Were careful where they went in public.

Q joked to her: "To protect my secret identity."

"Fine by me."

Quinn ached whenever she wasn't there. And when she was.

Lorri declared April to be "tourist month." She led Quinn hand-in-hand under pink-petaled cherry trees surrounding the Tidal Basin. They went to Smithsonian museums he'd been in only to search for radicals' bombs. Giggling, they took a tour of the Capitol building with a group of Hong Kong travel agents. They went to movies, to a jazz club, to a ballet. Late one Friday night she met him in a bar after he came off shift, a place where they knew nobody, and they slow danced to jukebox Righteous Brothers, her holding him so tight, rubbing against him for so long he almost exploded. The song ended, she stood on her tiptoes and snaked her scotch-tangy, fire-soft tongue in an electric circle around his lips.

Neither of them spoke the words.

That night, in his bed, she said, "Do you ever feel like you've lost who you are when you keep having to change from 'John Quarell' to 'Quinn' or 'Q' or whoever?"

"All the time."

"I don't care who you are," she whispered. "Just so you're here with me."

One spring afternoon she invited him to her apartment near National Airport. She opened the door wearing a wispy white negligee that swept to her ankles and musk perfume, perfect makeup she didn't need, a redness on her lips, her black hair flowing in the sunlight as he carried her to her bed, where he knelt in worship between her ivory thighs, then he was with her on the bed, behind her as she moaned *yes* and *John*, pressed her face into the pillow, her hips harder against him as she muffled cries and the words she promised not to say, as he pushed himself deeper into her than ever anyone before, and not saying the words was the most impossible thing he'd ever done.

Two nights later she came to his place, just to sleep, she said. Just not to be alone.

"You mean just to be with me?" he asked.

She curled into a ball in his bed.

He turned out the lights. Lay beside her. Felt her cry.

"I'll do whatever . . . whatever you need me to do." He knew he meant that; dreaded that.

"Let me stay here?" she whispered.

What he wanted to say was *forever*. What he was oh-so-smart-enough to say was yes.

She cried until she fell asleep. In the morning, she pressed her hand over his genitals, said, "I'll make up for last night, I promise."

"You never have anything to make up for," he told her.

Her smile was soft. He made her coffee while she showered. She drank it, kissed his cheek and hugged him. Left.

She phoned the precinct house that afternoon. "Thank you."

Didn't see him for two days because she said she was flying.

Ravaged him the third night, burrowed her face against him to muffle any words.

April, left town.

J. Edgar Hoover, the immortal head of the FBI, bastion of anticommunism, protector of the American way and Gary Harmon's boss, died in his sleep during the darkness of 1972's May Day.

"Everything changes now," Gary told Quinn, "like it or not."

"Sorry," said Quinn. "Guess I didn't know how you felt about him."

"Him the man or him the myth?" Harmon sighed. "The man disappears into the myth. I can tell you stories about the director that would make you laugh or curl your hair. Yeah, he was the nasty bulldog growling in the shadows, but he built the Bureau, and without it—"

"I'd be out here all alone."

"Something like that."

"So tell me the truth about the big myth," said Quinn. "Now that Hoover's dead, who's going to get his files?"

Harmon grinned. Shook his head.

"Come on! Hoover swung the big weight in this country because everybody thinks he's got files that could destroy all the powerful people by exposing their secret sins and crimes. Doesn't matter if he had files like that or not, doesn't even matter what's in them: Everybody's afraid of secrets, because we've all got something to hide."

"If the director had such files, he didn't share them with me."

"Who got 'em, Gary?"

"The director's estate is a long way from probate."

"Huh?"

"And I'm sure his office was sealed. Although . . ."

Quinn sensed a coyness enter his friend's tone.

"After Mr. Hoover died, the head of counterintelligence over at CIA, a guy named Angelton, showed up at the director's house with a truck to remove cases of spoiled wine."

"Spoiled . . . Nice of him to help out your dead boss. Clean up his house."

"Yes, wasn't it."

J. Edgar Hoover's public laying-in-state at the Capitol building coincided with a previously scheduled antiwar demonstration starring movie actress Jane Fonda and Pentagon Papers leaker Daniel Ellsberg.

Q's departmental handler told him, "The White House is freaking out. They say they got intel reports that the lefties are going to show up at the Capitol waving a Viet Cong flag."

"What else is new? Who's giving them their big scoops?"

"Sure ain't J. Edgar anymore. Unless he bugged his own coffin."

Q infiltrated that demonstration on the west front of the Capitol building. He edged through the crowd as speakers read the names of American servicemen killed in Vietnam. *Wonder if the movie star will look as beautiful as Lorri?* Q edged closer to the speakers.

"Traitor!" An accented man's voice shouting in the crowd. "Traitor!"

The man shouted again. Q moved toward the voice. He sensed white-shirted Capitol cops nosing toward that possible trouble.

There! Five, no, maybe ten older guys: scruffily dressed but not like the blue-jeaned college-looking lefties—older. The shifting crowd blocked Q's view. He heard an argument. The crowd parted, one stranger knocked a kid down.

Capitol cops jerked three of the beefy guys away from the protesters and led them toward the paddy wagon. The names of dead American soldiers droned through the air. Two military pallbearers got hernias as they struggled with Hoover's half-ton casket. Q drifted with a fist of older men following cops who'd arrested their friends. He hung back as the strange parade cleared the crowd, but saw a wispy-bearded skinny man in a gray suit materialize beside the arresting officers, whisper to them and to the rowdies. The cops shrugged, the rowdies walked away—free. The man in the gray suit vanished.

A cop jabbed Q with a nightstick. "What the fuck do you want?"

"Give peace a chance," said Q, backing toward the *de facto* tolerated zone of rebellion.

"Just give me a chance, faggot, I'll teach you about peace!"

"Sorry, Officer," said Q. "I'm going steady."

He turned to walk away.

The nightstick slammed his back. Quinn staggered. The second blow lashed his neck and shoulders and the day became fire. The steel shaft stabbed his ribs. A woman's amplified voice floated a dead soldier's name. Quinn crashed to the pavement, cut his forehead and got a scar he'd have forever. Powerful hands jerked him to his feet—*clearing. Sky going blue, white Capitol dome, can see, can*—His blood flecked the cop's white shirt. The shove and the kick spun Q toward the crowd of demonstrators. A kid from Michigan caught Q and pulled him into the dubious safety of fellow rebels as a dozen white-shirted Capitol Hill cops whisked their victimized colleague away from any press cameras or traitorous lawyers to never-happened.

"Oh God! You OK?" The Michigan kid gave Q a red bandanna to cover his wound.

" '*Policemen there to preserve disorder . . .*' "

"What?"

Q shook his head. The kid helped him through the crowd. Q focused on his rescuer; realized he'd once covertly photographed him and created a permanent security-risk file for this kid whose biggest crime was showing up where truly bad suspects might have been.

That night, as Lorri sponged his bruises while Quinn lay in a hot bath, he said, "Where's the world going?"

"Round and round, honey. Round and round." She gave

him a sip of her scotch to ease his aches, brushed her lips over his. "Let's just stay right here."

He closed his eyes in the cleansing steamy warmth.

THURSDAY, JUNE 1, 1972. Lorri called Quinn to say she was busy, Gary called him "for one of our nights." By eight-thirty, Quinn and Gary sprawled on the roof of a Chinese martial arts school not far from the wax museum. They had binoculars. A Telephoto-lensed camera. Across the street stood an Italian restaurant, a neon landmark with its own iron-pole-fenced parking lot presided over by a replica of the statue of David.

"I can't believe they're here," said Quinn as he scanned the restaurant's front windows with his binoculars. "It's like a bad ethnic joke. You sure this is the right place?"

Gary smiled. "Might be good if I'm wrong. You been too happy lately. You might be in danger of losing your edge."

A shaft of light fell into the parking lot across the street. Quinn trained his binoculars through the iron-pole fence.

"Oh, that's cute," he whispered to Gary. "Coming out the back door. Who's that big guy?"

"Some Big Easy button man who'll swear he's a tourist," said Gary. "He'll have a Louisiana pistol permit for what he's packing."

"That's right, tough guy," Quinn told the gunman he watched. "Check it out, make sure nobody's in the—"

"There he is! Told you so!"

Their binoculars filled with a barrel-chested man with silver hair and smoldering magnetism.

"Carlos Marcello," said Gary, "out on the town after a hard day telling Congress that he never knows nothing about gambling or mobs or rackets, that he's just a tomato seller adjusting to life after prison, that he refuses to answer on the grounds of the fuck-you Fifth and fuck the FBI."

Joe Nezneck stepped into the parking lot behind the men from New Orleans. He snapped a flame to his cigarette.

"Now," said Gary, clicking the Telephoto camera. "Aren't you glad you came?"

"Wouldn't have missed it for the world."

Women's laughter floated across the street to Quinn and Gary as a trio of miniskirted beauties on high heels sashayed into the parking lot's shaft of light behind Nezneck.

"That blonde touching Nezneck's back!" whispered Quinn. "She was there the night he and I—She's in the picture with Pat Dawson!"

Gary said, "Her name is Heidi Ryker."

"Heidi Ryker is in Pat Dawson's little book," said Quinn. "Now she's in a picture with Nezneck and Mr. Tomato Seller. What about the other two? The redhead sidling up to Mr. Muscleman, the other blonde trembling beside Carlos?"

"Hired talent," said Quinn. "If we could trust my department's Vice boys—"

"Whoa!" Gary clicked pictures. "There's your buddy Mel Klise! Bouncy little squirrel, isn't he? Look what's hanging on his happily married arm!"

Quinn peered through his binoculars.

Gary said, "She's a beauty. Good old Mel."

Through the binoculars, through the iron-pole fence, Quinn watched.

"OK," said the FBI agent, "that's right, say good-bye to the girls, see you later. Even you. Heidi, that's right, gonna be time for just men talk, just business. Pleasure later. Bobbsy twins taking off. Did you get their license plate?"

John peered through his binoculars.

"Sweet," said Gary. "A peck on the cheek for Nezneck . . . Ooo, Heidi! Way to score, girl! I wondered who that Corvette belonged to!" *Click.* "Got a good shot of it, plate too. Wave bye-bye—

"What's this?" said Gary. "Mel's leaving! Shaking hands with the guys. Holding on to his date like . . ." *Click.* "Classy Lincoln, Mel. That's nice: hold the car door for her! Great legs! Drive careful, Mel, back it out easy . . . Must be serious talk, them sending you off with the rent-a-broads.

"The slimeballs are taking Nezneck's ride! We'll never

make it to the street in time! Wish we had some goddamn official support! A surveillance team on—

"John? You OK?"

Quinn lied. Whispered, "Yeah."

Watched Mel's car drive away into the night with Lorri.

CHAPTER 21

Quinn opened his apartment door to her knock at eleven that night. Lorri wore the same damn dress and a fresh-lipstick smile she turned into a clinging kiss on his dead lips.

"*Mmm.* My bourbon man." She walked past his dangling arms toward the bottle on the coffee table beside John's holstered gun. "I'm a scotch girl, but you take what you can get."

Lorri splashed bourbon into the lone glass, raised the chalice to Quinn. "Besides, what's yours is great with me."

Liquid fire poured into her mouth and got swallowed down her long, smooth throat.

"Glad you're in a party mood," she said. "But try smiling. Unless . . . Promise me I don't have to worry about you being a blues-drowning solitary drinker."

"So how you been these last couple days? Busy, right?"

"Yeah. But tonight is different, tonight I want it to be just our time."

"Where you been tonight?"

"I'm here now, that's what matters. I'm finally here." She shrugged. "Earlier, I did a favor for someone who did one for me."

"That worked out swell, then. Good time was had by all."

"Honey, I came here to . . . What's wrong with you?"

"Guess I'm too much of a believer." He walked to her, around her. "God, you're gorgeous."

His cold hand traced her thigh, over her dress between her breasts, brushed her hair and down her back. She shuddered as he traced the curve of her hips.

"Why are you touching me like that? What's wrong?"

"I saw you. Tonight."

Lorri shrank back from him.

"How's Mel? Big car for such a little guy. Was dinner good? Spaghetti? Sausages? How much did it fucking *cost*!"

"You were spying on me?"

"I'm not that smart. Guess I'm just lucky. I was doing my job, and you walked your ass right into the way."

"I don't know what you think you're doing, but I . . . Where I was—You know our deal!"

"Evidently I don't."

She sobbed. "This isn't right!"

"Tell me how wrong I am! Tell me how wrong this is!"

"I don't have to tell you a damn thing!"

She stepped toward the door. He grabbed her.

"You gonna hit me now, too?"

"I wish to hell I could! How much? How much did they pay you?"

"Pay me?"

"To set me up. Get close to me. Fuck me up, fuck me good and get me so whipped I can't think. You get all and I get fucked!"

"John, what, no, I—"

"Nezneck: Is he your pimp?"

"Pimp?"

"Heidi, friend of his—and yours. One of the girls. Big dumb blind me. No full-time check, fly part-time, temp here, there—comes in handy for meeting johns, doesn't it?"

She wilted to the couch. "I'm not . . . That's not how it is, how it was. That's why I'm here now, tonight! That's what I was doing with Mel. He's a good guy, loves his wife. He wouldn't touch me. He was helping me fix it, walk away from Heidi and the kind of life where I was headed.

"Because of you, John." Her eyes bled tears. "No: not her, 'cause of you. Because of me, 'cause I didn't want that, because I saw what I'd been dancing with, where they were leading me to. It was me! Me finally figuring out how naive and bitter I'd been. I was on my way to stopping it when we met, not quite there but—"

"I should have known. You in Rendezvous—"

"Who were you expecting to meet there? The Virgin Mary?"

"That's not my religion."

"So what are you complaining about?"

"How it works with Heidi and Nezneck, Mel and the cast of thousands."

"Let me out of here. Just let me go."

"No!" Quinn slammed his fist on the coffee table. His holstered gun rattled against the bottle. "Tell me!"

"You want to know the truth? That's what I was so happy about! What I raced here to tell you: the truth. But you don't want that. You want to know what you already believe. I thought you were different."

"So did I," he said.

"So is this what it's like being a cop? You fuck somebody and then you *really* fuck them?"

"That's your business, not mine."

She laughed and cried. "No, that wasn't my *business*.

"You know Heidi? Another stewardess introduced us. You know how it goes: a friend of a friend is suddenly your friend. She listened to me. Just like I thought you—Guess I was wrong. Heidi, she's a good-deal girl. Want to meet interesting people? Party? She knows how and who. Want to get treated big-time? She's got friends who run escort services—legit places, college girls. You let her know, you get a date, what you do is up to you. The men know that, even if they never believe it. You want more? Some bonus payoff? Heidi'll fix you up.

"Last few months, she kept nudging me to try some real action, to . . . But I was never that ambitious. Just a party girl, good times, few laughs, no strings, no hearts on the line, something more elegant than a businessman pawing at me for drinks and a *give-it-up* in the airplane bathroom. Something on my terms. Of all the people in the world, I thought you'd understand that, Mr. Undercover Cop, playing at being whoever you get a chance to be, long as you play by your rules, keep yourself *unattached* to what's going on. I thought you'd appreciate that.

"Now," she said, "you happy? Satisfied?"

"All those *unattached* men . . . did you fuck them?"

"I fucked a lot of people. How about you?" She topped the glass with bourbon, drank half of it, set the glass beside his holster. "You get off on knowing? You should have told me that before.

"I went out maybe ten times. Kept it separate from me, from who I am. Heidi let me and other girls, when we had to get picked up or take a date somewhere—she has a special apartment.

"Two guys gave me presents—bullshit jewelry. I pawned it, didn't even let them kiss me good night. Some creepy Arab waved a roll of bills at me; I jumped out of his limo and walked home. That pissed Heidi off. Frenchman, government guy, in town from Paris—Yeah, I fucked him, I liked him. Afterward, he sent me a necklace. Threw it in the trash. Heidi wanted me to go out with him again. Wouldn't. Some guy: Seattle, he said, in town to meet with Hubert Humphrey, the senator. Slept with him even though I knew he was married. Is that what you want?"

"Nezneck, Joe Nezneck, how do you know him?"

"The guy at dinner? Not that iceberg Carl, the other old one. Heidi's always had this 'friend' she hints at. Tonight was the first time I met him. *Joe*. He sat in his chair like it was feeding time at the zoo when that wolverine kept staring at us. I knew enough to spend most of the time in the bathroom."

"What about Mel?"

"One of the guys I dated, just dinner, a setup when Mel was doing some business with him. Mel called Heidi for someone to 'class up the evening.' Mel figured out right away I wasn't . . . And that was more than OK with him. Mel's sweet."

"What else did you do for Mel and Nezneck and Heidi?"

"I thought all you cared about was fucking." She drained the bourbon glass. "Heidi knew the airline wasn't giving me enough work, knew the grab-ass shit I'd get part-timing. She set me up with some quick-cash deals. Ten, twelve times, she had me carry her extra purse in my flight bag. I knew better than to mule grass or cocaine or whatever. Didn't open the envelopes, but I felt them, made sure the most that was in them was money. Didn't matter. Wasn't part of me, who I am."

"You put your fingerprints on a deal, the deal rubs off on you. Where did you take them?"

"Dallas, Chicago, Vegas. Miami once. I'd give the envelopes to some 'secretary.' Different girl every time. None of them looked like they knew how to type, but so what? Not my business. I wasn't doing anything morally wrong, just walking the line a little. Being smart. A little jolt of *cool*. Different. Exciting. Choosing instead of just settling. The secretaries'd come to my hotel, meet me in the lobby, say hi, take the envelopes and go. I always said no to partying with them, meeting their friends. Since I helped Heidi out on 'tax things,' she got me a great deal on my car, gave me a hundred a trip for expenses."

"Did you ever meet a lawyer?"

"I met a hundred lawyers in this town. Bunch of them at parties, some Heidi invited me to."

"Did Heidi or anybody like her ever mention a lawyer named Bill or Will, a flashy guy who likes to defend girls in trouble."

"You mean *Phil* Bailley?"

"Madeline got the name wrong! Phil, not Will!"

"So how did you fuck some poor Madeline to get that from her?"

"Bailley, tell me about Phil Bailley."

"Going to read me my rights? You have the right to be fucked and fucked over. You have the right to lose your heart and your pride. You have the right to a lawyer named Phil. Do you want to know if I fucked him? Must have been the only woman who didn't. Heidi introduced us. He wanted me to go to a swingers party with him: government types, politicians, *Post* reporters. Couples only. Told him no. He didn't get that: the 1970s, everybody fucks everybody.

She choked down the last of the bourbon. "I thought I could have a real life. Silly me."

"And Mel—"

"Asked him, said he'd arrange to cover my walk away from Heidi, but I had to have dinner tonight with him and her. Said he needed a show date, somebody he could trust. He said if he had a date, he wouldn't need to stick around for business he didn't want to know."

"Did you tell him about me?"

"It wasn't about *you*. I told him about *me*." Her laugh was hollow. "We were so clever. Mel told Heidi I came to him for help with 'women sickness.' He'd called a doctor, got a diagnosis that would let me fade out of the high life. The big C: scares everybody, nobody'd want a woman who's got it there, no way would she . . . In the bathroom, I told Heidi the diagnosis. I knew she was lying when she said she'd help, be my friend. For her, I'm useless and useless is dead."

The whisper came from deep inside him. "Did you ever meet Pat Dawson?"

"Never heard of him."

Of her, thought Quinn.

"If nothing else is true, tell me: you, me . . ." Quinn couldn't finish that question.

"You," she wept. "I was on my way to getting free. Then I met you. Got happy. Got scared. Almost ran, hid. Then I got free.

"I came here tonight to tell you the truth. Not all that shit, I was never going to tell you about that, it doesn't mean a thing. I came here to break our deal. I came here to say the words. I love you. I have since that first night when you rode me away on your motorcycle."

She rolled her head on the couch, her bourbon-and-pain-drowned eyes staring at him as he spun a thousand miles away.

"What would you have said if I hadn't been too late?" she slurred. "What are you going to do now? Believe me? Love me, too?"

The great roaring around Quinn froze him solid.

She slid his gun out of its holster.

"Don't," he said.

"What do we got left? You and your job shot us all to hell so you can't, you won't think I'm ever true, ever trust me. Watching you fall away from me, seeing how you look at me now—"

"The gun, Lorri, the gun—"

"It's the first time I ever held one. So this is what it's like. Never held this kind of power before. Is it going to get us happily ever after?"

"I love you," he told her.

"Yes, you did. I know you did. But how can you now?"

"How can anybody love anybody? I just do."

"I want to believe you more than anything in the world." The gun waved in her bourbon-and-blues-shaky hand.

"It's the truth," he said. "I love you. I always have."

"Then you should kill me for hurting you like this."

"No!"

Her finger curled around the trigger. "Maybe all I can do is set you free. Set me free. Let you walk away to get OK."

"It won't work. You and I are welded together. And we're worth more than all the shit on us."

"How can I believe you?"

"Because I already did the hardest thing," he said. "When I saw what I saw, my love, my life . . . saw it all die when you drove away with Mel, the whole world and all the angels laughing, all I wanted was for the pain to just end. Tried to get drunk, didn't work, and I realized there is no escape. You got the easy way out in your hand. If we weren't worth it, then we could take the easy way out. But we can't take the easy way. I know, because instead I did the hard thing and took the bullets out of my gun."

She stared at him.

"If I did it, you can do it, too," he said. "Do you love me?"

"Yes," she whispered.

"I love you. Do you trust me?"

She nodded, pale and sad. He reached for the .38, felt her let go of the gun.

"You have to know you can trust me all the way." Quinn put the gun bore to his temple and Lorri screamed "No!" and he pulled the trigger—*Click!*

Lorri threw the gun across the room. They slid to the floor, slumped against the wall, holding each other, crying. He stroked her hair, her cheek, told her, "Everything will be OK!"

"Oh sure," she said. "Sure."

CHAPTER 22

Buck arrested Q on June 9, 1972. Red lights and siren on, Buck whipped his cruiser to the Dupont Circle curb where Q was jiving a bushy-headed hot-weapons dealer named Zep who claimed to be tight with both the Pagans motorcycle gang and political radicals. Buck leapt from his cruiser.

Q yelled, "Run!"

Zep fled.

Q sprinted, timed his stumble so he could fall on a patch of the circle's trampled grass.

"Don't fucking move!" yelled Buck. "You're under arrest!"

Buck cuffed Q, threw him in the back of the cruiser. Tore away for all to see.

As the cruiser raced down P Street, Quinn said, "This better be good! I been working Zep for three weeks to put together—"

"Shut up, motherfucker," said Buck. "You're under arrest."

"What?"

Buck cut the sirens and lights.

"Well then, shit," said Quinn. "You better read me my rights."

"You better have some *rights,* 'cause I know you got some *wrongs.*"

"Buck, what the hell are you—"

"Shut up!" The cruiser veered onto Rock Creek Parkway and sped through the swath of trees and jogging paths that bisects Washington. Centrifugal force knocked Quinn against the backseat door. Buck's eyes met Quinn's in the mirror: "How you like being handcuffed?"

Five minutes later, Buck parked the cruiser beside Lorri's car in a forested parking lot. She slouched behind her steering wheel. Quinn saw she wore her stewardess uniform.

"Never thought you'd treat me like a punk," said Buck as he uncuffed Quinn. Sweat rolled down the two men standing in the summer twilight.

"Is she OK? What's she doing here?"

"Pullin' into the house lot, I saw her parked by a pay phone, fly girl uniform. Desk sergeant tells me some woman called you a dozen times."

"I've been on the streets since breakfast!"

"Then the same girl's callin' and askin' since you ain't around, where's Buck? Can she talk to Buck? No call-back number, but I figure it. After roll call I roll up on her and find out how straight you been with me—maybe on account of her."

"Buck, I told you I was on the street!"

"See that newspaper she's hugging? Soon as I hear how she's just got to, life-or-death *got to* get to you right away, soon as I get her set up here and check your play with your captain . . . You think I didn't glom a copy of the same newspaper?"

"What does it say? What did she tell you?"

"She didn't tell me shit, and I don't want to know—from

her. It's you I hung my ass out with, it's you who owes me."

"Buck, I don't know newspaper from nowhere, but as soon as I talk to her, you wait, I swear I'll tell you everything."

"No. Don't swear 'everything' to me. Don't put either of us there." Buck put his cuffs away. "You got trouble. I could guess, but I don't want to know what I don't want to know.

"Something else," he said. "They're giving me my stripes back and a patrol command in Seven-D."

"Buck, that's great!"

"Means I can't ride with your posse. I'll help you all I can, but I'm on the bench. I'll clue our G-man Gary. Now go take care of your woman and your gotta-do's."

Buck pulled the cruiser away into the evening.

Lorri's car was air-conditioned but Quinn brought the heat with him when he slid inside. The chilled air smelled of tears. She handed him the *Washington Star*: "The FBI has uncovered a high-priced call girl ring allegedly headed by a Washington attorney and staffed by secretaries and office workers from Capitol Hill and involving at least one White House secretary. A 22-count indictment returned today by a special federal grand jury names Phillip M. Bailley, 30, as head of the operation."

"I got off the flight," she said. "This newspaper was in the taxi home—I couldn't find you!"

"OK, so far it's just—you weren't a call girl!"

"But I know him! And I—"

"Lot of women know him! So what?"

"I couldn't find you and I panicked. I know I shouldn't have, but I did, because I can't lose you and this could rip us up! Hurt you! A policeman consorting with . . . with me, so—"

"It's OK!"

"So I had to know, had to find out if I was going to hurt you! There's this ex-FBI guy, worked for the Un-American Activities Committee, Lou Russell—"

"What did you do?"

"Don't yell at me! Please! Let me tell you.

"Russell's one of the crowd around Bailley and Heidi. I

think he thinks that'll he'll save those kind of women. Heidi
said once he helped her out with 'security,' so . . . When they
said you couldn't be reached, I went to his place. Tried to
be clever. Asked him whether this would be trouble for Bailley's friends like Heidi and he wouldn't talk straight with
me. He said things like, 'All the players in town are jazzed
about this one.' Said to forget about Bailley, he was nobody,
but if they put 'big heat' on him, on call girl rings, people
like Heidi . . . 'Exposure.' He muttered 'exposure,' and getting 'caught in the nets.' Especially if the 'hard evidence'
turns up."

"Evidence! Hard evidence of what?"

"There are books," she said.

"Books? Address books? *Client* lists? Whore-girl lists?"

"I'm probably in Phil's address book, but what I'm worried about . . . Heidi steered me to a modeling job at a local
department store. All you could see of me in the newspaper
ad was my hair flying and my body and hands. The photog-
rapher took other shots. Face shots. Heidi kept some of them.
She put them in some books, binders, I think, with her
friends who . . . who she steered toward . . ."

"Books? How many? How do you know you're in them?"

"Because the man from Seattle, the Democratic Party guy
I . . . went with. He told me that's how he picked me to be
set up with."

John slumped against the car seat.

"A guy showed it to him in some office," said Lorri.

"Who? Where?"

"I can't remember. Some political office. Some old guy,
a hanger-on, a gofer kind of guy. A guy who makes himself
important knowing how to get things done, who to call. A
guy who'll do jobs nobody else wants. Guys who want to
be a big shot like Mel. Heidi knew a dozen guys like that.
They fit together. Help each other out. The Seattle man told
me there's always guys like that hanging around all political
campaigns."

"OK. But we're—you're still OK. Unless Bailley had one
of those books."

"Lou Russell said he didn't think so. And God, I felt great! Relieved! Then, out of the blue, he said Heidi knows there's a lot more to be nervous about. That there's bugging going on of girls and guys, phones, and . . . He said there were tapes. And he mumbled the word *films*."

"Films?" But Quinn knew of what. "Could you be in any?"

"Hate me. You have to hate me!"

"Lorri—"

"Ever since we blew up last week, careful not to talk about it head on, not to pull that weight down on us all at once. You asked me again and I said yes and moved in with you. It's OK if we touch it little by little, we'd have got there. Plus you working, me flying . . . so scared, praying—"

"I love you but you have to give it all up now!"

"There could be films." Her forehead hit the steering wheel. "I told you I kept it all separate from my life. Oh, that was so smart! The only two times—the Seattle guy, the French diplomat: I let them come back with me to an apartment Heidi has near the State Department. There were mirrors, phones . . . I don't know. I love you and I'm sorry and I wish I were dead and I don't know!"

Quinn stared through the windshield. "If somebody's making films, it's not home movies. Bugging, films—you do that for intelligence. And blackmail."

"But I didn't do that!"

"If it happened, you got used, just like a camera." He folded his hand around her grip on the steering wheel. "Something's happening here. When you live on the edge like us—"

"I don't live there now!"

"But you did. When you walk on the edge, being paranoid is the smart way to move.

"Blackmail," he said. "Double loading a call girl ring to get blackmail stuff—for power or bucks, doesn't matter, that's pure Nezneck. Heidi, he owns her.

"Lou Russell is right," continued Quinn. "Bailley gets

busted, maybe plea-bargains all he knows. Gives up Heidi, rumors of films and buggings—"

"I didn't do anything really wrong! Maybe I was around something illegal, but I haven't been caught!"

"No. But somebody you know has been, so now you're caught up."

Cop Quinn shook his head. "God, I love to find a participant like you in a crime mess! Turn you into a key. Make you help me unlock what's going on. Maybe you didn't do anything 'wrong,' but you probably broke laws or unwittingly conspired to help others do so. Even if you didn't know it, maybe money changed hands for your . . . liaisons. If you got filmed, you facilitated extortion. The cash you muled for Heidi? Call it tax evasion, conspiracy to commit. If I get your picture or your name tied to a call girl shopping catalog, rumors, bits, and pieces, whathafuck, who cares about a conviction, the threat of charging you is a big enough hammer. Sorry about that, Ms. Citizen, sorry about ruining your life and future and putting you on the crime line, but I'd turn you into a 'cooperating witness' and work my way up the ladder to Nezneck."

Quinn shook his head. "If he thinks that you could be part of a chain leading to him . . ."

Night enveloped their car.

Finally Quinn said, "How much does Russell know?"

"I don't know. I barely know him. He knows Phil. Heidi. Her activities."

"Going to this Lou Russell laid a trail back to you! Elevated you as an 'involved party'!"

"I was trying to find out how bad of trouble I was in! You weren't around!"

"Lou Russell. Phil Bailley. Heidi. Nezneck. Films and bugging. My hinked cops and the department headhunters. The good guys, crime busters. The fucking newspapers. They'll all get the sweats over this."

Cicadas sang.

"Leave me," she said. "I love you forever and you can

leave me and I'll tell the FBI and whoever that you didn't know anything."

"No." Quinn took her hand. "No. How could I leave you?"

Her hand came to life in his. "What can we do?"

"Be smart. Stay ahead of the game. Become invisible."

MONDAY QUINN STALKED the courthouse until he "ran into" Max and led the prosecutor to an empty stairwell.

Max whispered, "Why has the whole world gone nuts over one lousy prostitution case?"

"All I asked you was how far—"

"How far? You won't believe how far! The story's in the paper last Friday. That afternoon, the White House sends a chauffeured black sedan to our office to pick up the prosecutor on the case and bring him to the White House with the evidence seized on what should be a local felony! Talk about separation of powers, proper prosecutorial proced—"

"The White House is a building," said Quinn. "Who?"

"Some guy who's a White House counsel to President Dick fucking Nixon himself! Guy named John Dean."

Ice burned Quinn's bowels. "Why the hell does the White House care about a hooker case?"

"Why?" whispered the balding prosecutor. "You tell me. I'll tell you what they *said*. Concerns about some secretary on the White House staff being 'innocently involved.' This Bailley has hundreds of people in address books, some probably innocent of everything except giving out their phone number at a party. But whatever, this is a volcano case."

"And now you," said Max. "What's your angle?"

"You know I help Sergeant Madison with runaways," said Quinn. "Some of those girls . . . who knows. What's going to happen on this case? More grand jury? Other busts?"

"You tell me and we'll both know."

By the end of the week, *The Washington Post* reported that the White House had "special interest" in the case and was pressuring the prosecutors to stay silent. Bailley, over the objections of his defense counsel and the neutrality of the prosecutors, was bizarrely sentenced by the judge to a sixty-day evaluation commitment at the D.C. insane asylum. The judge issued a gag order covering prosecutors, defense attorneys and Bailley.

"That bought us time," Quinn told Lorri.

"To do what?"

"Be smart. Careful. Bold. Wisely paranoid. We're not sure what kind of exposure you have—*we* have. You're probably in Bailley's address books. Probably your picture is in some loose-leaf binders somewhere. But the big scare is something we're only projecting: film and tapes, and from that, felony blackmail. And there's only one place you could have been caught up in that."

"Heidi's apartment," said Lorri. "The one she—*we* used for—"

"For what is the key. If it's not bugged or set up for secret filming, then you're safe."

"How can we know if that apartment is . . . *No!*"

"Lorri—"

"I won't let you do it! It's too risky!"

"Hell, I got a secret government license for that kind of thing!"

"Not for this. Not for me."

"It's not for you," insisted Quinn. "It's for me. We can't reach out on this any more than I have, or I'll be spotlighted. No way can I go after Heidi: she even smells me, Nezneck will come straight at us, at you. Besides, given all she probably knows, her worries over a call girl ring investigation are nothing. And like you said, if it comes out that a police officer is knowingly involved with a woman linked to a call girl ring with potential related felonies, the best that happens then is that the cop gets fired."

"Oh, Johnny: only you could tell the truth to get me to believe a lie! You don't want to risk this for you."

"You and me are *us,*" he said. "A bullet hitting any of that makes me bleed.

"This won't go away," he told her. "Not with the damn White House and newspapers involved. We have to know how much trouble we could be in, and we have to know quick."

She shook her head. "I thought I'd be great for you."

"You are. I guess great doesn't come easy. We can just sit back and pray. The surest mistake is to know something and do nothing."

He won her over to the sense of his plan. She'd showed him the apartment building, which windows belonged to Heidi's unit.

"Nobody really lives in it," she said. "Heidi hands out the keys. You can send them back by messenger."

In the week after the first newspaper story, Quinn resurrected an absurd FBI report about left-wing "Yippie" women posing as hookers to feed LSD to politicians. He coupled that with Sergeant Madison's legitimate report about pimps targeting female runaways and "counterculture dropouts." Q fed a burned-out protester leading questions until the stoner mumbled into a tape recorder that Heidi's apartment might be "a hippie hooker place." Quinn filed a report that unless he received countermanding orders, he would follow up "as operationally necessary" on what evidence (including a taped informant) indicated were alarming subversive/criminal activities. Quinn filed his report where it would crawl through the law enforcement–security maze. By the time any decision could be made, he'd have done what he had to do.

"So we're ready," Quinn told Lorri. "If the shit hits the fan, my ass is covered."

"Is that the truth, the whole truth, and nothing but the truth?"

Quinn shrugged. "It's what we've got."

CHAPTER 23

Friday, June 16, 1972. Seven P.M. Hot. Muggy. Quinn sat in his car parked on Virginia Avenue where he could watch the windows of the high-rise apartment. He wore an untucked denim shirt to hide the .38 clipped to his belt and the CIA lock-pick case, Army surplus pants whose thigh pockets bulged with a black cloth hood and gloves. Black and white sneakers sheathed his feet. On the car floor beside Quinn was a plastic gallon milk jug into which he'd already peed. The scent of his own urine seeped into the lush summer air.

Stay dark, Quinn telepathically ordered the apartment windows.

Stay empty, he willed the apartment.

High above Kansas a jetliner flew westward with Lorri serving warm chicken. She forced her smiles, fought the shakes in her hands. Quinn had made her plead with other stewardesses and her supervisors until she got a schedule that jetted her safely far from D.C. that weekend.

Gotta go, he'd told her. Not be around. If it goes bad, that's the safest setup for both of us.

At 8:21, Quinn walked to the pay phone outside a Howard Johnson's family restaurant and hotel. The billboard on a bus stop held a poster advertising Leonard Bernstein performing *Mass* that night at the Kennedy Center a gunshot away. Don't let any FBI agents who know me be surveilling Bernstein, thought Quinn, who knew of the Bureau's interest in that Jewish conductor after his fund-raiser for the Black Panther Party. Every hour since he'd set up on target at 4:45 that afternoon, Quinn had walked to a pay phone in sight of the windows and called the two numbers assigned to that apartment. Luck was with him and no one answered. Now, as he shifted his eyes from the distant high-rise to the pay phone, Quinn saw Burt Lancaster.

What the hell—Quinn remembered hearing a roll call assign crowd control duties for a movie being shot in town, some spy versus spy story starring Burt Lancaster. There he is, strolling into the HoJo's restaurant, safe and bigger than life.

Fuck his Hollywood hero act, this is real.

No one answered the phones in Heidi's rendezvous pad. Those windows stayed dark as Quinn returned to his car to wait and watch.

Nine-thirty: dark windows, unanswered phones.

Ten thirty-two: same story.

Eleven twenty-seven: and Quinn used the milk jug.

Midnight: if there was a social event scheduled for the apartment, odds were the lucky couple would show up soon or never.

"What'll you do if you find cameras behind the mirrors?" Lorri had asked. "Microphones, bugs in the phones, or whatever?"

Then we'll know we're not paranoid, Quinn told her.

"The risk you're taking is a high price for just knowing."

Not when the cost of ignorance could be everything.

Twelve-fifteen, into tomorrow while it's still tonight. What would he be doing tonight *if* life were as it should be? Working for his badge, not the heart beneath it. Sleeping beside Lorri. If she was working a flight, probably reading, maybe back from the movies or the cops' bar, maybe filling the lonely hours by watching TV. He'd seen the late-night boob tube schedule: Scream Theater was showing a movie called *Attack of the Puppet People*. Quinn thought: I know how they feel.

"What if you get caught?" Lorri's eyes teared when she'd said it.

Then I'll say it was a national security job. Nobody will let me drop far, because I'd pull too much and too many powerful people with me. As long as we don't talk, there's only so far anybody can take it.

At 1:45 A.M., nerves sent him to the jug. He'd wait until three, after the bars closed and sent couples to bed. If the windows were still dark then . . . now work the phone. Scout the target zone.

The city'd grown quiet: a few cars whizzing past on nearby Rock Creek Parkway, cicadas, the buzz of a dying streetlight. He strolled, watching the apartment windows, scanning the shadows for derelicts or other witnesses, so intent on what he was pretending not to be doing that he didn't see where they came from.

Walking toward Quinn—three cops.

Shit!

Three cops, scruffy clothes, TAC Squad work. He knew them! And they knew him! The cop with hair down to his shoulders flashing him the "Be cool!" hand signal was Shoffler, Carl Shoffler, who worked Red Squad stuff, too! And the other guy was John Barrett, the third guy, a sergeant . . . Leeper, Paul Leeper!

"Act casual, like we're just friends," whispered Shoffler, slapping five with Quinn. "Did you monitor the radio call, too? Possible burglary in—"

"No! I'm working undercover surveillance."

"Come on," said Barrett. "Your surveillance is blown. Back us up."

They led him into the office, hotel and condo complex across the way from Heidi's apartment. The cops found an excited security guard who showed them the underground garage, where he'd found a door with its latch taped to stay open.

Had a burglary last week, explained the guard's supervisor.

"Where?"

Upstairs, the cops heard, in the Federal Reserve Board. The repository of security plans for banks throughout America.

Shoffler had the guards shut off the elevators, then the cops hurried up the stairwells.

"You don't look so spooked now," Shoffler told Quinn.

"I'm OK, this is gonna be OK," said Quinn. "But whatever this is, remember: I'm not here."

Panting, they reached the eighth floor. Found taped door locks. Couldn't enter the Federal Reserve offices.

"There's tape down here on the sixth floor!" hissed one cop. The others hurried to him.

They drew their guns. Eased their way inside a dark, cavernous office space. Hit the lights.

"This place looks like it's been trashed!" whispered Quinn; later they'd be told such a mess was a standard sight.

Inside, slowly, eyes sweeping, guns ready.

"Balcony door's open!" said Shoffler.

With the sergeant and Quinn covering him, Shoffler crawled out on the ledge, looking for bad guys. Across the street in one of the upper floors of the Howard Johnson hotel, Quinn and Shoffler spotted a male figure standing on a hotel balcony, staring back at them. Ghostly black-and-white TV flickers lit the room behind the man, and with pararational certainty, Quinn knew that he had been watching Scream Theater's *Attack of the Puppet People*.

"Sergeant!" called Shoffler. "Look at that guy! He probably thinks we're breaking in here!"

The sergeant radioed approaching scout cars that undercover officers were on the scene.

Quinn helped Shoffler back—

"Don't move!" screamed Barrett. "Don't fucking move!"

Leeper jumped on a desk, his gun thrusting down toward something Quinn couldn't see. Leeper screamed: "We are the police! We are the police!"

"Our backs! Watch our backs!" yelled Quinn, scanning the room with its hundred places where a shotgun man could be hiding.

Then he saw five pairs of surgically gloved hands sticking up between desks.

"Get up! Get out of there!"

Five men in business suits slowly stood. Bunch of 'em swarthy guys. Italians maybe. Mafia maybe. The tall one yelled, "Who are you? Who are you guys working for?"

"Police! Assume the position! Get against the wall! Put your hands on it! Lean!"

"They're the police!" yelled the tall guy. "Everything's going to be all right!"

Five clean-cut men in business suits pressed their surgical-gloved hands against the wall while a half moon of scruffily dressed, long-haired cops held them at gunpoint.

"What the hell is this shit?" mumbled Quinn.

They patted down the five men for weapons, found none and made piles behind the men of everything they stripped off them: lock picks, blank keys and screwdrivers, two cameras and thirty-nine rolls of film, a two-way radio, a stand used to brace a camera while photographing documents, ID's that looked shaky, hotel room keys, $100 bills, three high-quality electronic bugs, a smoke detector that had been wired to hide—

"Keep your fucking hands on the wall!" yelled Shoffler.

Quinn caught a glimpse of the fifth man on the far left of the line putting his right hand back on the wall as Shoffler shuffled to that burglar, gave him a second pat-down for weapons.

Fool has to know Shoffler could have shot him dead! thought Quinn. *What the hell was he thinking of? What was he doing?*

Shoffler moved back up the line. When his attention turned from that last burglar, Quinn saw the burglar's right hand lift off the wall, snake inside his suit jacket—

"Motherfucker!" Shoffler slammed him against the wall and pushed the barrel of his pistol into the burglar's ear, kept it there while Shoffler reached around and fumbled inside the man's suit until he came out with what was in there.

A twenty-nine-cent notebook, Quinn saw. Taped on its cover was a key.

Guy was willing to die for that? Quinn shook his head as Shoffler added the notebook with its key to the evidence piles. Shook his head and—

Wait a minute! Seen two, no: maybe three of these guys before! Where? Where?

The hollow of what he couldn't remember roared at Quinn's jangling nerves.

If I saw them somewhere, sometime, maybe they'll remember me—and I can't be here!

Quinn kept behind the handcuffed suspects; avoided their gaze.

Uniformed units arrived. Crime-scene techs. Out front, the paddy wagon rolled up. Shoffler, trying to break the ice with the burglars, trying to get them to say something, anything, told them the truth: "You guys are fucking up my birthday!"

A burglar told Shoffler, "You think you're gonna see another one?"

They took them to the cop house. Some burglars pretended not to speak English, but then raised their hands when Shoffler asked who wanted a Coke. Lawyers showed up. Feds in suits.

Shoffler took Quinn aside. "You know how we got a walkie-talkie radio off them? Those things only work in pairs. I think our citizen across the street at the HoJo's was a lookout."

"He's gone now," said Quinn. "If he's smart."

"All those guys in suits are so damn *smart*." Shoffler looked to be sure they were alone. "I figured a little pressure might help us find out what's going on."

He grinned: "I dimed *The Washington Post*."

Quinn had to smile.

"All that shit we pulled off them," said Shoffler. "Cameras, lock picks, electronic gear. That's beyond burglary. All those different kinds of tools. Like their work was grab bag collecting whatever was there, whatever they could do and get."

Shoffler stared at his colleague. "You gonna keep riding with us? We know you're a way-undercover badge and sorry we blew your surveillance, but how invisible do you gotta be?"

Get out! Quinn told himself. You were trapped on the scene of a crime you almost committed. Shoffler's dimed the press, there'll be spotlights everywhere. These guys already have some can't-remember-it link to you, some "undercover daze." If what you were really doing plus your undercover job gets dragged out . . . Sure, it's a great bust, cop work like you're hungry for, plus suit and tie burglars so close to Heidi's apartment is scary, but . . .

"I'll work it for you guys," he told Shoffler. "But figure I'm the ghost of Christmas never was, keep me way off the books. *Way* off."

Shoffler shrugged: *Do what I can.*

The exhausted cops banged out search warrants for the hotel rooms that matched the room keys they'd found on the burglars. At police headquarters the clock swung toward 10 A.M. Quinn kept an eye on the burglars shuffling through the system. Amid milling cops, lawyers, routine collars from a Friday night, a member of the police intelligence squad saw the burglars and did a double-take. He told his superiors what none of them wanted to believe: one of the burglars was James McCord, the liaison between the police intelligence squad and—

"The Committee to Re-elect the President!" a uniformed lieutenant whispered to Quinn. "CREEP! President Nixon's people!"

Head pounding, eyes burning, sneakers dragging, Quinn went back to the Watergate complex to search hotel rooms linked to keys the burglars carried. He was too tired to worry about why the burglars had carried incriminating keys to their own rooms, why they'd picked their "safe" quarters to be in their crime zone. That search found surgical gloves, electronic equipment, a $6.36 check made out to a D.C. suburban country club from E. Howard Hunt, and an address book containing the notation: *H. H.—W. H.*

The phone listed with those initials rang in the White House.

The FBI checked the Democratic National Committee office, where they'd caught the burglars, for electronic surveillance devices. That check turned up negative. Later that afternoon, the phone company checked all telephones in that suite of offices: again, no eavesdropping devices were found; the DNC was pronounced clean of bugs.

Get out of here! Quinn argued to himself. Get away from this!

But instead he went to the burglars' court arraignment.

Saturday afternoon, June 17, 1972.

Quinn slipped into the courtroom as the five men were led in. They wore their suits, but jailers had taken away their belts and ties. The burglars had coughed up their true names. Some were Cubans linked to Miami. The U.S. attorney prosecuting the case argued against releasing the men on bond. Max slid onto the spectators' bench beside Quinn.

"See the stocky guy at the bench with that defendant Sturgis?" whispered Max. "He's the columnist, Jack Anderson!"

"Jack—what the hell—"

"He knows Sturgis! Got to him in the cells—somebody's in shit for that! He's asking the judge to remand the burglar to his custody! Look at the other reporters going nuts!"

The judge declined the columnist's offer. He asked the arrested men their professions.

One said, "Anticommunists."

Others nodded in agreement.

The judge asked burglar James McCord his occupation.

He said, "Security consultant."

The judge asked where. McCord answered he'd recently retired from the government. The judge said, "Where in the government?"

"CIA."

Quinn whispered, *"Oh, shit!"*

CHAPTER 24

"What if you're wrong?" whispered Holloway to Jud Simon in a deserted White House hallway. Their watches ticked away the last seconds of that sticky June Sunday night.

"He's here." Jud Simon wore his Secret Service uniform,

his holstered .357 Magnum revolver. Carpet swallowed their cautious footsteps. "Feel it? Like in the jungle. Electricity. Hair on your neck, your arms. Tonight, this whole place is charged."

"Those five burglars D.C. cops caught at the Watergate yesterday: Think they—"

Jud's hand shot up; the Marine killed his whisper.

Nathan watched a doorknob turn in Jud's grip. Jud mouthed, "One . . . two . . ."

Jud threw the door open! *Inside!* Closing the door behind them as Jud snapped on—

Light engulfed the man sitting on the floor in front of a safe. His pale eyes blazed. Penzler said, "So, I was right. You two *are* together."

"And you're fucked," said Jud Simon. "Caught."

"I think not." Penzler frowned and told Jud, "Security sign-in sheets. You had your badge buddies watching for me."

"And now we've got you. This isn't your turf. Hell, you don't have a White House office!"

"This is nobody's office anymore. So me being here, being caught by you two of all people: Do you really think that anyone wants such a fuss? Especially this weekend?"

Penzler uncoiled, stood. "Keep up the good work."

He left them in the closed, quiet office.

"Son of a bitch!" said Holloway. "We won nothing!"

"We busted his play," said Jud. "Whatever it was."

"There's nothing in here but blank notepads, trash—"

"And this." Jud knelt in front of the metal safe. "Locked. He didn't have any tools, probably didn't have the combination. But if whoever shut this was lazy and only moved the dial a few numbers away so the handle would be secure . . ."

Jud painstakingly turned the combination dial as his other hand kept pressure on the handle.

"Either Penzler already finished, or he fucked it up, or the guy whose safe this is used it right." His fingers brushed the steel. "Wells Fargo vintage. Jesse James dynamited them."

"So we'll never know what Penzler was after."

"Give me your shoelace."

"What?"

"Your shoelace. And be quiet.

"Great safe," said Jud as he stretched Holloway's shoelace over the combination dial. "Stops brute force, a bitch to drill or peel. It's gravity drop-bottom locks."

Slowly at first, then faster, Jud seesawed the shoelace across the combination dial. The steel knob spun: first one direction, then the other. Fast. Faster. Steel whirred.

"When you hit the first number, the slot lines up, the lock bar is clear, gravity makes it fall fr—That's one!"

Holloway heard nothing.

"Two!" said Jud. He slowed the shoelace. "And . . . three!"

Cat-quick, Jud stopped the spinning combination dial. He turned the handle; the safe swung open.

"Where did they find you?" whispered Holloway.

"They made me. Use gloves."

The two of them left no fingerprints on what they found: a .25 automatic; CIA profiles of Pentagon Papers leaker Daniel Ellsberg; State Department cables about murdered President John F. Kennedy and the 1963 assassination of South Vietnamese President Ngo Dinh Diem; documents on a young woman's fatal drowning at Chappaquiddick involving Senator Ted Kennedy; two black cloth Hermès notebooks scrawled with covert-operations reports.

"I got nowhere near enough film!" said Holloway.

"Do the notebooks. Back to the front. Start with the most recent."

Holloway shot thirty frames. They replaced the material, locked the safe. Left the room dark.

"Dead-drop the film tonight," said Jud.

"For six months, they haven't even commo'd back a 'material received.' After they let Penzler set me up—"

"*If* they did."

"They did nothing before or after to help, they must have."

"Don't give them too much credit. Besides, since Radford's bust, we're all running scared."

"Who's office was that?"

Jud called a friend at Secret Service control, said, "Last occupant was a Howard Hunt."

"What now?" said Holloway.

"We stay alive. Hunker down. See who else runs through our jungle."

CHAPTER 25

On the sultry Monday morning, June 19, 1972, a manila envelope franked with the signature of his boss, the Senator, waited on Vaughn Conner's desk as he shed the linen jacket a friend had insisted that he buy, lifted the tie off his sunburned neck and hung it on a lamp. Inside the envelope he found newspaper articles and a note:

> *This looks like your kind of thing.*
> *Dane*

The first article came from the previous day's newspaper, Sunday's *Washington Post*. The bylined reporter was Alfred E. Lewis: *Five men . . . former employees of the Central Intelligence Agency . . . arrested in elaborate plot to bug the Democratic National Committee.*

At a place called Watergate. Never heard of it, thought Vaughn.

Surprised at gunpoint by three plainclothes officers . . .

Five burglars versus only three cops, thought Vaughn: Way to go, guys. The *Post* even identified them: Leeper, Barrett, Shoffler.

Saturday morning. Bad guys wearing surgical gloves. Cubans. A guy named McCord, retired CIA. Bay of Pigs links. No guns. Cash. Electronic equipment. Cameras. Agents from the FBI and the Secret Service also assigned to the investigation.

The bundle included follow-up stories from that day's *Post*. One story by two guys named Woodward and Bernstein linked the ex-CIA burglar named McCord to President Nixon's Republican Party. The White House was calling the affair "a third-rate burglary." An article by Ron Kessler said wiretap experts characterized the bungled operation at the Watergate as a slapstick comedy, a Mickey Mouse operation, "a blot on the bugging profession."

"Now that's a shame," muttered Vaughn. He settled in his chair.

"Apparently you survived." She poured a cup of coffee from the office pot. As she raised the cup to her thin lips, she told Vaughn, "Though you look a little overdone."

"The burn is only skin deep."

"Are you sure?" Crow's-feet at the corners of her brown eyes showed she'd been no stranger to the sun when she was Vaughn's age; the clean slash of her jaw showed that his youth wasn't far behind her. Whispers of silver lightened the shoulder-length brown hair she brushed back from a widow's peak. "So you stayed out too long in the surf and sun—"

"Plus there's this guy with a band in Asbury Park. Raw but amazing. Like a poet."

"Stayed out late rocking and rolling, and—"

"Got in on time at nine today. How was weekend duty?" She shrugged, and Vaughn said, "Thanks for the clips."

"They're just for amusement, not to get you in trouble again."

"What trouble? I haven't done wrong."

"That's not what I've heard," whispered Dane. "Heads up."

She went to her desk in the adjoining office. Public payroll records listed Dane Foster as an executive assistant to Senator August Martin, a volatile Democrat from a Western state. She ranked below Maggie Wallace, the Senator's personal secretary, and Byron Douglas, the Senator's administrative assistant, but above "executive aide" Vaughn Conner, a handful of legislative aides and caseworkers, and the cadre of secretaries.

Who's caught me doing what? thought Vaughn as he scanned mail routed to him by the back room: routine stuff destined for boilerplate paragraphs he'd architect into responses secretaries would churn out of electric typewriters for the Senator's signature.

Burglary at the Watergate office complex. Three cops. Guns. FBI. CIA. Surgical gloves. The Democratic National Committee. "A blot on the bugging profession." More interesting than casework or shepherding bills from committee to floor action so Nixon can veto them, thought Vaughn. Get in on it fast, before any other staff—

His phone buzzed. Byron Douglas, the AA, the staff czar: "You're in with the boss for a meeting in five minutes. Wear your damn tie and jacket."

"What—"

But the phone went dead. He cinched his tie around his tender neck, slid into the linen jacket, grabbed a pad and pen and hurried into the suite one door beyond his hallway desk. Maggie looked up from a pile of mail as Byron came around the edge of his green metal cubicle. Byron glared at Vaughn's tan linen jacket: "You look like a damn Boy Scout!"

Maggie smiled. "But chic."

Whatever I did, it's not fatal, thought Vaughn, or she wouldn't have defended me.

Byron belched his morning beer and tomato juice. He rapped on the closed door to the Senator's private office. Vaughn had time to take a deep breath, then Byron led him inside.

Unlike most members of Congress, Senator Martin had no power wall of pictures showing him shaking hands with presidents, generals and movie stars. The fifteen-foot ceiling of his private office looked down on leather couches and chairs, landscape paintings, law books, a framed eagle-feathered headdress given to him by an Indian nation whose barren reservation Martin had enriched with a federal dam project.

On the fireplace mantel sat two framed pictures: the one in the silver frame was a snapshot of his wife, killed two years earlier in a car wreck.

Gus Martin sat behind his paper-stacked senator's desk, a grizzly bear in a navy pinstripe suit. He waved them into his lair with his free paw as he held the phone to his ear:

"So he gets my vote to report it out of committee, then I vote no on the floor—if it comes up. And you'll get what you need from him in exchange for getting me to go that far? . . . Yeah . . . No, I hate conventions. Besides, I figure even if McGovern gets McCarthy to bring the antiwar people on board and picks up Muskie's broken hearts, Nixon's got it licked. Hubert's a good man, but this wasn't his year—again. Teddy's too smart to set himself up for the psychos who want to gun down the third Kennedy running for President . . . What's Mansfield say? . . . Yeah. OK."

The Senator hung up and lumbered around to the front of his desk with a jerky sway political sages chalked up solely to whisky but that Vaughn knew came in part from a *Wehrmacht* bullet that had shattered paratrooper Gus Martin's knee.

"First goddamned thing this morning, my home phone rings. I don't like my home phone to ring, Vaughn."

"No, sir."

"Especially first goddamned thing in the morning. Rang twice. First time was some guy from one of the cola companies that has plants back home. Asks me to see a guy today, squeeze him in because of something he says I'm working on. Since I don't know what the hell that is, I had to play along, and I damn well don't like *playing!*"

"Sir, I—"

"Hang up from him, and I get a call from the AFL-CIO downtown. Now I can say the hell with the cola guy. The most chamber of commerce bigwigs like him ever do is *not* drop money in the other guy's campaign. But the AFL gets out the troops, sends checks. So when I get a call from a union guy, I listen, even if he says he's asking a favor for someone who isn't AFL—draws a big line there so I'll be sure to see it. Turns out, this guy is the same guy the cola company exec called about, a guy who wants to do a favor for some group I've never heard of but apparently I wrote some damn letter about."

"Your thing, Vaughn," said Byron. "One of your 'routine' queries. My fault really, though, boss, I shouldn't have signed off so easy on it. No need for us to—"

The Senator's phone buzzed and he grabbed it from its cradle: "Now or never."

"I'm sorry," said Vaughn, "but I don't know what's going on."

There was a rap on the door, then Maggie ushered in a bouncy white-haired gnome.

"Hey, Senator! How are you? Thanks for squeezing me in." The gnome's hand disappeared in Martin's paw; in the Depression, Martin worked his way through Stanford law school boxing in roadhouse smokers. "Think the last time I saw you was that fund-raiser for the Democratic caucus!"

"Oh yes," said Martin.

Vaughn sensed that both men were lying, and that both men knew it. Their charade conveyed more important truths.

"I want you to meet my staff." Martin turned the smiling gnome to Vaughn and Douglas.

"Mel Klise," said the gnome. "Glad to meet you."

"What can we do for you, Mr. Klise?" said the Senator as they took leather seats.

"Call me Mel. I want you to know I'm here on nobody's dime. This is me helping out folks who are trying to do good by doing better."

Byron said, "And those folks are . . . ?"

"I'm here for the folks at the American Association for Justice, and they're—"

Son of a bitch! thought Vaughn. Got it!

"—they're just a bunch of decent private citizens who care about law and order in our great country, who figured that every now and then, it helps to have an outfront public voice to speak up on issues like helping Jimmy Hoffa get some fair justice. Helping recognize you hardworking lawmakers with awards and stuff. And then these good people, volunteers most of them, they got this letter from you, Senator, inquiring about who they are, their purpose, tax status, that kind of thing, and they were wondering the why and the what-for and how could they help you."

"That's my area," said Vaughn. "We were doing some follow-up on the President's commutation of Jimmy Hoffa. Newspaper stories said he was working with that group. Frankly, we'd never heard of them, so—"

"So the Senator thought it prudent to query," said Byron, steering the words just so.

"Totally understandable. But what I got the apples and oranges on," said Mel, "is, Senator, you're not on the Judiciary Committee. They're the ones who oversee pardons and commutations. While you've been a great friend of the working man and organized labor—"

"I work well with the AFL-CIO," interrupted Martin.

Saying nothing about Hoffa's "independent" Teamsters Union.

"So just for my own clue-in, how is it you come to be interested in Jimmy's commutation? It's not like you've got committee jurisdiction."

"Senator Martin is on the Government Operations Committee," said Vaughn. "And on the Permanent Investigations Subcommittee. Gov Ops has oversight responsibilities for all government organizations—including the Pardons and Commutations Office. Plus, as you know, that subcommittee has a precedent involving oversight of matters involving Mr. Hoffa."

The twinkle faded from Mel Klise's eyes.

Vaughn thought he saw the Senator smile: *Figure he did. So push.*

"So the Senator," said Vaughn, "consequently thought it prudent to inquire about any private organization involved in Mr. Hoffa's commutation. As a matter of routine."

"So this . . . routine inquiry," said Mel, his eyes on the Senator. "Are you just being sure all the *X*'s and *O*'s are in place? Because they are, wouldn't have it any other way.

And the way I read my *Congressional Record*, nobody has anything scheduled in the way of hearings."

"Not that I'm aware of," said Martin.

Mel leaned in. "That's the kind of thing our mutual friend downtown said he expects you would have nailed down, whether or not there are hearings planned."

"And he owes you a favor," said the Senator.

"We're just all helping each other out," said Mel. "I'm just arranging so that can happen."

"I anticipate no hearings on this." The Senator took the extra step: "Not by me."

Mel spread his hands wide. "Makes sense. Just wanted to clarify the what's what. Thanks again for your time. I know you're busier than bees at a wedding."

The Arranger stood, shook hands all around, continued: "And when our friends at the association get all their answers together, I'll make sure they send them right up.

"Attention to you," he told Vaughn. The Arranger's smile curved around the young man. "I got your name and number."

The gnome left. Vaughn imagined him bouncing down the corridor to the summer street.

"You do what you gotta do to get the best that you can," intoned the Senator. He sighed. "I've been able to keep that little squirt out of my office all these years."

He put his marble eyes on Vaughn: "Congratulations."

"Senator, I—"

"To hell with that smiling son of a bitch." Senator Martin thrust his forefinger toward Vaughn. "You let me know what's what on this. Keep Byron up on it. And no matter what this phony-ass lobby group sends you, think up more questions to ask them. Figure a way to shift the focus. Make it so it's not just Senator Martin picking on Jimmy Hoffa, the son of a bitch. We honored the favor from our friends, saw that guy, told him the truth. Now show them who's in charge."

Vaughn exhaled for the first time since he came into the meeting, said yes, sir.

"Give us a minute, will you, Byron?" said the Senator.

The AA left Vaughn standing there with his feet welded to the floor.

The Senator stared at the two framed pictures on his mantel.

"You did a hell of a job in the election," he told Vaughn. "Organizing phone banks, door to door, getting out the vote. I was lost, Bev just gone. What I didn't get as a sympathy vote, I owe to the campaign staff. Byron made me bring you back to the mailroom. If you didn't give us so much smart sweat, you'd be gone or still opening envelopes. Instead, we let you dabble."

"And I know how lucky that makes me."

"This Hoffa thing. No votes there, no jurisdiction despite that dance you gave Mel. But there *is* a chance for me to end up pissing somebody off—like when you had me support that hearing about the CIA in Laos and heroin smuggling!"

"I never—*you* never—said they smuggle heroin."

"Do you think they do?"

Vaughn paused, went to the core: "No. They're a bunch of government servants. Family men. Doesn't make sense that they'd help smack dealers target their own kids—*as a matter of policy.* But they're in a dirty business, and out in the field, wild guys on their own. Who knows what happens?"

"Until you do, don't set me up against the good guys again."

"Yes, sir. I mean, no, sir."

"Do you like my picture today?"

The framed photo near the portrait of the Senator's dead wife was the official photograph for Richard M. Nixon, freshman congressman. Nixon and Martin had served in the House together. Martin hated Nixon. When Nixon won the presidency in 1968, the Senator had Maggie dig the routinely received black-and-white photograph out of a storage box, put it in a glass frame and set it on the office mantel. Every week or so, he'd change the grease-penciled "autograph" on the photograph's glass. That day's inscription read: *To Gus Martin: Always great to listen to the best senator in history. Warm regards, your pal, Dick Nixon.*"

Took Vaughn a second. "Is *listen* because of those guys they caught on Saturday?"

The Senator grinned.

"Maybe this isn't the time, but Dane gave me clips on that break-in at the Watergate."

"I hear the DNC's going to sue Republicans. Get some headlines, but it's not worth it."

"Yes, well, there may be some federal oversight angles we should explore."

"*We?* And *should?*"

"The FBI, Secret Service, they're on the investigation, and my guess is the new federal elections office will get some piece of it."

"Nixon's going to win anyway." The Senator looked at the portraits on the mantel, the wife he lost, the President who'd win again. "Dane gave them to you? With what suggestion?"

"She said it was my kind of thing."

"You're learning how to massage a fact real well, aren't you? So what do you want?"

"Let me call down to the Subcommittee on Investigations, see if they're looking into this."

"I'm not detailing you down there. Byron's been down that road with you."

"Like that Mel said, just let me work out what's what."

"Hmmm. OK—and since Dane is already in on it, she's your chain holder."

"I don't really need—yes, sir. Thanks."

"Un-huh." Martin frowned. "I never asked you: Why the hell are you working for me?"

"Your voting record and—"

"Yeah, yeah, yeah. What do you want? Where are you going?"

"I just want to see the whole thing."

"You think there's one 'whole thing'? Is that what politics is for you?"

"Politics is any human interaction involving power."

"My, but you went to college! Son, politics is who gets what."

"And the degree of consciousness and commitment that—"

"Go do your job."

Vaughn walked to the door, his shirt soaked despite the air-conditioning. The Senator called out: "Remember, Vaughn: whatever you do, I'm the one who ends up tarred with it."

Finesse it now. Vaughn smiled his way past Maggie, found Byron rummaging through the paper piles that filled his cubicle.

"You skated on that one," said the AA, lighting a cigarette. "You mad?"

Byron shrugged. "No harm done. So damned if I give a shit."

"I got my orders. Plus the boss agrees with Dane that she and I should keep a hand in on what Permanent Investigations downstairs might do about that Watergate mess."

"That's DNC troubles, we got our hands full with the Senate."

"Don't think it'll interfere with what I need to do up here," said Vaughn.

"You're right," ordered Byron. "It won't."

Because Vaughn had time to spare after work, he slung the linen jacket over his shoulder, drifted to the west front of the Capitol building to gaze at the Mall's sprawl of grass, trees and sandy pathways stretching out two miles from Congress's marble steps. A red ball sun pulsed in the city's humid air just beyond the ivory obelisk of the Washington Monument. On nights he drove home from downtown, Vaughn cruised the opposite direction of where he looked now, toward the Hill with the Capitol dome gleaming ivory beyond his windshield, coming ever closer as he drove, a vision straight off the cover of his high school government textbook. That June sunset, he stood on those marble steps, told himself for the millionth time: *Here I am.*

When he got home, he cranked up his AC, took a shower. He put on a polo shirt, cutoffs, popped a tab on a beer from the refrigerator. Got the plastic bag of marijuana from the table beside the couch, took a rolled joint out of the baggy of green stems and powder, fired it up. The hot smoke burned his lungs; he held it in as long as he could.

Not bad.

He wandered to the bookcase with shelves of record albums filed alphabetically *and* categorically. He smoked the joint as he reasoned his way to the proper aesthetic for the day.

When in doubt, go with the classics.

He eased the black vinyl circle out of its rainbow red album sleeve, let the marijuana cloud drift up his spine, billow inside his skull, sweep him into the sounds of the Beatles' *Sgt. Pepper's.*

Some time later. The joint was gone. The Beatles sang "Lovely Rita." The door buzzer startled him back to earth. He pushed the Admit button without thinking to intercom down to see who he'd let in. *What the hell: worst it could be is salvation sellers.*

A double knock on the door. He fanned the smoky air— *like that would make a difference!* Opened the door.

Dane walked in, a bulging briefcase in one hand, a paper sack in the other. Sweat glistened along her widow's-peaked brow.

"So," she said, sniffing as he shut the door. "Relaxing after a hard day's work?"

"Well," he shrugged, stoned. "You know."

"I do now. You should be more cautious."

"If I were more cautious," he said, walking toward her, "you wouldn't be here."

Then he kissed her, softly, his fingertips barely daring to touch her flushed cheeks.

She returned his kiss, but he felt her hold back.

"Bringing work home?" he said, taking the briefcase from her hand, and she let him.

"Not work. And I've already been home."

"But if home is where your heart is . . ." He kissed her again.

She handed him the paper sack. "Doesn't need to go in the fridge. I figure you're hungry."

"Dinner can wait."

"Then get me a beer. I want to hear about this weekend when a good time was had by all."

He laughed, took the sack to the kitchen. Dane ran her fingers through her hair so it lifted off her sticky neck for the cool air to touch. She stepped out of her shoes. When Vaughn came back with a beer for both of them, she was sitting on the couch.

Vaughn let her take a cool drink, then said, "Two couples. Three solo guys. Beach house. Sun, sand, surf, rock 'n' roll. Fruit stands and traffic on the bay bridge coming home."

"No . . . drop-by guests?"

"You can just ask if I got lucky."

"You got lucky when I rang your doorbell."

"I never even thought about it." He was amazed by that truth, encouraged by her curiosity despite their excruciatingly delineated boundaries of commitment, enraptured by her sitting beside him, long legs curled on his couch, skirt riding high on her trim thighs.

This is crazy, she thought. Dangerous. Looked at his goofy smile, his seven-years-younger body, his Woodstock-generation shaggy hair, intense eyes that perceived amazing things yet never noticed street signs. Thought: *OK*, this is great.

The Beatles chorded to silence on his stereo. He put on the Supremes, music cooing with a rhythm as warm as a virgin's heartbeat. On the way back to her, he got a joint out of the dope drawer—*Damn, I wish he wouldn't call it that!* He fired the joint—*as if he needed more!*—passed it to her. She took two deep drags.

"I missed you," he said.

She felt her goofy smile. Took another hit. Before she felt the stone wave roll her around, she said, "I missed you, too."

They kissed again, deeply this time. The joint burned her fingers and she jerked away from their embrace. He dropped it into his beer can. She heard the sizzle, the *phut*.

"You wasted—"

"Who cares." He led her to his bedroom. Pulled his shirt off as she worked the buttons on her blouse, found the zipper on her skirt as he kissed her neck. Her head floated inside her hair. His cutoffs snapped off and he was naked against her. He hooked his thumbs inside her panty hose and peeled them down, pressed his face against her, kissing her. They sprawled on the bed. He caressed her thighs, his fingers not jabbing or probing but gentle, seeking/finding. She rose above him, crossed her arms, pulled her bra down, turned the hooks to the front and unfastened it. His mouth moved on her breasts until her head spun. She turned her back to him, mounted him. He reached around, covered her breasts with his hands. Time rode away until she heard him scream *"Dane!"* and *"Yes!"* and she was already there, gone, but without freeing a word.

Naked, they picnicked on deli salads and beer on his living room floor, laughing, talking about how gaunt billionaire Howard Hughes had come out of hiding to visit Nicaragua's fat dictator Samoza and thus expose a "Howard Hughes autobiography" scam, how Democratic senators schemed to counter President Nixon's approach to controlling Congress by impounding—refusing to spend—money that Congress appropriated using its hallowed "power of the purse," how marijuana would be as legal as cigarettes or beer by 1990, about a civil war massacre in El Salvador and would it become another Vietnam for the U.S. and how the Marxist President of Chile's nationalization of ITT would encourage such a strategy by White House fanatics. Dane ticked off violent flashpoints in the world: Iran, Iraq, Libya, Ireland.

Vaughn said, "The best and the brightest see everything as just who is on our side, and who's with the Soviets."

"I told you that you'd look great in that linen jacket," said Dane. "Only one in town."

"Byron didn't like it."

"Byron has to find something wrong with everyone," said Dane. "Otherwise, in his mind, he's got no reason to be the boss, and no defense in case someone jumps him about drinking."

"I've got no defense against you," he said.

She flicked a plastic fork of macaroni salad at him.

"I got the boss to let me keep an eye on that burglary."

"Don't look too hard."

"To make sure I don't, the boss says you're supposed to keep an eye on me."

She took a long sip of beer. "I don't like that."

"Why? You and me—"

" 'You and me' is why. Now I'm not your boss, but if you create a project and rope me in . . ."

"Without you, I don't have enough clout in our office to keep this on my desk."

"Whatever happened to the wide-eyed, all-up-front kid we hired?"

"He was inexperienced, not stupid. And he paid absolute attention to you."

Night darkened the room. He lit a lemon candle, a lamp he'd salvaged from a trash can. They talked and listened to record albums, Vaughn jumping up to change from one band Dane might have heard of to another he said she just *had* to know. His exuberance infected her; his joy and hunger. She fell into the music even without the next joint that they smoked. Somehow the two of them were naked, waltzing to Van Morrison's "Tupelo Honey," one minute swaying to the song's lyrics of love, then, with no change or rhythm or melody, the song segued into pledges of political rebellion.

"It's all in the music," he whispered to her.

"If you can understand the words."

"Doesn't matter what you don't understand, only matters how it makes you feel. Plato said: 'When the mode of music changes; the walls of the city shake.' Music scares kings and churches because it touches people where they can't be reasoned with."

She laughed. "You're kinda cute when you get intense and on your soapbox—*kind of*."

"Is that why you're crazy about me?" Leading her as they danced.

"Who said I'm crazy about you?"

"You're too sensible to be here, tomorrow's clothes in your briefcase, risking Byron and Maggie finding out, unless—"

"Maybe I'm just plain crazy."

"No. You're brilliant and beautiful—"

She kissed him to shut him up. He swept her into his arms, lowered her to the cold linoleum, pierced her, thrusting again and again and again while she arched her knees to the candlelight's wave-shadows on the white ceiling. He glowed as he said, "You know where we're going?"

"Where?" she whispered.

"Straight to the heart of everything."

CHAPTER 26

John Quinn rocketed to a sitting position—naked, trembling beside a dark shape in his bed. *Where am I?*

His police revolver lay on the bedside table next to a clock radio with glowing blue numbers. 3:13 A.M.

Wednesday. I worked the Watergate break-in from zero-dark-thirty last Saturday to Tuesday night. Now it's a safe Wednesday, June 1972. The burglars are locked up.

Before I woke up, what was it I saw? *Dreamspeed slow-mo . . . Burglars hanging on the wall . . . Mel! Mel Klise dancing on a sidewalk . . . Lorri naked crawling up the bed, hair brushes my chest as she whispers in my ear, "All the players in town are jazzed," licks me . . . Sign hanging on a wall, white letters, black background, CREEP gas fireball . . . Shoffler lights a killer cigarette says, "These guys were a grab-bag collector job" . . . And . . .*

"John?" Lorri nuzzled her thick black hair on his chest.

" 's OK. What's wrong?"

"The key!"

"Mmm?"

"The key! The one taped to that cheap, nothing-written-in-it notebook! Why was one of the burglars in the Watergate trying to eat that key? Ditch it. Why would he risk a move like that—them up against the wall? Hell, one of us might have blown him away! All for a key."

"You said the FBI guys showin' up means you're off the case."

"Fuck the FBI! It's the key! It's the damn key!" Quinn snapped on the bed lamp. She shrank back like a vampire from the sun. "Can't remember—damn it! Still can't remember where I saw some of those guys, but I did, I know I did, and that means . . . Maybe they weren't just ripping off the Democrats! *Grab bag* . . . The FBI's turned up links to Nixon's CREEP—and that was where Mel took the sack of cash! Maybe this is also about us! Our thing! Your—"

"I didn't do anything!"

"Lorri: The man from Seattle. The big-shot Democrat you . . . you went out with."

"I want to forget all that!"

"How did he pick you?"

"I'm sorry! I know I'm not perfect like you deserve, but—"

"You and I are fine. Great. I love you—"

"I love you, too!"

"—but how did that guy, the others Heidi set you up to date, how did he choose you?"

"I told you, she got ahold of my modeling pictures. The guy said they were in a folder. Like high school. Black vinyl folder."

"Where did he see it? Who showed it to him?"

"Some other guy, political hack, he called him, a hanger-on. Where it was, I don't—"

But she was talking to an empty bed, the bathroom light snapping on, shower water spraying.

WEARING A SUIT and tie felt funny, but Q's undercover days taught Quinn the importance of the correct disguise. The property-room sergeant smiled when the radical-shagged but conservatively dressed Officer Quinn strolled up to his wire cage.

"You got court or you goin' on TV?" said the sergeant.

"I try to stay out of court and TV's not my style," answered Quinn.

"Must be a rush, being on TV. So what are you doing here? Ain't even dawn."

"I need to pull notebooks we took off those three hippies locked up on gun charges. They jumped bail, but they were college guys, so maybe they wrote down their grand plans."

The sergeant buzzed him inside the storeroom. Quinn searched shelves stacked with the debris of evil. He fished the plastic-bagged notebook with a key rubber-banded to it from the Watergate stacks, shuffled that evidence bag in with spiral notebooks seized from the skipped-town bad boys. The sergeant barely glanced at the "bagged notebooks" Quinn logged out.

At 5:15 A.M., Quinn parked his car in an alley on Sixteenth Street. At 5:25 A.M., a pickup truck parked in the street in front of a locksmith's. A wheezing, straw-slim white guy in blue jeans and cowboy boots climbed out of the pickup, lit a cigarette, shuffled into the shop. Quinn marched through the shop's front door, his badge held in front of him like a crucifix.

The smoker standing behind the counter shook his head. "You called, I came, I don't need to see your shine. Nobody but a cop would be asshole up at this hour of the day."

"Tell me about this," said Quinn, dropping his burden on the business counter.

"It's a fucking notebook in a condom. One of your crime-sized condoms."

"You ain't about condoms. But you could be about crime."

"I'm a locksmith. You show me that notebook, and yeah, I can ID it's got a key on it."

"What kind of key?"

"Can I take it out of the baggie?"

"Do you have to?"

Smoke drifted from the cigarette dangling in the locksmith's lips. "Never mind. The little voice of God in my ear tells me I don't want my fucking fingerprints on your shit."

"Got a guilty conscience?"

"Hell, yes. Don't you?" The locksmith rustled a magnifying glass from a drawer, twisted a snake-necked lamp and snapped a cone of light onto the bagged notebook with its rubber-banded key. Gray ash flecked the plastic as the locksmith peered through the eye-expanding lens.

"Furniture key," said the locksmith. "Most likely for desks."

"You mean *a* desk."

"If you're going to tell me what I mean, why bother to ask? Yeah, for *a* desk, but check those scratches. Might be a master key. Or maybe somebody lost a key, and makes this one do the job of the one what got lost *plus* its own thing. Whatever, this gets used for more than one lock."

"And you can tell all that from glassing it for just one minute."

The thin man coughed, stubbed out his cigarette, lit another. Over the stroke of the match and the rasp of blue flame, he said, "Ain't that why you came to me?"

The summer sun dropped warm light on Quinn as he walked to his car: almost 6 A.M.

The private guard stationed in the hall outside the Democratic National Committee's Watergate suite fidgeted beside a folding chair as Quinn stepped off the elevator. Quinn wore his badge on his suit jacket, carried a camera in one hand, an attaché case in the other.

"Pose a minute, will you?" said Quinn. "I got to check the flash."

The nervous guard snapped to his minimum-wage version of attention. A blast of white light burned stars into his sleepy vision.

"Thanks a lot," said the shimmering image the guard saw. "Could you get the door?"

As the cop stepped past the door he'd unlocked, the security guard heard him say, "You think they'd have got it all and got it right the first time they came."

Inside, the guard's mumbled "Yeah!" faded behind the closing door. Quinn stared at the office chaos. No wonder we thought those guys were done when they'd just started. Politics must be innately messy. He thumbed the camera's flash button for a burst of light in case the guard was expecting to see a flicker and—

Ghosts in water shimmer with that blast of light.

Surgeon-gloved suit-and-tie burglars spread against this office wall, scruffily dressed Shoffler and Barrett and Leeper, guns out, their mouths grotesquely moving silent commands . . .

Scruffily dressed rowdies harassing demonstrators at J. Edgar Hoover's funeral party, Capitol cops lead the rowdies away, skinny half-seen guy in a gray suit walks the rowdies to freedom . . .

Nightstick slamming—

Burglars and rowdies: the same crew.

Who are *those* guys?

Can't go back and do it better. Do it right. Work it now.

Nobody here. Not yet. They work late in politics, in Washington, not crack of dawn.

Quinn slipped on surgeon's plastic gloves like those worn by the burglars. Twenty-some offices, lots of secretary stations. Closed doors. CIA lock picks inside his suit jacket. He freed the key rubber-banded to the notebook.

The first desk the key fit turned out to be used by secretaries.

The second desk the key fit belonged to nobody.

Quinn found it in that nobody's desk: a black vinyl binder with slip pockets. The binders held scrapbook pages mounted with photographs of women, the slip pockets carried Polaroids and pictures of models torn from newspapers, a few eight-by-ten—

Lorri smiled at Quinn from an eight-by-ten black-and-white glossy.

Quinn hid the binder in his attaché case, relocked the nobody's desk: 7:17. He probably had more time, but his cop mind said there would only be one stash: What more could there be?

No one paid any attention as Quinn returned the logged-out notebooks—including the one taped to a key—back to their proper stacks; thought: I got this first. Before grab-bag burglars. Before crime scene searchers. But where the hell am I now?

TWO DAYS LATER, Vaughn smiled his way through a ring of two thousand women surrounding the Capitol to protest the Vietnam War, settled behind his desk and had the Library of Congress pull press clippings on the American Association for Justice. The photocopied pages from the Library included a story on a D.C. gambler named Joe Nezneck, who said he planned to work for the AAJ.

For the Senator's signature, Vaughn wrote another letter to the AAJ, thanking them for sending Mel Klise to "help my staff develop our inquiries." The letter reminded the AAJ that their answers about finding and staff had still not been received. The Senator had said to shift the focus off him, so Vaughn wrote the AAJ: "In order to avoid duplication that may create an undue burden on the AAJ, my staff will share our correspondence with relevant Senate committee staffs, including the Senate Permanent Subcommittee on Investigations." Finally, Vaughn noted: "It has also been brought to our attention that a Mr. Joseph Nezneck may be associated with your organization, and a clarification of his press-reported role would be appreciated."

Vaughn also got his boss to send a "letter of concern" about the Watergate burglary to the new Federal Elections Office. Vaughn stuck a copy of the letter in his own "W'gate" file.

You want to go someplace in Washington, thought Vaughn as he daydreamed of Friday-night movies and Dane, you make a paper trail.

THE WEEKEND DISSOLVED into a workweek. Quinn "happened" by the U.S. Attorney's office as he had almost every day since the Watergate break-in. A secretary who thought he was part of the case let him check the file: a field report said the FBI discovered that the key "affixed to a notebook confiscated by WPD from a suspect's personage" fit a desk linked to a DNC secretary. The FBI agents found nothing of significance in that desk. Their search complete, the FBI didn't try to match the key to the unassigned desk Quinn had rifled. Quinn slid the slim FBI memo back into the growing mountain of Watergate reports, went home to Lorri. "I think we're clear."

Her shoulders slumped off a boulder. She took miniature bottles of vodka and bourbon from her purse, poured them into glasses over ice, handed him the bourbon.

Quinn said, "When did you switch to vodka?"

"Sometimes it's all a poor flygirl can score." Lorri clinked his glass, dazzled him with a smile. "Here's to getting away with it."

He wanted to smile back. Couldn't. "Maybe yes, maybe no."

"You don't—Those Watergate burglars: you don't think they were after me?"

As he turned away to set down his drink, he said, "Nobody gives a shit about you . . ."

He didn't see her arms cross as she hugged herself.

". . . or me," said Quinn, turning back to her. "What they were doing . . . Bugging is what everybody says. They were ready to take pictures, too. Grab bag. One of them had that key. Maybe they didn't want that binder, or *just* that binder, or even know what it was, but—"

"All they would have gotten is a bunch of pictures of women!"

"One of whom is you. You used that apartment across from the Watergate for . . ."

"Whoring! Go ahead, say it! *I'm a whore!*"

Quinn heard his cop voice say, "If that's the way you want it."

"Does it still matter what I want?"

"To me," he said. "To you."

"Can't that be enough?"

"If we can keep the equation that simple," said Quinn. "You and Heidi. Heidi and her boss Nezneck. That lawyer you both knew who got busted for prostitution stuff that scared the White House so much that they sent a car to fetch the prosecutor and the evidence. The key taped to a notebook, a key that fit the desk with the binder of pictures of you and other women that's now locked in our closet. That key being on a Watergate burglar and those guys being ghosts from Hoover's funeral who could maybe recognize me. The burglars and Mel all being linked to CREEP. Lou Russell's jazz about buggings of men and women, about films. The apartment across from Watergate where *maybe* somebody *might* have a two-way-mirror that filmed you or bugged you while you were . . . fucking."

Lorri didn't flinch.

"All that's . . . a whole lot of *wow*," said Quinn. "Just because we've got a lot of nasty pieces doesn't mean they fit together as one big monster. We better pray Watergate stays a simple burglary and bugging case. That all the suits don't focus on evidence that's not there anymore. On who could have made it disappear. Or why that happened and who that protected."

The air conditioner hummed against the heat. He picked up his car keys.

Lorri kept her eyes dry. Exhaled. "Where are you going?"

"Back to work. Gonna play cops and robbers."

"You don't have to be there for at least an hour."

"Thought I better check in early. Take some time to practice which side I'm on."

THE NEXT AFTERNOON, Holloway spotted Penzler walking up the White House circular drive from the check-in gate at the black iron-pole fence and remembered him saying, "Keep up the good work."

The hell with that! Holloway followed the bearded raptor in the summer suit. Penzler carried a slim briefcase into the Sit Room. *Don't follow him in there, he'll spot you.* Holloway hid around the corner until Penzler and briefcase emerged, headed to the outside walkway connecting the White House to the Old Executive Office Building. In the EOB, Penzler entered an elevator.

Third floor, the NSC offices, that's where he's headed! Holloway ran up the circular marble staircase in time to see Penzler walk past the NSC door to a men's room.

Holloway threw the door open: saw Penzler standing in front of the urinal. Saw the open and empty stall. Holloway grabbed the briefcase leaning against Penzler's leg and shoved the spy against the porcelain urinal. He pulled a file out of the briefcase, said, "So what's new?"

"You will never do that to me again!"

Holloway risked a glance at the memo in the file, saw the stamp reading EYES ONLY. Saw "SUBJECT: Watergate Affair."

"Are you supposed to have this?" Holloway took the memo. "Hope you've got a copy."

Penzler's face cooled to an annoyed smile. "Keep the briefcase, too, Marine. Call it your coffin. Check it out: you and your boy Jud are boxed in, while I'm covered."

Holloway said, "You peed on yourself."

"I'll dry off and be fine. How about you?"

Penzler's laughter echoed from the bathroom as Holloway stalked down the halls with the hijacked memo and sour guts: Won this one, he told himself, didn't I?

That memo he photocopied for the admirals had been written the day before by CIA Director Richard Helms to one of his deputy directors:

"The Agency is attempting to 'distance itself' from this investigation," read the memo about Watergate. Helms said he "wanted no free-wheeling exposition of hypotheses or any effort made to conjecture about responsibility or likely objectives of the Watergate intrusion.. . . . it is up to the FBI to lay some cards on the table. . . . we still adhere to the request that they confine themselves to the personalities already arrested or directly under suspicion and that they desist from expanding this investigation into other areas which may well, eventually, run afoul of our operations."

Holloway got no response from the admirals about that stolen memo.

CHAPTER 27

On the first, steamy afternoon in August, Dane gave Vaughn a coworker's smile as she leaned against his desk. "Are you still playing around with that Watergate mess?"

"I can't even find the game," said Vaughn.

"I have a friend over on the House side. You know Congressman Wright Patman? Head of the Banking Committee? The *Post* says twenty-five grand from Nixon's CREEP ended up in one of the burglar's bank accounts. Patman says that's money laundering, and he's going after it."

"Patman's a damn lion! Nobody crosses committee chairman! He'll grab the whole issue! I won't get—I mean *we* won't—"

"Sure, Patman will run the show on the House side," said Dane, "but we're over here. And if you're on top of what's happening . . ."

She heard Vaughn punching numbers in his phone as she walked away, smiling.

On August 24, Vaughn clipped the *Washington Post* story about the district court judge who wanted to start the trial in the civil suit that the Democrats had filed against the Watergate burglary suspects before the coming November elections "to ensure the right of the public to know." As he scissored that story from the front page, the story above it caught his eye: campaign contributions by dairy farmers to Nixon's re-election campaign influenced the President's decision to raise the 1971 federal milk price supports. The key Nixon player in the dairy affair was Murray Chotiner, a "controversial" aide to Nixon.

"He's got a rep as a bag man for Nixon," a Democratic investigator for the Permanent Investigations Subcommittee told Vaughn. "And a political shiv artist. Been with him forever, worked on the last campaign. California lawyer. Represented, shit, I don't know, maybe a hundred mobbed-up guys."

Vaughn dropped the Chotiner/milk fund story in his "W'gate" file.

QUINN'S BEEPER WENT off that August afternoon as he sat in an unmarked car with other TAC Squad cops staking out a boardinghouse on Georgia Avenue for a suspected bomber.

"It's the job," he said after reading the beeper—not quite the whole truth.

"We got this," said a cop who knew the departmental "he's a spook" rumors about Q.

Heat shimmers off the blacktop swept him into their waves. He was sticky by the time he walked to a pay phone in this neighborhood that after the Martin Luther King riots had gone from middle-class, blue-collar Jewish and Greek to blue-collar, poverty-stricken African American. He called the number he knew without having to re-read the beeper, got orders from a familiar voice. Quinn hopped a bus to downtown. The cab he caught there wasn't air conditioned. By the time he arrived at the Irish cafe, sweat soaked his blue jeans and the red polo shirt draped over his .38.

The cafe was a dark arctic cave with a neon jukebox and a waitress whose smile promised she'd forget Quinn before the end of her shift. He turned down her offer of a table, watched her plump hips sway away with an intriguing excess Lorri didn't have.

Sitting at the bar was the wispy-bearded skinny man who'd worn a gray suit and walked Watergate burglars free from their bust at Hoover's Capitol memorial service.

SHIT! Quinn's stomach churned.

The gray suit had been replaced by summer linen. He perched on a barstool in front of a glass of golden brew.

Be cool! Don't say what you don't have to! Maybe he didn't see Q at the demonstration. Maybe this doesn't have anything to do with that. Everything doesn't always string together. Don't tell him anything he doesn't need to know! Don't let him make any links. *Be cool!*

Quinn slid onto the stool next to the man, smelled the cool green of his cologne. Quinn muttered the recognition code, got the *one-two, one-two* response patter and an engaging smile.

"I've been dying to meet you!" said the CIA exec. "My name's Penzler. Bill Penzler. Should I call you *Quinn?* Or should I use your work name, *Quarell?*"

"Call me John. Simpler."

"Simplicity is worth its effort. Looks hot as hell out there. Let's get you a beer and take that table in the corner.

"I'm not supposed to tell you," said Penzler when they'd settled at the shadowed table, "but so far, you've gotten the highest marks on our performance-review sheets."

"You guys keep written records?"

Penzler laughed. "Well, not of everything. Records can be helpful, if they show what they should. Your high marks are more whispers than writings. You're quite the legend."

"Flattery? What are you guys setting me up for now?"

"Sounds like I'm not the only one who's been used and abused."

"I wouldn't know about that."

"You don't have any trouble with my *bona fides*, do you?"

"We never worked together before, right?"

Penzler smiled.

"I figure we both know we're legit," said Quinn. "All I'm supposed to need to know is that you and my command have a working arrangement."

"A deal that's good for everyone."

Quinn shrugged.

"I wish we had the time to get to know each other better," said Penzler. "Especially since our professional and your personal interests are so intertwined. Do you sail? I know you're the kind of adventurous guy who likes fishing in strange waters. Perhaps someday I'll take you out on my boat. Sailing teaches you so much. Me the captain, you the crew. But thanks to you, we don't have time for just fun and games now."

The air-conditioning sent a chill down Quinn's spine.

"You're silent. Officer Invisible. You should stand up and take your credit. Go down as one of history's heroes. But anonymity has its uses, right? Take for instance . . . Watergate."

"You take it."

"We have to. The Agency is being cast as the fall guy behind that bungled mess. We weren't, but there's a danger that unraveling the Nixon boys' sins to the public's satisfaction might expose some of our operations. Can't have that."

"Not my problem."

"Don't lie to me," said Penzler. "You don't have that luxury.

"We make alliances to make things happen. Comingle operations. Cover one operation with another, with someone else's game. Happens all the time. But so do accidents. Like Watergate. We're not involved, nor are our allies, but because of those arrests, it became necessary for friends of ours to retrieve something from the 'crime scene' DNC headquarters before investigating badges found it."

Vomit boiled in Quinn's throat.

"But when our friends sought that something, it was gone. That concerned them. Their concerns became my concerns. So I went looking. You know how it works. Begin at the beginning. Understand something by peeling away its layers, then seek the connections. As you said, all things are not written down. But people *witness*. People *whisper*. Love to tell secrets. That's how at the beginning, at the scene of the burglary, I found a ghost. A ghost who later signed log books at the evidence room. Odd enough, but odder still, you shouldn't have been a ghost: you should have been a step-forward guy seeking rewards as a hero. So I wondered why. Some pictures were snapped of you and yours, discreet inquiries made with your Internal Affairs Division, with mutual acquaintances. *Poof!* Suddenly a legend appears."

"What do you want?"

"Keep the binder with the picture of your whore girlfriend. It was to be destroyed anyway. I don't care about her. I want to save you."

Quinn whispered, "How come I'm so lucky?"

"Because you're not so smart. You left trails. If there are any questions, they'll lead to you. And in this life, you've made more enemies than friends."

"Which are you?"

"I'm your savior—if you do the smart thing. If not, I'll help a lieutenant at Internal Affairs break you. I'll feed you to liberal crusaders as a Red Squad cop gone psycho."

"You can't go after me without exposing yourself and the Agency!"

"Oh. *Really.* Let's pretend you're right and you have nothing to fear from us good guys. Are we your only enemies? My guess is all that's kept you alive this long is the price of terminating a badge. One word from me, and you're a freebie. Your whore will be a bonus."

"Was Watergate a CIA-Op?"

"*Not mine.* I wouldn't have sent in the clowns."

"But they might pull a spotlight on you."

"You were there, not me." Penzler waved the waitress away. "Now you have to go back."

"What?"

"Watergate must stay simple. A chord of burglary with a theme of bugging. If everyone holds to that story, then no one will ask what *else* was going on there that night. What booty Nixon's thugs might have acquired. Where else the evidence leads. Then you're home free.

"But now, a complication exists. The DNC phones have been swept three times—nobody, not even the FBI, found any installed electronic listening devices."

"So the guys didn't have time to—"

"Or maybe they were repairing bugs they'd removed. But when you brave cops caught the burglars, the phones were clean, even though an ex-FBI agent working for the plumbers—"

"The who?"

"—even though the FBI has one of its former agents as a cooperating witness, and he was monitoring bugged phone calls. So you see the problem? If phone calls he was taping weren't from the Watergate because the bugs weren't in place when the FBI searched, and if a thesis about repairing bugs doesn't hold, then the forces of justice face bizarre questions. Like who else could have been being bugged. Like what else could the burglars have been doing there. Looking for."

"This is way over my head."

"That's why I'm here. To keep you from drowning. To help you save yourself."

Quinn sank his face into his hands. Dizzy.

"You see it now, don't you? By being there, your implicated as the criminal answer to dangerous questions. You have to keep the questions from being asked. You must keep the whole affair simple. Or it will run wild. Trample you and your poor girlfriend. You said it yourself: simplicity is worth its effort."

Penzler leaned across the table, his whisper hissing beneath jukebox songs of whisky and Irish rebellion, beneath the hum of the air conditioner, beneath the last edge of the cop's badge. The whisper became a drone became a roar until Quinn heard nothing else, until, dizzy, he fell away from certainty and honor, knew only that what the whisper told him to do made sense, even though it was crazy.

That evening, he stole a Neanderthal phone bug from a stockroom of McCarthy-era spy gear, waited out the howling night until the quiet before dawn. The security guard fixated on a gift photo of himself as he unlocked DNC doors for the guy who had to be OK because he'd been there before.

"Guess a good cop's work is never done," said the security guard.

"Don't say that," whispered Quinn, the Neanderthal bug burning in his shirt pocket.

"You must like it, though," said the security guard as Quinn stepped inside the deserted Watergate suite of offices. "You here, ain't you?"

"No," said Q. "It's somebody else."

The guard laughed as he closed the door and left Quinn alone in the dark.

When he finished at the Watergate, Quinn stumbled through his official eight-to-four day shift until he got home and collapsed on his bed. Call it sleep but not rest. He jerked awake as crimson shadows filled the bedroom. Lorri sat in the chair, watching him.

Their apartment building's resident manager let them use the barbecue chained in the passageway between brick walls that led to the garbage cans in the alley. Lorri gave the manager a three-quarter-length mirror she'd bought at a flea market so he threw in a bag of charcoal briquets and a can of starter fluid. The manager was so eager to get his bargain mirror locked in his apartment that he didn't notice the young couple had no hamburgers or chicken or corn to grill.

Quinn lit the coals with a kitchen match. Lorri flinched as the barbecue erupted in chemical-stenched blue flames. That shimmering inferno bathed them with waves of heat. Cicadas sang from trees in the alley. Quinn and Lorri heard other sounds of the urban evening—car radios, music and TV from apartments forced to rely on open windows instead of humming air conditioners, walkers hoping their shouts would slice through the swamp air to reach someone who cared. Quinn and Lorri knew that they alone could hear themselves speak; still, they whispered.

"You planted that bug," she said. "But what if nobody finds it?"

"That's not my job. That's not what I had to do. That can't be me."

The coals glowed.

Lorri said, "Tell me again why you think this CIA guy works for Nezneck."

"Not *for*," said Quinn. "*With*. Because it all fits. Because nasty deals like that get made all the time. Cops and crooks cut deals so the cops can bust other crooks. Whathafuck, we wink and walk away from our bad-ass buddies. Protect them. Hell, we even give our bad boys some under-the-table action, cash or a get-out-of-jail-free card."

"But what do Nezneck and Penzler, the mob and the CIA, what 'deals' do they have?"

"I don't know. Maybe Heidi's girls come in useful to the CIA. And having a powerful fed on your side . . . Nezneck and Heidi, when their call girl ring got too close to the Watergate mess, Penzler wouldn't want them exposed, because if he's crossed too many lines, Heidi or Nezneck getting heat might burn him."

"There's gotta be some really horrible shit they're hiding." Lorri shook her head. "And now they've got us trapped in it, too. Because of me. I'm sorry, John."

"Me, too, but sorry doesn't matter now. This is what it is. Penzler can't burn me for playing games at Watergate without exposing himself. That's the last thing he wants. Nezneck and I are in the same standoff, only now I know more about him, who his friends are. Guess that makes us more dangerous to each other. But I'm still a cop. I cost too much to whack. And if I can get him first . . ."

A car rolled by in the alley. Quinn watched the machine glide past, its woman driver intent on getting somewhere else, somewhere safe, somewhere happy. As she drove out of sight, he noticed the apartment building's Dumpster and the two mirrors leaning against it.

"Those mirrors," he said. "Aren't they ours?"

Lorri stared at him as he pictured a blank space on his bedroom wall, an empty hook inside the hall closet door, the bathroom medicine cabinet door that held their home's only remaining reflective glass. Lorri said nothing.

Quinn took the black vinyl loose-leaf binder from her and fed photographs of women to the white-hot barbecue coals. Lorri's modeling session portrait vanished in a shimmer of orange flame. He dropped pictures of two beautiful blondes into the inferno. He thought he heard his phone ring as the briquets melted a Polaroid of a black woman naked except for a discreet white feather boa.

"Maybe now it's even better for us," said Quinn. "We know where we stand. Maybe they think that they've neutralized me, or even made me their man. Scared me."

"Two days ago, I thought I couldn't be more lost. Goes to show you what thinking gets you." She said, "Now we're truly, deeply lost."

"We're OK as long as we're not found."

Flames shimmered on her face.

"Penzler has the right idea," said Quinn. "Keep Watergate contained. Away from him and Nezneck and thus away from us. We're all on the edge of it. We've got to stay there and stay hidden. But we can't count on that just happening."

"You can't help them anymore! That's wrong!"

"It's not them I want to help. It's us. Is that wrong?"

"Maybe. Probably. Yes. I don't know." She stared at the shimmering blue flames. "What can we do?"

"We've got to fight back like they can't expect. We can't touch Penzler. But we can't let up on his friend Nezneck. Especially now. He'll carve us up an inch at a time if we let him."

Quinn muttered, "Before I let him do that, I'll whack—"
Stop that! Don't be him!

Flames ate the last of the women's photographs.

"Control," he whispered. "We can't *control* the Watergate hunt, but if we can *deflect* . . ."

Again from inside the building came the sound of their ringing phone; Quinn wondered whether he could make it if he ran.

CHAPTER 28

"I've got you nailed," the federal narc told Quinn as they ate noon cheeseburgers in a drug buster's unmarked cruiser.

"What?" Quinn broke into a sweat despite the car's humming air conditioner.

"Last time it was me doing a favor for you," said the narc, "so you owe me. Worked out, scored a bust on that David Strait creep you left hanging from the fire escape, but you damn near got us all killed."

"Is that all?" muttered Quinn.

"That's all I got, man! That's enough!"

"How come this off-the-books shit? You say you working NY fucking C these days, not the D of C. You called me at home last night. Set this up outside my department's house. Outside your local office. What happened to your Mr. By-the-book?"

"He got serious." The narc wadded his burger wrap into a ball and tossed it to the backseat. They were parked in an "OK" neighborhood of Capitol Hill. "We all finally got serious, thanks to President Nixon officially declaring 'war on drugs.' Give us five, six years . . ."

"Tell me about today," said Quinn. "I'm short on tomorrows."

The narc handed Quinn a manila folder, watched him slide out eight-by-twelve black-and-white surveillance photos of the parking courtyard of a motel with a neon sign that read VALE INN.

"This place is up on Bladensberg Road," the local cop told the federal narcotics agent. "Just this side of the Maryland line. Redneck and poor black, some sneaking-around spouses, some college trade from the U of M up the road."

"Not that day. It's two P.M. eight days ago, and the whole place is No Vacancy. Check out those Caddys, Lincolns, a Porsche, for Chrissakes. That Mercedes? Me and my partner followed it all the way down from Harlem. Three street boys plus one superfly lieutenant to a smack king named Nicky Barnes. We thought they were going to Midtown. Lucky we had a full gas tank."

"And I care *how*?"

"Because I'm asking you to. Because with a magnifying glass, you can read fourteen of those license plates, eleven of which are D.C. tags. I want you to run them. Run them quiet, run them deep."

"You can run them as easy as me."

"But then the system bounces a report to your Motor Vehicles bureaucracy that the plates have been scanned by a New York fed. And if I formally ask someone from your department to cover this for me . . . Sometimes it's interesting dealing with locals."

"Locals here?"

"Locals every fucking where."

"You want to tell me more?"

"No." The narc who'd started his career as a suit-and-tie cop now wore blue jeans and a T-shirt; with their beards and long hair, he and Quinn could have been hard-eyed graduate students.

"You still a good guy?" asked Quinn.

"Fuck if I know."

"Then OK, I'll handle this. But don't put me in your jackpot." Quinn stared at the fed. "You really believe we're fighting a righteous 'drug war' that somebody can win?"

"I got out of Nam alive," said the fed. "I've gotta believe."

Three nights later, Quinn sat at a table in a dimly lit, isolated corner of the Fraternal Order of Police blue shack bar at the base of Capitol Hill with Buck Jones and Gary Harmon.

"I spread the license plate runs out through half a dozen sources," Quinn told his ex-partner and the FBI agent as he passed them copies of reports. "Covered the background checks, too."

"Damn!" said Buck, scanning Quinn's research. "You got a shit pile of truly bad-ass black motherfuckers here! This guy, double murderer we never broke; these two—no, these *three*—they all big in the smack trade, couple steps up from corner boys. This guy's a Mac with a couple street pimps and their stables coughing up to—this guy, Greentop, the reefer daddy for the Southeast. This guy: my lieutenant wants him for narc *and* numbers so bad his brass aches!"

Buck blinked. Fell silent.

"What?" said FBI Agent Harmon.

Buck stared at Quinn through the smoky darkness. "You sure this is right?"

"That's from the plate on the car," said Quinn, enjoying— finally enjoying—the moment.

"What the hell is he doing there—hell, doing *anywhere* out in the street!"

"Who?" said Harmon.

"Jake R. Winston," answered Quinn. "Registered owner of a brand-new Caddy."

"Jake the Jar," said Buck. "That fat fuck never, *never* leaves his squat over his homebrew on K Street! I never figured him to own a ride."

"He hasn't before," said Quinn. "At least not in D.C. I checked."

"What got him out of his house to a tea party with badder-ass motherfuckers than he'll ever be? What the hell is Jake doing anywhere but in his squat with Elma? I didn't even know he had a driver's license!"

"He does, also new. And he can't drive for shit: He's gotten two moving violations and a bunch of parking tickets over the last three months."

"He's moving. He's out and about in the open and moving!"

"But here's the best part," said Quinn: "The Vale Inn is owned by a limited partnership. Three citizens I can't figure and the DelaRyke Corporation. The DelaRyke Corporation—"

"Owns Nezneck's wig place downtown!" said Harmon. "It's his Delaware corporation!"

"His place, his numbers and loan shark manager, and a crew of bad-ass mother—" Buck frowned. "The Vale: what's it supposed to be? Like the mafia meet at—where the hell was it?"

"Appalachia," said FBI Agent Harmon. "But Nezneck wasn't at the Vale. My buddies in Customs and State say that during those days, he was in Nigeria."

"Africa?" said Buck. "He's no tourist!"

"Do you trust your 'foreign affairs' friends?" Quinn asked the wire-thin FBI agent.

"What?"

"We've got to be certain," said Quinn. "We've got to be careful. We've got friends, but so does Nezneck. But if we realize that and figure a way to drive a wedge between him and them, put such a stink on him that they push him away—"

"What are you telling us?" said Harmon.

"Nothing," said Quinn. "Nothing. Just thinking."

Harmon looked at him. Buck looked at him.

Ignore that. "Gary, your Washington field office organized crime section. You say all they're doing is busting gambling operations like number banks, small-time players."

"Gambling is a crime with federal implications," said the FBI agent, "and by its very nature, organized."

"And it's Nezneck's background, but besides getting a bunch of show-and-tell stats, you and I both know your guys aren't ever going to work their way up from runners and bankers."

"Do you want me to nudge my colleagues toward Jake?"

"Not yet. But plug into them. Get them primed—just in case."

"Do what I can," said Harmon. "But that won't be much. Them, me, every agent in the D.C. field office is getting sucked into Watergate."

Harmon blew smoke across the table to Quinn. "I heard you have a piece of that, too."

"Not really," said Quinn. "I was . . . near the scene. Lent a hand."

Harmon's eyes registered the hollowness of Quinn's answer. Then Harmon shrugged, a gesture Quinn saw Buck catch. Quinn felt sick as he sensed his friends withdraw into themselves. But they stayed at his table.

"Do what you can, guys," said Quinn. Thinking: Sorry for not being straight! Forgive me!

"Let's roust Elma again," said Buck. "I'll come out from behind my desk, roll her up with you. Hell, driving to work the other day, I saw her walking around in a new dress, spiffy shoes. That's probable cause right there."

"No. She won't know enough, and she'll rat back to Jake."

"So?"

"So I'm going to keep my promise." Quinn got a handful of change from the barmaid, walked upstairs. Uniformed cops playing pinball in the next room added to the *ding*'s as he dropped silver coins into the pay phone.

"Yeah?" answered the narc on the phone in his divorced man's sparse apartment across the river from Manhattan's mean streets.

"I got what you wanted," said Quinn.

"Good for you, and guess what my other call from your Death City just told me?"

CHAPTER 29

The deserted prison chapel smelled of summer dust and concrete. Quinn stood beyond the empty altar and the bolted-down pews. The damp skin on his arms tingled. Morning sunlight oozed through colorless shatterproof windows. The cavernous silence felt full of inaudible screams.

An unseen door boomed shut somewhere in walled-off recesses.

Keep the suspense as long as you can. Quinn disappeared into the chaplain's alcove, a windowless gray box with two chairs and a door that closed. He listened to the shuffling tinkle of approaching chains.

A corrections officer pushed David Strait into the alcove then shut the door.

"So I figured right," said the convict. "There ain't no sky pilot waiting to save my soul."

"Who did you think'd be here?" said Quinn. "A con with a shank waiting to finish the job?"

A white bandage on Strait's noir cheek offset the goatee he'd added to his mustache. His elbows V'ed out from his ribs, where under his gray prison shirt bandages covered other wounds, a posture made difficult by handcuffs that manacled him to a waist chain and a set of ankle irons. "That misunderstanding's been cleared up."

"Yeah, killing those two guys who jumped you clarified things for them."

Strait lowered himself toward an empty chair. "You pigs got a self-defense rap my—"

Quinn kicked the chair out from under the chained man. Strait hit the floor with a cry of pain. "I didn't tell you to sit down."

Churning eyes glared up at the cop from the prison floor.

Quinn righted the chair, jerked Strait into it. "Aren't you glad it's just me and you in here?"

"Oh yeah, motherfucker, you made my day. Don't worry, I'll pay you back."

"Start now. We both want to be where I owe you."

"You set me up, hung me up, got me sent here. Now you soliciting a bribe, Detective Quinn?"

"I'm looking to help you out."

"Out of the frying pan and into your fire. No way."

"Not the same-old, same-old anymore, David, or we wouldn't be here. You lost your protection. Somebody put a hit on you."

"Look what happened to them."

"Those were just button boys and you got lucky. What about next time?"

"You ain't getting what you want from me. I ain't no rat."

"Sooner or later, everybody's a rat. You used to be a king rat in here, but now you're just a lone, lonely mouse looking to get hit."

Strait didn't blink.

"Maybe you got heart, don't want to give up everything. I respect that. Maybe you don't want to put yourself out on the rat line until you know it's a solid bet. I understand that. But if you want to save your ass, you're gonna have to move me toward where I'm going. Hell, it's only 'cause I'm sentimental that when I got the call about you being stabbed, I drove down here to give you a chance. I should play this the easy way, roll up your pal Jake. He's made being a rat a regular art form, now that he's taken your slot on the team, become your replacement."

"That fat punk sack of shit couldn't shine my shoes, let alone walk in them."

"He shined at the Vale."

Strait shifted in his chair. His hands rose to stroke his chin, but the chains stopped them. He licked his lips. Sniffed. Couldn't stop the flick of his eyes toward the closed door.

Gotchya!

"You givin' me . . . what?"

"As good as I get," said Quinn.

"You know why they call Nezneck 'Possum'?"

P! In Pat Dawson's address book, Nezneck's numbers were listed under P!

" 'Cause," continued the chained con, "he plays dead like a possum, but he ain't, and when you ain't looking, he'll bite your ass off."

"Like he did yours. With the two guys who put the blade to you."

"Possum didn't send them. He's stepped back enough so as not to care if some fools think they can grab my action because of my current situation. 's all right, I'm a big boy, on my own now, that's the deal. 'Course, he could have given me a heads-up, for old time's sake."

"Instead he put Jake in your place—for new times."

"Jake's a clerk! An errand boy! All he's been 'promoted' to is the up-front guy. Somebody need to take a fall, it'll be him. I never stood in those chump shoes."

"No, you're sitting here and Jake was at the Vale. He's Nezneck's man, that's Nezneck's place, Nezneck's meeting."

"Two out of three, cop, not bad. Wasn't Possum's meeting, and Jake, he just emptied ashtrays, showed the damn flag. Possum 'facilitated' the party, like he and his wop friends set up suits like lawyers and bankers and—"

"Cops. Friends in the feds."

Strait shrugged. "I know what I know."

"The Vale."

"Bunch of big-dreaming niggers. Our mob, our maf. Know why that action will never work, even with guys like Nicky B. from Harlem pushin' it? Even with Joe in the background like . . . like Henry fucking Kissinger? Because this is America. Ain't gonna be no black President in the White House. Not in your sorry lifetime. Those 'organization' games come from the theology that you can build your way to the top. But look at Martin. Malcolm. Whitey ain't gonna ever let no black man get to the top. Whatever organization you build ain't ever gonna get to leave the ghetto. So cutting a bunch of buddies in on your action—especially when the wops don't have the only product connections anymore—all that does is take money out of your pocket. Let you play big-time mobster. But look in the mirror, you're still a nightshade motherfucker. All you ever gonna run are the projects, the concrete and steel ghettos like this place, and corners you got the guns to hold."

"So what do all those tough guys at Vale think they're doing?"

"What else, man? They trying to 'regulate' the smack biz. Possum knew he'd be cut out total if he didn't help. But hell, all he's got going, he don't really care about that taste no more."

Keep him going with what pisses him off. "So when Jake took over your spot—"

"Jake is the chump, man. Possum got a couple of brothers auditionin' to be me, but they ain't got the brains or the balls to walk the walk."

"Which one called the hit on you?"

Strait stared at the cop.

"You can't still think that Nezneck's going to cover you. Get you out. Keep you around."

"He's got the biggest, baddest game going. Maybe he didn't step *up* for me, but he didn't step *on* me neither. We'll be tight again. Meanwhile, you knowin' enough to keep those Vale studs on their toes while I'm coolin' my heels in here—Possum taught me that. Never miss a trick. Do just enough. Make allies where you can. Keep your rivals busy. Divide your enemies. And when you whack somebody, graveyard 'em."

"If he's backing off dope, what's he moving into?"

"You got all you're gonna get, cop. Plus now you owe me."

"You didn't play your whole hand, Strait. You folded, you get nothing."

The chained con yawned.

"Worse than nothing," said Quinn. "When they patched you up, they ran a tox screen on your blood. Guess what?

You been using the smack you sell, haven't you, Mr. Dealer?"

"I got no needle in my arm!"

"You got a nose. How'd it start? You get bored? Test the product you sell in the yard?"

"Maybe I got a little recreational thing. Like smoking. Just a habit, no addict-junkie shit."

"You're too smart for that, right? Too on top of your game. It's a shame you couldn't help me, but that doesn't mean I can't help you. You're the victim of attempted murder. Said so yourself. You get out of the infirmary in three days. They got you on pain pills now, so you're cool. You'll go back into general population. Without meds. But I'm a cop—*your* motherfuckin' cop. I know that in gen pop anybody can get to you—and you can get damn near anything. So to do my duty, to *protect* you, I'm gonna put you in admin lockdown. Protective security. Round-the-clock isolation. No one's going to be able to get to you—or, come to think of it, you aren't going to be able to get *anything* from any—"

Strait lunged from his chair. "You gonna die!"

Quinn stiff-armed the con back down. "We're all going to die, Strait. But first some of us are going through hell screaming our motherfucking junkie guts out cold turkey.

"Unless," he said, leaning into the con's face, "unless you got a whole lot more to say to me."

Quinn heard the snort start in the back of Strait's throat. He slapped the con's face to one side so the spittle hit the cement wall. Quinn turned his back on the manacled man in the chair; hesitated at the door for a moment, heard no voice calling him back. Quinn left a man chained to nothing but who he was and what he'd done.

CHAPTER 30

"Our life-or-death rule is that I don't exist," Quinn told a handsome man in the tan corduroy blazer who sat across from him in the booth of the Virginia-past-the-Beltway redneck bar. "Not now. Not tomorrow. Not ever. Not to your bosses, your wife, your priest, not to nobody."

"Guys like me don't have a priest," smiled the good-looking man, whose hair was not as long as Quinn's. His levity broadcast nervousness.

"You think this is a joke?"

"Hey, no, no joke!"

"If you don't want to do this . . ."

"I need to do this! This is all I've been doing for months! This is my big thing—the most important thing going! You've just got to—I mean, we've got to—"

"Do what's right," said Quinn.

"Yes. Precisely. What's right. Not just for us, but for the country."

"That's why I called you," said Quinn.

"Why me? I mean, you were right to, and thanks, but why me?"

You're the first one who was there to pick up the phone. "Who else would I call? Only a few reporters in this whole damn town are working to get the truth. I suppose I could meet with one of them, too."

"*No!* I mean, I'm . . . you can do the most good with me— *us,* with us."

"That's all I'm after."

"So you haven't talked to any other reporters."

"No," said Quinn. *Not yet.* "We aren't here talking either, remember?"

"This is deep background. You're a cop, you know how that works."

"My best informants, somewhere down the line, I've got to tell somebody where what I know comes from: tell a prosecutor, my captain . . . somebody. You got bosses who say what gets printed. How do I know you'll do the right thing?"

"You've got my word."

"Oh." Quinn drained his beer, as if to leave.

"Wait! . . . Look, I'm working this night and day. I talk to a hundred people. A thousand! There's other want-to-do-the-right-thing sources like you. I can combine you with one or two of them, make you . . . somebody who you are, but nobody who really is. No real names. That'll work to get to the truth. That'll be fine, OK. After all, getting the story out, that's what's important."

"Your game, not mine." Quinn shrugged, signaled the barmaid. "You want another one?"

"Thanks," said the reporter, unable to hide his exhale. "I'm thirsty as hell."

"Bet you are. And guess I need to bet on you. Just don't put me out there to get shot."

"Don't worry. It'll all be on me."

If you get it big-time, that's just what you'll want anyway. What the hell: you get it like I need it to be, you deserve any glory you can get.

The barmaid swung two iced bottles of Miller beer to their booth. Her gaze said, Long-haired, un-American freaks don't belong here. Her mouth said not a word.

Quinn whispered, "This Watergate thing is bigger than it seems. *Way* bigger."

The reporter nodded like a bobbing plastic dog mounted in the rear window of a car that was rolling toward where he wanted to go. "What do you know?"

Make him work for it so he'll believe it's gold. "I don't know what I should tell you."

"I thought you wanted the truth out."

Take a swig of beer. Show the wheels turning. How hard this is.

"I'm telling you stuff I'm not even supposed to know." *True.*

"But the public has a right—"

"What do you want to know?"

"The burglars, the Watergate break-in, all—"

"That's not what this is about." *Give him the spin.* "That's just a random piece of another puzzle. You think something this big is about one simple breaking and entering? I'm a cop, I know burglaries, and this isn't that."

"What can you tell me about the new bug they found at the DNC, at Watergate? Weeks later, they find another bug on a phone. A source says it doesn't match the others. Doesn't make sense."

Quinn felt sweat on his brow. Shrugged. Lied. "Must have been left over from the burglary night. Feds must have missed it when they searched. No big deal. But now their bugging case is solid."

"The bugging, and what else they were—"

"It's not what they were doing *there*. It's what they were doing *everywhere else*."

"Everywhere—where?"

Quinn wanted to say, Nowhere near the Watergate or a neighborhood apartment building, but said instead, "Some of those guys, the Cubans, they were doing stuff all over town, not just at Watergate. I can give you an eyes-on fact that they were spying on the antiwar movement. I can't tell you where or how."

"We've heard they were gathering political intelligence." *Confirm what he wants to know.* "Absolutely no question."

"What? Specifically."

Quinn dodged: "What do you know about the money?"

"I know that so far, that's the key."

"You got it." *Christ, I wish I could feed you Mel! Let you link back straight through the burglary to CREEP to Mel to Nezneck, but that road might lead to Lorri.*

The reporter frowned. "You said you're a street cop. But you aren't one of the arresting officers, plus my sources say the FBI took over the police work right after the bust."

"What does that tell you?"

The reporter shrugged. "So how do you know anything?"

Give him the sigh. Scan the crowd—he caught that; good.
Quinn pulled a stolen laminated plastic clip-on ID tag from inside his jacket and held it so only the reporter could see:

FBI—D.C. FIELD OFFICE
CLEARED VISITOR

"I get around," said Quinn. "That's my real job. I tell you zero about that."

"Then tell me about Watergate. Is it a CIA operation?"

"I doubt it. Don't know anybody in the Bureau who thinks it is. Aren't CIA guys better at doing things than this? They never get caught, right?"

Memories of what had never been reported playing in his eyes, the journalist nodded.

"Besides," said Quinn. "It all comes up political—not criminal or spy stuff. Forget about penny-ante local stuff. There are Mexico tie-ins. Florida. The FBI is going hard at CREEP, the national re-election—"

"I know what it is. What are they finding out? How do you know?"

Three visits to Gary Harmon at the D.C. field office before that FBI agent began to wonder. Buzzed through the visitors room into that cavern with file cabinets crowding the halls outside the private offices and squad room. Sitting at Gary's gray desk, Q becoming accepted despite his freaky hair and clothes. He sneak-peeked a field report on the desk and heard a conversation between two agents who didn't think they needed to whisper. An order for travel forms shouted from a supervisor to a road-weary agent.

"I can't tell you how I know. But if you're good, you can confirm what I say with other people."

The reporter sipped his beer. Circled back, a sly hunter. "What about the burglary?"

"Nothing there."

"Why are you so sure?"

Because you have to believe me!

The reporter pressed, "I need what you know so I'll go after the right stuff."

"So far the three prosecutors aren't talking deal with the guys they got locked up."

"Why?"

A humid grass softball field near the Mall. A languid after-hours slow-pitch coed game, a team from the Montana Senate staffs versus the Washington U.S. Attorney's office. Quinn in cutoffs and a T-shirt hanging with prosecutor Max as he coaches first base. Max with a baseball cap over his balding head, a tattered Red Sox jersey. "Why do you care about that Watergate bust? It's not your case. Or mine—Pitch them fair!" Quinn: "Come on: if you can't office gossip with the guy who collars crooks for you, who can you talk to?" Max: "Nobody, if I do my—Go! Go! Take three! Good hit. Cool case, wish I was on it. Even the White House cares—'course, they should, those guys probably thought they were doing the boss a favor." Quinn frowned. "What do mean, 'cares'?" The prosecutor shrugged. "They got a hotshot lawyer named John Dean working with the FBI on the investigation—That's OK, swing it level! Smart trio of guys on that team for us. They're gonna make those men sweat until they get prison terms, then try to turn them. Those bad boys are keeping their mouths shut so—Aw, shit! It's OK, he's got a golden glove!" "So?" said Quinn. Max told him, "So forget about it. You promised you'd come to play, not talk shop. Grab a bat and swing hard."

"What if the prosecutors don't get convictions?" asked the reporter.

"Then they better run back to law school," answered Quinn. "Shoffler and Barrett and Leeper caught them red-handed."

"With gloves on."

"Got to be careful not to leave fingerprints on what you do."

"So there's a lawyer named Dean monitoring the FBI for the White House. Who else do you know that's involved in any way?"

Quinn whispered two names he'd overheard in the case agents' banter.

The reporter slid the coaster out from under his beer bottle. "I've got a terrible memory. Do you mind if I write them down?"

"Why don't you use the notebook that's burning a hole in your pocket?"

"Not gaming you, it's just that some people freak when the pen and pad come out."

"As long as you only write the names I told you, not where they came from."

"We've got a lot of sources. A lot of sources."

"Not me," said Quinn. Said Q. "Not ever me."

"What else can you give me?"

"If you let me know what you need to know—"

"Everything; we need to know everything."

"I'm a D.C. cop," said Quinn. "I've got my limits."

"That's good to hear. Everybody in this town thinks they know everything." The reporter spread his hands wide. "All I'm after is the story."

From his heart, Quinn said, "I'll tell you everything I can."

From his heart, Q said, "If you hit something about D.C., street stuff or crime stuff . . ."

Like prostitutes or call girl rings or party girls, he hungered to specify—but didn't.

Like the mafia or mobsters or a guy named Nezneck, he ached to say—but didn't.

Like how the Watergate bust really went down, like how the bugging really worked, like who's really linked to who and to that third-rate crime, like keys and desks that belong to nobody, like what is/might be and not just what fits, he wanted to scream. But didn't.

"I can call you?" said the reporter.

Give him a sigh. Give him a nod. Give him phone numbers and a phony name to use, warn him not to use his office or home phones that might be bugged or traced; watch his eyes widen—drama never fails and every Movement veteran knows that street theater dazzles.

Quinn said, "I'll try to steer you straight."

"Thanks. Hard to say where this is all going to go."

"Yeah. I just want to help you make it come out right."

They shook hands. Quinn caught the reporter checking his watch; said nothing.

Late, Quinn knew, but the reputation of one of the other reporters on his list said he had no personal life, so no call came too late, and any call after dark . . . drama, street theater.

"Hey!" said Quinn as this reporter walked away. *Keep control. Have the last word.* The wild-eyed street cop made his fist into a pistol. Pushed his forefinger barrel against his own temple.

Said, "Be careful."

Eyes widening, the reporter saw the cop shoot himself in the head.

CHAPTER 31

Autumn's symphony of colors brought a knock on Holloway's door. Sandy stood in his hall, a suitcase in each hand.

"I haven't done anything wrong," she said.

"Come in," he told her and closed the door when she did. "Don't freak out about the suitcases, OK?"

"First thing I thought of wasn't to freak out."

She let him hold her close. "I need someplace to stay. I've got to get away from them."

"From who?"

"Reporters. From *The Washington Post*. This Watergate thing. They're going around at night to everyone who works for CREEP, showing up on their doorstep with questions. I can't lie. What a bizarre thing for a 'press spokesman' to say." She smiled. "At least, I can't say a lie if I know it's a lie, which is why nobody tells me the whole truth. And I don't want to be a . . . a traitor. Or a patsy. Our official line is that we agree with what the Justice Department said after the grand jury indicted the five burglars plus Hunt and Liddy: there's no evidence to charge anybody else with anything. I've told a dozen reporters that. What I don't tell them . . ."

"You can tell me," said Nathan.

"Like you tell me those secrets behind your smiles?" She looked at him for a long time. "Love in Washington means not asking your partner his secrets."

"I don't love you just in Washington."

She hugged him and wouldn't let go. Whispered in his ear, "I'm so afraid to be where I am. It's absolutely the top and I feel like any door I open could be the long drop."

He held her close. She felt him nod.

"I hear whispers," she said, "rumors. People are lying to the Watergate grand jury. I don't want to know who or why, because then I'd have to . . . I don't want to make that choice.

"But I do know about money. Shoe boxes full of money. In it comes, away it goes. And here I am." She shook her head. "My mother thinks the pressing issue is you getting to take advantage of me. She said 'good girls' don't shack up."

"You're better than a good girl."

"Then how did I end up here? Not here with you, but—"

"I know what you meant."

"What are you going to tell your father? About us?"

"As long as I don't rock that admiral's fleet, he doesn't care enough to want to know. About us or . . ." Nathan shrugged. "What do you want to do? Not about us. About you."

"Same thing I've always wanted. I want to work where it's exciting. Where things matter. I want to work for the President of the United States."

"Congratulations."

AUTUMN IN WASHINGTON is wonderful; the Capitol grounds have trees from each of the fifty states. Dane made Vaughn take a walking lunch around the grounds with her that first week in October when the branches above them were filled with gold and russet poems.

"Patman's in trouble," she said. "The Justice Department wants him to delay his hearings until after the burglars' trials, so they can get a fair trial."

"And just because that means the hearings wouldn't happen until after the election—"

"Pure coincidence," said Dane. "Plus, the White House is putting on a full-court press. They had one of the Democrats on Patman's committee down to 1600 for a picture with Nixon. In that congressman's district, a Democrat needs Nixon's stamp of approval to avoid being chained to our guy McGovern, who'll be lucky to get *any* of those hometown votes for President. Another Dem is suddenly getting White House smiles about a two-million-dollar HUD appropriation for an old-folks apartment building in his hometown."

"Assholes! Who's leading the charge for the White House?"

"A Republican from New York. A prosecutor in the Justice Department told me that Nixon's buddy John Mitchell—when he was attorney general—blocked a grand jury from investigating that congressman for steering government contracts to a postal service firm with 'mob ties.'"

Vaughn got a phone call the next day from a Patman committee staffer he'd cultivated. By the end of the call, all Vaughn could do was shake his head. He went straight to

Dane. "Patman's committee colleagues voted to refuse him subpoena power."

"That never happens!"

"Tell that to Patman. Or Nixon. But you gotta give it to that old Texan: he's 'invited' Mitchell, John Dean, CREEP's new head and its money man to show up at a hearing."

"When?"

On a Thursday in October, Vaughn watched Patman gavel in his committee and fail to muster enough members to constitute a quorum. Patman's "guests" also refused to appear. Vaughn felt the old man's rage as he lectured four empty chairs at the witness table, as his colleagues avoided his gaze, as he told the tense room that the President "had pulled down an iron curtain of secrecy to keep the American people from knowing the facts."

IN OCTOBER, CAPTAIN Nathan Holloway, NSC aide, flew to Saigon.

Saigon. Again. Forever. The damp heat/barbecue/fish oil smell engulfed him when he stepped off the plane at Tan Son Nhut airport. His .45 hid under a diplomat's suit. Unseen gunsights made his spine tingle as jeeps with mounted machine guns escorted American diplomats' cars through Saigon's crowded streets.

Boyd grabbed him in the lobby of the Nash hotel and steered him to a deserted corridor: "Kissinger's done it! He busted ass in Paris and got Hanoi to agree to a peace treaty! We got a timetable to get President Thieu here to sign, then we jet up to Hanoi for a public ceremony where they'll initial it! There's a few details to be worked out, but our war here's all but over!"

"This is Saigon," said Holloway. *Sniper could have a line on that window!* "In Saigon, everything goes wrong."

"Not this time." Boyd licked his lips. Looked away. Sighed. "OK. There's one possible glitch: Henry's kept everything secret. Not from Nixon, though from what I hear, keeping Nixon happy has been as hard as dealing with Hanoi."

"If Henry gets peace before the election, Nixon'll surf back into the White House."

"And if Henry blows it, like LBJ did in sixty-eight . . ."

If you knew what I knew! thought Holloway. "Who's Henry keeping secrets from?"

"The South Vietnamese." Boyd shrugged. "This deal will structure South Vietnam, decide the war and what follows, but Henry never told Thieu what was going on. Figured, why complicate the negotiations? Now Henry can convince him this is the best deal for everyone."

"Then get on the plane to Hanoi for a hero's ceremony and bring peace home to Nixon. The Democrats might as well pack it in if that happens."

"It will. It's got to. This whole damn war . . ."

"Did you see those banners over the roads?" Holloway asked. *Or the covered baskets the street vendors carry? Or the eyes of the shoeshine boys?* "They went up in the last few days."

"I can't read Vietnamese."

"Our intel guys can. Banners don't just appear by magic. They demand no cease-fire without a North Vietnamese withdrawal from the South. Did Henry get Hanoi to agree to that?"

"We can handle that issue," insisted Boyd. "Won't be a problem."

Holloway, Boyd and a sirens-screaming convoy of aides and bodyguards followed Kissinger to the Presidential Palace on October 19, marched into its grand halls . . .

Stopped cold in front of closed doors and cool, polite apologies for "the delay."

In the crowded anteroom, Holloway listened to his heart beat, his watch tick: *eleven minutes* . . .

Boyd nodded to an adjoining corridor crowded with reporters. "How the hell did they get there?"

"Witnesses to us losing face by being kept waiting. Them

being there must be just a coincidence—a *Saigon* coincidence."

Holloway, Boyd and other aides lined the walls of the conference room where South Vietnamese President Thieu, Kissinger, and Thieu's Oklahoma-educated nephew, Nha, sat. For half an hour, Kissinger eloquently lectured on geopolitics—and a breakthrough treaty he had brought as a triumphant victory for Thieu to sign. Finally Kissinger put the document on the table. Thieu asked for a copy in Vietnamese. Kissinger didn't have one, so the thirty-one-year-old Nha translated the document for his uncle. Thieu smoked a thin cigar, his face impassive as his nephew tensely read.

"This isn't going right," whispered Boyd.

Kissinger took out his address book full of Hollywood actresses.

"What the hell is he doing?" whispered Holloway.

America's supernegotiator jokingly offered his phone book to Nha in exchange for a "friendlier" atmosphere.

Nha pulled out his own address book; offered a straight trade, not connected to business.

Holloway avoided the next round of meetings. He hunkered down in Saigon's Nash hotel, not venturing to the rooftop garden, or outside to the ice cream stand, or to the adjoining movie theater. He kept his curtains and blinds pulled shut, peered around their edges at irregular intervals, his air conditioner turned low so he could hear the sounds of the street.

They won't send me into the jungle.

They won't let me go to the jungle.

That patrol. Broke out of the ambush, ran for the stream.

Crashing through jungle, lungs on fire, and Mardigian chucks a grenade behind us. A roaring push: shrapnel hits my pack, rips my thigh. No gunshots behind us, no brush-crunching sounds on our trail. Stream, four feet wide and twenty-five feet away, twenty, almost to the helicopter landing zone extraction and why isn't Charlie charging right behind—

"Hit it!" Marines slam to earth. "Grenades! Hit the treeline across the stream!" A rolling chorus of grenade bursts/deafening thunder: sympathetic detonation or maybe the Viet Cong holding the switch on the stolen GI Claymore mines panicked when the grenades popped. Claymores, set across the stream to wait for the whites of our eyes. Each mine blasts seven hundred steel balls over our earth-fucking bodies. Mizell full auto sprays the swirling green powder fog across the stream. Splashing across that water, through the trees—branches dripping wet red, dripping—

Then it's Saturday. October 1972. *I'm in Saigon.* Back in/ just in/still in Saigon. Hotel room. Phone ringing. Ordering Holloway to the embassy to staff another conference between Kissinger and Thieu, who didn't care about Kissinger's timetable for the ceremony in Hanoi.

NSC aides from Washington and Marine guards crowded the fortified block of Saigon given over to the American embassy. Holloway carried a red security-sealed folio of documents to the room where Kissinger prepared for the day's negotiating battles with Thieu. The second hand swept around the clock, knocking down the odds of success with each second that fell into history. A phone rang; an aide answered, yelled for quiet, handed the receiver to Kissinger. Senior aides grabbed headsets as Kissinger took the phone. Holloway muscled a headset from a State Department flunky.

Through the earphones Holloway heard:

"I'm sorry," said Nha. "The President cannot see you now. He will see you tomorrow."

"I am the special envoy of the President of the United States of America!" yelled Kissinger. "You know I cannot be treated as an errand boy!"

"We never considered you an errand boy but if that's what you think you are, there's nothing I can do about it."

Kissinger raged through the embassy after the phone call; raged again when two hours later, a siren-screaming convoy of South Vietnamese white-mice military policemen and

Army bodyguards roared past the American embassy with Thieu in his limousine—going nowhere.

Sunday, Holloway stood in the background as Thieu told Kissinger he'd never sign that peace agreement.

Kissinger yelled, "If you don't sign, we're going out on our own!"

He whirled to translator Nha: "Why does your President play the role of a martyr? He does not have the stuff of a martyr."

"I'm not trying to be a martyr," said Thieu, who knew some English. "I am a nationalist."

Thieu turned his back on Kissinger—Holloway saw tears on Thieu's cheeks.

Kissinger intoned, "This is the greatest failure of my diplomatic career."

"Why?" snapped Thieu. "Are you rushing to get the Nobel prize?"

Holloway bartered his way onto the first planeload of diplomats headed back to Washington. In the droning darkness of the flight, he sat closeted in the dimly lit bathroom to write his secret report on the trip for the admirals.

His internal clock hadn't fully adjusted to Washington, D.C., time when he went to Kissinger's televised press conference on October 26. Holloway carried a *Washington Post* that claimed Nixon's number-one staffer Haldeman controlled a slush fund that had financed the Watergate burglary; Nixon's appointments secretary had resigned because of the scandal, though the *Post* noted few Americans cared. Holloway knew Kissinger's press conference strategy was twofold: convince Saigon that the U.S. was serious about the peace plan and that they had better fall in line, and convince Hanoi that the delay in signing the plan came from minor problems and not a deception cooked up by Nixon, who often played the nuclear-armed madman. Other strategies—like boosting Nixon's ratings—went unspoken in the NSC's White House lair.

Standing in the TV spotlight, Kissinger announced, "We believe that peace is at hand."

A voice behind Holloway's ear whispered, "Did you miss me?"

Penzler! Keep your eyes straight! "No."

"I've missed you. How was it over there? Still fun?"

Reporters scribbled Kissinger's words in notebooks.

"No need to be this way," said the whisper. "Times have changed. Listen to Herr Doctor: peace is at hand."

"Not for us. Not my hands."

"Are you sure?" breathed Penzler. A thin manila envelope slipped into Holloway's newspaper. "Consider that a peace offering. Use it to redeem yourself."

"What is it?"

"Did you wonder why Thieu was so cold to Herr Doctor from the start?"

A reporter Holloway didn't recognize shouted a question.

"Cat got your tongue? All you have to do is listen. Figure out what's your duty. What's best for you. Your troubles began when you chose Jud Simon over me. What I've learned about that psycho . . . Promise me you'll be careful around him. People who weren't ended up dead."

"What's in your damn envelope?"

"Gold for you," said Penzler. "Thieu knew our—*your*—Paris secrets. Henry doesn't know that, Pentagon doesn't know that, but at the Agency, we know. For once, Saigon's army did its job. Do you know Quang Tin province? I've been there. Choppered in-country once or twice to help Bill Colby with Phoenix. No hero stuff. Such wet work we delegate to our gooks and grunts."

"Not my billet either."

"ARVN troops knocked over a Viet Cong bunker, took a ten-page document off a dead political commissar, flew it to Thieu. Our boys bought it from Thieu's aides. It's the deal Henry cut in Paris. When Henry showed up at the palace mouthing 'breakthrough,' Thieu knew the captured VC document was genuine, knew Henry had cut him out of the loop, knew even Viet Cong commissars in the boondocks had closer links to Henry and Uncle Sam than he does.

"If I were Thieu," whispered Penzler, "I'd have drawn my

pistol and blown Henry's brains out all over the marble floor. Nixon would've covered it up, called it a lone Viet Cong sniper, had a lovely state funeral for Henry *and* gotten the point to not fuck with me."

"You make it so easy to trust you."

"You don't have to—not on this. Tell your Pentagon masters that you 'acquired' the report from a CIA source. They'll applaud your ingenuity."

"Why do you care? And why so good to me now?"

Penzler shrugged. " 'Peace is at hand.' The Radford debacle of the Navy White House spy who confessed is locked up in secret files. Nixon's witch-hunters are hiding because some of them got caught at Watergate, so they're no longer looking for our shadows. Watergate is being tidied up—the FBI caught the bad guys, the op team is maintaining cover silence, a few low-level aides will be sacrificed. Congress or the press might make noise, but they can't do shit. Nixon will get re-elected, so the problems that brought us here will be around for four more years. Our masters need us more than ever, because now's not the time to try new insertions, not with the post-Watergate sensitivity. They need us, we can help each other. Simple as that."

"And I should just forget how you tried to take me out."

"You should remember where you are: thirty years ago, we were allies with Russia and would have used the atomic bomb on Berlin, if we'd had it. Today we'd use the atomic bomb to stop Russia from attacking Berlin. Politics requires adaptation—if you want to survive. Do you want to survive, Captain? Who would Sandy fuck if you were gone?

"Whatever you think of me," hissed Penzler before he vanished, "you *could* be right. Or you *could* be wrong. But you *should* be flexible and smart. Can you do that?"

AUTUMN PROVED PENZLER right: news stories about Watergate fell like dead leaves on the Capitol grounds, small, quick to crumble and unseen outside of Washington. In the November contest that overwhelmingly re-elected Richard

Nixon and Spiro Agnew, Quinn voted against Nixon and saw his father's ghost recoil in horror. *Dad, if you only knew.*

In the quiet of the Congressional election recess, when losers in the Senate buildings were sealing their résumé envelopes with tears and winners sighed relief, Vaughn realized he'd never heard from the AAJ. The letter he wrote them over Senator Martin's signature was scathing, but staring at four more years of Nixon-Agnew made Vaughn not give a damn about diplomacy. He saw his original letter to AAJ concerning Hoffa's pardon: *Why let the assholes slide on anything?* Vaughn crafted a letter from Senator Martin to the Justice Department "requesting" notification of all pardons and commutations granted by the President.

Vaughn meant to tell Dane what he'd done, but she flew home when her mother slipped on ice and broke her leg. Byron was drunk when Vaughn put his proposed pardons letter in front of him to approve. Byron's nephew had fled to Canada rather than be drafted into the Vietnam War, a move Korean War vet Byron hated because he believed a patriot answered his country's call, a move Uncle Byron embraced because he thought all America would gain from the Vietnam conflict was row after row of white gravestones. What Byron knew was that his nephew could never come home again without going to prison, "So fuck it," he slurred to Vaughn as he scrawled *OK* on the pardons letter's draft, "let's see who gets to stay out of jail under Tricky Dick Nixon."

CHAPTER 32

December 1972, the sky fell.

Holloway shivered as he retrieved the Saturday *Post* from outside his door. He checked the newspaper for envelopes, found none, decided to let Sandy sleep. Though Watergate was old news—at least until the burglars' trial scheduled for January—FBI agents and reporters snooping around CREEP made her toss and turn at night. Nathan poured a cup of coffee. On Page 3 of the *Post,* a wire service story said that Admiral Burt Petersen was dead.

Killed in a helicopter crash while on a routine inspection in Vietnam for the Joint Chiefs of Staff. Mechanical failure brought the chopper down. The last paragraph noted that his naval officer son, Todd, was in a Honolulu hospital recovering from wounds suffered in Vietnam.

The paper didn't call Admiral Petersen a spy master.

We bury our heroes well, thought Holloway that Tuesday as he sat in the crowd of dress-uniformed men and their coiffed wives at Arlington cemetery. Jackhammers and blowtorches had opened the frozen earth for the coffin. Graveside rows of mourners' chairs were parallel and perpendicular. Flags snapped in the biting wind. The bugler and the honor guard rifle squad were statues while a chaplain delivered a eulogy.

Holloway stood out in that crowd of officers from all four armed services because he was young and because he was only a captain. He scanned the rows of gold-braided admirals, telepathically imploring: Look at me! See me! Tell me what to do now! I'm here in the cold where you put me! Rescue me!

Hearing it first, the funeral crowd swung their eyes toward the naked branches of the treeline and the *whumping* of a helicopter coming closer, closer—

The machine cleared the treeline and veered away so its chop and drone wouldn't stop the funeral below. The bird touched down in the distant parking lot. Holloway spotted a sailor holding his white cap on his head as he ran through the winter morning light toward that helicopter—

Run/rip free of the jungle! Stumble into a smoke-painted veldt flooded by lemonade light. Charred earth, blackened tree stumps. Every thudding step kicks up choking charcoal dust and the afterburn

*whiff of napalm. Get somewhere, set up LZ perimeter.
A chopper! Rotors beating against the setting sun.
Coming in fast and door gunner firing. Bullets zing
past—but horizontal, not from above! From behind
us! Victor Charlie, never gonna quit and the chopper
kicks up a black swirling stinging fog of charred Nam,
hovers off the ground, door gunner rocking through
ammo belts as my men tumble aboard. Is that Mardigian smeared black and red? We toss Sergeant in
and Mardigian gets grabbed up, too. O'Brien and Waters limp on, turn to pull on the last two and me, and
those guys, both of them, bullets pop dust off their
packs. Screams. Holes punch in the chopper! Fuel
tank will explode, kill us all. Hear myself yell: "Break
off! Break off!" A sucking whoosh. Chopper rises,
cinders fly. Stagger blind, my ride roars up, up and
gone while bullets lance through the swirling black
dust. Run away! Run alone.*

Bagpipes . . .

Bagpipes, graveside, not my grave and it's freezing.

The bagpiper played "Anchors Away." All eyes were on
the flag-draped coffin.

Except for those of Marine Captain Nathan Holloway, who
blinked back from where he'd been to where he was and saw
a white-haired admiral hurrying up from the parking lot, his
face bent over to watch where he stepped. Holloway knew
even before the admiral turned his face up that the man the
helicopter had brought to this time and place of the dead was
his father.

Admiral Samuel Holloway hesitated when he spotted the
young Marine. Then a smile lit his face as he hurried to his
son.

"Attention!"

Every soldier, sailor, airman and Marine snapped to and
faced the grave. At the back of the crowd, an admiral stood
shoulder to shoulder with a Marine captain.

"Present . . . Arms!"

The two Holloways swung right hands to hat brims in salute.

"Shoulder . . . Arms!"

The bugler blew "Taps." The honor guard fired one volley, then two, then three as the coffin sank into the earth. The military men snapped off their final salute to Admiral Petersen. The chaplain and honor guard finished the formalities. Bundled lines of aging men with their patient wives broke ranks to shake hands, whisper ritual comforts, hurry to waiting vehicles and the land of the still-living. A dozen faces turned to the Holloways: Nathan saw them nod or smile greetings to his father, a decorous wave or two. But no one came over to them.

"Still can't believe Burt's dead," said the admiral who'd been his roommate at the Naval Academy. "Not going to be the same from now on."

"I know," said Nathan.

"Damn near didn't make it. Feel like I'm still in Brussels."

Car engines started. Limo drivers held doors.

"Got time to take a walk with your old man?"

" 'Take a walk'? Four years, a handful of checking-in phone calls, all your official holiday cards and you . . ." Nathan shook his head. "Take a walk? Yeah, I can take a walk."

They drifted through the harvest rows of white stones.

"Don't have much time," said the father. "Got a jet back to Wiesbaden waiting out at Andrews. Don't have to tell you, the Soviets and Warsaw Pact boys, gotta stay on top of that."

The son said nothing.

"So . . . How you been?"

Nathan laughed, then his voice grew cold, jagged. "I guess it's good to know you care."

"Care? I've always cared! I'm your father!"

"Right. You are. Yes, sir."

"Sometimes I just don't get you young people."

"Yeah. You only command us."

The wind whipped their coats.

"Everybody salutes somebody," said Nathan's father as

they stood in the field of white stones. "That's the way things work."

His father stared at him; had to look away; said, "Hear good things about you. Hear you been doing a damn fine job. Outstanding."

"Who told you? What do you know?"

"Admirals' mess is not just a dining room. Word gets around—no details, mind you. No break in chain of command, operational components, but . . . We're family—even you Marines."

Stones strained to hear Nathan's whisper: "Imagine that."

"Heard more. Think—*hope* I'm the first one to tell you. You're going to make major. What I hear, keep doing the outstanding work, keep doing what you've been doing, fast tracking you, put colonel birds on your shoulders before your next posting. Young as you are, you could beat your old man's record to getting a star."

"Oh, Jesus!" sighed Nathan. "They sent you."

"Nobody *sent* me. Came to bury my friend, see my son—"

"Is that who I am? Or am I a Marine in need of subtle command guidance. A pat on the back, a push to the lines, some new *motivational* brass on my collar."

"Nate—"

"Sent you? *Of course they sent you!* That's your life, following the orders wherever they send you. Jumping at the chance to volunteer to go."

"Let me tell you about my life, mister! I wasn't there as much as I wanted to be for you and your mother, God rest her soul, but I did my duty by both of you! For both of you!"

"Worked out good for you, didn't it? Doing your duty. The job. Answering the call of your grateful country. Nothing less than that. Nothing petty or messy or personal. No questions, no if's, and's or but's. No situations worthy of challenging such a grand responsibility. Everything shipshape and four square as long as you, *you* got that duty to do."

"What's your point? You've seen the hell most people live

in around the world. I made sure you never suffered like that."

"Gee, thanks, Dad."

"What more could you expect? Look at you: if I'm so wrong, such a bad guy, why'd you follow in my footsteps?"

"I didn't," whispered Nathan. "I went my own way."

"Did you? Me, I'm proud of what you've accomplished."

"How could you be? You don't even know."

"I know what I see."

"Or know what they tell you? Tell *me*, Father. You say you care, so please, tell me. I need to know. I need *you* to know. Bet they didn't tell you a damn real thing. Just a whisper, a nod, old-boy-to-old-boy phone call, a jet and a helicopter. And you saluted. But I need your help."

"I already told you. You know what you need to know. Duty. Long as you do your duty, what's expected of you—"

"Duty? Let me tell you about—"

"Don't you dare break your command structure! Don't you dare make me a part of some insubordination! Make me have to report violations by my own son, my own flesh and blood!"

"Yeah. Wouldn't want to let any of that smear your record."

For the first time in years, father touched son. He grabbed the young man's arm. "What the hell do you want from me?"

Nathan needed a heartbeat, needed a lifetime to answer. "Nothing you've got."

"This is the way it is. You know that. Be a man about it."

" 'Be a man'? OK! Yes, sir!"

Nathan snapped to attention and threw a salute.

"Don't worry, *Admiral*. Tell your brass buddies not to worry either. I know all about duty. About 'the way it is.' "

"And don't worry, *Dad*," added the Marine standing in a stone field of Arlington. "You've done your duty. You'll still get to end up here."

Samuel Holloway went as pale as the infinity of white gravestones. Then he marched to the waiting helicopter.

Chopper engine whined to full power. The dark machine lifted off the earth, flew over acres lined with white stones, over a lone Marine, vanished beyond the winter trees. The rotor blast beat down on Nathan; the vacuum *whoosh* of the flying machine's wake swept him with terrible freedom.

THE NEXT AFTERNOON, Nathan rode with NSC aide Boyd in a caravan of White House cars headed toward Camp David, the Presidential mountain retreat two hours' drive from Washington. The windshield wipers beat a metronome rhythm against the blowing snow. In his suit pocket Holloway carried the official letter notifying him that he'd been promoted. Their boss Kissinger was in Paris, frantically trying to hammer out a new peace proposal with the North Vietnamese.

"Henry's all ripped up," said Boyd. "Thieu won't play Henry's game plan because he thinks Henry fucked him and sold out to Hanoi. Henry didn't deliver a signed peace proposal in October like he promised, so Hanoi figures Henry lied to them. Nixon knows he's gonna get blamed for the screwups and Henry shooting off his mouth."

Boyd shook his head. "I wanted to bring some sense to all this shit. Stop the war by being smart."

"The best and the brightest got us there," said Holloway.

"I keep thinking it's almost over. Then I wake up, read the papers, see what we see . . ."

"You know why we're going out here. You know what their fallback is."

They rode the rest of the way in silence as snow fell.

When the aides and advisers arrived, they found the President swimming in his new half-million-dollar heated pool. The frigid air formed a steam cloud above the water, a fog that drifted around Haldeman and Ehrlichman as they watched Nixon paddle toward them. They all averted their eyes as he climbed dripping wet from the steaming water, wrapped himself in a terry-cloth robe.

Holloway stood in the mist. *No one will believe this.*

Nixon toweled his hair as Haldeman and Ehrlichman reported on the war stalemate.

"The South Vietnamese think Henry is weak now because of his press conference statements," said Nixon. "That damn 'peace is at hand'! The North Vietnamese have sized him up. They know he has to either get a deal or lose face. That's why they've shifted to a harder position."

Nixon dictated orders for Kissinger to get Hanoi's Le Duc Tho to quit waffling. To make sure that the communists knew the consequences if the peace process broke down. And to be sure he deflected the heat from Nixon.

As the Paris talks stalled, cables flew from the White House to Paris, including orders for Kissinger to check his staff and see how many of them had supported antiwar Senator George McGovern's failed bid for the presidency. Kissinger got two cables from Haldeman telling him not to smile in any photographs taken of him and Le Duc Tho. One week after the swimming pool session, the Paris talks fell apart. Kissinger flew home.

"They're just a bunch of shits," Kissinger said to Holloway and the NSC staff of the North Vietnamese. "Tawdry, filthy shits. They make the Russians look good."

For the first time in the history of America's thirteen years of warfare in Vietnam, every available B-52 bomber was alerted for conventional bombing missions targeting Hanoi. The giant B-52's had obliterated large chunks of jungle along the Ho Chi Minh trail (and secretly in Cambodia and Laos), as well as South Vietnam, but never before had they been sent to blast the communists' capital of Hanoi, a city of one million people that had been progressively armed with surface-to-air missiles. Only one B-52 had been lost in the war's combat.

Monday night, December 18, B-52's hit Hanoi to begin the twelve-days-of-Christmas bombing. The port city of Haiphong made the buffs' target list, too.

Holloway and Boyd all but lived in the White House Sit Room during the Christmas bombing. Their desks piled high with newspapers, with reports of worldwide protests.

On Christmas Day—observed by Nixon with a twenty-four-hour halt in the bombing—those two NSC colleagues and thousands of other Americans watched TV cameras capture Kissinger attending a Washington Redskins football game.

As bombs fell, Holloway and Boyd saw what the world didn't.

Their desks sagged under classified Air Force reports on crews of America's Strategic Air Command who refused to fly the missions because they were being sent to a SAM shooting gallery in an escalation of a war their Commander In Chief kept promising was almost over.

At Torii Station, Okinawa, the Air Force Security Service's 6990th unit continuously eavesdropped on North Vietnam and the Viet Cong's communications; now these American servicemen staged work stoppages to protest the bombings. Their eavesdropping had told them that enemy MIG warbirds had been disarmed to prepare for a Hanoi air show celebrating Kissinger's collapsed peace plan—a deed curiously far from the duplicitous, aggressive strategy attributed to the North Vietnamese by administration spokesmen. The 6990th radios also heard the "real time" screams and "Maydays!" from the fifteen B-52's and fifteen other American warplanes as SAMs blew them burning and smoking from the deadly sky.

Under the bombers' sky, few children ran through the streets of Hanoi: thousands of them had been evacuated. Thousands, but not all. Two children died when a string of blockbuster bombs from a B-52 missed their target and blasted Bach Mai hospital, killing them and twenty-eight other people. The lowest estimates of target casualties averaged out to one human bombed to death every 7.6 minutes, every hour, twenty-four hours a day, for those twelve days of Christmas.

As bombs and bombers fell on Hanoi, Holloway used the anonymous power of the White House Situation Room to reach into the bureaucracy for a classified document on another plane lost to the sky. The wife of arrested Watergate conspirator, ex-CIA agent E. Howard Hunt, had died in a

Chicago plane wreck the day after Nixon's steaming swim.
Crash scene investigators found $10,000 in her purse. Hol-
loway stole a copy of a classified federal report: no evidence
of sabotage existed in the plane wreck.

Holloway dead-dropped a copy of that report along with
a copy of an anonymous letter Penzler gave him one night
in a White House bathroom: "We've got to quit meeting like
this," Penzler'd whispered. "People will say we're in love."
The unsigned letter was a warning: "Jack . . . if the WG operation is laid at the CIA's feet, where it does not belong,
every tree in the forest will fall. It will be a scorched desert.
The whole matter is at the precipice right now. Just pass the
message that if they want it to blow, they are on exactly the
right course."

"Make sure your commanders get this," said Penzler as he
stroked his wispy beard in the bathroom mirror. "They may
know, but let's be certain."

"Know *what*?" said Holloway. "Who's this for and from
and—"

"Jack is Jack Caufield." Penzler straightened the knot of
his tie. "Good man. Ex–New York cop, hunted commies.
Worked for the White House, CREEP. Now he's at Treasury.
The letter's from his friend McCord—"

"The Watergate burglar who worked for the CIA."

"And now he's upset. We—*he* keeps hearing that his burglary buddies are going to claim that Watergate was a CIA
operation as part of their defense. That Nixon's boys are
going to push that line, too. As a man passionate about truth
and loyal to his old comrades, McCord's justifiably angry.
Nobody wants an out-of-control free-for-all."

"Especially not you. The White House has finally admitted
that the plumbers exist. You waved me off looking at that
little shop. You were one of their CIA contacts—"

"Oh, *Nate*." A schoolteacher's chiding smile lit Penzler's
face in the mirror. "There's only that one document linking
me to those people. Even if it surfaces, it shows me as merely
another inconsequential bureaucrat."

Penzler faced the Marine in a civilian suit. "Just be sure

your commanders get the message. Perhaps it will help them serve truth, justice and the American way. Right, Major?"

Penzler's bony hand flushed the urinal.

On the ninth-day-of-Christmas bombing Holloway walked past that bathroom and smelled the stench of vomit. He caught that scent again when he entered the Sit Room; it grew stronger the closer he got to the desk where Boyd sat.

Boyd's suit jacket was nowhere to be seen; his tie hung askew like a noose. Stubble dotted his pallor. His hands trembled on the desk, where White House condolence letters to Air Force family members lay scattered with photographs of Hanoi's burning houses, shattered buildings, corpses in the streets. The eyes he raised to see Holloway were tattooed with webs of blood.

"You know why we're doing this?" he whispered.

"Boyd, come on. Let's go for a walk."

"We're not doing this just to break Hanoi at the Paris peace table. We're doing this to convince our Saigon allies we'll cover their ass. We're killing our own guys, killing thousands of people—not numbers: people. To placate a dictatorship we know is rotten to the core with corruption from the black market to heroin to . . . That's us, that's 'never gonna lose a war' us. This is how we protect democracy?"

Faces turned toward them. Holloway crouched beside Boyd's chair, the stench of sweat and vomit enveloping him like a fog as he whispered, "Easy, go easy. Intel reports say that no matter what else, the bombing's working, the North Vietnamese are coming back to—"

"Back to where we were two months ago in October? Aren't we the smart ones. You and me and Nixon and Herr Doctor and—"

"Look where you are!" snapped Holloway. "You're in the Situation Room. You chose to get in this situation. Maybe you thought it was something else. Maybe they told you it was something else. But here you are, and trick is, thing to do is, only right thing to do is—"

"Moral choices, Major? You're going to tell me about it—"

"You gotta use what you got, where you are, how you can. What you can't do is give up. Can't surrender, walk away. Never gonna be clean that way. You're in the situation but that means you got the power of being there, the responsibility of being there, duty of being there. And if you're there, if you're smart, careful, got the guts, you can take some shots and maybe, just maybe, *change* the situation. Make things more like they should be."

"What are you talking about?"

Holloway fell silent.

Boyd looked around like a man in a daze—or just out of one. A sigh trembled from him. "I can't be this anymore."

A heartbeat before he floated from the Sit Room, a day before his resignation came back, he told Holloway, "You're just as lost as I am. Only you don't know it."

CHAPTER 33

Vaughn and Dane went to their separate homes for Christmas. Vaughn told his parents he was seeing someone special, Dane told her mother to quit bugging her about getting married. The older woman insisted there was something Dane wasn't confiding. Especially when Dane blushed every time the phone rang.

"If he's married, forget him!" said her mother. "Once he's left his wife, he'll feel too guilty—and too damn free—to stay with you!"

On the plane back to D.C., Vaughn read *Time* magazine's "Man of the Year" issue. *Time* picked Nixon and Kissinger as 1972's most important newsmakers, labeling their reign "triumph and trial," citing the Kissinger "peace is at hand" euphoria's strange elusiveness, Nixon's bombing of North Vietnam, their leadership in facing terrorism from the Munich Olympic Games to the year's 393 skyjackings. The article quoted Nixon proclaiming: "1972 has been a year of more achievement for peace than any year since the end of World War II."

Vaughn found Nixonian scandals confined to the tag end of one paragraph in the six-page story, a double-barreled summation. First, the "suggestion" that the Justice Department dropped antitrust suits against ITT in exchange for at least a $200,000 subsidy of the GOP Presidential convention. Second, the arrest of "agents with ties" to CREEP for breaking into the Democrats' Watergate headquarters "to remove electronic bugs planted there earlier.

"Yet," noted *Time*, "none of these issues took hold in a serious way, none of them seemed to make much difference."

On January 8, 1973, the trial of the Watergate break-in team began in Washington. Vaughn sat at his desk, knocking out routine replies to constituent queries. He almost missed the envelope from the Justice Department marked to his attention that contained a list of year-end Presidential pardons and commutations, "as per Senator Martin's request." The list showed that on December 20, Nixon had commuted one Angelo DeCarlo from New Jersey.

Never heard of him or any of these guys, thought Vaughn. He photocopied the list, sent it to the Library of Congress to identify who the pardoned were and their crimes.

Dane walked off the plane at Washington National Airport on Tuesday, January 10, and slid into Vaughn's hug. They worked late the next day. The phone on Vaughn's desk buzzed at six-twenty.

"The boss wants to see us," Dane told him.

They found Senator Martin filling one of the leather easy chairs in his inner office. A java mug scented with bourbon sat on the coffee table not far from a long-necked bottle of Pabst Blue Ribbon beer belonging to Byron, who lounged in the chair to the Senator's left.

"You guys want one?" asked Byron, lifting his beer as Vaughn and Dane entered.

"No thanks," said Vaughn.

"Sure," said Dane. She fetched a bottle from the fridge by the private bathroom between the Senator's office and his AA's desk, came back and sat beside Vaughn on the couch.

Like kids in the principal's office, thought Vaughn, wishing he'd taken a beer.

"You two have to make some choices," said the Senator.

Dane knew both she and Vaughn tensed on the couch.

"This has been going on quietly for a while, but that's changing now."

"No more tiptoeing around," said Byron.

"Senator Ervin's agreed to go after Watergate," said Senator Martin.

"What?" said Vaughn.

"What do you mean, 'what'?" snapped the Senator. "What the hell have you two been doing, keeping an eye on since this summer?"

"Kid just got excited, Gus," interrupted Byron, nudging his old friend and boss away from the abyss that barely hid his explosive frustration. "Didn't understand."

"You better understand," snapped the Senator, but the fire in his eyes cooled to a twinkle. "We don't make them bleed a little now, in four more years the same bunch of rustlers will shove Agnew down our throats! Majority Leader Mike Mansfield made Kennedy and Proxmire and me and a few others wait until after the election so we couldn't be charged with playing politics. Then old 'Iron Mike' wrote Ervin a 'Dear Mr. Chairman of the Judiciary Committee' letter, urging an investigation. Ervin's been talked into it, but only with a special committee."

Vaughn said, "Are you in line for it?"

Martin sighed. "I won't get on that committee in a million years. Nor will a few other well-known Nixon fans. But giving that up gets me some chits.

"We're putting it together squeaky clean. Nobody gets on the committee who's ever shown the slightest interest in running for President, and nobody who's up for re-election next time, so the committee won't look like anybody's springboard or grandstand."

"What about Ted Kennedy?" asked Vaughn.

"If we let him on a select committee, the whole thing will just become another chapter in Nixon's feud with his family."

"Tricky Dick versus the Camelot clan." Byron burped. "Never underestimate personal grudges in politics. Shakespeare was a better journalist than the whole *Washington Post*!"

Martin said, "What I'm hearing is that everybody figures this is about wiretapping."

Vaughn shook his head. "What's going on doesn't feel to me like just bugging."

"What do you think, Dane?" asked the Senator.

"They hit Patman on the House side harder than they needed to if this was just about wiretapping." Dane took a long swig of beer. "You said the two of us had to make some choices."

"I won't get on the committee, but I'm owed for it. However they set the Select Committee up, I'll get to stick a staffer—or two—on it. Detail them there, if nothing else. Vaughn, you have been on this from the start, and I put Dane over you on it because—"

"Because I'm the kid."

"Because she's a trench fighter and you're more of a . . . you're a crazed lone sniper. Now the three of us—Byron, he's not so sure—the three of us smell more than rats running around with wiretaps. Question is, if I only get to put one staffer on the committee, which of you two goes?"

The room grew quiet and close. The air smelled of bourbon and sweat, of fine leather furniture, beer, law books on the shelves and electricity.

Vaughn said, "Send—"

"Him," interrupted Dane. "He spotted it from the start, not me. Ervin will get a dozen good trench fighters, but for us—for you—they'll need at least one clear, crazy eye."

Byron said, "Vaughn's got a clear eye?"

They all laughed.

"Understand," said Martin, "odds are I can send both of

you. Not as honchos—they're gonna want lawyers—but I'm owed one slot, I'm going for three, so maybe I'll get two.

"The thing is, son," said Martin, leaning—looming—toward Vaughn, "the Republicans will be gunning for everybody on the other side. And if they can knock you off with a cheap shot, you falling might tip the committee off balance. So don't screw up."

"I understand," said Vaughn, certain that he did.

Dane said, "If you do get a chance for two slots—"

"Then you go. We'll lose two hands, but we'll pull in a fellowship guy from the state university to pick up the slack, pick up some hometown chits for that, too."

"That's not it . . ." She took a deep breath, let it out. "Vaughn and I are a couple."

"What?" said Byron.

"A couple," she said as Vaughn's face caught on fire. "You know. Social . . . Dating."

"Oh, shit!" said Byron. "Right under my nose!"

"The only reason I—we—told you now is because if we both get lucky enough to have you put us on the committee, I don't want it to be an issue."

"At least you didn't make me hear about it from somebody else." The Senator rubbed his brow. "If you're up front about it from now on, Ervin and his people still might take both of you."

He raised his coffee mug of bourbon over the low table. Byron leaned in with his beer bottle, as did Dane. Vaughn felt foolishly empty-handed.

"Here's to you two," toasted the Senator. "Hope you're always this damn lucky."

CHAPTER 34

Holloway felt hunters' eyes on him as he walked home from work on a cold February night.

Where are you? A station wagon grumbled past the sidewalk where he walked. A woman's heels clicked as she turned the corner, gone from his building's street of sleeping cars and curtained windows. Dirty snow crunched under Holloway's step.

Car headlights winked on, yellow eyes swinging from the curb, pulling toward him. Thirty feet from Holloway, the car stopped, bathed him in its headlights' yellow glow. The car's passenger door opened—*No dome light, they'd rigged*—a man climbed out to the street: wind-blown long hair, a winter coat. Headlights blinded Holloway as the car accelerated . . .

Raced past him in the night.

A gravel whisper came from the shadows: "Long time no see."

Holloway said, "Is that you?"

Jud Simon stepped into the light. His hair hung over his ears. A beard stubbled his face.

"You've been nowhere. Thought you were AWOL or—"

"Dead?" Jud shrugged. "Maybe you're right."

"Who's in that car?"

"Come on, Major. We've got a cab to catch."

They caught three, traveled in silence. Jud's eyes rode the mirrors. The last taxi dropped them in empty shadows beyond Fourteenth Street's prostitution stroll.

Jud made the Marine hide a manila envelope inside his shirt.

"I've been gone from the Secret Service for weeks," said Jud. "But I still got friends there, sources. They passed me the copy of that Secret report. Eighteen days ago, February ninth, four of Nixon's White House boys hunkered down at La Costa resort in California: Haldeman, Ehrlichman, Dean and Moore. The FBI report to the Secret Service says that showing up at La Costa the day before for their own secret meeting were mafia and Teamster types. The guy who replaced Hoffa as head of the Teamsters, Frank Fitzsimmons. Another labor guy named Allen Dorfman. The mob types are Peter Milano out of California, Mo Dalitz who owns La Costa, plus two Chicago boys, Tony Accardo and Lou Rosanova."

"Did the White House guys and the mafia guys meet?"

"Don't ask me, I don't know." Jud led Holloway west. "Next tick comes three days later, February 12. Searchlight's at San Clemente. He invites Teamster boss Fitzsimmons to fly back to Washington on *Air Force One*. My guys say a fine time was had by all."

They reached Fourteenth Street, where the night burned with a neon-yellow blaze from the "World's Largest Adult Bookstore."

"Jud that makes my skin crawl. But—"

"But *wait*! What's also in there is the routing slip for the report. Guess who demanded a copy? Our pal Penzler."

Ice sliced the length of Holloway's spine.

"Penzler fought hard to set it up. Never mind that the CIA is legally barred from stateside ops—Hell, you and I are proof of what laws like that are worth. And now, as a CIA Office of Security exec, Penzler gets a copy of all White House–related Bureau or Secret Service reports concerning the mafia or mobsters."

Holloway's feet froze to the sidewalk.

"You got it now, bro."

"Got what?" whispered Holloway. "Ugly coincidences?"

"Maybe," said Jud. "Mixed it all together: Nixon's boys, the plumbers Penzler is linked to, the mafia, CIA. Sure, in this town, everybody knows everybody, but still . . ."

"What am I supposed to do with this?"

"Turn those docs over to our commanders. I'll confirm

their *bona fides*—long as you make the play before I disappear."

"To where?"

"Nowhere on my own, you can bet on that."

"If we turn this over . . ."

"Then our hands are clean, plus we tie a can to Penzler."

"Only if he's not supposed to be into all this shit."

"Hell, only a handful of spooks dance across that many dirty lines. I don't think he's sanctioned to be one of us. He gets burned, the Agency sizzles. Nothing better at self-defense than a spy house. So they might decide to do the smart thing, a preemptive burn. Gets him off your back, my back. Makes the world a better place."

"Give me until tomorrow night. I'll dead-drop it then."

"Make a copy for your ass-covering self."

"You didn't do our taxi dance just to pass me this."

"When I say good-bye, I go all the way." Jud led Holloway across the street. "Come on. I'm going to give you the big secret of the Nixon White House."

Jud led the way to the entrance of a trapezoid-shaped building facing New York Avenue with a small front running around the corner to Fifteenth Street, across from the Treasury building, whose west wall faced the White House. The brass sign above the revolving door read SOBEL BUILDING. The door spun Jud and Holloway inside a mutant architecture of time.

The Sobel was a vast hollow hive with an ancient caged elevator running up its center, an ambience part post-Depression, part pre-millennium. Must filled the air. Brown wood paneling covered the walls. Scars marred the black and white tiles.

A black man wearing janitorial shirt and pants sat behind a desk thirty feet from the door. His clothes said *minimum wage*, his hulking mass said *never made it to the football pros*, but Holloway saw his warrior eyes, which said *death*. Jud nodded to the desk man, scanned the upper landings until he spotted a blond guy holding a push broom. Jud flashed a hand signal. Broom Man disappeared.

"He's turning off the cameras," said Jud. "They filmed us coming in, but only footage of those who go up to the hot zone gets reviewed. Never take the elevator: can't shut that camera off."

Broom Man reappeared by the railing, nodded.

Jud and Holloway climbed flights of wide stairs.

"Outside is seedy, inside is low rent," said Jud. "Speak-English school. Court reporter service. Some guy who runs a newsletter about right-wingers and Klan types. A private eye famous for big-time sleaze. Singing coach for opera wanna-be's."

Yellow bulbs brightened the top-floor landing. Most doors bore no signs. Jud pushed a five-beat code on a doorjamb buzzer. Holloway heard no buzz, but a moment later the doorknob gave an electric *click*. As Jud led Nathan inside the office, he said, "Say whatever you want as long as they're not watching."

Not much more than a closet, thought Holloway. The door shut behind him. An empty—

The wall opposite the door swung open.

They entered an electric sanctuary. Two men sat facing a wall of reel-to-reel tape recorders rigged with red lights and dial monitors. A third man with a trim mustache beckoned Jud and Holloway deeper into the room, then he closed the "wall" he'd opened for them and reached for a ledger. Jud caught the mustached man's wrist, shook his head. Mustache sighed, crossed the room to watch his colleague work knobs that made monitor needles jump.

Windows are gone, noted Holloway. Bricked over. *Bet they built a false back for the "real" windows so from the outside, looks normal still, like shades drawn. Must have cost—*

From behind Holloway came the *ratchet-clack* of an automatic pistol as a bullet got jacked into the firing chamber.

Holloway whirled around to face the noise.

Jud stood beside a trash stack of Washington phone books, a .45 in his fist cocked and aimed at the top volume of Yellow Pages as he squeezed the trigger.

The pistol roared! Flashed! The stack of phone books jumped. Even Holloway, who'd seen it coming, flinched. Smoke swirled from the gun barrel as Holloway turned back—

Saw the three men at the monitors turning their heads, frowns but no jitters from the ear-splitting *Bang!* still echoing in the office. The mustached man glanced at Jud. Saw the smoking gun. Saw the gunshot phone books' pile sliding apart. He shot his middle finger at Jud.

"I had to prove to him you could be trusted," Jud told the man.

The mustache man shook his finger, then turned away.

"Got them via Gallaudet University across town," Jud told Nathan as he holstered the pistol, picked up the ejected casing. "Totally deaf-mute. You saw how that gun blast didn't even register with them, so you know I shit you not. One way or the other, they made it known they were pissed off that they were physically unqualified to soldier for their country. So we gave them this chance. Good men. Smart. Loyal. Deaf as can be working in this soundproofed lair. They can lip-read, but can't hear what's being taped on the systems they monitor twenty-four hours a day. They don't know who or what makes the needles jump. Impossible for them to put their ear on the op."

Jud led Holloway into a room filled with enough neatly shelved reels of tape to fill a dozen moving boxes.

"The White House is bugged," said Jud. "Nixon ordered us Secret Service badges to set up the system—voice-activated bugs in the Oval Office, his office in the Executive Building next door to the White House, his lodge at Camp David, some phones. But what Nixon doesn't know is that there are two *other* taping systems."

"You're telling me—"

"The real truth. Hard as it is to imagine, huh? One system bugging and taping private Presidential conversations shakes the shit out of you. But *three*?"

"If Nixon runs one," said Holloway, "and this one is ours, who's got number three?"

"The boys across the river."

"CIA."

"No: the strata of them matters," said Jud.

"Penzler?"

"I don't think he's wormed his way into that tight loop."

Dazed, Holloway followed Jud to the street. They walked a block. Two. Nathan wasn't aware of such details until the cold air chilled his lungs and he realized he still breathed. He cupped his hands to his face. "Why did you do this to me?"

"Because you needed me to. Because I'm gone. Our commanders have launched me into the great dark river, so you got no one watching your back. Because maybe you'll need this someday, someway. Because in our op, we're set up as throwaways if shit hits the fan. Because fuck them: they made us, so let's play."

Holloway stared at the long-haired soldier in the night.

"Hey," said Jud, "look at this: block behind us is 1600 Pennsylvania Avenue. You're damn near back where you started."

Jud leaned closer. "Only now you know where you *really* are."

Then he gave Nathan a ragged salute. Vanished into the darkness.

Leaving me, left me—

OK, I'm fuckin' lost in the nightjungle. Charlie's gonna kill me—Think! Don't panic! Escape and evasion. First rule STAY CALM. What was—Bird! Bat! Wings beat and Charlie's got no flying machines, just myth 'bout vampire bats. Chopper, my men, got off OK. "They" made my mission. "They" let young Marines die so I could measure their damn holes! In the course of greater events. "They made me executioner to their bureaucratic clean hands. Judge and jury and I let them! Concentrate, focus: Marines'll be back! They'll come get me! If Charlie knows, and sees I'm an officer, he won't make me kneel. Fuck them! I've

*got my .45! My M16 and six magazines left! Two gre-
nades, K-bar knife! I'll get them first! Leeches on my
thigh, let 'em eat, fuck 'em too! Two days' rations,
four canteens. They'll come get me in the morning! I
just have to make it through tonight! White Coat Doctor sorry your mother won't make it through the night/
are you in Little League/you'll have her with you
forever. Nightbird screams and I slip on a wet log.
Tumble but drop nothing and didn't lose anything.
Academy dress white graduation Father taking his salute and no tears/pissed off Marines don't cry, won't
help. Bowels on fire. They'll be back. Notheywon't.
Gotta do it myself, I can do it myself. Cherry pie on a
November trees morning/fucking trees every reach
won't let me/will hide me/hot, sticky, dress whites
smeared with napalm soot/cherry juice not mine promise not mine/rotting green jungle guck—were those
whispers? Scurrying? What is the sound of a cobra?
Bump into tree, just a tree, didn't make a bonk! They
couldn't hear—Behind! Thumb click to full auto, is—
scurrying Rats! Dozen rats running over my boots—
Run—Bounce off tree! Run—Don't panic! Floppy
hat's ripped off—by a branch—no a monkey—no,
gone, fuck it! Run! No—hide! The jungle is your
friend. The night is your friend. Love lasts forever.
Semper fi. OK, you're OK!*

The next afternoon, Holloway dead-dropped the report on
the Nixon crew, mobsters and Teamsters that showed Penzler
in the loop. Holloway added a coded message:

SUGGEST PROBLEM RE: Penzler MISSION PARAMETERS.

Then he went back to work—helping the NSC work
through the rejuvenated Paris peace process, spying for his
veiled commanders. And he waited.

CHAPTER 35

Quinn didn't want to believe what he heard.

"I'm telling you," said the federal narc in the courthouse cafeteria, "he sweated us out. Waited it through. Beat the monkey. Now it's March, and the warden won't keep Strait in admin lockdown anymore. I signed the original confine papers like you asked, but I've used up all my federal chits. If you sign as a D.C. cop—"

"Then N—somebody can track it was me who locked Strait down. No."

"He's probably told somebody anyway."

"He's too smart for that."

"Well, forget it then: in two days, smart guy is back in general population."

Visions of David Strait screaming through heroin withdrawal haunted Quinn as he walked from the courthouse to police headquarters. *What makes Nezneck worth fighting that monkey for in prison solitary?*

Quinn dropped by the desk of a friendly traffic sergeant.

"You been 'not around' for two weeks. Ain't we colleagues anymore?"

"Been working, Sarge." Working radicals who stole dynamite from a Maryland construction site. Working with Lorri, working it out, working it over, working so much what "it" was and what "working" was no longer seemed clear.

"That license plate you flagged picked up some parking tickets." The sergeant handed Quinn computer printouts— and a sly grin. "You know, if I didn't have only four months, six days and this shift left before my thirty, I might inform myself as to why you got the eye on that car."

"But we are who we are."

"Well, it's lucky this car owner always, um, clears his parking tickets, or he'd be of legitimate interest to this here police department."

"Yeah," said Quinn. "Lucky."

"Hey, you get your transfer to the Intelligence squad or you still doing that shit under the badge while TAC carries you on their books?"

"You're the sergeant, I'm just an ordinary law dog."

Laughter followed Quinn all the way down the hall to the elevator.

Jake the Jar, thought Quinn as he sat in his cruiser, staring at the reports of parking violations listed for Jake's car. Out and about. Where? Why?

The addresses on Jake's two parking tickets were around the corner from each other, one dated on one day, one the next. But the location made no sense: Connecticut Avenue, up from the K Street canyon of lawyers but not north enough for the stately homed Cleveland Park neighborhood where they lived with their first wives and golden retrievers. And *way* west of Fourteenth Street's hooker and porno stroll where Nezneck swung weight, even farther west still from Jake's clapboard, Capitol Hill ghetto rowhouse. Quinn pictured the block, but didn't believe the image.

Until he drove there.

"A hotel," he said, though no partner rode with him to hear. The Commodore, a sprawling beehive of ballrooms and meeting halls, a one-thousand-bedroom warren for tourists and out-of-town lobbyists, expense-account businessmen who knew how to order room service from escort services.

Quinn traded his windbreaker for the black leather blazer he kept bagged in the trunk, along with a button-down blue shirt and a black tie that was years away from the proper fashion width.

The concierge's eyes over his half-moon glasses billboarded "You don't belong here" to the shaggy-bearded, déclassé leather-jacket-and-blue-jeans-clad freak as the hotel man's arctic voice said, "However can we help you . . . sir?"

The flash of Quinn's badge made the concierge frown.

Quinn laid a trio of surveillance photos of Jake the Jar on the desk.

"An individual such as this is not likely to be one of our guests."

"You mean because he's black."

"Absolutely not."

"Un-huh," said Quinn, wishing he'd brought Buck. "You mind if I ask around?"

"Do as you must, but may we suggest some discretion in waving your badge?"

"Hey, for *we*: anything."

Quinn struck out with the front desk, the bell captain, two doormen, the parking valet, the bartender, the barmaid (who offered her phone number, just in case), and the coffee shop hostesses.

Two times you were here, Jake, thought Quinn. Two tickets, two.

He went outside. Jake got one ticket for parking too near the mouth of the alley beside the hotel. Maybe this was the only place you could find to park. Must have pissed you off: you're no walker, and the front entrance is around the corner.

A loading dock jutted out from the hotel halfway down the alley.

Quinn vaulted onto the loading dock, banged on the locked double doors until a gray-haired black man in a custodian's uniform stepped outside to be badged and shown Jake's photos.

"The hotshit at the conceirge's desk said you might know this guy."

"What's it to you?"

"Mister, please: all I want is to do my job."

"Guess you just a regular-sized man after all. Not like that guy. Only thing fatter than his gut was his damn head. But he was sweatin' so much, I figure he's one of those puffed-up guys who's afraid he really ain't as big as he fronts out."

"What did this guy want?"

"To be sure I know how to fetch and carry stuff to the

Coolidge banquet room for the big event, that party night for the Advancement League."

"Who the hell are they?"

"Some charity group. That guy was bringing in boxes and stuff for a wingding fund-raiser. Stuff he says only he gets to set up. Fine by me and my crew; we'll dolly it in, let him sweat the rest. They gonna have a fine old time. If you plan on going," said the old man, nodding at Quinn's wardrobe, "this ain't the kind of black tie they mean."

"And if you see this guy or his pals, they don't need to know we talked."

"Neither does any damn court or my Mr. Peepers out front."

"Deal. One more thing: When is this wingding?"

"When else: after dark, April Fools'."

CHAPTER 36

Carpenters nailed a plywood cover over the sloping floor and chairs of the Senate auditorium, building a hollow-floored cave of partitioned cubicles. Vaughn sat inside a Magic-Markered black square on the plywood floor of the staff offices for the Senate Select Committee on Presidential Campaign Activities—turf the new committee's Chief Counsel and Staff Director Sam Dash had taken *weeks* to negotiate out of a foot-dragging Senate. Paint and sawdust scented every breath as Vaughn opened a box of documents labeled "Arrest Reports" while he waited for the green plastic walls of his partition to arrive, for his phone to be hooked up, for a desk and chair.

I'm here, he thought. I'm really here.

Above the hammering, Vaughn heard her call out: "Swell digs."

Dane walked toward him through the swirl of construction dust, a cardboard tray of wrapped sandwiches and Cokes from the Senate cafeteria in her hands.

"Maybe someday I'll actually have a chair to offer you when you come to visit." Vaughn pushed a box over for her to sit on, took the tray as he realized he hadn't stopped for lunch.

"I don't have to depend on your hospitality to come here," she said. "Remember how Gus ordered me to ride herd on the Library of Congress's computerization? Dash got the Library to put together a computer system to process all the dirt you hotshots are going to dig up. It'll be the first time a congressional operation uses a computer. And Gus convinced the powers that be that I'm a natural 'expert' to help coordinate that whole historic operation."

"Does that mean you're still my boss?"

"Well, that hasn't changed."

He raised his middle finger at her.

"Not now, we're working." She smiled. "Call us colleagues. Check this out."

She showed him a stiffly new black leather wallet-like folder that opened to reveal her laminated I.D. picture as a member of the Senate Select Committee.

"That's cool! Regular staff ID's look like driver's licenses. This looks like we're cops!"

"Don't get carried away," she said. "Or you'll get carried away."

By the following Friday, they both were working ten-hour days. Vaughn's desk had been delivered and the green walls of his cubicle were in place, but he still had boxes instead of file cabinets. He'd just set his breakfast cup of coffee and cafeteria-line chocolate doughnut on the only paper-free section of his desk when one of the committee lawyers hurried into his cubicle: "Hey, Conner: you got a car? Judge Sirica asked our boss to be in court when he sentences the burglars and we need a driver."

Vaughn's new ID let him stand against the crowd pressed shoulder to shoulder in Judge Sirica's courtroom. Dash and senior committee staffers sat near the front of the courtroom.

But at least I'm here, thought Vaughn.

Before imposing sentence on the found-guilty Watergate defendants, Sirica announced that defendant James McCord had given a letter to the judge in chambers.

Next to Vaughn stood a balding man with a "U.S. Attorney" ID clipped to his lapel; that prosecutor muttered, "What the hell is this?"

Judge Sirica asked his clerk to unseal the envelope containing the letter and hand it to him.

Sirica read ex-CIA exec McCord's letter: "Political pressure had been applied to the defendants to plead guilty and stay silent . . . Perjury occurred during the trial about the burglars' intent and motivations . . . Other people had been involved in the Watergate operation who had not yet been identified when they could have been by those who'd testified . . . The Watergate operation was not a CIA operation, though the Cubans may have been 'misled' by others into thinking it was."

A drone of voices filled the courtroom.

Sirica gaveled a recess.

When Sirica gaveled back into session, he postponed McCord's sentencing, pending hearing his testimony about the matters raised in the letter under oath, then hit the other defendants, especially the defiant Liddy, with heavy fines and prison terms, and urged them to cooperate with the grand jury and the Senate Select Committee.

As the judge banged his gavel for the last time, Vaughn whispered: "Yes!"

THAT NIGHT THE reporter sitting in Quinn's car stared at the horizon at the end of the city street as it turned from black to gray. He rubbed his eyes. "I don't know if I remember how to sleep."

"Me either," said Quinn.

"Do you believe McCord? What his letter said in court?"

"What, you taking a poll?"

"I'm talking to everybody who might know anything. Since we first started back in that bar, you wouldn't believe who I've talked to."

"Did you tell them about me?"

"They wouldn't have wanted to know." The journalist shook his head. "No."

An empty city bus rumbled past them.

"Do you believe him?" asked the reporter.

"Beyond me. But I was right about the CIA not being involved. About it being more than a burglary. Right to tell you to forget that petty-crime burglary stuff." Quinn said, "Do you think they get it yet? The Senate people? The FBI and prosecutors?"

"They have to, all the shit . . . Do you think now people will finally start reading our stories?"

"Sure. Maybe believing them, too."

The reporter's head bobbed, too tired to stop.

"You're doing the important thing," said Quinn. "Keeping the story straight. Defining it. Keeping it focused and headed out and onward, not stalled on the stupid burglary."

"Yeah. Sure." The reporter slumped until his head rested on the back of the car seat. He rolled his face until his eyes saw the cop he'd called. "You, your people, FBI friends: Can you tell me anything? Give me something new that I can use?"

"I'll keep an eye on it like it was my case. Make sure it keeps going the right way."

The reporter stared at him. After a moment, he grabbed the car door handle.

"Hey," said Quinn. "Good luck. I'll help you all I can."

CHAPTER 37

April Fools' night, 1973.

The tuxedo Quinn wore came from the police department's unclaimed-property room and fit him like a grocery sack. He'd vouchered its "duty use" in the hope that such a tangential "documentation" could provide evidence that he'd done whatever he would do as official business. He knew that such an obscure papering of his trail would not alert his bosses to his intentions.

What are my intentions? he wondered as he spun through the Commodore Hotel's revolving doors. The doorman stared at the bearded, long-haired freak in the bulky tuxedo; so did a tourist from Maine, at whom Quinn winked and said, "It's OK, I'm a rock star."

Quinn left the tourist staring in his wake.

Quinn joined a flock of other penguin-suited men who all feigned to know one another—by obvious substance if nothing else. They joked and called out greetings as they rode the escalator up to the banquet rooms. One or two of them nodded at him, smiled.

You wear the suit, you're part of the flock. But his fellow penguins' glances at Quinn's baggy tux and bearded shag told him that at best they thought him a distant, eccentric cousin.

Penguins streamed toward the Coolidge ballroom. Quinn spotted two tuxedoed gatekeepers seated behind a table at the Coolidge entrance checking names and taking handouts of green cash: *Guess you need more than just cash and a penguin suit to get in.*

He followed the red carpet past other Presidentially named meeting rooms to the exit, through those double doors to the

stairwell. A swinging door off to his right read HOTEL STAFF
ONLY. He pushed through it to an aluminum-bright cavern
of waiters with trays and rolling tables.

"What do you want?" snapped a fat waiter, a platter of
canapés balanced on one hand.

Quinn badged him. "To follow you."

Five minutes later, Quinn stood against the back wall of
the Coolidge ballroom. Perhaps two hundred men in tuxedos
milled about laughing and backslapping as they made their
way from spinning roulette wheels to card-snapping blackjack tables to clattering dice tables. Off in one corner waited
five round tables where men played poker with stacks of
clinking red, white and blue chips. Women merely dotted the
black-suited room: as pixie-dress, black-mesh-stockinged,
cleavage-prominent cocktail waitresses, as bow-tied blackjack dealers; they were accouterments, servants, decor in that
cacophonous atmosphere of marbled checkerboard floor,
green-clothed tables, testosterone, sweat and booze, cigar
smoke and the static tingle, the preening electric tingle of
money.

The Advancement League, thought Quinn. Tonight, you're
a casino.

One plump penguin twenty yards away was a lawyer who
Quinn had seen in the courthouse. Quinn spotted an aging
hero of the Washington Redskins surrounded by big-bucks
men who'd boo him when he faltered on any given Sunday,
who'd claim athletic insight for every yard of his success,
who'd brag that they knew him. Quinn counted zero Asian
or Hispanic and exactly five black faces among the penguins,
five who'd made it here with the downtown boys. Quinn
wasn't sure which shocked him more: that only five blacks
had cracked their way into this moneyed elite, or that the
moneyed elite had been cracked only five years after the
King riots.

An old man reeking of scotch stumbled into Quinn, recovered, said, "Don' worry 'bout it. After all, 's why we're
here. Rub some elbows, slap some backs. Am I or right or
am I right?"

"One or the other."

Internal Affairs Lieutenant Cleve Godsick stood fifty feet away in the crowd, a monstrous mutant penguin with hooded eyes, his pinky ring glistening on the fist crushing a highball glass.

" 'Course, w' tell the missus 'bout the charity bucks. Let 'em know what a . . . a sacrifice all this is. Hell, they don't care if we don't come home anyway. As long as they get to keep it." The old man drained his glass. "Women. When I's your age, I had that all figured out."

"You're ahead of me." Quinn slid behind the old man to screen himself from Godsick.

The old man mumbled something Quinn couldn't have understood even if he'd been paying attention as Godsick drifted toward a bar across the room. Quinn slid the other way through the crowd, keeping taller men between him and the Internal Affairs lieutenant Nezneck owned.

The crowd parted—Mel Klise, smiling, laughing, introducing two men to each other.

Work it, Mel, arrange—Quinn blinked. Saw Joseph R. Nezneck. "Possum." Penguin-suited. Thinning black hair brushed flat and polished to perfection. Pall Mall smoking in one thick-fingered hand.

Quinn ducked behind a waiter. Lost a minute knifing through the crowd, finding a pay phone near the men's room. Gary Harmon was home to answer Quinn's call.

"The Bureau's organized-crime gambling squad!" Quinn whispered into the phone. "I'm a law enforcement officer who's uncovered and on the scene of a huge gambling operation in progress at the Commodore! That's probable cause up the ass!"

"You know how long it takes to organize a raid?"

"This is no April Fools'. If you can roll out your FBI, we can hang a collar on Nezneck and Godsick and even Mr. Arranger Mel, and that one collar will give us a peg to hang—"

"Hang up! I need the ph—"

Quinn slammed the receiver in the hook. And smiled. His watch said 9:23.

Ten o'clock. Quinn stood against a wall by a potted palm, where he could hide from Godsick or Mel or Nezneck's roaming eyes. Quinn's heart clutched every time he lost track of one of those men. He'd nod, joke, make small talk, all the while scanning through the acrid smoke.

Godsick hung near the bar at the opposite end of the room. The IAD lieutenant glared at the wall behind the liquor bottles; talked to no one; every so often swept the room with his hooded eyes and made Quinn slide behind the palm tree or some conveniently nearby penguin.

Laughter roared. A fresh cloud of cigar smoke burned Quinn's eyes and throat.

Mel never seemed to stop talking, shaking hands, bringing this penguin together with that one, sometimes even pulling men away from a craps table or a fan of blackjack.

Roulette wheels spun. Dice clattered on craps tables.

Nezneck moved like a lion in the crowd of penguins. He talked to a few revelers, let some shake his paw, played blackjack, put chips on roulette bets and walked away with a bigger stack. Quinn watched him crumple an empty cigarette pack, drop it to the floor and walk on without a second glance.

Twenty-two minutes after ten o'clock: Quinn saw Mel Klise wave good-bye to a cluster of friends and skip out the door to go home to his Mimi.

Come on! Hurry up! People are starting to leave! Lost Mel, he's home free and . . . and . . .

Godsick shook himself free from the bar, buttoned his tuxedo jacket over the Magnum holstered on his belt, marched toward the men's room.

Nezneck, standing alone by the craps tables.

Checking his watch, he's checking his watch! Heading toward the door to leave!

Quinn shoved his way between two wobbly penguins, elbowed through the crowd, Nezneck's thinning hair locked in his vision. Nezneck gestured recognition to someone, lumbered past the last craps table between him and the door.

"Hey, Possum!" yelled Quinn, scooping the thrown dice off the craps table as three startled players and the croupier watched.

Nezneck turned—eyes widening as he saw Quinn, saw two white cubes flying toward him. Nezneck dropped his smoking cigarette, caught the dice before they hit his heart.

"Thought I'd check out the action tonight," said Quinn. "See how to 'advance' my league."

The croupier stepped near, coughed. "Ah, gentlemen, we're in the middle of a game."

Quinn smiled. "You remember me, Possum. Please don't say you've gone senile."

"Well, I'll be damned. Quinn: bullshit walking and bullshit talking." Nezneck kept the dice in his hand and his eyes locked on Quinn. He fished chips out of his tuxedo pocket for the croupier. "Here, this'll cover the play. Close the table."

"Sir, I don't know if I, if we, can do—"

Nezneck pressed a bill from his pocket into the croupier's hand. "You don't need to know how to do nothing but walk away."

Quinn heard the croupier argue with the customers, usher them away to other diversions, but his gaze never left the black holes of Nezneck's eyes.

The dice shook in Nezneck's fist.

"So . . . Johnny boy: How's your mom back in Ohio? How's your tasty flygirl?"

"*You*—They aren't here tonight. Or in this. Ever."

"But I'd bet they'd love to play."

"You mess with them, even if you put me down, my guys won't stop."

"Ever wonder why you haven't had an accident . . . *yet*?" The dice shook in Possum's paw. "You're not so careful or so cool you can't take a fall. Figure it's because I don't care about sacks of bullshit like you."

"Such a big shot, huh, Possum?"

"I'm any shot I want to take." Nezneck shook the dice,

stepped to the craps table, the rattle of bones in his fist. Quinn moved with him, two dancers who didn't touch facing each other from opposite sides of a green felt table. "So you want to fade my action? Last time, you crapped out."

"New time, new game."

"Well, hell, I got the fuckin' dice. But forget about craps, we're down for snake eyes."

"Sure."

"You don't even fuckin' know what you've stepped up to. Said yes to. Never a smart play. It's OK, trust me, I'll bring you along."

"You can try."

"Two of us. Two is the hardest point. The lonely point. Shooter who rolls the deuce, hits snake eyes, loses."

"Who wins?"

"The guy who's still in the game. Which'd be me." Nezneck threw the dice: three and four.

"Should have played craps," said Quinn. "You'd have won one."

"I win 'em all. Only us in this game here, cop. All those other smart people in this place who look over here, what they think they see isn't what's happening. They think they see us playing craps, but we're shooting snake eyes. What's the matter? Can't you even pick up the dice?"

Quinn threw the bones: two and six.

Nezneck shook the dice. "You didn't even ask the stakes. Do you wonder what you'll lose?"

He threw two fives.

Quinn scooped up the dice.

"How'd a guy so dumb as you ever get to be a cop anyway? How do you think that happened—huh, Cleve?"

Quinn whirled. Lieutenant Godsick stood just out of striking distance, his jacket unbuttoned. His face was flushed, his hooded eyes boiling with blood.

"Other people make mistakes," rumbled Godsick.

The dice shook in Quinn's hands. He kept them shaking.

"Other people make mistakes," said Nezneck. "Ain't that the fuckin' truth. Other people like you, Quinn. You're a gambler not a player. You gotta know when to pick up the dice. You gotta control your shake, rattle and roll. You don't *know* the odds: *set* the odds. Cut the right people in. Cut the others cold. Let the suckers make their move and help 'em the whole way, and always, always fuckin' collect. But you don't play gamble. You become the action. You run the game. Throw the damn dice."

"When I'm ready."

Nezneck shook a Pall Mall from a pack to his lips, flicked it to fire with his gold lighter. "You're gonna be buried still gettin' ready."

Godsick laughed.

Quinn threw: three and five.

"Eight and late." The cigarette bobbed in Nezneck's lips. "Too late for you, Quinn. Unless you came here to turn smart all of a sudden. You gonna do that?"

The dice bounced off the table wall: six and six.

"Boxcars," said Nezneck. "You gonna be smart? Or you gonna be one of those suckers who we ship out in boxcars?"

Quinn took the dice and felt them rattle in his closed fist.

"You got asked a question," snapped Lieutenant Godsick. "You gonna be smart or fucked?"

On the edge of his vision, Quinn saw the double doors to the staff service area swing open. From behind him came a rising murmur of voices.

"I didn't come here to answer your questions," said Quinn as someone behind him yelled. "I didn't come here to play. These are my dice now, Possum. I came here to nail you to a wall."

"FBI!" came the shout from the door behind Quinn. "This is a raid! Stand clear of the tables! Hands at your sides!"

A roar from the crowd drowned out the commanding agent and all words except the guttural bellow from Lieutenant Cleve Godsick, who charged toward the front door through the crowd of panicked penguins, shouting, "What the hell are you doing? This is covered! Don't you know who I am?"

Nezneck raised his cigarette to his lips, his eyes locked on the cop shaking, still shaking the dice. Nezneck exhaled a cloud of smoke, strolled over to join the crowd of other citizens being herded into processing lines by the feds.

Shaking the dice. Quinn folded his badge from the tuxedo handkerchief pocket, scanned for Gary Harmon in the squad of G-men. Tossed the dice onto the table without looking, heard them hit and roll and stop in could-have-been-snake-eyes, walked away and ordered himself, forced himself to obey: *Don't look back.*

CHAPTER 38

The Senate Watergate cave became a maze of green cubicles assigned to attorneys, investigators, research assistants, and secretaries. Vaughn Conner was the lowest investigator, bounced from one project to another, including the "nut" file, citizens' suggestions that poured into the Select Committee—everything from depositions swearing Nixon had been set up by a Mormon Church plot to newspaper photos of Watergate conspirator/ex-CIA agent E. Howard Hunt taped beside photos of the three tramps arrested by Dallas police after JFK's assassination.

On Monday, April 9, Vaughn paged through *The Washington Post* to find that Lou Russell, a former congressional investigator, had been hired by Watergate burglar McCord's post-Watergate private security firm.

Where does that stop being odd? thought Vaughn. He clipped the story, photocopied it and made sure that nugget of information made it onto the McCord satellite chart—a graphic system that staff used to follow who was connected to whom. The original he stuck in his "W'gate" file that he'd brought down from Senator Martin's shop.

If I come up with something that's hot, they'll have to let me run with it. End up somewhere besides the bottom rung of the staff ladder . . . Don't think that way. Work. But he smiled.

QUINN STALKED THE courthouse for three cool April mornings before he "accidentally" ran into Max on the way to a show-cause hearing in a routine homicide.

"What are you doing here?" asked the balding prosecutor.

"You know cops," said Quinn, "we spend years hanging around the courthouse."

"Yeah, and then you fail to show for testimony when we need you."

"It's too nice a day to beef." Quinn steered his friend to a deserted alcove entrance of an unused courtroom. "So what's going on with the Watergate grand jury?"

"Why do you care? You stuck me prosecuting gamblers, so . . ."

"Come on: I didn't get the Watergate case, you didn't get the case, we both want a piece of it, it's history. I'd tell you if I had anything."

"This isn't junior high." Max sighed. Shook his head. "You wouldn't believe who's dancing with our guys! They can't even work it in the office!"

"So where and how is who doing what?"

"Come on, man, back off: That's all I can tell you!"

"I'm just curious. Like you."

"Yeah, well, I might go home to my empty bed every night wondering what's going on while I'm trying to sleep, but I know enough not to open my mouth during the day."

While I'm trying to sleep. Quinn randomly picked one of the three Watergate prosecutors to shadow after hours. On the third night, parked up the street from the prosecutor's townhouse, he fought to stay awake as the clock ticked toward midnight.

Go home. Lorri's right. Nothing you can do here now. The pace's killing you.

Headlights filled Quinn's rearview mirror. The growl of a sports car engine drew closer, drove past where he'd slumped below the steering wheel. Quinn watched a brown Porsche nose into a parking space. The German engine died. From the other direction, a second car drove up and parked alongside the Porsche.

Car doors opened. Two men stepped out of their rides. Doors *ca-thunked* shut. Those men walked to the prosecutor's front door.

The prosecutor's door swung open before his visitors needed to ring the bell. Light from inside the house spilled out to the midnight visitors. Quinn couldn't put a name to one man, but the other, the handsome blond driver of the Porsche . . .

Motherfuck! thought Quinn as the men he watched went inside and closed the door. With all that guy knows about Phil Bailley's bust for call girls, about intel operations, the FBI investigation . . . If he's looking to jump ship, I'll need every friend I can get. And someone I can work for intel. Someone who could back-channel for me if . . . Think: not the reporter from the bar—got him already. And not the one with gray hair. Go to the wild one, the one who doesn't sleep.

Quinn drove away with his headlights dark. At Dupont Circle, he found a pay phone.

The man's voice shouted in the phone: "Yeah? Yeah? Who is this? What do you—"

"You recognize my voice?" said Quinn.

"Shit, you, yeah, sure. This hour, what do you want?"

"Nixon's White House lawyer John Dean's secretly meeting with the Watergate prosecutors. Now. Right fucking now."

Quinn hung up. Went home to not sleep.

APRIL CREPT TOWARD May.

"Every day, you pick up the newspaper, and it's something else," Vaughn told Dane.

"Just be glad the news cycles give us breathing room," she replied. "Between the morning papers hitting our doorstep and the TV evening news, we have time to absorb what we find out ourselves. Even if a wire service radio story breaks, it's not real until it comes out in the *Times* or *Post* the next day."

"Hell, I've absorbed amazing realities," said Vaughn. "Liddy ran a secret tough-guy program called Gemstone and burglarized the psychiatrist of the Pentagon Papers leaker. Dirty money trails crisscross everywhere. Weird characters keep popping up, like the ex–New York Red Squad cop who carried a beer vendor's coin dispenser on his belt so he could make pay phone calls when he was passing out laundered cash. I've absorbed all that, but what are we really seeing?"

"America in action," answered Dane.

On April's last night, she, Vaughn and the rest of the Senate committee staff gathered around the TV to watch Nixon address the country:

"Today," said the President, "in one of the most difficult decisions of my presidency, I accepted the resignations of two of my closest associates in the White House, Bob Haldeman and John Ehrlichman, two of the finest public servants it has been my privilege to know. The counsel to the President, John Dean, has also resigned . . . We must maintain the integrity of the White House, and the integrity must be real, not transparent. There can be no whitewash at the White House."

The TV program ended—to groans and to cheers among the partisan staff.

"That's it," Dane told Vaughn, "it's all over but the sound and the fury."

"What? You're crazy!"

"Right there in public, in Hometown, America's living room, he sadly, bravely tossed two pounds of flesh to us political junkyard dogs. And Dean! Didn't you like the way he separated him from the others, cast him out like a Judas? Americans might lynch a murderer, but they loathe a Judas rat fink. Everything will swirl and settle around those three musketeers, maybe Mitchell, too, but Nixon capped it, took the bold step, made himself the victim and the sacrificing, heroic leader. If we nail some bad guys, he might get bruised, but only because the great American 'they' will think he's been fighting the good fight."

"You can't be serious!"

"It's not a question of being serious." Her smile was sad. "It's facing reality."

"Reality is for people who can't handle drugs." He shrank from her angry glare, went for redemption with "Reality is just what we've got the guts to do."

"Yeah," said Dane. "And people in Washington are renowned for their courage."

May swelled toward June. Reporters and TV camera crews hung around the guard's post in the corridor outside the cave. Men who'd been shielded inside White House bunkers of "executive privilege" and "lawyer-client confidentiality" and "national security" came now one by one to march through gauntlets of shouting journalists, white-shirted Capitol cops, the curious and the crazies in the Senate halls to be interviewed by staff investigators. The once untouchables came like a drumbeat, a cadence: Haldeman, Ehrlichman, Dean, McCord, Magruder, Moore. Theirs was a chorus of denials, deals, nonremembrances, evasions and explanations, counteraccusations and confessions. The cast varied but played similar acts downtown in the secret grand jury.

Dane had all but officially moved in with Vaughn. Her apartment was a twenty-minute drive from work at the best of times; his apartment was a nine-minute walk, and they could fumble into their clothes on the way. Even before Nixon purged Haldeman, Ehrlichman and Dean, exhaustion muted the passion between Dane and Vaughn, who thought: We didn't even get to the just-routine-sex phase before we sank into Watergate. As the heat of summer built toward public hearings, and scandals spider-webbing out from the defeated burglary became more numerous than the sum of his digits, Vaughn comforted himself with the memory of one dawn when Dane scared the hell out of him as she pulled back the plastic curtain of his shower. Steaming water pounded down on them. She held onto the towel rail while he slammed again and again against her hips, a nostalgic, hopeful coupling that they washed away without a single word.

On May 3, Vaughn's eyes drifted from *The Washington Post*'s comics page sarcasm of "Doonesbury," heroism of "The Phantom," and sophistry of "Peanuts" to a story reporting that Nixon crony and former White House aide Murray Chotiner was the key man in the White House for getting Jimmy Hoffa out of jail.

Vaughn blinked; blinked again. *Should have gotten two Styrofoam cups of coffee from the cafeteria.* He stuck the Chotiner story in his private "W'gate" file, but forgot to ink Chotiner's name onto his personal satellite chart, an artistry that would have linked mob lawyer and dairy-fund/price-support-scandal Chotiner to Hoffa to the American Association for Justice to a guy named Joe Nezneck and to a smiling gnome called Mel Klise.

The next Monday, as Vaughn zigzagged through the maze of cubicles toward his desk, a white-haired Republican staffer all the Democrats privately called Frosty pulled him close.

"You might be the savviest guy on your whole damn side of the cave," said Frosty, smugness lighting his face beneath his snowy hair.

"Then the world's in deep trouble," said Vaughn.

"You had them put Lou Russell up on the satellite chart, right? Well, now you're gonna see, all you guys are gonna see. Hasn't been easy for us, right? The poor President and the men downtown, we're kind of like their defense lawyers, and they haven't always—they can't be easy clients. They got jobs to do and a whole mess of shit from lefties like—"

"Me?"

"Nothing personal, you're entitled to whacky beliefs, long as they don't contradict America, right? And that's where you acting so smart just might make you smarter than you think."

"Ah, OK, but I have to get back to earth, now, so . . ."

"You linked Lou Russell to McCord. I always wondered

about that McCord, him and his letter to the judge. Old-hand CIA guy like he was, why didn't he keep his honor up and his mouth shut like the rest of the good soldiers."

"Good soldiers?" Vaughn shook his head.

"Russell used to be a damn good man,. too. Ex-FBI. Fought the good fight over on the House Un-American Activities Committee. We got a guy, another private eye, John Wolf Leon—"

"*Wolf?* There's really a private eye named Wolf and he's not in the comics?"

"Like I could make this up, right? If I didn't trust you, if you hadn't shown you can look at the forest and see the trees that might really be bent, I wouldn't be telling you all this."

"Thanks—I guess. But what are you telling me?"

"Word I'm getting via the Wolf and others is that Russell knows the bones about what really was going on in this town and the . . . the context of this Watergate mess, so us guys're gonna drop a subpoena on his ass."

"Ah . . . great."

"You'll say great. Believe me, you'll say great!" Then he flashed the two-fingered V peace sign spawned by the Vietnam War; Frosty's smile implied he thought he'd used one finger too many.

THE REPORTER FROM the bar called Quinn at home that night. "What do you know about a guy named Lou Russell? Maybe tied in with McCord and the bugging?"

As she unpacked her flight bag in the bedroom she shared with Quinn, Lorri saw him snap to rigid attention and press the phone to his ear; heard him say, "Nothing."

Whatever you're talking about, she thought, you just told somebody a lie.

"He's an ex-badge type who lives in D.C.," said the reporter. "My sources say the Senate Watergate Republicans just subpoenaed him."

"Wh-why? What about?" asked Quinn, but he thought about how Russell was a teddy bear for call girls and other women in trouble, whether he'd told a stewardess that he knew something about bugging and covert filming of Lorri fucking and Heidi and Nezneck and what happened to the hard-evidence call girl picture book at the DNC . . .

"Damned if I know," the reporter told his source. "Before I doorstep him, I—"

"Want me to find out if he's worth anything. Ask my badge buddies about him."

"That'd be great! I'm so swamped I can't afford to run down blind alleys to nowhere."

"Don't worry. I'll help you out on this one."

Quinn hung up.

Lorri slumped onto the bed, heart thumping, waiting for him to say their lives were over.

"But they haven't got us, not yet" is what he claimed.

"It just doesn't stop! Won't stop!"

"After what we've done, neither can we" was all he told her, not even saying good-bye as he trudged out of there, not daring to answer her whispered, "What are we going to do?"

Quinn huddled in his car parked across the street from the address he'd scored for Lou Russell. A light shone in the window of the apartment registered to him, to the target.

You're home. Ex-FBI. Ex-congressional communist hunter. Private eye. McCord employee. Do you remember Lorri? When she came to you after Phil Bailley got busted? When you told her there might be films? What do you have up there in your lighted room? In your ex-cop's head? Who and what can your testimony put on the firing line?

Quinn unscrewed the dome light in his car. Near midnight. Deserted street. Most of the windows in the homes are dark.

But not his, thought Quinn, thought Q.

The DNC's hooker picture book is gone. Nobody's mentioned a fourth cop busting the Watergate burglars or proved the September bug didn't come from those bad guys. No linkages to me. To Lorri. Nezneck and Heidi and Penzler—they're still hidden, still stand-off/status quo with me. I abused police power. Falsified reports—like perjury. Broke-and-entered the Watergate DNC twice. Obstructed justice by stealing evidence and planting false evidence. Knowingly consorted and cohabitated with a . . . a woman who might be and thus—because of my law enforcement official status— is a criminal suspect in possible federal tax fraud, illegal wiretapping, felonious prostitution and blackmail.

And the lighted window to all that is an ex-cop named Lou Russell, who might be innocent and ignorant of everything in this guilty world, who might know sins and horrors unimaginable, who might remember Lorri and loose the scandal hounds to start turning over every rock and following every trail and finding and . . .

Lou Ru—Don't give him a name.

Target. How much does he know? What does he have? Who can he hurt?

Us.

Q got out of the car, eased the door shut. The night was cool. He wore an Army fatigue shirt unbuttoned over his sweat-soaked pullover. He'd liberated the Luger stuck in his waistband from a Weatherman who'd boasted about "gonna glide up behind him with a smile and, man, execute some fucking pig cop" and whom Q couldn't bust without blowing his cover.

He crossed the street. Saw no one see him. Felt no real eyes. Put his hand on the top of the target's apartment building black iron-fence gate, memorized that spot so later he could—

All the burning night flew away and left him caught with his hand on that gate. The iron scorched his hand and he jerked away.

I'm not this far gone. Can't be. Won't be.

Quinn got in his car and drove away. Threw the Luger into the Potomac.

From a pay phone outside a closed drugstore he called the reporter. "Forget about Lou Russell. He's a nobody nobody will care about. The Senate guys must just be shooting blind."

Then he hung up and drove home to Lorri in that dark city.

*   *   *

DAYS LATER, FROSTY pulled Vaughn from the line in the Senate cafeteria.

"Look," he whispered, "that stuff I told you about Lou Russell, you didn't take it anywhere, did you?"

"You know, I've been kind of busy, and I don't think it even came up. Why?"

"Good—I mean—OK, I . . ." Frosty dropped his voice again. "Well, Lou, he, he might be more of a problem witness than I—we—thought. We subpoenaed his entire ass, but he wrote us back, said he can't be any help, he doesn't have diaries or log books or even a bank account."

"Sounds weird."

"Maybe, but do me a favor, right? Don't link him to me. It was you who got his name up there; anything else anybody did, why, they could be just doing their job."

"Don't worry, Frosty, we all got our problems."

The Republican staffer nodded, let Vaughn go. The long-haired kid was three steps gone when the Republican muttered, "*Frosty?*"

At 10 A.M. on Thursday, May 17, in the Senate Caucus room, Senator Sam Ervin hit his gavel on the dais before a packed audience, and in his thick Southern drawl announced, "Today, the Select Committee on Presidential Campaign Activities begins hearings into the extent to which illegal and improper or unethical activities were involved in the 1972 Presidential election campaign."

Hot lights and television cameras recorded that and every other day, though most stations across the country featured their regular programming of quiz shows and soap operas. Select Committee staffers crowded into the hearing room to watch Ervin open the public show of their work, then trudged back downstairs to the long hours of cave-dwelling wars that had to be fought even as the hearings were unfolding. Dane stood next to Vaughn; under her arm, she carried that morning's *New York Times*. Page 1 trumpeted that Henry Kissinger had asked the FBI to wiretap his National Security

Council aides and that the head of the Securities and Exchange Commission had resigned amid allegations that he'd covered up a $200,000 contribution to CREEP from Robert Vesco, the fugitive financier who was on the run from an ever-expanding list of criminal investigations, including the business of heroin.

Hearing Day One meant opening statements read into the record by the seven senators, then "foundation" witnesses: an administrator from CREEP, an assistant to the President— and the policemen who officially arrested the Watergate burglars.

Quinn watched every televised instant of his fellow officers' Senate appearances, his heart slamming against his ribs with each word spoken.

Sergeant Leeper testified first.

Then Barrett.

Neither cop revealed that a ghost named Quinn had been swept up in their adventure.

Before the last of the arresting officers' testimony, the chairman gaveled a recess until the next day. To Quinn, the chairman's gavel sounded like a hammer pounding nails in his coffin.

The next morning Quinn sat in a police station's locker room, transfixed by the TV set. On Capitol Hill, his fellow D.C. badge Shoffler sat at the witness table, stared into the cameras—

And like Leeper and Barrett, told the world the truth and nothing about a fourth cop.

Thank you! whispered Quinn in his heart. You did your job and still kept faith with me. Told the truth and kept me safe from it out of pure honor.

"Yeah," said the lieutenant who stood beside Quinn as they watched the hearings playing on the TV in the locker room, "I'm relieved, too. Our boys did great, and even those blowhard politicians can't muck that up."

The lieutenant frowned. "You look like shit. Go home, get some rest."

"Yes, sir," said Quinn, as on TV, a senator swore in burglar and court confessor/ex-CIA official James McCord to testify. "Yes sir."

In the cave, as McCord was finishing his testimony on the television, Frosty hurried into Vaughn's cubicle, whispering, "Lou Russell just had a heart attack! He isn't dead, but lucky break, right? After all, now you're off the hook for the nothing you were gonna get from him, right?" Frosty put his finger to his lips, walked away.

That same day, Acting Attorney General Elliot Richardson appointed Harvard law professor Archibald Cox as the special prosecutor for Watergate.

"It's a damn shame," Max told Quinn as the exhausted cop bought him another beer in a bar after work. "Means us locals have been trumped by the feds. The crime done on our streets isn't our case anymore. And I never even got a piece of it!"

"Damn shame." Quinn sipped his beer.

"Means nobody cares anymore about the actual crime that started the whole mess that's now oozing out everywhere."

Quinn said, "Damn shame."

MAY NIGHTS NEVER seemed so dark. Vaughn and Dane would often not see each other all day. Once, when they were both too exhausted to sleep, she lay on his chest, said, "I'm glad you're in this with me, too. If there are two of us, we can't be insane."

He knew her well enough to ask, "What's wrong?"

"We got a warning passed back to us. Might have come from law enforcement, but I don't know how," she said. "The whole 'Dean team,' maybe all of us staffers, you and me: they're watching us. And maybe it's a thing where control has been lost. Where rules might not . . . Where they might try something extreme."

" 'They'? Who's 'they'?"

She held him. "Nixon's people, maybe. White House. Spooks. Whoever. Just *they*."

"Rock 'n' roll," said Vaughn. He felt Dane drop deeper

into herself as she lay in his arms. "What's the matter?"

"Nothing."

"You feel like there's something."

"It's just . . . rock 'n' roll. Life's more serious than a song."

"That's just the way I talk about it, keep things in perspective." He hesitated. "Are you pissed off at me?"

"OK, I said it's OK." Dane felt him frown. *Should kiss him but . . .* She squeezed his hand. "I'm just tired."

"Me, too."

They held each other tight. He fell asleep. She eased over to her side of the bed.

CHAPTER 39

All through the spring of 1973, Holloway dead-dropped coded pleas to his superiors: Confirm mission. Reply concerns re: Penzler. Recommend aborting mission due to potential compromise from escalating Watergate probes. Advise re: mission and multiple Watergate-related investigations. Request orders. Request contact. Request transfer.

The Marine's "real" job haunted him, too.

Kissinger and Nixon resumed bombing Cambodia to crush the communist insurgency there before America pulled out of South Vietnam. American B-52's and other bombers flew 22,900 sorties. Holloway read a secret CIA report that said the genocidal Marxist enemy Khmer Rouge turned the terror of the American bombing campaign into a successful recruiting tool.

One hot June '73 night Holloway couldn't fall asleep. Rather than disturb Sandy, he moved onto the living room couch, lost consciousness, only to be jarred awake in darkness by the thump of a newspaper outside his door. He put the coffee water on to boil. Wearing only boxer shorts, he opened his apartment door—

No newspaper.

What—Where the—Cut off, I'm cut off!

Newspapers lay in front of every apartment door in the long hall. Every door except his . . . and a door three apartments away.

The crack between that door and the carpet glowed: lights on inside the apartment. The doorknob turned in Holloway's grip. The door eased open—froze. The chain was on: urban paranoia victorious over careless sloth. Holloway heard a radio inside the apartment.

Holloway slammed his shoulder into the door. The chainlock screws burst out of the doorjamb. Holloway staggered into the apartment, pushed the door closed behind him.

The man standing near the kitchen table wore a softball shirt and cutoff sweatpants. He held a powdered sugar doughnut. His jaw hung open and eyes behind his glasses bugged out toward the damn near naked madman. Next to a steaming coffee cup on the table lay a *Washington Post*.

"Who the fuck are you! Get out of my kitchen!"

"You stole my paper!"

"The hell I did! I'm calling the cops! You can't—"

The doughnut man crashed against his kitchen wall, a steel vise gripping his throat. The monster's other hand slapped him.

"I can do anything I want! I killed better men than you'll ever be! You gonna tell me what to do? You gonna rip me off?"

"No, I—"

"You gonna call the cops! What you gonna tell them? Huh?"

The monster slapped him again.

"Oh shit, mister, I couldn't wait to find out the Mets score. I'm sorry. Don't, I won't, don't—"

The sound of a warm trickle hit the tile by their feet. Doughnut man sobbed. They both knew that even if he decided that someone would believe a bizarre story about a near naked intruder, now doughnut man would say nothing about this morning. Ever.

Holloway took the newspaper. Left.

In the hall, he heard his tea kettle scream, then stop.

Sandy opened his door. She wore one of his T-shirts, morning hair and a puzzled frown.

"I was getting the paper," he said.

"Like that?" she asked as he brushed past her to flip through the *Post*: Nothing. No envelope, no nothing.

"Yeah. Like this."

SPRING SWELTERED INTO the Watergate TV summer. One Saturday evening after they both got back from White House work, Sandy sat on his couch, drained the beer she held and told Nathan: "I keep thinking I've gotta get out of here. Go somewhere else."

Holloway blinked. "What?"

"Do you ever listen to me anymore, Nate?"

"I heard you, I just . . . I don't think that's a good idea."

" 'A good idea'? What the hell does that mean? Are you asking me to stay? Or are you giving me advice?"

"I don't want you to go."

"For weeks now, just being there is all I've gotten from you. You don't even fuck me like you're here anymore. You've fallen way back into your eyes."

"Sandy, all this shit that's going on, for both of us—"

"We don't need it. When I moved in, I thought it was worse for me, but now I wonder." She leaned toward him, *reached* toward him with a hopeful smile. "We can both go!"

"What?"

"Get of here! Quit our jobs! You don't want to quit the Marines, make them give you a transfer! Pentagon people owe me; I can help! I'd rather be missing you when you're serving on some battleship at sea then missing you sitting across from me!"

"I can't."

"Oh. Oh, yeah. I forgot. Duty. Honor. Always faithful."

"That means—"

"That means what you want it to mean! I still don't get why, you hating your old man—"

"Not hate."

"Whatever. Why'd you go academy and join the Marines?"

After a moment, he answered, "The dark horde."

"What? 'Dark'—that's a new one."

"It's always been there. I was raised on it. Not just because I'm a Navy brat. We all were. Our parents remember the dark horde that ambushed them, killed them. Nazis. Pearl Harbor. Stalin got the bomb, and now Mao, too. Communists: Hoover and the chamber of commerce warned they were everywhere. They were gonna rape you and put me behind barbed wire. Brainwash us. Unless we stand up to stop them and be willing to fight them. Kill them. Die. And do it right. Not to get bars on your shoulders or medals on your chest, but *right*. Do it right."

"Like you."

Nathan Holloway needed a minute to say, "I don't know."

"Let's just go!"

"No." As she leaned away from him, he grabbed her hands. "I can't. If you quit your job, you won't be in their way, but that's OK. There comes a time to retreat, and maybe this is it for you. But don't go away. Don't leave."

"Are you asking me to stay with you?"

"Yes."

"God, you look like that hurt more than getting shot!"

"I just never had something to lose as important as you before. Something out of my control. Something they could take."

"I'm not a thing. And the only one who can make me leave is you."

"Don't go."

She stared at him.

"It won't always be this crazy," he said. "It can't be."

Sandy sat motionless except for her eyes skimming this place where she found herself living. Nothing was new;

everything seemed alien; outside waited unknown fears.

"Please! Stay with me."

Her forehead sank to his shoulder and he wrapped his arms around her. Nathan felt the wetness of her cheek, and she didn't pull away.

The envelope came hidden in the next day's newspaper. Holloway decoded the message in his newspaper while Sandy showered:

> **TRANSFER DENIED. CONTINUE MISSION. CONTINUE**
> **PROTECT COVERT OPERATION. REMAIN ON ALERT.**
> **MAINTAIN/PROMOTE NSC/NATIONAL SECURITY STABILITY.**
> **COOPERATE AS CAN WITH PARALLEL OPERATIVES**
> **KNOWN TO YOU. HIGHEST SANCTION YOUR MISSION.**
> **ENCOURAGE/ALLOW EVENTS NOW IN MOTION TO EVOLVE.**

CHAPTER 40

The summer of '73 meant heat and humidity swallowing Washington, D.C. The summer of '73 meant the Oakland A's slugging their way to October's World Series to defeat New York's Mets, a fall classic whose splendor for sports fans was equaled only by the amazing football halfback O. J. Simpson, who set a new rushing mark. The summer of '73 meant *Gravity's Rainbow* by Thomas Pynchon came screaming across the sky and Pablo Picasso died. Coffins still flew home from Saigon, and televised Watergate hearings starred former Counsel to the President of the United States John Wesley Dean III.

Dean got a haircut for his performance. He traded his contact lenses for glasses and wore conservative suits and ties. As he sat at the witness table in front of the senators of the

Select Committee on Presidential Campaign Activities, behind him sat his beautiful blond wife.

Senator Ervin gaveled to order the packed Senate Russell Office Building on the morning of June 25, as the air conditioner in the cave blew with a gale force. Dane wore a stocking hat and mittens to keep from freezing while she watched Dean on TV and cursed staffers who'd forsaken work in the cave for the hearing room upstairs, where they could crowd in behind the seated senators, elbow in beside their necessary fellow aides, and be televised as part of the big show.

In a calm monotone, Dean gave a four-day confession.

"Watergate was an inevitable outgrowth of a climate of excessive concern over the political impact of demonstrators, excessive concern over leaks, an insatiable appetite for political intelligence, all coupled with a do-it-yourself White House staff, regardless of the law. However, the fact that many of the elements of this climate culminated with the creation of a covert intelligence operation as a part of the President's re-election committee was not by conscious designs, rather an accident of fate."

Dean told about a meeting with then Attorney General John Mitchell, CREEP official Jeb Stuart Magruder and G. Gordon Liddy: "Liddy said that the operations he had developed would be totally removed from the campaign and carried out by professionals. Plans called for mugging squads, kidnapping teams, prostitutes to compromise the opposition and electronic surveillance. He explained that the mugging squad could, for example, rough up demonstrations that were causing problems. The kidnapping teams could remove demonstration leaders and take them below the Mexican border. The prostitutes could be used at the Democratic convention to get information as well as compromise the persons involved. I recall Liddy saying that the girls would be high class and the best in the business."

In the cave, Vaughn sat at his desk. I wonder where exFBI agent Liddy would get prostitutes? Especially "high class" and "the best in the business."

Vaughn scratched a note on a yellow legal pad: *Find out/ prostitutes—how, where, who. Liddy n/talking. Ask FBI? D.C. cops?*

On and on and on came Dean's litany of sins. And when, after four days, Dean was through, the stunned Republicans focused in on one question: "What did the President know and when did he know it?"

"Forget about that," Dane told Vaughn. "These kinds of things, it's like a 'he-said, she-said' affair. And hell, who are the American people going to believe? Some burglars and Dean, an admitted snitch, or the President of the United States and a cadre of his public servants?"

Dane handed Vaughn a file. "But we do what we can. Dean brought this in. I saved it for you to check out."

In the file, Vaughn found a memo to Dean from White House Counsel Chuck Colson, who wanted Dean to get a codefendant of Jimmy Hoffa an expedited parole. The plusses for Nixon, thought Colson, included winning Jewish votes because the convict was a Jew.

I never got the report on the other pardoned guys' crimes from the Library of Congress, thought Vaughn. He found the request he'd made while still on Senator Martin's staff, called his old office to be sure nothing had come, then rewrote his request on the Watergate committee's stationery. Vaughn sent a copy of the letter to the federal pardons office. *Crazy as things are, you never know.*

"Impeachment of a President," he whispered to Dane as they lay in their midnight bed.

"We can't take this that far. And maybe we shouldn't. That's what the ballot box is for."

"If it's not rigged or tricked-out. But politics obeys physics 'a body in motion tends to' and 'chain reactions.' If we keep moving like we have been, where else is there to go?"

"You can impeach the President for high crimes and misdemeanors. The House acts like a grand jury. If they vote articles of impeachment, then the whole thing goes over to the Senate, and the Senate tries the President. If the Senate throws him out of office as guilty, he still has to be convicted in a court before he faces jail."

"And we're the cop on the beat."

"Forget it, Vaughn; we barely got a badge."

ON JULY 3, cop Quinn found Lou Russell's obituary in the *Post* as he drank his breakfast coffee. He told Lorri, "Now he can never testify about a stewardess who came to him terrified about a call girl scandal."

"Should I feel lucky?" She sipped coffee Quinn hadn't seen her pour.

"Don't ask me how you should feel."

Lorri raised the cup to her lips and drank.

ACROSS TOWN, THE *Post* obituary for Lou Russell leaped out at Vaughn. The *Post* noted that Russell was an ex-FBI agent, a witch-hunter for the House Un-American Activities Committee, and "had been connected at times with McCord and Associates," the security firm founded by the ex-CIA Watergate conspirator who blew the scandal open with his letter to Judge Sirica.

But nothing about how Frosty thought he was a linchpin in the Republicans' alternative theories and counterattack for Nixon, thought Vaughn. With that private eye Wolf-something. Nothing about that.

At 10:45 that night, Dane found Vaughn slumped in his cubicle.

"Are you awake?" she said.

"Beats me. You've always been like a dream, so who can tell." He drained the last of a warm Coke, dropped the bottle in his wastebasket. "Who else is still here?"

"Us. Plus the boss is upstairs in his office. I've got to take these files to him. Most of our guys went across the street to the Monocle bar. You working on the Howard Hughes stuff?"

"I'm so burned I can't keep straight who did what to

whom for why, and how much money got passed or laundered. If you're going upstairs, I'll walk a ways with you."

The Capitol policeman on guard outside the cave smiled at them, went back to his paperback novel. Reporters on stakeout duty had long since left: The news cycle didn't start again until regular hours tomorrow. Dane and Vaughn went as far as the men's room door together.

"The hell with the elevator," she told him. "I'll get some exercise."

He watched her walk away, all alone as she started up the stairs.

Bright light in the bathroom made Vaughn wince. His urine reeked of caffeine. He washed his face in cold water: the eyes staring back at him from the sink's mirror were maps drawn with lines of blood.

Exercise, he thought as he walked into the cave: what an intriguing concept. He entered the cubicles maze, took an aisle leading into Republican territory. *But I'm just getting some exercise.* Cubicles he passed were silent, their government-issue chairs empty, desk lamps snapped off. Somewhere someone sneezed. The air conditioner kicked off, let Vaughn hear radio jazz tuned in and turned low by a Democratic lawyer still working back on "their" side of the cave. *Wish I really did like jazz.* Vaughn swore he'd buy an album by Thelonius Monk. He passed a cubicle dimly lit by the overhead lights. A long table held a paper cutter, a three-hole punch, a box of file folders . . .

Stink, what's that smell: Electric burned dust.

Vaughn blinked. Saw no one in the maze but him. Heard only the whisper of radio jazz.

The electric-burned-dust smell pulled him into the workroom, around the long table to the latest high-tech photocopy machine. The burning scent came from there. The machine was warm beneath his palm. A dozen collating metal slots along the left side of the machine were empty. So was the feeder load tray on top of the machine. Vaughn turned to go back to his own turf, his mild caution about fire sated—

There: down low on the right side of the machine, easy

not to see in the discharge bin—half a dozen sheets of paper that had been fed into the machine for multiple copies.

Classic. Typical. A harried staffer zaps out a bunch of photocopies, hurries away to distribute them, forgets the original document that's been discharged and stored safely out of sight. Happens all the time on our side of the cave.

But this is not "our" side. We're all employees of the same government, but . . .

Framed photos of Richard Nixon and Spiro Agnew stared at Vaughn.

If I just take a quick look, that's not wrong. I can do it and get away with it.

Vaughn scanned the documents from the discharge tray: A memo stamped "From the White House" and "Secret." Tables compared Dean's testimony with what the President and others "actually" said in Oval Office meetings.

This is how the other side will counterattack us!

Radio jazz played muted and slow.

Vaughn thrust the memo into the load tray, hit 1 for number of copies, pushed the green print button.

The machine hummed. Whirred. Flashed: *Warming Up.*

Don't have time for that! You were already hot, for Chrissake, when—

Laughter—*Someone laughed*! Close by. Out there in the cubicle maze. Radio jazz that wasn't playing loud enough to cover the sound of a machine working and laughter: coming closer.

Humming photocopier heating . . .

How do you shut it off? I can't be caught here with it running. Where the hell's the switch? Pull the—

Footsteps! Voices!

Vaughn crouched against the cubicle wall.

Walking past the entryway, two Republican staffers, one saying: ". . . so we've got to figure out what the hell is that prick Dean getting for lying about the President, then put stink all over—"

The GOP staffers turned a corner, headed deeper into Republican turf.

The photocopy machine whined, *ca-thunked* out a copy of the memo and spit the original pages back into the discharge tray, where Vaughn had found them.

Vaughn stuffed the warm photocopy inside his shirt.

The lawyer whose radio played jazz jumped when Vaughn suddenly loomed beside him. He reached to turn the radio down.

Vaughn stayed the lawyer's hand; whispered: "You know we've scooped up tons of documents."

"What are you doing?"

"Just listen! So many documents in here, this," said Vaughn, displaying a sheaf of warm papers, "this got in our system. Doesn't matter, really, how I found it, but I think this is something you need to look at. Maybe pursue it somehow."

The lawyer dropped his eyes to the document the young staffer put on his desk. Twenty seconds; thirty; two minutes passed. When his face turned from the paper on his desk, the eyes behind his glasses were wide. The lawyer started to speak, then closed his mouth.

"You got it now," said Vaughn. "What you do with it is up to you. But if it's useful, could I be part of the followup?"

Then he left the lawyer to his jazz.

Don't run! In his cubicle, Vaughn collapsed into his chair, caught his breath. *Where's Dane?*

After she left Vaughn, Dane climbed the stairs. She heard the echo of her footsteps.

Private enough in here you could make love—God, it's been a long time! Vaughn must really be tired. At least when it's still there, that part of us is still—Don't think like that!

All the office doors in the dimly lit Senate hallway were closed. For a second, she feared she'd grabbed the wrong file, so she dropped her gaze to the manila folder as she started down the hall. When she looked up again, she realized she'd turned the wrong way.

Guess I'll really get some exercise. She continued the long way around the building's loop of hallways. The path of locked office doors stretched in front of her like a tan canyon. Each heel click echoed, and she heard her cadence—

Doubled: her echoes *plus* . . . thuds.

Dane stopped, whirled, looked behind her.

Silence. No footsteps. No echoes. She opened her mouth to call out, "Who's there?" Closed it: *What answer would make you happy?*

She turned, resumed walking. The first of three corners was fifty feet away, forty . . .

Footsteps, padding behind her, around the end of the corner in her wake. She turned to look. They stopped. As if waiting.

Don't run, don't really run, walk faster . . . Why is he waiting to start walking? Nobody's really there . . . Corner, here's the—Look over my shoulder, make the turn—

"Hi."

Some man loomed in front of her. She wobbled in her shoes and only his strong hand catching her arm saved her from falling, only the breathlessness of her rush kept her from screaming.

"Hey, you OK? You look like you've seen a ghost."

White guy, jacket—Is it cool enough outside for a jacket?—smile, pleasant face and a strong, strong grip on my arm. "Let go!"

"Oh. Sure." His hand drifted off her arm. "I didn't want you to fall. Split your skull."

"Who are you?"

"I work down the hall. I know you."

"You do?"

"Well, we've never truly met. Funny about that. Small town, Washington. Smaller town up here on the Hill. You think you know everybody, then *Bam!*"

She flinched as his hands clapped.

"You run into a stranger. You're Dane Foster. What kind of name is Dane?"

"My . . . my mother named me after the movie star." Edge around him.

"Of course!" he said. "That actress. Always played the girl

who didn't get it, or who really got it, if you know what I mean. She had great death scenes. Remember? Movies are dangerous, when you come to think about it. They warp your sense of what's not real and what you fucking well better pay attention to. Especially if you're not a star."

"My boss is wait—waiting for me."

"Bet he is. But you went down the wrong hall, didn't you? Got to be careful about that."

"I'm leaving now!"

"Sure," he said as she edged away, retreating down the narrow canyon toward the bright light at the corner. He stood there, still—No, not still: his feet weren't moving, but the rest of him, turning with her, shifting in his clothes . . . *coiling.* "See you again sometime, Dane."

Then she was around the corner, running to Dash's door . . . In! A weary secretary looked up.

Dane said, "Nothing's wrong! Really, nothing's wrong."

Next morning, the phone on Vaughn's desk rang. An investigator for the Permanent Investigations Subcommittee said, "All that mob stuff you were always asking about, you should come to our hearing today. It's not as glamorous as Watergate, but you might want to be there."

Vaughn made it in time to hear the subcommittee's star informant testify that the Justice Department threw him out of the witness protection program when they learned he was going to help the subcommittee's investigation of the mob's use of stolen securities, secret foreign bank accounts and Nixon's pardon of mafia capo Angelo "Gyp" DeCarlo.

Oh shit! thought Vaughn. Before he ran to take advantage of the chance he'd been given, *won,* he called the Library of Congress and ordered them to finish and deliver their research into Nixon's other pardons "like, yesterday!"

Friday the thirteenth, thought Vaughn: lucky day for me.

But not for Washington private investigator John Wolf Leon, who'd been working with the Select Committee's minority staff on alternative theories of the Watergate scandal: like Leon's obstreperous target witness Lou Russell eleven days earlier, Leon dropped dead from a heart attack.

And not for former White House aide Alexander Butterfield, who that afternoon was interviewed by committee investigators Scott Armstrong for the Democrats, and Donald Sanders for the Republicans. Off to the side sat another Democratic staffer named Vaughn Conner. A majority counsel had convinced the two investigators to let "the kid" tag along.

Armstrong displayed an incredibly precise White House memo rebutting Dean, winged a question to Butterfield: "Where might this paper have come from?"

Vaughn sat still and silent. Invisible.

Butterfield picked up the document, said, "This is very detailed, very detailed."

"Well, where could that have come from?" said Armstrong.

"Let me think about that a minute." Butterfield set the memo down.

Armstrong moved on to other questions—for three hours.

Then it was Republican investigator Sanders's turn. Inspired by the precisely detailed memo Butterfield was still thinking about, Sanders asked if there might be any validity to the suggestion made by John Dean that there might be a taping system in the White House. A direct question. A late-Friday-afternoon shot in the dark.

Butterfield sighed. Said, "I'm sorry you fellows asked me that question."

Monday, July 16, 1973. Butterfield sat at the Senate Watergate Committee's witness table. Vaughn sat behind the senators in a view-of-history chair mandated for his use by a committee counsel. Chairman Ervin gaveled the hearing to order.

Democratic Counsel Sam Dash said, "Mr. Chairman, at a staff interview with Mr. Butterfield on Friday, some very significant information was elicited by the minority staff member. Therefore, I would like to change the usual routine of the questioning and ask minority counsel to begin the questioning of Mr. Butterfield."

Republican counsel Fred Thompson led former military

intelligence officer Butterfield through his history and his duties in the White House, where he worked with the Secret Service.

"Mr. Butterfield," said Thompson, "are you aware of the installation of any listening devices in the Oval Office of the President?"

Count them off, the last seconds before the answer. *One. Two. Three. Four. Five.*

"I was aware of listening devices . . ."

CHAPTER 41

Quinn yelled at Max as that assistant U.S. Attorney sat behind his desk in the cramped, barely air-conditioned office. "Don't do this to me!"

"To you?" Max shook his head. Must be the summer heat. Or the humidity. "What a team player way to look at this mess you made!"

"I did my job!"

"Congratulations! You engineered a federal gambling bust of 179 prominent Washington citizens at a charity gambling night!"

"Gambling is gambling is—"

"Illegal, thank God, otherwise we'd all be looking at false arrest charges. The agents rolled up fifteen attorneys! And three D.C. police officials, including that drooler lieutenant from Internal Affairs, who, by the way, damn near nailed you with his investigation!"

"He's crooked!"

"And thanks to you, that's nickel-and-dime official now for him and two other cops, too. They all get a letter of reprimand in their jackets, which has gotta make you popular as hell with your fellow officers. If it wasn't for your FBI buddy Gary Harmon going to bat for you . . ."

"You can't just drop this!"

"Have you completely lost track of reality? We're in the middle of a national legal earthquake! We got half of the Justice Department trying to get their hands on White House tapes the President made, and the other half fighting to keep those tapes in Nixon's hands, and you got a hard-on for some local gambling to help charity!"

"They knew it was illegal." Quinn stared at Max.

"Cream-of-the-crop civic leaders like that, *if* they knew, they and the hotel and everybody figured they had a noblesse oblige do-good escape clause, like the churches and fire halls that run bingo nights. That's illegal, too. You want to put on the sirens and lights? Chase around the countryside? Bust them, too?"

"So you're going to let them all walk?"

"The cops get reprimands. The hired help and the hotel never existed. The citizens, they'll be allowed to plead to misdemeanor gambling, local charge—and believe me, if they plead innocent, they'll be nol pros'ed. The forty-one-year-old Advancement League agreed not to hold casino nights anymore, the gear we seized gets trashed, the money we seized will get shipped to the United Way or impounded, I don't give a damn. End of story."

"But—"

"No but's," said Max. "Good-bye."

"What if I bring you a cooperating witness who'll link the gambling equipment to a known criminal of record for a limited conspiracy case that your leading citizens won't want to fuss about because we'll use that charge to build stepping stones to other indictments *way* away from them?"

Max stared at the cop. "Who helped think that one up for you?"

Gary Harmon, before he disappeared into overwork he won't talk about. "What if?"

"What if I'd have gotten into Harvard?" said Max. "Could I have found a Japanese poet to love me? Would my life have soared above this everyday shit?"

"You wouldn't want it to."

"Try me."

"Look, if you go for this, you might get a piece of the big guy you missed with your police corruption probe—and that's way above everyday shit!"

"Or I might get a chunk ripped out of my hide."

"There is that."

Max looked around his cramped office stacked with yellowing files of commonplace sins and sorrows. He looked at the cop who he thought had never gamed him. "Shit. *If* you bring me a conspiracy case—a solid conspiracy case that leads somewhere beyond gambling equipment but not to the kinda clean and certainly powerful . . . *If* nobody has accepted my applications to be on the Watergate special prosecution team or the Senate committee or any history-making place like that, I'll see what I can squeeze into a grand jury."

As the office door swung closed, the prosecutor yelled, "You're welcome!"

THE RED BALL sun floated in the haze as Quinn parked in front of Jake the Jar's rowhouse. Quinn banged on the front door.

Elma opened it a crack. "We ain't got nothin' for you here no more."

He shoved his way inside. She staggered back, then straightened tall in her shiny new shoes and gave him a look colder than the river flowing from the window air conditioner.

"I didn't come here for you," said Quinn.

"You got that right."

Quinn surprised Jake as he trudged upstairs from his basement still. Quinn pushed the fat man across the kitchen. "Long time no see."

"Look, sorry, but any business we done is done. You ain't—"

"I 'ain't' leaving, and I 'ain't' coming here empty-handed. I got your balls in my pocket, and you're gonna have to buy them back. Who knows? They might even be bigger than before."

Jake stared past the crazy cop. "What you lookin' at?"

Quinn turned and saw Elma watching them from the doorway.

"Go on," Jake told her. "Get out o' here."

Never seen her smile before, thought Quinn. Then Elma's expression twisted into a snarl. She turned on the heels of her new shoes and marched out to the sunset swamp air.

"Upitty bitch," muttered Jake.

"A lot has changed round here." Quinn spotted a gold timepiece on Jake's wrist, grabbed the man's arm and twisted it as if to admire the jewelry. "Nice watch."

Quinn shoved him into a kitchen chair, then pulled up the other chair and scooted close to the fat man's sweating face. "Your new watch says 'time's up.' Time has fucking come today."

"I got nothing to say."

"David Strait and the heroin biz. Yeah, I know about that. And the Vale meeting—I got great pictures of you there. I'll call ATF for moonshining charges. But the easy federal rap I already got lined up: witness statements, your fingerprints on gambling equipment in a legitimate bust. Doesn't matter that the bust goes away for the big people. You're not big people, Jake, even with your new watch and Cadillac. You're my people. And the FBI's meat. Between them and you stands only me. They want you for gambling racketeering. They've got something called a 'jeopardy assessment,' which means they'll total up the bucks seized at that casino night, multiply it by 365, then figure that's the size of the annual take you ain't been paying taxes on. They'll slam you hard time for that haul."

"I don't have no haul."

"Al Capone. Biggest gangster around. Got him with taxes." Quinn softened his face, his tone, the truth. "But it doesn't have to be history for you, Jake. Not if you pay what you owe. Pay what you can. Not if you give the FBI, the grand jury, me, give us just that little more help on the whole package we're wrapping for Mr. White Boss Joe Nezneck."

"Oh, man! Oh, man! Why you doin' this to me?"

"Because I can, Jake. Because it's my job. Because I have to."

For an hour, for two, what Quinn had to do won nothing. Sundown mist turned to streetlight haze. The second hand swept round on Jake's new gold wristwatch. Quinn threatened, reasoned and pleaded with the fat man sweating in the kitchen chair. Quinn even whacked Jake's head. Nothing.

Streetlights outside sent their pale glow through the window to give the kitchen its only illumination. They sat in thick shadows. *Too dark in here to take a picture.*

Quinn snapped on the wall switch. The blast of light made Jake flinch.

"You watch TV, Jake?"

"So what."

"Only thing on TV most of this summer is Watergate. You know about that?"

Jake shrugged. "I don't do politics neither."

"But you know about it. Have to. Picture it, what do you see? The guy who *you* could be!"

Jake truly looked at Quinn for the first time that night.

"*John Dean!* That blond guy with glasses and the wife to die for? He sat there, on TV, got famous, probably gonna get rich and gonna skate free or at least only bullshit air-conditioned honor farm time. John Dean: ratting out his boss's whole gang. The fucking President of the United States! The most powerful man on the face of the earth, ratted out! John Dean got away with that rat job, got famous for it, got the sweet ride for it, all because he had the right guys to help. All because he sang when he had to, sang when the badges were closing in on his boss. Dean's smart! A lawyer. Third-rate shit goes down, gets caught, so Dean probably figured Nixon would feed him to the cops to keep them satisfied. Or worse. So Dean did the smart thing, made his move first. Doesn't matter if he doesn't have all the goods on the bad guys. Doesn't matter if Nixon walks or not. Dean made his move first, came clean, got on TV."

Quinn shrugged. "That could be you, Jake. You could be John Dean. You could make your move first. Or you could sit here after I leave. See what kind of hand Nezneck deals you. Personally, I think he's smarter than Nixon when it comes to guys who could be rats."

Jake couldn't turn his eyes from the cop.

"Here we are," said Quinn. "On the road. Let the FBI come after you with their 'jeopardy assessment' and Al Capone bustin' games. I won't be here to see what Nezneck deals you. You want to be John Dean? Or Jake the shattered fucking Jar?"

The second hand swept twice around Jake's new watch.

"I could get the John Dean deal?"

"Don't know," said Quinn, carefully edging back toward the full truth. "Depends on you. How good you are. How truthful. How much you know. How fully you cooperate."

Jake licked his lips. Dried them with the back of his hand. "We gonna do this, we gotta do it now. Right now."

"Whatever you say. You're the man."

He let Jake stand, commit, then before the fat man could waver, Quinn led the way outside. The July night was hot, sticky; humidity so thick Quinn saw it shimmer. The streetlight's glow bounced off the scummy windshields of parked cars. He let Jake walk free, without handcuffs, let him feel the illusionary power of clearly being nobody's prisoner.

Quinn said, "What happened to Elma that's got her so tough?"

"Puffed-up bitch," Jake said as they reached the unmarked cruiser and Quinn unlocked the front passenger door. "She ain't gonna be walkin' so damn high and mighty no more now."

The cop frowned as he opened the door for Jake. "Where'd she get those new shoes?"

The crack of a carbine from a car idling at the corner sliced through the summer night as its bullet slammed home and Jake's head exploded in a crimson mist.

CHAPTER 42

Spinning red lights on police cars and the ambulance rainbowed the ghetto street. Quinn slumped against a patrol car with its uniformed driver pretending not to be standing nearby so as to keep an eye on the undercover officer wearing blood-flecked clothes. Quinn stared at his cruiser still sitting across the street, corralled by strips of yellow crime scene tape.

The lead homicide detective wore cowboy boots with his suit, had a chipped-tooth grin. Quinn watched Buck jawboning that tan detective who the black sergeant outranked everywhere but on the scene of a homicide. The night stank of weeds and beer bottles. Quinn smelled car exhaust, sweat from everyone, the memory of butchered meat.

The ambulance turned off its party lights and motored away, back end full, siren silent.

The murder cop motioned for Buck to stay where he was, heel-toed his cowboy boots to Quinn. The hand he made Quinn shake felt like steel.

"Just for the record, I'm Nick Wetzel. I got your name and badge. You're not a suspect and since this is an officer-involved shooting, IAD has a part of it, but I'm the man and that is that. You figured out yet that I'm your best shot here?"

"I figure you're a good cop." Quinn watched the ambulance vanish. "Not like me."

"So who was waiting up the block in a car with a carbine?"

"IAD gets this?"

"Fuck them. I'm the murder police."

"I should have brought him out in handcuffs. Then they'd have seen him as being in custody. As holding his mud.

When he walked out clean with me, they knew."

" 'They' being this white bad-ass Hollywood crime czar named . . ." Wetzel checked his notes. "Nezneck."

"He probably has ten solid citizens for an alibi."

"And he somehow has a hard-on for a two-bit hustler—moonshine, numbers, loan shark—who only about fifty cops used for a snitch. Figure bad boys aren't stupid forever, so I've got what: a couple hundred suspects with motive, means and opportunity?" Wetzel shook his head. "How'd the shooter know to be waiting up the street?"

"Elma. Had to be her. She left. Called somebody. Told them I was there."

"Why would his old lady turn rat on Jake after all these years?"

"Way back when, Buck and I'd popped that cherry for her. Gave her practice." Quinn cupped his eyes with his hand. "Nezneck must have wanted to be sure he had a close eye on Jake after he upped him. Elma . . . He bought her new shoes."

"But that's just what you think, not what we know or I can prove in a court of law."

Quinn made no answer.

"All this wild shit you told me is probably what you think is true. But thinking doesn't make it so. Your ex-partner vouches for you. That prosecutor says you were here legitimately. But all this still adds up to you smelling like trouble, looking like trouble, and a dead source from a bad tactical play makes you for-sure trouble. From now on, you will give me no trouble."

A new cruiser pulled to a stop. The cop who climbed out wore deputy chief stars on his white shirt. Wetzel cowboy-booted to the department prince.

Quinn let himself fall away from that night to a vision mirroring long-gone yesterdays when Lorri and he always smiled. That world of time was warm and cool, lilacs; that time seemed swallowed by the great fucking now.

"My turn," the deputy chief was saying when Quinn blinked back. "Do you recognize me?"

"Sir, we've never met."

"I'm in uniform now, so you probably don't remember me. Probably didn't recognize me before. I was at the casino night you arranged to be busted."

Oh, shit.

"Twenty-five years on the force. Never got a letter of reprimand. Until you." The deputy chief leaned against the patrol car beside Quinn, so close their shoulders almost touched.

"Hell of a night tonight. Twenty-five years on the job, you do a hell of a lot. Some of it good, some of it just done. Sometimes you find yourself in a place where you'd rather not go, but you do. You go along to get along to do as much good as you can. Maybe that means politics. Maybe that means being sure to show your flag with the can-do people. Maybe you go along because everybody says you should, because you know it's dangerous arrogance thinking you got the angle on good and evil all by your lonesome. You do something, and you get hit with shit. You deserve it, you take it.

"Been on the phone a lot about you, a cop I never met. An IAD lieutenant I can't figure how to get rid of wants you shot first, fired second. Back when feds seconded you for long-hair work, I had to nod and smile. I dragged my kid to the barbershop, but you . . . I let them take you. Now those feds call to say you're too valuable an asset, too in-the-groove to lose. But another fed I never dealt with before calls to say purge your rogue ass. Wish I could get real answers. Never gonna happen. So you do what you can.

"Wetzel over there is our first Cherokee-blood detective. Damn good. If he clears you here, you're clean, though IAD will chew you raw. You're not getting any promotions or your transfer to Intelligence—guaranteeing that for now is a chit I spent. Plus you still play for Uncle Sam's team. The negotiated change there is that now IAD gets to review and monitor all your 'special duty' case file—past, present, future. The only other choice is for you to give me your creds and gun, right here, right now."

"I do that, I'll be naked."

"And alone."

"Thank you, sir."

"Do what you should. You owe all us other guys with badges that. Plus, if I ever ask a favor . . ." The deputy chief pushed off the cruiser. "We done here tonight?"

"Sir, I—it's been so crazy, like every road I've got or tried to use to get me . . . When Jake . . . his head . . ." Quinn blinked.

Felt it hit him like a roaring freight train.

"*Oh, shit!* I need a cruiser!"

Quinn needed a dark highway hour to get there, even with the red light spinning on the unmarked cruiser's dashboard. Then he hurried with the guard captain and two keys-clanging corrections officers through the dark prison, cell block lights banging on, muffled sounds and shapes stirring in rows of cells tiered three levels above Quinn's head, the stench of urine and nightmares arcing away from their frantic dash like waves from the prow of a ship.

"This way!" said the captain as he climbed a metal staircase. He yelled to the Control Pod: "On the gate!"

A CO charged ahead, had his steel key in the cell door lock even as the control pod officer hit the electronic release with a loud buzz.

A withered man of thirty-one cowered on the top bunk. Quinn shoved his way past the prison officials to where David Strait lay sprawled on the bottom bunk, his evaporating eyes pointing toward cemented-off heaven, his mouth slack, dried scum crusting his nose and where it had foamed out of his mouth. He wore a white tank-top undershirt. His right hand slumped across his boxer shorts, his left hand dangled off the bunk and above the floor, where an unfolded chessboard square of paper lay beside the crinkled condom that had carried it to its destination. Quinn saw the cement by the paper dusted with a spill of white powder.

"Overdose," said one of the CO's, his palm confirming that Strait's heart beat no more.

"How'd he get shit that pure?" said the other CO, then he

remembered the captain and a D.C. cop were standing there, so he shut up and looked away, watched as across the open cell block shapes filled the cell doors, arms and hands dangled out; someone over there lit a cigarette.

Homicide detective Wetzel phoned Quinn in the warden's office as Quinn numbly typed a statement for the prison files.

"We found Elma," said Wetzel. "Somebody stood her in a phone booth, single knot tied the pay phone cable around her neck and pulled on the receiver while she thrashed her new shoes off onto the booth's steel floor. Left her hanging there. You're a hell of a cop, Quinn."

The sun was well up when he left the prison. FBI Agent Gary Harmon had arrived, a representative of the federal authorities who had secured the narcotics conviction that had incarcerated the man slated for the hearse idling inside the prison walls. A CO escorted Gary and Quinn outside the wall to the visitors' parking lot. They were almost to Quinn's borrowed cruiser when the doors on the Cadillac parked three spaces over swung open and a gray-skinned, fish-faced man in an expensive suit climbed out into the morning accompanied by Joe Nezneck.

"Hey!" yelled Nezneck. "Mr. CO! There's a rumor going round that one of your residents died in custody."

Quinn charged—but wire-thin Harmon grabbed his wrist, spun him this way and that and then somehow swept Quinn's foot so that he stumbled back into the grasp of the CO.

Harmon reached inside his jacket. Trapped in the CO's grip, Quinn knew that only the FBI agent's brains made him choose his ID over his pistol.

"You're on government property. My jurisdiction. I own you—"

"I'm Mr. Nezneck's attorney." The fish-faced man met Harmon's credentials with a business card. "He's here in a public parking lot on legitimate business working as a volunteer with a recognized nonprofit group for prisoners' rights."

"Yeah." Nezneck shook a cigarette to his mouth, snapped the gold lighter. Blew smoke. "Convicts. What a bum deal they get. Who knows what you guys do to them in their cells. Even if they set themselves up askin' for it. They're in your care and custody. What'd you let happen?"

Nezneck shook his head. "It's a crying shame."

His attorney spread his flipperlike arms and addressed the parking lot like it was a court of justice: "I believe that individual being restrained knows my client. I am ethically compelled to inform all of you that though you may be officers of some limited authority, the laws of slander, libel and defamation of character still apply to you, and should negative aspersions about my client circulate in the public or the press, we will vigorously seek prosecutions. Furthermore, any harassment or civil rights violations will be swiftly addressed."

"You going to lick that envelope and make it stick?" said Harmon.

Nezneck leered. "He don't have to. You're the lawmen. That's your job."

He laughed so hard he coughed, hacked—then laughed more.

In that coarse laughter, Quinn envisioned Pat Dawson's smiling face; a red mist exploding in the night; David Strait on his prison bed; Elma hanging in the phone booth, her new shoes.

CHAPTER 43

On Sunday, August 15, Vaughn let Dane sleep in. He left *The Washington Post* delivered to the apartment for her, drifted to work. At a corner drugstore, he bought a Styrofoam cup of coffee plus another *Post*, the *Washington Star,* and *The New York Times.* Each paper bulged with analyses of Watergate; of a resolution for Nixon's impeachment that accused the President of "high crimes and misdemeanors" for the secret bombing of Cambodia, secret tapings in the Oval Office, "impoundment" of funds appropriated by Congress, and the plumbers; of Nixon's battles to keep "his" secretly recorded tapes out of the hands of all investigators. When Vaughn got to the cave, he found an envelope from the Library of Congress waiting on his desk.

"Pursuant to your requests, we have been able to identify . . ." Pages of pardons and commutations, for convicted criminals with a bullet description of the presidentially forgiven crime. But was a pardon for "marijuana" some guy (*like me*) caught holding a joint and sentenced to twenty years, or was it the only charge a good cop could make stick on a maximum gangster who boasted murder notches?

Before his coffee was cold, he had totals scratched onto paper: Nixon pardoned or commuted the sentences of sixty-six people charged with narcotics (and, *yeah*, marijuana) offenses, twelve other people jailed for heroin, three people convicted of racketeering and kickback crimes, and four murderers.

Some of them must have been innocent, he thought. Some of them must have gotten travesties instead of fair trials. Some of them must have been sick. Some of them might have reformed, saved a guard's life in prison or finally named to the FBI the evil crime king of Kansas City. Some of them must have been given disproportionate or even totally wrong sentences for their crimes.

But all of them? And what about the rest, the page after page of cases? And what the hell does it mean? Figure it out later.

He put the documents aside, drained his cold coffee and flipped open the papers.

Found a story in the *Star* about a sensual blonde who'd been hired for $1,000 a week by Nixon political adviser Murray Chotiner to pose as a reporter and spy on Democrat George McGovern's Presidential campaign.

Murray Chotiner, mob lawyer, thought Vaughn as he stared at his personal "W'gate" file with its satellite charts.

Chotiner had arranged the pardon of Teamster boss Jimmy Hoffa. Hoffa was linked to the American Association for Justice along with some D.C. guy named Joe Nezneck. And a smiling gnome named Mel Klise. Chotiner hired blond spies for a White House where Gordon Liddy boasted of call girls, a world of *ratfucking*. And off in a White House corner was a list of pardons, name after name of orchestrated Presidential fixes in an administration where it seemed nothing was done for free.

"But you know what you got?" said the committee lawyer, who went over the swirl of charts Vaughn put on his desk. "You don't know what you got. I don't know what you got."

"We don't know *yet*! But if it ties together—"

"Then it'll be a miracle, and I don't think you can walk on water." The lawyer shook his head. "Sure, something stinks here. But we're under the gun, with or without the tapes. If we give Nixon the ammo to say we're a runaway investigation, chasing phantoms who we weren't set up to hunt, our whole operation will go down the drain, with the public doing the flush."

"We can't ignore this!"

"I can't take this to the chairman or other senators." The lawyer took off his glasses to rub his brow. "You're in charge of the nut file, aren't you?"

"Officially, we don't call it that."

"Officially, this is a bipartisan investigation." The lawyer tapped his glasses on Vaughn's file. "Since you're in charge of the whatever-we-call it . . . If you push this a little further, maybe we can justify it as you just doing your duty."

"Wouldn't want to make a premature, incomplete report," said Vaughn.

"No, you wouldn't want to do that." The lawyer returned his glasses to their perch. He stared at the staffer who'd gone from being a gotta-take-him legacy from Senator Martin to an innovative if erratic asset. "I've got something you *will* want to do."

Tuesday Vaughn sat in a downtown office that cost more to decorate than his parents had paid for their family home.

The craggy-faced fifty-something man in the tailored British suit sitting behind his huge mahogany desk hadn't bothered to rise when his secretary showed Vaughn in, hadn't offered to shake hands—so Vaughn hadn't bothered to ask before he pushed a chair closer to the desk than it had been placed, sat down, took out his yellow pad and clicked his pen.

"I'm surprised they sent . . . you," said the baron of that office.

"Why?" asked Vaughn.

The man shrugged. Made something like a smile. "No matter. Perhaps someone so young will not be so short-sighted. I'm sure you'll do."

"This is an interview. The committee may also subpoena you later, but all this is still on the record."

"I'd check on that if I were you."

"The committee is investigating one hundred thousand dollars your employer, Howard Hughes, funneled to election efforts for President Nixon."

"Mr. Hughes employs and has employed a vast number of people for a variety of services. I know that senior members of your committee have had many discussions with such people. For example, Larry O'Brien, the Democratic Party official whose Watergate office those men burgled, he'd worked for Mr. Hughes. As for political donations or oth-er . . . financial help or technical assistance for our public ser-vants, I'm surprised you want to get into all that."

"Why?"

"You're a Democratic staffer, correct? If you poke into Mr. Hughes's private business, into money he may have given politicians, you may expose information that will be as damaging to Democratic heroes in the Senate as it is to the President."

"We're a nonpartisan, bipartisan investigation," said Vaughn. *You smug son of a bitch.* "We're about politics, but not po-litical parties. If you have information on Democrats to give us, that's cool."

" 'Cool'? You really think so? Well, I'm sure *cooler* heads will prevail."

"If you were sure, you wouldn't have seen me without a subpoena."

The man glared at Vaughn but Vaughn wouldn't blink.

"You mentioned 'other technical assistance' besides money that Howard Hughes gave public servants. Explain that."

"You don't want me to put all that on the record. You may be smarter than you look. Your superiors will agree with us that nobody wants to start down that road. You know where that leads. That ship of Mr. Hughes that the CIA is using in the Pacific. Plus all the help he let his people give the agency when the *nonpartisan* Kennedys wanted Fidel Castro eliminated."

"Excuse me?"

"Surely you're cleared and in the loop to know about that."

"Know about what? Cleared for what?"

"How the agency asked Mr. Hughes's people to put them together with certain mafia individuals to, I believe the phrase is, 'put out a contract' to assassinate Castro. Mr. Hughes is a patriot, so he obliged the Kennedys. Contacts were made here in Washington, elsewhere; various individuals with experience in Cuba came together with certain officers from the CIA. There were several such connections. All ultra hush-hush, though that damn Jack Anderson reported the heart of everything. When was that? Back in 1967?

"At any rate," continued the man, "even though success was never—or not yet—achieved, do you think your nonpartisan political bosses want a country that's ripping itself up over the horrors of Vietnam to get smacked in the face with how their heroic, martyred Democratic President arranged a deal with the mafia to commit murder? That the Kennedy saints wanted murder blood on their hands? That's what will happen if you and your committee go too far down the road toward Mr. Hughes. I, for one, don't want that on my conscience, so before we continue . . . Go report to older and wiser heads. If you come back, you better have that subpoena."

Vaughn left the office in a daze.

"Can't call it blackmail," the committee counsel said as he edited yet another line out of the memo Vaughn gave him.

"But that's what it is!" Vaughn yelled as quietly and discreetly as he could.

"No, not even according to your memo. Blackmail is a specific crime. That asshole was too smart to phrase it specifically. Indirectly . . . Shit, Hughes has dirt on our senators, plus this mob and CIA and assassination . . . And some of the burglars were ex-CIA, Cubans. I can't believe—"

"Nobody does. I had the Library of Congress find the Jack Anderson column, 1967, all about the mafia, named names, a bunch of attempts . . . Got zero reaction in the country, from the rest of the press. It's like Anderson chopped down the biggest tree in the forest but when it fell, everybody heard and nobody cared."

"Nobody wanted to believe him. Journalism, history, politics, lawsuits, criminal trials: they're not about the truth, they're about what you can get people to believe."

"Even if it isn't true, even if we can't get a blackmail charge going against Hughes for trying to keep us from figuring out why he gave Nixon one hundred grand—"

"The anti-trust stuff for the Vegas hotels and airline—"

"That's *nothing* compared to the CIA working with the mob and murder! Even if that's not true, we've got to investigate!"

"Maybe."

"What?"

"I'll rework your memo, bump it up through the system to the chairman to let him decide what to do with this. You and I have that responsibility. And hey: you did good."

"But it doesn't matter!"

"You never know." The lawyer shook his head. "But now forget about all that. Plus you're off everything else."

"I step on some Democrats' shadows and you—"

"Give you a moving target you gotta nail dead center and

true, and real, *real* fast. As of right now, you've got to prove that in our shit storm called Watergate, the highest and mightiest and most sanctimonious Nixon asshole in town is innocent."

CHAPTER 44

"We don't need your help," the prosecutor in the office four floors above September trees told Vaughn. "We've got him laid out on the cross, just waiting for the nails. So you can drive back to D.C. and play politics. Up here in real town Baltimore, we're about crime and punishment."

"More power to you," said Vaughn. "But with all the press speculation—"

"Your boss said you had nothing on Mr. Big. Now you're here to cover your own asses."

"If my boss needed his ass covered, he'd get somebody better than me to do it. When *your* 'secret' grand jury investigation sprang some leaks and the press started calling *us,* my man told them the truth: Vice President Agnew is not a target of the Watergate committee. That's your job."

"So what's yours?"

"To be sure we aren't missing something. If you guys found dirt on him . . .

"Mountains, man! We found . . . You'll see. Soon there'll be two impeachments going on in D.C., and when your bosses kick Agnew out of office, he's ours. He's a fucking crook."

"And no fan of mine. I was one of those antiwar-protester 'nattering nobobs of negativism' he gave speeches about."

"No shit. I was a Huey door gunner. If they'd have let us go all out, we'd have already had our victory parade."

"We aren't here about Vietnam," replied Vaughn. "I pored

over mountains of documents, talked with everybody on both sides of our committee. We got nothing on Agnew in Watergate. The weird thing is, seems like Nixon didn't trust him, only used him for a cheerleader. You might have him for shit he did when he was governor of Maryland—"

"And in the White House."

Vaughn froze.

The door gunner grinned at his direct hit. Shrugged. "But not stuff about Watergate. Legacy stuff. Just between you and me?"

Vaughn nodded.

"Back in 1969, after he was vice president, Agnew made a guy he'd done a corrupt deal with in the old days come to the damn Office of the Vice President in the damn White House and put an envelope with ten thousand dollars right smack damn in Spiro's hand."

"Oh, man! But we're about CREEP. Did Agnew—"

"Spiro didn't share it with the Nixon boys or CREEP. Kept it all for himself."

"Get him," Vaughn whispered.

"Got him." The Air Cavalry door gunner held out his palm to the war protester.

Vaughn slapped him five. Started to get out of his chair . . . sat back down.

"I know you can't officially tell me details," said Vaughn, "but the stuff you got Agnew on, the bribe taking, corruption . . . *where* is it about?"

"You mean is it national? Not like you mean. Except for where he collected illegal gains and how he kept reaching his hand out after he won in sixty-eight . . . Most of it's tied into dirty deals around Baltimore and the suburbs between here and D.C. from when he was governor of Maryland."

"Look at these," said Vaughn, passing photocopied pages from his briefcase to the prosecutor. "I found them in the stacks Nixon's people sent over to the archives. These are photocopies of scribbles on yellow legal pads. Haldeman and Ehrlichman in a cabinet meeting on March 31, 1970, passing notes back and forth like a couple of bored teenagers in civics class. Ehrlichman starts it, asks Haldeman: 'Do you know about the V.P. taking over all GSA patronage for Md., Pa., W. Va? Appointments? Architects? Favors for Congressmen? Construction, etc.?' And then at the bottom, he scrawls, 'Add District of Columbia.' "

"Agnew grabbed all the patronage and contract awards for everything around Washington, D.C.?" said the prosecutor. "That's how he worked bribes here!"

"But Haldeman shut Agnew down. My guess is Nixon's people controlled all the goodies."

"Why the hell would Agnew risk bucking the Nixon guys to control federal money on the streets of D.C.? Billions of dollars in local business and being the ex-governor to the state next door to D.C. make him damn near a local politician down there, but who were his connections?"

"If either of us finds out . . ."

They shook hands, and Vaughn drove back to politics.

ON SEPTEMBER 29, Vaughn was at his desk catching up on the Hughes investigation when Dane charged into his cubicle: "Come on! Your guy's on TV!"

They made it to the front of the cave in time to see the network news cut to the convention of the Federation of Republican Women in a hall bedecked with American flags, swell balloons and red-white-and-blue banners. Vice President Spiro Agnew stood tall behind a podium and proclaimed to the beaming faces of adoring women: "I want to say at this point, clearly and unequivocally, I am innocent of the charges against me! I will not resign if indicted! I will not resign if indicted!"

Women danced in the aisles. Waved placards bearing Agnew's likeness high above hair-sprayed heads as they chanted: "Fight, Spiro, fight! Fight, Spiro, fight!"

Vaughn said, "They're so damn *cheerful!*"

*   *   *

IN THE WHITE House Situation Room, the only cheer centered around the news that Henry Kissinger was named secretary of state, the job in title that he'd wielded in fact. American soldiers still served and died in a Southeast Asian quagmire. The only clear victory for Nixon and America's foreign policy was one they didn't dare brag about: with multimillion-dollar covert American encouragement, Chile's military overthrew democratically elected Marxist President Salvador Allende in a bloody coup that killed Allende and thousands of Chileans.

Holloway sat at his Sit Room desk, shuffling through a stack of photographs—wire photo shots, embassy pictures, CIA and other intel agencies' photos. Looking through the photos let him focus on realities far, far away and not the skeleton truths grinning beside him.

He stared at a black-and-white photograph taken inside Chile's National Stadium.

A picture taken from the soccer field through the helmeted, machine-gun-toting coup troops toward the stands where hundreds of suspected "traitors" had been rounded up and deposited, awaiting interrogations, incarcerations, executions. Two men seated in the stands caught Holloway's eye: they had broad grins; every other face in the stands showed fear. He blinked, looked closer. . .

Got a magnifying glass. Felt his bones go cold as the lens pulled up the grinning, long-haired, bearded face who'd left him alone in the streets of Washington. Jud Simon, caught in the midst of Chile's bloody coup.

They sent you there, thought Holloway. To do what? He knew about the two tracks: track one, the diplomatic pressure and propaganda against Allende; Track Two, the secret money and encouragement to Chile's military to do what they'd just done. Two tracks: a little push here, a little pull there. What track are you on, Jud? What did you do?

Get out of there! Holloway mentally ordered the grinning image captured in time already past. They're taking people out of the stands, questioning them in the locker rooms, shooting them one after another after—

Hope you got out of there alive.

Holloway slipped the photograph out of the stack and hid it in his shirt. *That's all I can do.*

His home phone screamed on Saturday, October 6, moments after Holloway'd picked up his empty morning newspaper. The NSC watch officer told him that Egypt and Syria, nominal allies of the Soviet Union, were exploiting the Jewish Yom Kippur holiday and invading Israel, America's blood-brother ally in the Middle East. He kissed Sandy awake. Said he'd see her when he could.

"Sure." She lay in his bed, her eyes on his ceiling. "Sure."

FOUR DAYS LATER, Vaughn answered the phone on his desk and heard the Baltimore prosecutor yell, "Get up here now! Son of a bitch, get up here right damn now!"

Vaughn needed almost an hour to get to Baltimore, and then police barricades barred him from entering the federal courthouse. He saw Secret Service vans, limos, and as he argued with a longhair-hating Baltimore cop who didn't give a damn what credentials the punk had, Vaughn spotted the prosecutor shuffling down the steps, his tie askew, his face pale. The prosecutor heard Vaughn's shout, and his beckon overrode the city cop's restraining arm.

"Son of a bitch!" The prosecutor fought tears. "Agnew, just as we're gonna pound the nails in . . . He limos up here with the goddamned Secret Service taxpayer cars and cops to lousy income tax evasion! We got him taking more than thirty-two grand in bribes, and the judge . . . the judge gives Agnew three years unsupervised probation and a ten-grand fine! So Agnew makes a minimum damn twenty-grand profit from being a crook and selling out every citizen who . . . Look at him!"

The crowd of reporters and bystanders roared as silver-haired, just-resigned, former Vice President Spiro Agnew hurried down the courthouse steps and into the back of a limousine. Vaughn glimpsed his patrician face through the rolled-up glass: vacant black eyes locked on nothing.

The limo roared away.

"Tell me you guys are going to get him!" whispered the prosecutor. "Or the special prosecutors! Tell me somebody's going to get him!"

Vaughn watched the limo disappear. "No."

CHAPTER 45

Forever afterward, Dane associated Saturday, October 20, 1973, with the sound of car horns, the scent of autumn leaves at night and burning fear.

Kissinger was in Moscow, asking the Soviets to help control the Yom Kippur War that had led to the Organization of Petroleum Exporting Countries instituting a boycott of oil sales to the automobile-addicted United States. Nixon had chosen House Republican Leader Gerald Ford to succeed Agnew as vice president. The headline across Page One of *The Washington Post* read: "Nixon to Give Hill Court Summary of Tapes." The story quoted Nixon saying a deal for him to give transcripts to the Senate and prosecutors, rather than actual tapes of Oval Office conversations, had the blessing of Senators Ervin and Baker, the heads of the Select Committee.

"Takes the wind out of our sails," Vaughn told Dane in his apartment that morning.

Dane frowned. "A short article, wire service instead of *Post* guys. This must have come in right before deadline. Wonder what's happened since?"

Vaughn shrugged. "You know how we talk about taking a day off? Let's do it. Today. *Now.*"

"But I've got to go in."

"OK, go in for an hour or so, but you don't have to stay in."

Guilty pleasure lit their faces.

"Let's do something so absolutely . . . normal it boggles the imagination!" said Dane.

"A movie!" he said.

"The art gallery!" she said.

"A movie *and* the art gallery! And dinner in a restaurant somewhere far, far away from Capitol Hill! And home in time . . . not *exhausted*."

"I don't know," said Dane: "The Impressionists' wing can tire out a guy."

"Not tonight," said Vaughn. "Believe me: not tonight."

They ditched the news pages of war and scandal for the movie section.

"We can finally see *American Grafitti*!" shouted Vaughn. "You know what the ad says? 'Where were you in '62?' I can't believe my youth is already marketed nostalgia!"

"Modern life," said Dane. "You're nostalgia the minute you're born."

An hour later, as they strolled down the Senate corridor, Frosty strutted out of the cave. "Well, the damn tape mess is about over. Dash and Ervin got some flap up about the deal—you guys are never satisfied."

"What do you mean, 'flap up'?"

Frosty yawned. "They claim they never agreed to it. Like the President would give out a wrong story! Oh, and some reporter called to ask about the press conference at one."

"What press conference?" said Dane.

"That Harvard dandy Cox. Dollars to doughnuts he resigns right in front of the TV cameras. Those TV vultures would put cameras in a plane crash if they could." Frosty's smugness warmed. "You kids ought not to be here. Workaholics are like booze hounds, only boring. Fine Saturday, you got each other . . . Find something better to do."

With a wink, he strolled to the sunlight streaming through the glass doors and was gone.

Vaughn cleared his throat. "I think . . ."

"If he thinks everything is OK," said Dane, "somewhere, somehow, something stinks."

At 1 P.M. they tuned in the press conference televised from the National Press Building. Sitting alone at a long table in front of a deep blue curtain and an American flag, Special Prosecutor Archibald Cox told reporters, "Criminal wrong-doing is the subject of investigation. . . . It is simply not enough to make compromise in which the real evidence is available to two or three men operating in secrecy."

A reporter asked, "Do you consider the tapes absolutely vital?"

Exasperated, Cox answered, "I think it is vital to know! I had started with the naive belief, if you'll forgive me for being corny, that what's right will prevail in the end."

Dane turned off the TV, looked at Vaughn.

"Figure we can catch a late movie," he said.

They spent the afternoon doing paperwork. Afternoon became evening; they had Chinese food delivered for dinner yet again. Phones rang. Rumors poured in: The Attorney General had resigned. The Justice Department was being purged. Reporters were told, "No comment." Staffers phoning in were told, "All we know is what's on the radio and TV!"

At 8:25 P.M., the TVs in the cave showed them the press room that Nixon had built over a White House pool where John Kennedy used to swim naked. Press Secretary Ron Zeigler, who'd called the Watergate burglary a "third-rate" affair, stood behind the podium to announce, "The office of the Watergate Special Prosecution Force has been abolished as of approximately eight P.M. tonight."

Phones screamed in the cave as Dane and Vaughn watched television flicker its rainbow in the darkness. Dane felt Vaughn take her hand as NBC's John Chancellor stared out of the screen:

"The country tonight is in the midst of what may be the most serious constitutional crisis in its history. The President has fired the Special Watergate Prosecutor Archibald Cox, and he has sent FBI agents to the office of the special prosecution staff, and to the attorney general and the deputy attorney general, and the President has ordered the FBI to seal off those offices. That's a stunning development, and nothing even remotely like it has happened in all of our history. . . . In my career as a correspondent, I never thought I'd be announcing these things."

"They'll come for us next," whispered Vaughn.

Dane bolted from his grip, dashed to the door. Vaughn ran beside her.

The patronage-appointed Capitol policeman stationed outside the cave heard their door slam open; a kid, as they'd later recall, from South Dakota, a weekend part-timer with a senator who'd gotten him this no-sweat job with its limited badge and not-quite-rusted gun so he could work his way through college pulling easy weekend shifts.

Tears streaming down her cheeks, Dane clutched the young policeman's arm. "You work for Congress, do you understand! The Senate! You work for the people of the United States of America! Not the goddamned FBI! Not any fucking President! You don't let them in here! Nobody, *nobody* but us staff and senators gets past, you motherfuckin' *die*, you understand me! You work for us, not them! The people, you hear me? *The law!* This, all this, you and I are the line where they all stop! Right *here*! Right *now*!"

The man who wasn't much older than the cop spun that officer from the woman's grip. "Don't let anything happen to her!"

Then he turned and ran back into the committee staff office.

The woman paced. Tears streaked her face, her breasts heaved. She stiffly held both hands out like a mother calming a child. "It's OK! Calm down. Do our job. Going to be OK!"

But the cop knew she was lying. He put his hand on his holstered revolver.

The cave door flew open—that guy, with a jacket on now, runs up to the woman, looks around. Nobody here but us, thought the cop, his thumb on the holster's safety strap. The guy took the woman in his arms, kissed her.

"Stay here. You'll be OK. Don't—Keep all this safe."

"Where are you going?" she yelled after him as he ran out of the building.

The cop, just a kid really, a heartland rube with stars and stripes in his eye, stepped in front of the woman as she paced back and forth in front of the committee door. And knowing only that he'd die to make what he said be true, told her, "Don't worry. I'm here."

Vaughn ran—ran harder than he'd run since high school track, got his car and busted one red light after another as he raced toward downtown.

They caught him at Twelfth and Constitution: night cries slicing through his rolled-up windows, dozens of tones, long beats and rapid-fire machine-gun staccatos—*car horns*, car horns honking from the streets circling the White House, car horns honking at the White House and the craggy-jowled, ski-nosed President burrowed inside.

Roll down the window! Damn, he couldn't roll down the window fast enough! Cold air rushed over him, he hung his head out the window and screamed *"Yeah!"* to the darkness, screamed and blared the horn on his rusted Dodge as he tore through the night.

This is where the action is, he thought as he parked behind TV trucks and cars with press placards on their dashboards. Select Committee ID folder in hand, he bullied his way through the office building's crowded corridor, squeezed into an elevator jammed with reporters and rode up to the "secure" floor, where Cox's Special Prosecutor Force rented office space.

The elevator dislodged him into a corridor of bedlam. Uniformed policemen tried to maintain order. Photographers held cameras above their heads and flashed pictures. Microphones on sound poles angled over everyone like tree branches in a jungle. Vaughn saw prosecutors streaming off the elevators, rousted from their Saturday night in whatever clothes they'd been wearing when they heard the news, their faces set in wet stone.

One prosecutor yelled at a man with an FBI ID folder hanging from his suit pocket, "You were with us, investigating this all along! Now you're here busting us? Whose side are you on?"

"Please!" pleaded the FBI agent. "I don't want to be here doing this either. I'm just doing my job! We're keeping everything safe!"

Another prosecutor spotted Vaughn's Senate ID. She pulled him inside the prosecutorial office suite.

Time swirled. Swept him up with faces he didn't know, upstairs to a law library where dozens of reporters crowded against walls lined with law books. TV cameras' hot lights laced clouds of cigarette smoke. Microphones thrust across a brown conference table at a lean young prosecutor named Henry Ruth, who wore a long-sleeved, collared gray pull-over. His hair was neatly trimmed, his eyes were red, his lips were taut and his skin was the color of death.

"I must say I suppose, ah, that human emotions take over, ah, in this kind of occasion, because one thinks that in a democracy maybe this would not happen, and that maybe, ah, we could proceed in good faith to prosecute those who have violated the criminal law. Apparently that is not to be the case, and we have been abolished."

That night, Vaughn heard Jimmy Doyle, the prosecutors' black-haired, bespectacled press officer, tell reporters, "Mr. Cox's comment when he was told that he was apparently about to be fired was: 'Whether ours shall continue to be a government of laws and not of men, is now for Congress and ultimately the American people to decide.' "

Somebody asked Jimmy Doyle what he planned to do.

"I'm going home to read about the Reichstag fire," he replied, his eyes full of visions of that arson in Germany that empowered Hitler.

A voice hissed in Vaughn's ear, "Senate committee?"

After he said yes, and the face checked his ID, Vaughn found himself in a room of a half dozen men and women, all only slightly older than him.

"What are you prepared to do?" asked one of them.

"Whatever we need to," said Vaughn.

Documents appeared from desks, file folders from behind

bookshelves where they'd been hastily shoved. Vaughn, two women and one man stuffed as many of them under their shirts as they could, down their backs where just maybe a quick pat wouldn't find them.

"Let's go."

Led by a woman prosecutor, they elbowed their way back through the crowd, avoiding reporters and men sporting FBI folders. In the hall, Vaughn saw a prosecutor holding a framed copy of the Constitution and yelling at a wire-thin FBI agent: "Can I take this home, huh, Gary? Please? What the hell, just stamp it null and void!"

A uniformed cop made Vaughn open his jacket wide, but the argument over the copy of the Constitution distracted the armed guards from all but cursory inspections of Vaughn's group.

They raced in Vaughn's Dodge to Capitol Hill.

Dane and the young cop paced in front of the cave entrance. As Vaughn and the staffers from the prosecutors' office neared them, an ebony slab wearing the white shirt of a Capitol Hill policeman came round the corner; the black cop wore three blue stripes on his sleeves. He smiled at Dane. "How you doin', Miss Foster?"

"I've been better, Sergeant Jones."

"I've been watchin' my TV. Ruining another perfectly good Saturday night. Figured I best come on down and stand watch with my young officer." Sergeant Jones smiled at Vaughn, who knew him only by sight. "My, we havin' a noisy time. You're a staffer: Can I assume that these folks are with you, and therefore that don't necessitate me ID'ing them and signing them in?"

"Yes, sir!"

"Don't 'sir' me, son. I work for a living. Well, all right then. All of you can go on inside and do what you're supposed to do. Me and this young officer, we'll be sure nobody who ain't staff or senators gonna . . . disturb you."

Dane hugged him.

Half a dozen more Democratic Senate staffers had congregated in the cave by the time Dane and Vaughn admitted the first wave of secret bearers from the prosecutors' office.

"We were worried about something like this," said a prosecutor. "The irony is Nixon's guys're right: we were—are—taking evidence, copies of evidence, out of our offices, but only to safeguard it! If they get control . . ."

She looked around the cave. "Here . . . Are the Republicans staffed in here, too?"

"Bipartisan committee," said Dane.

"If they come in here tonight before the courts can . . . These copies we've brought you—"

"Don't worry," said Vaughn. "We're safe here. This is Congress, we got cops."

"We were special prosecutors—with the FBI protecting us." A heartbeat later, she asked, "Who lives closest?"

They ran photocopy machines until the enormity of deciding which documents to copy became paralyzing. Vaughn and Dane crammed photocopied documents into briefcases, found a shopping bag with handles in a secretary's trash can.

"It's past two in the morning now," said Dane. "TV camera crews will show up out front by first light. Soon as the building opens for regular Sunday hours, they'll fill it up. There probably are reporters and photographers staked out on the staff entrance doors right now."

"If somebody besides reporters is staked out . . ." Vaughn didn't finish his thought.

"Come on," she said.

They left the cave with a pack of other staffers and their "guests;" other Senate staffers volunteered to pull an all-nighter in the cave "just in case." Outside the cave, the pack of government servants walked toward the building's door, blocking a clear view of the hall behind them as Vaughn and Dane slipped down the corridor in the opposite direction.

Beneath the Capitol grounds and the main buildings of Congress runs a labyrinth of tunnels and passageways. Some tunnels are polished thoroughfares complete with the subway trains designed to rush members to their chambers for votes. Some tunnels are shoulder-width yellow-brick corridors with rows of overhead pipes, cramped humid gaps smelling of

stone and cement, rat poison. Congressional aides learn how
to navigate from the Senate side, through the Capitol, across
Independence Avenue, and into the House office buildings
without ever leaving the tunnels. Since the Weathermen terrorist bombing of the Senate barbershop two years earlier,
the guard posts at each building entrance—and at major tun-
nel junctions—supposedly checked and logged each person
who passed by. As he followed Dane, a briefcase weighing
down each hand, his eyes on the shopping bag and briefcase
she held, Vaughn *knew* a cop would stop them, demand to
inspect what they were carrying. But Dane's bravado carried
them past all the guards.

They emerged into the night behind the Cannon House
Office Building, all the way across the grounds from their
Senate turf, past the Capitol itself and the columned castle
for the Supreme Court with its chiseled-in-marble motto of
"Equal Justice Under Law." Vaughn joked, "All we have to
worry about now is getting mugged."

"Wasn't that Liddy's plan?" said Dane.

They reached a white stucco building on Pennsylvania Avenue three blocks from Congress's Cannon Building, a per-
petually sealed flat-faced building with a garage door.
Vaughn knew what most Capitol Hill residents only believed: the white building housed a secretive FBI unit. According to what the Bureau'd told him, an officially inquiring
aide to U.S. Senator Gus Martin, that albino FBI fort a
stone's throw from Congress was for "translation" work.
When Dane and Vaughn saw the Bureau's lair that night,
they quickly crossed the street.

Sweating, exhausted, they limped into the tree-lined resi-
dential neighborhood of Capitol Hill. Vaughn said, "Gus told
me a story. When Kennedy was inaugurated, there was a
huge snowfall. Gus lives just over there, behind us, and he
can walk to work. When he woke up that morning, him a
World War II vet, he heard what he could never forget: the
rumble of tanks. His first thought was Vice President Nixon's
pissed off about losing and there's been a military coup. Gus
figures they're coming for senators like him, says fuck it,

fuck them, he's in his bathrobe and throws open his front door.

"And there, clanking up his street headed for the Capitol where the inauguration will be, is an Army tank—with a snowplow mounted on its front."

"What does a tank sound like?" asked Dane.

They walked through the October night, forcing their footsteps to fall fast and softly.

"Listen!" whispered Dane. "Do you hear that? What is it?"

Off in the not-so-distant city, damn near 3 A.M., muffled . . .

"Car horns!" said Vaughn. "Holy shit, it's car horns! People, the damn people, they're still driving round the White House blasting their car horns!"

Laugh, they had to laugh, and they knew that there, stumbling in the darkness, they were also crying. They shuffled through the night on a cracked sidewalk beside an old red-brick church with a famous history Dane didn't know. She looked up at the trees: hanging from them were yesterday's leaves. She smelled their musty rot.

CHAPTER 46

"Where are we?" muttered a White House Sit Room staffer behind Holloway as they watched pandemonium televised from the nearby press room where Sandy's boss, Ron Ziegler, was announcing the purges of the Special Prosecutors Force: "Chile?"

"I'm going home," said Holloway.

Electricity charged the city streets he walked; whirling red lights from police cars seemed everywhere. No one he met looked at his face; everyone hurried over the sidewalks.

He opened his door and found Sandy sitting on the couch.

She stared at him with bloodshot eyes. "You're one of them."

"What? One of who?"

"The *them* who—you know! *Them!* You're one of *them*!"

"I'm the guy who loves you."

"Then tell me who you are."

"I'm a Marine officer."

"And that's it. And that's a lie, because that's not it. You're twisted up into some big secret knot. I know you have a gun, sneak around, do stuff, know people—"

"My job at the NSC means I have to be secretive, careful."

"Bullshit. You're not at the NSC, not truly. You're one of them. A White House basement boy. A plumber. A conspirator waiting to be caught."

"No! I'm not one of those guys! I'm not a bad guy!"

"Then prove me wrong. Do the right thing. Quit."

"But I can't just leave! I've got duty, I owe—"

" 'Owe'? You signed on to a job, not a war."

"I need to make it work! I need to do it right! Because that's . . . because of what I did . . . Because everything I've done is wrong if I don't make it come out right at the end."

"The end is when you make it. One way or another, you're making an end now. If it were another woman, then loving you and losing you would at least be personal. Still hurt like hell, but—"

"Don't go!"

"I quit tonight," she said. "Left my badge on my desk. Walked out, walked away. I'm going home, back to Illinois, land of Lincoln. Out of this town. I have to believe in something besides being here. Here belongs just to *them* now, and I quit it. If I quit them and you won't, you're them."

"No!"

"Look at you: you're not just burned out, you're burned up. Whatever secret things you're doing, whatever big secret you're hiding in your heart, all that's come together into one big fire and Nate Holloway is what's feeding the flames."

Slumped in a chair, can't raise my hand. Can't reach her. Can't tell her anything.

"It would have been great to be somebody else, someplace else."

She picked up her suitcases crammed with rumpled clothes and Nathan's screaming heart. As she left, she closed the door.

He sat on a chair in a blaze of lights in the dark night.

Jerked awake, sitting in the chair, all the lights on bright as day, bright—

Asleep, must have fallen asleep. Sunlight. Clarity. Jungle—I smell smoke. Beetle crawling across a log. Sound of . . . music. Must have run ten miles from the ambush. Creep low and . . . Jungle's edge, a ville with a dozen huts and . . . American Soldiers! Army troops! I made it! Safe! There's a dozen grunts, M16s at ease, one of them raises his shiny hand near a thatched roof, a lighter, a Zippo patrol. Yell—No! Don't spook them! By the nearest hooch, three more GIs—M16s beside them as they squat. Smoke from burning homes mingles with . . . marijuana. Whose slack men are these? Radio HQ so they won't send Marines into the shit looking for me. Radio, one of these toy soldiers. His rock 'n' roll transistor radio playing Beach Boys.

Use an irrigation ditch to come in close, keep low, scram—

Corpses line the ditch: old men, four women, a goat, a pencil-limbed boy.

Walk tall and easy to the three smokin' and jokin' GIs . . .

"Who the hell are you? All smeared ash black like that, you look toasted!"

Say: "Marine officer. Where's your radioman? Your CO?"

"Everybody else's with the trucks."

" 'Cept Kansas. He's still in that hooch. We never even seen sign one of old bad-ass Victor Charlie, commie cowards. We rule this dink shithole."

Tell three mind-blown marijuana faces sent here by

hometown draft boards: "Get me your radioman."

One of their voices sings through the Beach Boys: "We already got the radio on, man!"

Laugh, they all get it and laugh. Then freeze up, the push from Officer Eyes they can't meet shuffling them away through the smoke. The transistor steps out an oldie-goldie, the Four Seasons singing: "Walk like a Man."

The farmer's home pulls like a magnet. Inside: stench of burned rice, fish sauce; an M16 and pack dropped on the floor; pale girl sprawled on a pallet, ebony hair, glazed eyes pointing at a rafter. Exposed swells on either side of the red star punched in her chest. The pants around her ankles are farmer cheap.

Tear scars line Kansas's cheeks: "She wouldn't stop crying."

Flies buzz.

Say: "Easy, soldier. I'm an officer. We have to—"

"Where were you? You were supposed to be here."

"You're not one of my men."

"Then who the hell do I belong to?"

Flies buzzed.

"You were supposed to be here. To tell me what to do."

"I got cut off. Lost in the jungle."

"Whose fault is that?" A tear cut his cheek. The nineteen-year-old nodded to the pallet: "Look what happened. I'm not supposed to be here, and I can't get out that door. Ain't that some shit."

Look what now forever haunts the wheatfields in those eyes of the man in the mission. What are the measurements of those holes. Guess what, Mom and Dad. Hey, America! You sent us here to keep you safe and look what's comin' home. "The course of events, the mission is always the greater good." Hear those rock 'n' roll flies buzzin'? Who opened the door and let them in? Always the greater good. The man or the mission. Who's the judge. Forget about everyone who

*was supposed to be there but it's just Kansas and her
and the officer who came too late, and wouldn't it be
nice, but it's not. How do you walk like a man.*

Kansas says: "Wish I could go home."

Say: "OK."

*Kansas smiles the whole time the M16 raises to kiss
his heart.*

*Later, walking past the smoldering huts on the far
side of the ville, here come the three grunts from before, plus a radioman and a young sergeant. Tell the
sergeant: "You got an American KIA back in the last
hooch."*

*As the military radio transmits a casualty report, one
grunt says: "There it is."*

The transistor plays rock 'n' roll.

CHAPTER 47

November's chill filled the air the morning Vaughn lingered
at home while Dane went to the cave. He felt guilty stealing
the time from work to write checks for the electric, phone
and credit card bills so the "real world" wouldn't kick in the
door to repossess his life. The day's *Washington Post* beside
the envelopes stacked on his cheap dining room table glowed
with stories about an eighteen-and-a-half minute gap in the
tapes Nixon had finally turned over to Watergate investigators, a gap Nixon's secretary said she'd "accidentally"
caused. Yeah, thought Vaughn. Right. He finished his to do,
dressed for work and had walked to the end of his block
when a man called out his name.

"Do I know you?" asked Vaughn as the shaggy-haired
man in the rumpled suit and overcoat hurried across the street
to join him.

The man spoke his name, said, "I'm a reporter."

"And you just happened to be walking down A Street at nine-fifteen in the morning."

"You don't want me to lie to you. That's not what I'm about and neither are you."

"I'm sorry, but I don't talk to reporters. You can call the committee and—"

"And get the runaround. My job is to get the story. The truth. That's what I think you want to happen, too."

"Yeah, well . . . sure."

Vaughn walked toward the Capitol five blocks away. The reporter fell in step beside him, his eyes oblivious to the dog shit on the sidewalk.

"Look," said the reporter, "we don't have to do this on the record. You don't need that, neither do I. You can talk to me on background—a committee source. We can go with deep background, where I won't link what you say to anybody, any source. But if we do that, you've got to really be certain, and really give me something."

"Wait: How did we end up that I 'got to' do anything?"

"We all have to do what we can. If we don't, the bad guys win, Watergate keeps on going even after it's over, and every time we look in the mirror, we'll know who to blame."

"I do my job."

"That's what this is about, you doing your job. Me helping you do your job."

"How are you going to 'help' me?"

"If it wasn't for the press, there wouldn't be any Watergate."

"Actually, I don't think Hunt and Liddy and McCord and the Cubans were reporters when the cops busted them."

"You know what I mean. We kept them from getting away with it."

Vaughn said, "So the prosecutors and FBI and Senate staffers are just along for your ride?"

"Look, we're talking semantics, and that's not the issue. I've got sources—several sources—who tell me Ervin is going to push to keep the committee alive beyond its scheduled expiration date, expand the probe beyond the Howard Hughes money stuff."

"If that's true, then when the votes are taken, it'll be out there—"

"For everybody to see and report and nobody will give a damn."

"You mean *you* won't give a damn."

"Once it's out there, it's not a story."

"No! That's not . . ." Vaughn stopped, shook his head. "Tell me something."

"Trade back and forth? Sure, that's a good way to go."

"You're right. Without a few tough reporters at *The Washington Post* and Jack Anderson's column, Hersh at *The New York Times*, *L.A. Times*, *Chicago Tribune*. Without the stuff you guys dug up, the heat you kept on the White House and Congress, maybe this whole mess wouldn't have busted open, but—"

"No buts about it!"

"Maybe not. But in the beginning, what you guys were doing was *investigating*, reporting stuff that nobody else wanted out, that the good guys didn't know or couldn't get to. That was hard as hell—I mean, we've got subpoena power, and it's still hard as hell!"

"But lately," said Vaughn, "you guys are just after scoops—twelve inches of 'news' about something that *if* it's true will be released to the public in a few days anyway. Hell, you're even writing about each other! Now you guys aren't trying to get the truth out to the public, you're scrambling to get a story, any story, *first*—and get credit for it."

"What's your point? That's the news business."

"I'm not a businessman, I'm a public servant."

"Look, I don't want to have to play hardball with you—"

Vaughn laughed.

"—but you staffers are investigating Howard Hughes's Watergate role beyond money. Sources tell me Nixon was afraid Democrats had proof that he and his brother took bribes from Hughes. So the burglars hit Watergate to clean up dirt about Nixon and Hughes, not just to bug the DNC. Hell, I've been told those burglars had multiple agendas, that none of them knew what the others were totally doing! There's whispers about Vesco, his ties to Nixon. Last week that DEA guy testified that the White House blocked investigating Vesco as a heroin kingpin. You can help me figure out what's bullshit and what's not, then the senators on your committee will know which way to go."

"Wait a minute; what's your story again?"

"As much as I can get. Right now, I'm trying to keep you and the Watergate committee from having a problem because of it."

"Huh?"

"Look," said the reporter as they walked over a brick path flanked by the head-high bushes of the Supreme Court. "I'm going with the story about Howard Hughes being a target of the Senate Committee and a possible motive for the Watergate crew. There's two ways I can write it. We're walking along here, you and me. Who's to say this conversation that's close to the Capitol is not also close to the White House? It's only sixteen blocks away. So I can attribute my story as coming from 'sources close to the White House.' And you and the committee staff won't catch another bullet for leaking. Or I can attribute it to 'sources close to the Select Committee.' And you guys will catch another rain of heavy artillery."

"What's the difference between your blackmail bullshit and the stuff Nixon's boys pulled?"

"Hey! The difference is—"

"Save it," said Vaughn. "Doctor it up in your story."

He hurried toward the shimmer of the Capitol in November light.

So much for the good guys, he thought as he entered the cave. Everybody's got an agenda, ambition or something, and maybe most of us are too close to being whores.

Reminds me. Vaughn went to his cubicle. On Select Committee stationery he typed the letter he'd been unable to get around to as event after event had overrun him, a letter to the Metropolitan Police Department, Washington, D.C., requesting that their vice department inform him about any known or suspected contacts between known or suspected prostitutes and current or former employees of the Executive Branch, including any individuals arrested in connection with the Watergate burglaries or any individuals or "entities" related to current federal and Senate investigations "no doubt familiar to your department."

Let's see if Nixon's boys were locally recruiting the call girls they kept talking about, thought Vaughn. Maybe figuring that out will lead someplace interesting.

CHAPTER 48

Night-side, November 1973. Holloway sat parked in front of a department store warehouse building in a riot-scarred section of Washington, D.C. The radio played news stories about President Nixon standing tall, standing fast. Holloway turned the radio off. He got out, locked the car. The cold wind skittered trash along the gutter. Squatters' lights flickered in two boarded-up townhouses. Holloway unzipped his nylon jacket to clear the .45 tucked near his belt buckle.

Walk it slow and easy, he thought as he headed toward the warehouse. Walk like a man.

Instincts told him not to go in there. Experience told him to stay out of there. Tactical doctrine told him never to go it alone.

But that's who I am. A man alone. With a job to do.

Since Sandy left, he'd numbly moved through his NSC hours, coming home where there was nothing but his bedroom ceiling and his morning paper. Holloway felt as unattached as the padlock hanging loose in the warehouse door's lock. *There it is. Just like it's supposed to be.*

Streetlights filtering through smudged windows grayed the vast darkness inside the warehouse. The cold air smelled of dust and cockroaches. Two red arrows glowed on the freight elevator panel. When Holloway reached them, he found the cage door closed, the elevator gone. He pushed the down arrow, heard the creak and groan of dry winches and rusty cables.

The elevator cage sank to his level, a golden-lit box behind bars. He chose the button labeled "Top." The machine clanked and groaned and rose through a dark shaft. Holloway held the control lever with his left, not his gun hand.

Levels of darkness rolled past the bars in front of Holloway's caged eyes: up, ever up. The machine stopped. Through the slats of the elevator, Holloway saw a vast floor dotted with islands of trash, continents of refrigerator and dryer boxes. Near the distant edge of this dark world, a dangling ceiling light dropped a cone of white light around a standing man.

Holloway jerked the rattling slatted door up, leapt out of the cage's golden glow and into the shadows. The man in the cone of light didn't move. Like radar, Holloway's eyes swept the warehouse as he sidled toward the man in the light.

Penzler called out, "We live in amazing times."

The raptor spy wore an overcoat, buttoned to his collar. Hard to draw a weapon out from under there. Penzler's hands hung open and empty at his sides—gloved, but after all, it was cold. If his hands drifted into his pockets . . .

"This town is in danger of flying apart," said Penzler.

Forty feet separated them. Thirty-five. No one hid behind any of the huge cardboard boxes.

"Why did you ask me here?" said Holloway.

"Why did you come?"

"It's my job."

"Ah, yes, your job. And your duty. Your power. Tell me, which one of those imperatives compels you to keep putting me at risk, to keep fucking with me, your comrade in arms?"

Holloway stopped within easy pistol range of Penzler. Who said, "Why do you focus attention on me with your reports? You've forced me to develop an 'arrangement' with your commanders. They wouldn't give you up, but now they recognize my value. That's sufficient, providing this town holds together during Nixon's implosion. But then there's you. Why do you persist in meddling in my business?"

"Guess something about you just pisses me off."

"I'm the one who has the right to be angry—at you," said Penzler. "Stealing that Helms memo. Then linking me to the plumbers with the memo you stole from them. Plus reporting to your commanders that I'm keeping a close eye on mobsters linked to the White House. None of those areas are your mission or concern."

"Maybe they should be."

Penzler shrugged.

Holloway watched the CIA exec's gloved hands.

"What are your ambitions, Major? What do you want?"

Holloway laughed.

"That's always the question. What do you want? Really want, at your core. If you don't piss off the Pentagon brass more than you already have, I can give you guidance there."

"One way or another," said Holloway.

"Yes. One way or another. But doing what you're supposed to do will ensure a comfortable career for you. Maybe even a stellar career. If you want money . . . helpful investment advice is yours for the asking, financial assistance. If you're looking for more excitement than that red-white-and-blue mouse Sandy—"

"That's—"

"—then you'd be delighted by the help I can provide."

"As long as what?"

"As long as you focus your eyes and your interests away from me. You can't hurt me anyway. Your commanders forbid it."

"But like you said, this town is flying apart. If I keep shining flashlights on you, maybe somebody else will notice. And care. And the Agency won't cover you."

"National security is a discreet affair. You're a sworn Marine officer."

"Don't whine to me about 'national security'!"

"You don't even know what you're doing or what you've got."

"Neither do you, asshole."

"Ah. Well. Perhaps not, *dude,* but—"

The *rackety-clack* of a shotgun slide and whir of a cardboard box bursting open cut the air. On the cue of *dude,* the huge black man with the shotgun popped out of the stove-sized cardboard shell like a jack-in-the-box.

Holloway grabbed his belt-tucked .45's grip.

The shotgun giant in the box bellowed, "Freeze, motherfucker, or I blow you up!"

Holloway froze.

"Position and timing, Major," said Penzler. "Marines should know that."

Holloway stood still, silent.

"You're alive," said Penzler. "Let's keep it that way."

"You're over the line. No going back."

"Good: you think clearly under fire. Your time in Vietnam was not wasted."

"Kill me and the admirals will come after you. Fuck the law and the CIA and your deal: their pride won't let you win over a Marine's dead body."

"So we agree: I can make a dead Marine. Here and now. Or later if I choose."

"You can try. But you don't dare."

"Then you have nothing to fear by surrendering your weapon. I knew you'd have one. You're too schooled not to. Before we continue, I need it. Otherwise, I'm the one here who's at risk. You've not been overly stable these last few months. Ask around the Sit Room."

"You got the man with the shotgun. You don't need any more."

"Move, motherfucker! Come on! Fucking honky soldier boy!"

"If I wanted you dead, he'd have dropped you when you stepped into the killing zone. Give me your gun, Nate. Set it on the floor and slide it to me. Your eyes show so much.

You've been seen lost in the thousand-yard stare. Living in your own world. What can one expect, tossed out in the cold like you have been? Admit it: you've fantasized about killing me. Maybe you even came here half convinced that tonight was that bloody night. These are times of casual death. I don't intend to let that happen to either one of us. I need you to listen, I need you to know, I need to be safe to do that. You need to know, too, or else you wouldn't have come here."

"Keep your piece, motherfucker! Make your sweet ass play! Maybe I'll only blow an arm off. Maybe I'll let you live to give me a sugar kiss!"

"What Ivy League college did you CIA guys get him out of?" Holloway asked Penzler.

"Oh, he's not with the Firm. And you should know who he is, in case anybody asks. They call him Manster in D.C.'s streets: 'man' plus 'monster.' Charming, yes? Those he's close to—men and boys only, a taste Manster picked up in jail—they might get to call him Jerome. I wouldn't know, Mr. Jerome 'Manster' Smith and I aren't that—"

"Shut the fuck up!"

"Well-trained, disciplined help," said Holloway.

"What can you expect? I borrowed him from a friend who employs Manster on a more regular basis."

"Whach you talkin' 'bout my business!"

"Easy, Manster," said Penzler. "The major is about to put his pistol on the floor and slide it to me. Once that's done, we can all relax. Nothing very bad is going to happen here. It can't, and the major knows that. He knows that here, rationality is in charge. After all, this isn't Saigon."

"If you—"

Penzler rolled his eyes: "*If, if, if, if!* Nathan, if *what?*"

Holloway said nothing.

"Want to find out?"

There it is.

Holloway eased the .45 from his waist, slid it toward Penzler. Braced for the shotgun blast . . .

Penzler smiled. Walked to the pistol, cradled the .45 in his gloved hand.

"There," said Penzler. "Was that so hard? Manster, lower your cannon. We're past that."

Reluctantly, the giant standing in the cardboard box lowered the shotgun. The bore pointed at the floor. The terror weapon looked like a toy in the big man's hand.

"Thumb the safety on," said Penzler. "I want no accidents."

The click of the shotgun safety going on filled the night.

"We can relax," Penzler told Nathan. He stood twenty feet from Holloway, ten from the giant in the box. "Now you belong to me."

Penzler swung the .45 up and shot Manster in the chest.

The pistol's roar boomed through the warehouse, the muzzle flash lit their faces like a flare: Penzler's leer, Manster's surprise, Holloway's dumbfounded stare.

Manster staggered but still stood in the cardboard box. He looked down at the golf-ball-sized oozing red splotch on his chest. Raised wide eyes to Penzler.

Who said, "Need another?"

Manster's knees buckled. His shotgun clattered to the floor and he crashed to cold tile.

"Apparently not." The .45 in Penzler's gloved hand zeroed in on Holloway.

"What—what?"

"That's the question, isn't it?" Penzler backed toward the elevator. The black bore of the .45 pulled Holloway past the gurgling, dying Manster. "What happens now?"

"That's up to you. You're a major in the Marines, an NSC aide and a can-never-be-revealed spy. Who has a gun logged out to him. A weapon ballistically traceable to a bizarre murder of a thug tied to narcotics. A black homosexual thug. What does it mean that the personal weapon of a bachelor Marine killed poor Jerome? On a lie detector test, you'll show up as knowing his name, that he did jail time, details that muddy up answers about your 'innocence.' But such an 'official' scenario assumes that your commanders would permit that much scrutiny of you. That's what car accidents are for. Heart attacks. You and I both want tonight to stay a mystery forever. All that has to happen to make that so is for you to fuck off. To forget that I ever existed. Ignorance is never too much to ask. Especially when everyone wants that. Even your commanders."

"You just murdered a man!"

"Utilized a throwaway." Penzler backed into the elevator cage. "Think I'll hold on to your pistol. Do you mind?"

"I'll report you!"

"Who would believe this? Who would want to? And who would care?"

Penzler pulled the cage door down, a rolling racket clunking, dropping lines of steel between him and Holloway. Penzler kept his aim on the Marine through the gap in the bars.

"That's OK, don't thank me," said Penzler. "You're safe now. As long as this gun doesn't come to local cops who know what questions to ask. A wild story like yours, who'd believe it? But in this rational age, ballistics is science, science never lies, and the good guys always win."

Forever after, even during the horrors of the hour that followed when Holloway used his Swiss Army knife and, *screaming,* cut his way through the perfumed corpse's chest wound, soaking his own clothes in steaming blood and gore as he sought/found/fled with the slug from Manster's heart, Holloway heard the benediction Penzler delivered as he pushed the button and the elevator slipped him down, away into the night, gone:

"Besides, you have no reason to complain. You're free of me now—if you leave me and the way things are supposed to be alone. Think of that as your penance. Think of tonight as justice: even if you somehow skate clean from this mess, you have to be guilty of *something!*"

CHAPTER 49

On Tuesday, December 4, in a Senate office turned into a formal interview room, Vaughn and other Watergate staffers argued with Howard Hughes's lawyer, a blustery attorney who'd fought the committee's subpoenas for Hughes's records and for the $100,000 in cash that Hughes had given—but that had supposedly never been used—to help CREEP finance its questionable activities.

"Don't telegraph this," one attorney had explained to Vaughn. "If we can get the cash they've supposedly been keeping and never used, then we can check the serial numbers. If the serial numbers on the cash checks out to bills not circulated until *after* the date that Rebozo says he got that cash from Hughes, then they've switched the money, replaced 'gone' cash with new bills. And then we've got them in a lie. If we get Hughes before our committee, we're suddenly more interesting than the soap operas the TV networks have put back on."

Just as a Committee counsel started to swear him in, Hughes's lawyer jerked open an attaché case, yelled, "There's your goddamned money! Take it, burn it, do whatever you want with it!"

Stacks of hundred-dollar bills slid across the table.

My father's worked his whole life and never seen money like that, thought Vaughn. And he voted for Nixon, too.

"We can't keep that!" said a committee lawyer.

Vaughn helped other Senate staffers photocopy both sides of all the bills before they returned them to Hughes's simmering attorney.

As Christmas drew near, the photocopied and returned bills were but more bricks in the increasingly complex edifice called Watergate being built by the Select Committee, the grand jury, the new special prosecutor, by the press and other law enforcement investigations in Washington, in New York, in California, in Nevada, where a grand jury was investigating Hughes for stock manipulation and conspiracy, and in Kansas City, where the Justice Department was filing an antitrust suit against dairymen linked to the milk fund contributions to Nixon. Nixon was simultaneously taking credit for releasing "his" tapes and fighting over releasing specific tapes and transcripts (in which expletives and "national security matters" and "privacy issues" were deleted) subpoenaed by the committee and prosecutors.

Dane handed Vaughn a *Chicago Tribune* story on Friday, December 11, as they ate sandwiches in his cubicle. According to the *Tribune*, Nixon's plumbers, while trying to uncover one of Jack Anderson's sources, had accidentally discovered Pentagon spies targeting Kissinger.

"We going to do anything with this?" asked Vaughn.

"I'm not sure. It's not about the campaign, so it's not on our table."

"You ever read *Mad* magazine?" asked Vaughn.

"I'm not culturally illiterate," answered Dane.

"They have cartoons in the margins. Two guys, one white, one black, but otherwise, exactly the same—sharp noses, weird hats, always killing or tricking each other: 'Spy versus Spy.' "

"Nixon and his boys and these military guys are a lot more than cartoon characters."

Vaughn said, "Are we sure?"

For the first time in his life, Vaughn did not go home for Christmas. While regular Senate staffers boarded crowded jetliners for pine-scented holidays in their childhood beds, he and the other committee staffers labored for a new round of public hearings on the milk fund and Howard Hughes's contributions, even though officially the committee was scheduled to deliver its final report and die before March roared into town like a lion.

On New Year's Eve, Vaughn and Dane went to a sedate

house party with a dozen other couples linked to the Selected Committee, even though they'd received dozens of A-list invitations, many of which, remarkably, were linked to reporters and TV correspondents they knew not at all. Because they were a slightly drunk drive closer to her apartment than his, they spent the first night of 1974 there. Her rooms smelled of dust from another planet. "We haven't made love for a long time—I mean here," he'd said. "I know," she'd answered. "Still want to, right?" he'd asked. She held him on top of her for a long time; it lasted a long time. Then he wasn't sure which side of the bed was his. She lay in the dark of the new year, wondering where a hundred steps she hadn't noticed taking would lead. She made herself sleep.

On Thursday, January 24, back at his apartment, Vaughn climbed out of his bed, fetched the newspaper, and discovered that Murray Chotiner, Nixon's hatchet man, the mob-representing lawyer tied to the milk fund scandal and Hoffa's pardon, had been in a car accident at a sober 9 A.M. the day before. A government truck had struck Chotiner's Lincoln Continental in front of Senator Ted Kennedy's house, knocking it into a car driven by a doctor named McGovern (no relation to the Democratic senator Nixon beat in the Watergate-tinged election). Chotiner was hospitalized with a broken leg. Vaughn thought: Guess he's temporarily out as a witness.

Richard Nixon delivered his "State of the Union" address on January 30, 1974, the same day that Murray Chotiner died unexpectedly of complications following the car accident.

Two hours before Nixon's speech, Q hiked up Capitol Hill. He'd volunteered for surveillance duty before he'd been asked.

"What the hell," his captain had said, "lately you been putting in every damn hour you could. Are you building up a bank account to buy a house, settle down?"

"Not that."

"Guy your age, you think you'd have something better to do than work and someone to do it with."

"I got someone, Cap. Now do you need me?"

"Yeah, Quinn, I do. So that makes one of us who knows what he needs, right?"

"If you say so, Cap."

On that January night, thirty minutes after he'd hit the undercover street, Q turned west on East Capitol Street toward the ivory dome glowing in the misty winter night, forced himself to concentrate on where he was and what he was doing, not where he'd been, not Lorri, not the weight of the target nailed on his back by Nezneck and Penzler, by crooked cops Godsick and Bruce.

Can't do anything about what's already been done. Quinn's boots crunched dirty snow. *All you can do is watch where you're stepping now.*

And don't think about the meet tomorrow: routine biz.

Three blocks from the Capitol, he spotted the churning mass of demonstrators.

The antiwar people, Q thought as he walked toward the lines of bundled figures carrying placards around their necks and signs on sticks. Has to be at least one thousand demonstrators. The next day, many journalists reported only that the demonstrators were "students" carrying what Q abruptly realized he was seeing in reality and not in some LSD hallucination—signs that read PRAY FOR UNITY! SUPPORT THE PRESIDENT! PRAY FOR AMERICA! WE LOVE THE PRESIDENT!

Q's mouth gaped as he stood in the night, watching the orderly crowd of young demonstrators parade with the brightly lit Capitol as their backdrop.

"Hey!" He beckoned a cherubic Asian girl in a parka to him. The placard around her neck read STUDENTS FOR NIXON! WE BELIEVE THE PRESIDENT! "What's happening?"

She smiled brightly and replied to Q in a fast babble of Asian.

"I'm sorry," he said, "I don't . . . Do you speak English?"

"I so happy be he'e!"

"What is this group?"

A smiling young Asian man joined them. His placard read SUPPORT AMERICA! He and the girl talked rapid-fire Asian to each other, then beamed at Q.

"You don't speak any English, do you? You don't know what your signs say or mean."

They beamed. Nodded. The boy chanted, "Amer'ca, yes! Nixzon, yes!"

A stubby blond girl joined them, her smile as bright as the glow from the Capitol.

"Hi!" she told Q. "Do you support America and the President, too?"

"Where are you from?" he asked.

"Gosh, Seattle!"

"No, I mean . . . this group. Who organized the buses, your signs? Who paid?"

"Everything comes from the Father! We're helping him help President Nixon because that's what God needs and wants!"

"The father?"

The Seattle smiler thrust pamphlets into his hands, gave him a limp pink carnation, told him if he'd wait right here, she'd get him a book.

Q melted into the crowd, dropped the pink flower on the rain-black street as he read the pamphlets. *The hell with this.* He lifted the badge chained around his neck out from under his Movement sweatshirt and got waved past the police barricades at the base of Capitol Hill. Quinn followed thick black power cables snaking over the pavement from portable generators to a command post trailer. A dozen high-ranking cops ignored consoles of radio receivers to crowd around a black-and-white portable TV filled with the snowy image of Richard Nixon speaking to Congress inside the white-domed Capitol looming outside the trailer's windows.

Quinn held the pamphlet toward his commanding officer. "Hey, Captain, who the Hell is Reverend Moon and why'd he ship in those demon—"

"Quiet!" snapped the captain.

Quinn faced the flickering image of the President of the United States giving Congress his "State of the Union" message as Richard Nixon said, "One year of Watergate is enough!"

Congressmen leapt to their feet with wild applause.

CHAPTER 50

Quinn muscled the TAC Squad's blue Volkswagen Beetle through the cold morning of the last day of January 1974. The rusted bug chugged up Pennsylvania Avenue, past yellow barricades still lining the sidewalk from Nixon's "State of the Union" speech the night before. Six blocks past the Capitol dome, Quinn spotted his man shuffling on the sidewalk: black leather motorcycle jacket and all alone in front of the McDonald's across from an Art Deco–towered movie palace marqueeing *Pig Keeper's Daughter*. Quinn parked around the corner, thrust his gloved hands into the pockets of his Army parka and hiked back through the icy wind.

"Long time no see, Zep," Q told the pale man. "Let's hit Mickey D's, get out of the chill."

"Too many ears in there." Zep leaned close. "Where you been, Quarell?"

They shuffled from foot to foot on the deserted winter sidewalk.

"Low profile," said Q. "Watching my step."

"If I hadn't run into Lonny, you and me'd never hooked up again. I lost your matchbook phone number after we ran from that cop in Dupont Circle two years ago! He jail you?"

"Naw," said Q: he'd set up Lonny in a dope bust, then turned him into a registered informant who faithfully dropped dimes—as he had yesterday.

"You hear about my man Skeet?"

Pulling five years in a stolen grenades sting Quarell had engineered with ATF agents. "Don't want to hear about anything except why we gotta stand out here in the fucking cold."

"Crazy days." Zep shook his head. "Everything's bent out

of shape. Can't trust nobody, and none of us make it out here on the streets all alone."

"I hear you," said Quarell. Said Quinn. Said Q.

"Skeet's in the slam, and I need a backup."

"Being somebody's butt-boy ain't my style."

"Come on, Quarell! It's not like that. And no rough stuff: just low-key deterrence, like Kissinger's always talking about."

"When did you start reading the paper?"

"All that political rap we had to hear to sell meth and M16's to the rev-o-loots . . ." Zep shrugged. "Guess some of it rubbed off. But now it's get-real time. For both of us. Your antiwar hippie shit: that's just a gig for you to get pussy, peddle dope, mix with flower children so the man can't spot street dudes like us so easy. But those Weather-bombers are too whacko to deal with anymore. Them good old days are over. So I got me a real business."

"Sure, I can see you got the Wall Street look."

"You don't know what you're seeing. Remember how I was tight with the Pagans?"

Pagans: the Mid-Atlantic states's most vicious motorcycle gang.

"I remember you talkin'," said Quarell.

"Hey, I'm doin'. You stand with me, I'll earn you two C-notes a job."

Q laughed. "You hookin'?"

"Naw: ferrying. See, the Pagans are holding hands with the racket boys."

Cold beyond the chill brushed Quinn's spine. *Should have worn a wire!*

"Real mafia action," said Zep. "They use the Pagans for heavy shit. Hire 'em as hitters. Plus you gotta figure there's deals about the meth the Pagans peddle, the chicks."

"What's your angle?"

"I'm the cutout artist the John Laws never notice. I'm Mr. Clean."

A Metro bus roaring past showered them with icy pellets.

"Think about it: With my chains and biker jacket, the cops

think I'm just another rider on the scene. I shave, put on some square-John civvies and I'm Mr. Invisible in downtown."

"Downtown? Here?"

"Last few times. Pick up a bag from a bitch or suit in a bar. Hold it on ice at a houseboat. Get a call. Deliver. Works both ways. Rumble my bike to a 7-Eleven, mix in with a bunch of riders, buy a six-pack and leave with extra weight in my saddlebags. Get from one team, pass off to the other so they're not made as connected and everybody's safe. Dope, cash, papers, whatever. They don't tell me and believe it: I do not never check out the package."

"Hand-to-hand?"

"Gotta be, man. Can't leave anything laying around in this town. Too many thieves."

Can't ask who! screamed Quinn's street smarts. Can't even describe Nezneck! But in this town, he's the one behind this! Has to be. Hand-to-hand . . . Even if Nezneck's not on the receiving end, I can set up a chain, make a bust right away. One, just one of the links has to be breakable! Turnable!

"Getting faced out by the big guys ain't my style," said Quarell.

"Nobody knows I come to you. Skeet's down, so you're the ace up my sleeve. We'll work it out so you stay in the shadows—but you better be there, motherfucker, if I need to wave you in to show I ain't no all-alone sucker chump!"

Don't let him know you're dying for this! "If I go with you, I get to say how close I'm going to dance. If I'm there, I'm there. But if I say no go—"

"Shit, man, you don't like a scene, I'll walk away, too. You didn't survive out here this long by being stupid. That's why when Lonny told me you were still around, I picked you, not him or some done-hard-time loser."

"If you're offering me two C's, you're getting a lot more, plus maybe some side action. Keep your side action, but it's three C's a dance for me."

"You robbing me, man!"

Risk bargaining to make the play seem real. Quarell shrugged.

"Two-fifty," said Zep.

"Deal."

The men slapped five, Q's glove against Zep's frozen blue palm. Zep yelped in pain.

"Easy money, man," said Zep as he thrust his throbbing hand inside his black leather jacket. "You know me. Take it easy, take it cool, take it big."

Quarell scrawled a phone number on a piece of paper he got from Zep. "I liberated an answering machine, so I don't answer my phone. Leave a message, a callback number."

The phone number rang at an answering machine in the TAC Squad room.

Q stuck out his hand for the power shake. Zep kept his frozen fingers inside his jacket, nodded good-bye, climbed behind the steering wheel of an empty Mustang, fired it up, roared away.

Not perfect, thought Quinn as he hurried to his car. Far from perfect. But good. Damn good. A new chain to wrap around Nezneck.

The wind burned Quinn's face as he turned the corner in front of the drugstore and jogged toward the blue Volkswagen punch buggy: *Damn heater and defrost in that thing never work!* Everything rang true: the Pagans connecting with the mob, Nezneck structuring that to keep it hidden. This was Zep's kind of score: He was streetwise enough for a bagman gig, schooled enough for the players to gamble that he wouldn't rat, dumb enough to take the job, cool enough to follow orders, crafty enough to want Quarell secretly in his corner—and weak enough to break if Quinn could truly scare the dog shit out of him. ₊

Work it off the books. IAD lieutenant/Nezneck dog Godsick tracked all of Quinn's cases. Can't let him spot this or it's dead. Quinn fumbled in his pocket for the car key, couldn't feel it, pulled off his glove. The cold air burned his hand. Like plunging flesh into fire. Quinn grasped the car key. Mr. "Take it easy, take it cool" Zep—

Why didn't we talk in his right-there car with the heater going and no "ears" to hear us?

Why did we have to stand out in the arctic wind on a daylight street?

Quinn ran back to the corner drugstore, entered through a side door, scanned the empty aisles and the blank face of a cashier as he ran to the window facing Pennsylvania Avenue. Quinn peered around a pyramid of toilet paper rolls. His panting breath fogged the windowpane that let him see both sides of the street past the McDonald's; as secretly as possible, his gloved hand wiped the glass.

Two minutes ticked away.

Feet cold, sweat trickling down his sides, the nauseating tang of commercial air freshener.

Another bus roared past. Three trucks. Half a dozen family-looking automobiles.

Across the street, the movie castle showing *Pig Keeper's Daughter*.

Under that red-lettered marquee two overcoated men let themselves out of the theater's glass doors, relocked them and hurried toward a nondescript sedan.

Lieutenant Cleve Godsick, Metropolitan Police Internal Affairs Division. Carrying a tripod that required time to disassemble and a Telephoto-lensed camera.

Joe Nezneck. Cigarette dangling from his lips.

Setup.

Godsick mined Quinn's reports. Found Lenny. Zep. Nezneck strategized the scam. They strong-armed, bought or both Zep, told him Quarell was a cop, so he'd enjoy playing him. So he'd keep Quinn standing out on the street with a story that was true at its core. So Godsick could take pictures to prove . . . *What?*

They'd know Quinn would work this off the books—they were making their own official version, making their own reality to . . .

Setup.

Not a bust: undercover investigating officer Quarell could possess any drugs or contraband and walk clean. Not any-

thing Zep would capture on a wire: Quinn was too good for
that, they knew it. They could smear him with bad police
work, maybe get his badge with engineered events, but so
much effort for so little—

Dead.

Somehow. Someway. They were setting him up for the
big hit. Doing it right and doing it oh so carefully because
he was a badge with federal friends. Maybe collide Quarell
with the Pagans. Ironically prove that they were contract killers. Or maybe Zep would pull the trigger himself. Nezneck
ached for that pleasure, though he wouldn't put himself in
such jeopardy. But he had to be there today, savor his genius.
They'd play it like a symphony. Sweet. Secure. Then somehow, someway, the photos Godsick had of Quinn meeting
Zep would hide his true murderers.

Set up to die.

Don't know how. Yet.

But after all this time . . . Why now?

What propelled them to pull the trigger now?

CHAPTER 51

Dane and Vaughn slogged home from work through the evening drizzle of February 6, 1974. Vaughn held *The Washington Post* over their heads. Rain spattered the front-page
picture of a convoy of trucks in the wildcat strike of truckers
that had spread to forty-two states, despite opposition from
the Teamsters union. The soggy newspaper bled ink onto
Dane and Vaughn's heads: Nixon had rejected new Special
Prosecutor Leon Jaworski's demand for additional Presidential tapes. Vaughn had been fascinated by the Page 3 article
"Hearst Granddaughter Kidnapped at Gunpoint by Trio in
Apartment." No ransom had been demanded for the heir of

a man who had founded a media empire, sold newspapers that pushed America and Spain into a news-generating war fought in Cuba, and had his life doppelgängered into Hollywood's *Citizen Kane*.

"All I want to do is dry off and get warm," muttered Dane as they hurried up the brick steps to the apartment building's outer door.

"Nobody wrote," said Vaughn as he checked the mailbox mounted inside on the first-floor canary-yellow hall wall. "Guess I won't know how popular I am until Valentine's Day."

Dane shook water off her coat sleeves. Headed toward the stairs to Vaughn's apartment.

He climbed the stairs behind her, continued, "Good thing work has eased off for us. Gives us more personal time together."

Dane said nothing.

Vaughn unlocked the dead bolt first, then slid a second key into the doorknob and gave it a twist. He froze—stood there; the knob turned but the blue slab of his door remained shut. Dane was trapped in front of him, unable to push ahead until he let her. She turned to meet his eyes. He said, "Are you going to tell me what's wrong?"

"It's nothing, all right? I'm tired. Can we just go inside?"

He kept their gaze locked as he pushed the door open and they took three steps into home. The door shut behind them. He heard a crunch, looked down and saw he'd stepped on a Four Tops album. They raised their eyes to the trashed living room and saw a man standing in front of them holding a police ID folder and badge in a rubber-gloved hand, a smile on his face as he said, "Hey, kids, how you doing? Come on in."

Vaughn felt like he'd been punched: his 247 record albums lay tossed on the living room floor like colored squares on a chessboard made by a drunken madman. Books had been thrown off their shelves. The sofa cushions jutted at awkward angles. Their clothes lay scattered on the bedroom floor; the bureau drawers gaped open.

"Quite a shock, huh?" said the man in the business suit and surgeon's gloves.

"Who are you?" said Dane.

"Police."

"What happened?" said Vaughn.

"Where are the other policemen?" said Dane.

"There's just me and you and you, and nobody else."

"I've been burgled!" said Vaughn.

"Yeah," said the cop, stepping on the Beatles *White Album*, circling to the door, locking it. "Hell of a deal. Sit down."

"I don't want to sit down!" said Vaughn. "I want to know what happened!"

"Well now," said the cop, "that kind of depends."

Dane said, "Let me see your ID again."

The cop smiled. "Whatever turns you on."

He let them read his ID, the number on his gold badge. Told them, "Detective Bruce, Billy Bruce. You can call me 'Detective.' Or 'Sir.' Now sit down."

Vaughn said, "I don't want—"

The cop stiff-armed Vaughn onto the sofa. He pushed himself back up.

Dane pulled him back down on the couch.

"So she's the smart one. Nice legs, too."

Dane held Vaughn on the couch, sat beside him, her arm around his trembling shoulders.

"Feels like shit, doesn't it? The whole world upside down and unjust, banging on your chest. You come home, find your pad messed the hell up. Some guy with a badge and gun muscles you in front of your woman. Gotta shame you. Make your balls shrivel up."

"You have no idea who you're messing with!"

"No, Slick: you have no idea, no fuckin' idea whatsoever, Mr. Vaughn Conner, Ms. Dane Foster—what a sweet name you got, babe."

She said, "We already know that."

The detective toed one of the wooden captain's chairs closer to where he stood, stepped on it with a well-shined

Italian leather shoe so he could lean on his thus elevated knee, so his suit jacket gaped open and the couple huddled on the couch could see his belt-holstered gun.

"You gots to understand the way things are," said the cop. "I'm cruising, followin' up unrelated crimes, and in your alley. I glance up, see some jamoke burglar on the fire escape lifting your window. So I climb the fire escape and *Wow!*: Out tumbles one jamoke; he knocks me back and gets away. But all I seen, the open window: more than enough probable cause—Hell, duty!—to pop inside for a look-see.

"And look what I found!" His surgeon-gloved fingers reached inside his jacket to lift out a plastic baggie with a quarter cup of green leafy powder, a few home-rolled joints, a pack of adhesive gummed cigarette papers. The cop held the bag high above the wide eyes of the man and woman on the couch, both of whom knew that this morning, it had resided in the now-dumped-on-the-floor drawer of the end table.

"This," said the cop, "this saw-it-in-plain-probable-cause-sight item is narcotics."

Vaughn's stomach fell away. His eyes seared into the baggie. He started to say, "That's mine, only mine!" but Dane dug her grip into his arm and killed his confessional protest.

"You know what our lab can do?" said the cop. "They can lift fingerprints off of this here plastic, prove who handled it so no lawyer can deny that said load of dope was once 'in the possession of.' And when I wave my hand over my crystal ball . . ."

Detective Bruce waved his free hand over the baggie.

"Look! There's two jamokes I know. One's a college boy, one's a poor, oppressed street cat, they both gonna swear some white dude off of Capitol Hill sold them evil marijuana, and that's trafficking, Jack, possession with intent to sell, Jack, that's felony, Jack, that's hard time big-time . . . Vaughn. And you know, maybe there's some lady's prints here."

Dane said, "What do you want?"

The cop nodded. Smiled.

"So you are getting to understand the way things is. Maybe there's a bright and shining happily-ever-after for the two of you after all. But before we go there . . .

"You're thinking you got the clout to ride this out or turn it around. You know prosecutors and FBI agents and senators up the ying-yang and *fuck* all that, because you ain't with them in this, you're *alone*. Over the line and onto the street and *that's* our turf! Even if you beat the rap . . . All you've worked for and want? Down the tubes, and you'll be the ones who flushed the toilet. Think of the headlines: *Senate aides! Watergate investigators! Living in sin! Fucking! Dope!* Your whole committee will drown in your shit. Plus your boss, your *real* boss, the guy you owe: a crazy juicer like Gus Martin, what are the voters going to do when he's smeared with fucking and dope? This is America: nobody's got time to read past the headlines."

The cop smiled as he tucked the baggie back inside his suit pocket.

"Why?" said Vaughn.

" 'Cause you're a fuck-up, man, and you're good at it."

"What did he do?"

"Sorry about that, honey, but it ain't just him. You being his partner jammed you right alongside him. Of course, I'll help you all I can."

"Leave her out of it," said Vaughn. "Help me."

"Since you asked so nice, how can I say no?" The cop sat across from them. "You and your damn letters, kid. Don't you know to put nothing in writing?"

"Letters? What letters?"

"I'm a Morals cop. Keeping hookers knocked in line. It's a hard job, but somebody's got to do it. Then you come along with a damn letter, not giving a shit how you fuck up the way things are and how I gotta work."

"You and the plumbers."

"Those amateurs got nothing to do with it unless you put them in it, and you're bustin' my balls to get there. See, everything works now, but if you keep pushing where there's nothing to get, you're gonna make trouble. Trouble for me."

"Because you're crooked," whispered Vaughn.

The cop slapped him.

"You could say that again, but then you'd get to hear the sound of your teeth hitting the floor. Dane there, she won't like kissing no gummy face. 'Course, no teeth will make you popular in prison, and I can help her out with a missing-you social life.

"My guess is, though, your days of being a fuck-up are through. You realize now what your real job is. You do what you're supposed to do, nail President Dick or not—I don't give a shit, he's not on my street. Nobody cares about my world but you and what's there ain't gonna help you do what you're supposed to do, so forget it and be fine. Hell, be a hero!

"Be smart," he said. "No more letters about whores. No more wrong questions from you to anybody. No nothing about nothing that's about any of our something."

"Letters," said Vaughn. "And before, you said . . . letters. I only wrote one about prostitutes to your department; they bucked it down to you. What other letters do you care about?"

"Well, now, Vaughn, that's something you're gonna have to figure out. You're about politics. From now on, you just do your political hack job. Stay out of stuff like law enforcement, prostitutes, street crime, then you'll be fine, just fine. Both of you.

"If not . . ." The cop lost his smile. He smelled of leather aftershave. The couple on the couch smelled of fear, rage and tears. "If not, who knows who'll come in through your window next time, or what they'll do? Vicious people out there. That's why you got cops like me."

Detective Billy Bruce stood. "The good news is, you two might be dumb enough to leave your window unlocked, but you ain't so dumb you don't know how to close it."

He tossed an overcoat over his shoulder just like Frank Sinatra on a record album Vaughn once saw, heavy-shoed over crunching rock'n'roll records and left without looking back.

Door closing, echo gone. Vaughn said, "I'm sorry!"

"I'm going to be sick!" Dane pulled him with her to the bathroom, shut the door and flushed the toilet, whispered, "We can never talk for real in here again!"

"What?"

"In here, the apartment."

Vaughn got it; nodded. Water rushed into the toilet tank. He turned on the sink faucets.

"I'm—"

"No time to be sorry," she said. "It's not just him. He said 'our' and 'we.' And he's too certain. Plugged in. Knows too much about us and Gus and how the Hill works. He's not just one lone crazy crooked creepy cop!"

"Then who did this?"

"I don't know. We were stupid about the dope, but you did something dead-on right. If we hadn't given them the dope handle on us, he'd, *they'd* have found some other way. Every lie he told us shows some truth and every truth is somehow a lie. Maybe we're lucky we gave the 'vicious people' an easy handle, a dope bust."

They whispered as water whooshed in the sink.

"He's right," said Dane. "It would smear Gus, the committee, blow it up and smear. . . We'd have to confess we were dopers and the only evidence that we're not paranoid liars is in his gloved hands. The least that would happen is we'd be fired because we must be crazy. Then we'd just be citizens: ordinary, average, vulnerable . . . He's right about that, and how we're alone, framed."

"They'll never let us go," said Vaughn. "Even if all they want right now is for me to not get into whatever their shit is, someday they'll want more. They'll come for more. Or they'll see us as a problem."

Water whooshed in the sink.

"We can't fight this alone," said Vaughn. "We need somebody who'll believe, who we can trust, who cares, who can do something. There's nobody. I don't know anybody who can or knows how or will. How to start. I don't know anybody."

"I do," said Dane.

CHAPTER 52

They'll kill me tomorrow, thought Quinn as he trudged home through the snowy night.

Zep had called. "I made a pickup, got the call for the delivery. We're on for Valentine's Day. Tomorrow night. Meet me at the houseboat nine o'clock."

Sure, Quarell had told him.

Sure, Q had said.

Nezneck humor: Happy Valentine's Day. Time to die.

Can't tell Harmon. Great FBI agent. He'd take this into the system—where Penzler rules. If Harmon moves, Nezneck'll know it, fold his play. Next time, the trap will be invisible.

Can't tell Buck. Got a "call me" message from him, a great cop, but bent cops Godsick and Bruce have Buck nailed in their eyes. Go to Buck, they'll see that their setup is blown.

Plus if I tell my law enforcement friends, I have too many sins to confess for Lorri to walk away clean, free and safe. Too many sins for either of us to win absolution.

Zep told the truth. "Everything's bent out of shape. Can't trust nobody, and none of us makes it out here on the streets all alone."

I made this personal. That put me outside the system. With Lorri. And that's alone.

If I live, I've busted some Nezneck and Penzler plan. Maybe I'll even send them a bullet.

If I die, the truth hidden, they won't hit Lorri right away: Why risk sparking questions? They think we don't know. It's ripping Lorri up, but she'll hold together. She'll tell Buck and Harmon. Get my department life insurance. Escape on a plane before the earth eats my coffin.

Spinning snowflakes burned his face.

What a mess I've made of my life.

"Don't stop!" whispered a man behind Quinn. "Don't turn around! Forget about your gun! If I wanted you dead, you would be."

No! Not now! Tomorrow night, it's supposed to happen tomorrow night!

"Keep moving!" hissed the voice Quinn didn't know. "Been reconning you for a week. Got your name from Gary Harmon."

Quinn found his voice: "Who's that?"

"An FBI agent who's thinner and sharper than a needle. With all the Watergate eyes on the Bureau's Washington field office, I barely snuck under the radar to contact him. He didn't want to risk reaching out for you."

Plausible, thought Quinn. Too damn plausible. So it can't be coincidence. True.

"We can't stop in the open. Take a right at the corner. One block down. That ugly apartment building. Rear staircase opposite the front doors. I'll meet you at the top landing."

Snow-muffled footsteps faded away behind Quinn.

Setup! They can't know you know! They tried to lull you to sleep with tomorrow-night's Zep setup, so beat feet! No: bust their play from the inside! You're good enough!

Quinn's head spun as inertia pushed him forward.

Fuck it: live or die *now*.

Out of the storm, through the glass doors of a sour chunk of architecture. A shabby lobby. Gray walls. Drafty. Steamed essence of ammonia and urine. Tan faces with black hair, dark eyes. Saigon and El Salvador whispers. Gun thrust in front of him, Quinn ran up the rear stairs until, panting, he zeroed onto the fifth-floor landing with his .38—found only a locked steel exit.

Boom! The slam of the first-floor door reverberated up the stairwell.

Footsteps scraped on the concrete stairs. Climbing up. Climbing closer.

Quinn twisted the handle of the fourth-floor door—unlocked. He slid into a musty hall, one hand clinging to the doorknob, the other gripping his revolver. The only other human being in the hall was a woman wearing a torn parka over an *audai*. She saw *American*, saw *gun*, melted into the shadows with the ghosts.

Footsteps in the stairwell, passing the door, climbing . . .

Quinn threw the door open and locked his aim on an overcoated back. "Gun on you! Don't stop! Don't look back at me!"

The man climbed until he reached the steel roof door. His gloved hands hung open by his sides. "There's no place left to go."

"So turn around."

Short haircut, not as old as he looked. No flinch as he stares down the bore of my gun.

"Killing me solves my problems," he told Quinn. "Not yours. Not ours."

"Why not?"

"Did you know a gay street thug named Manster? Butchered last fall in a warehouse?"

Manster, flashed Quinn: *man*-plus-*monster* strongarm for overdosed David Strait, who'd been a black street boss and chauffeur for Nezneck. A stone-cold mystery homicide.

"I'm a cop. If you're confessing, it goes into a court of law."

"I'd never make it to a court of law. Besides, I only did the butchering. A psycho killed Manster, a CIA freak named Penzler."

"Why are you giving me that?"

"Because it's true. Penzler tried to box me into a murder frame. Stuff he said then, what I knew before . . . He has to have ties to local hoods. Plus he uses his power as an agency exec to track everything that comes through the White House about the mafia, organized—"

"The White House!"

"Penzler's a leech bleeding the country. I can't let that happen anymore. He knows I want to take him down—I have to take him down. So I need help. I need a local badge who can work the links between Manster and Penzler."

"Me? You need me?" Q's .38 trembled. Sure you do. "Who the hell are you?"

"Major Nathan Holloway, United States Marine Corps, seconded to the National Security Council, White House. Your FBI buddy Gary Harmon gave me his card."

And you're truly a spook, one of Penzler's kind. "Seconded" to Nezneck. For what?

"So just like that," said Q, playing along. "I should trust you?"

"That would be crazy," said the man who claimed to be a Marine, who'd have all the right credentials to back up his cover story. "How sane are you feeling these days?"

Quinn's gun arm ached.

"Look," said Holloway, "even if you check me out with our friend Harmon, you won't know any more than what I just told you . . ."

So you've got him snow-blind.

". . . because that's all he knows. So maybe it's smart not to trust me. But if being smart is so good, why are you here, gun out, not knowing who to shoot?"

"Maybe I'm not smart enough."

"Who is? But times like these, when everything is supercharged and colliding, it comes down to pure faith. What you feel in your guts. All the regular things I had faith in are twisted up or broken, so I'm looking to go back to who's a good guy and who's not. Or who wants me dead and who doesn't."

Let's do it now. Quinn lowered his gun to his side, daring the spy to make a move.

"Come on, cop: we're the two crazy guys running through the jungle of the sane. We might not get out of here, but burying both of us *together* will make them bleed."

"Is Harmon in this with you?"

"No. I figure he can't be. If we reach out to him, we'll touch the Bureau and the whole damn law machine. Then we won't have to worry about Penzler; the system will crush us rebels for him. All Harmon knows is I need a D.C. cop who fights the real monsters in this town. He told me you were the only one to trust.

"You're stuck in some bloody horror, too, aren't you?" continued Holloway. "Otherwise you'd be playing this differently. Penzler rang a bell with you. So did Manster. So here we are. Time's running out. I'm through playing a puppet. I won't surrender or retreat, I won't hide. Hell, they wouldn't let me. What I got is you and here and now. So shoot me or stay with me, but do *something*."

The Marine sat on the cold concrete stairs.

Q eased down to the floor opposite him with his gun in his grasp.

Holloway told Quinn about the admirals. His father. The spy ring. Jud Simon in Chile. Penzler. The three White House taping systems. Cutting the frame-up bullet out of Manster. Sandy. But not about Vietnam. Nothing about Vietnam.

That's mine, thought Holloway. Mine alone.

Q thought, Whatever's true is wrapped around a hole to make a big, solid lie.

"I keep thinking it's over," said Holloway as they huddled in the cold stairwell. "News stories broke about Yeoman Radford getting caught. Senate Armed Services Committee held hearings on the military spy ring in the White House. I watched the clock in the Sit Room. Waited for some higher authority to come tap me on the shoulder. But 'press exposure' didn't matter. 'Senate oversight' didn't matter. Some admirals testified. Radford. And the whole process skipped along the cover story of tin soldiers playing kid games. Once the secret got packaged, nobody wanted to check what was true or what it all meant. Plus everybody was distracted by the House Judiciary Committee authorizing an impeachment investigation."

"Amazing," said Q.

Bullshit, thought Quinn. Even though I fogged them on the Watergate burglary stuff, the press and Congress can't be that nearsighted.

"After the Senate hearing," said Holloway, "my commanders sent me a message: Cover intact—proceed."

"Proceed where?" said Q.

"You tell me, then we'll both know."

That's it! You're the Make Certain Man. Make certain what Quinn knows. Make certain what Quinn does. But I am Q. Give him what he's certain I know. What Quinn should give him.

Q told Holloway about Lorri. About planting the September bug. About Penzler. Vice Detective Billy Bruce and IAD Lieutenant Cleve Godsick. Garbage disposal–vanished Pat Dawson. Shotgunned Alvin. David Strait's evaporated eyes. Jack the Jar in the red mist. Elma's shoes. And how everywhere was the stench of Joe Nezneck's cigarettes, the origami of their packs.

"But you say you don't know him," said Q.

"No, how could I? I mean, I didn't know the name, but I knew he had to exist."

"Sure you did. That's only logical, that Nezneck and Penzler work together. Penzler and the Agency are Nezneck's get-out-of-jail-free card. How he gets to run gambling casinos overseas, behind the Iron Curtain—Hell, do you think that might even be why such a pure capitalist pig does business in communist 'enemy' countries?"

"Linkages," said Holloway. "Alliances of convenience—"

"Convenience," interrupted Q. He smiled. "Use it when you can."

"Cover one operation with another, each with their own secrets, each helping the other, each protecting the other."

"Yeah," said Q. "Convenient and so fucking *logical*."

"The women: MICE." Holloway revealed Penzler's *M*oney, *I*deology, *C*ompromise, *E*go acronym. "All spy agencies love honey traps—setting up the opposition with unsanctioned sex, filming them, 'compromise' blackmail. Our Ivy League boys sure aren't going to whore out their sisters just for patriotism. So they link up with a man who has those kinds of women, who can operate at arm's length from them, plausible deniability, and still give them the take. Hell, the fools they trapped probably paid to. . . ."

Backing away from graphic analysis: *As if he cared about brushing against Lorri.*

"Was Pat Dawson in the black vinyl Watergate binder?" asked Holloway.

"No." *Use the truth.* "But she'd been long dead by the time I got the binder. Heidi wasn't in it either—she's been promoted to management, don't you think? But Pat Dawson . . . Somehow she's something powerful to Nezneck. Got any ideas what?"

"No."

"Too bad." Q shook his head. Shrugged. "What the hell can we do?"

The two men sat in the icy cold of a concrete stairwell.

Wait, thought Q. Let the Make Certain Man lead.

"Penzler and Nezneck's strength is that they don't exist," said Holloway. "Ironically, in a way, so is ours: they don't know we're not alone anymore, that we've got each other."

"Guess we're lucky."

"Not too. They're men who don't believe in living enemies. From what you've said, what I know, they'll take us out—probably not until all the heat around Watergate dies down, but then for sure. Sooner if we toughen up. We can go cowboy and grease them first—"

"*Huh.* That's interesting, but not my style. Guess I'm not as deep in the jungle as you."

"It might not work anyway. It might put us in bigger jeopardy, but as long as they don't exist, we can't get them with the system. Maybe we can pull them out into the street. Or maybe we can make a chain back to them, one or the other. Whatever—I've just got to. I wish there was something I could do that's hands-on. We need a break. And we need it now."

A break. Like you just happening to appear now, when Zep's set the ticking clock.

Q smiled. "Funny how right you are. Tomorrow night I'm running undercover against a low-life boom-boom supplier for radical bombers. Now he's a go-between for the Pagans and the mob. I'm going to turn him into a link in a chain to drop around Nezneck."

Holloway frowned. "Why didn't you tell me this before?"

"With so much to sort out and get straight . . . Timing just happens. Because of Godsick, I've kept this off the books. I haven't told anybody: not Harmon or Buck. Not Lorri. I won't tell them either. So if my play doesn't work, I'm going to need a survivor to tell them the truth. You'd do just fine for that, wouldn't you. Plus . . ."

"Plus what?"

"Nobody makes it out on the streets alone. I could use a backup man."

"That's what I'm here for."

"Yeah," said Q with a welcoming smile. "I know."

CHAPTER 53

Valentine's Day brought a crimson freeze to a deserted Washington marina.

Dozens of battened-down sail and power boats rocked secure in their hibernating berths. Dozens of the slips were filled only with the lapping indigo water. Most boats wintered at more hospitable marinas than this meager harbor of the urban Potomac, where "security" meant a droopy chain across the gangplank leading down from a ghetto street, and the marina master's office fifty feet from the no-longer-used light tower was locked shut for his Jamaica vacation.

Quinn was sure no one had seen him work his way along the water's edge, dodging from trash bin to tool shack to utility box in the pale morning light until a calculated dash brought him to the deserted light tower's walled stairs. He dragged his gear up three zigzagging flights to the drafty shed where the homing beacon and spotlights had long since been stripped out, where electricity no longer flowed, only a backless chair remained and the window ledge on which he rested his binoculars was covered with pigeon shit.

Carefully, quietly, he eased the broken chair to the shed's corner that overlooked the boats rocking in their slips. That corner let him see the street and the boardwalk leading down to the boats. Quinn stayed low, though he doubted anyone on the docks or street had the angle to spot his profile through the filthy glass. He pulled his sleeping bag up around him and settled into the broken chair.

Perfect perch for a killing zone.

When they come to set their ambush, I'll be waiting.

He checked his watch: 10:19 A.M.

Eleven hours before the shit hits the fan. Coffee thermos. Sandwiches. Hershey bars. Granny Smith apples. Two hits of wakey-wakey speed from a bro of Quarell's. An empty milk jug, tissues and a corner for privy business. Bullets, lots of bullets for his .38 and extra ammo magazines for his Colt .45.

The flat morning light let binoculars zoom close the deserted, glass-cabined deck of the motor houseboat moored fifty yards away between two empty slips. Zep's Harley was chained near the marina gate. Odds are, he was on the houseboat now, bunked down below and sleeping late like other night shifters.

"Part of my gig, man," he'd told Quarell. "Dude I know tricked me a caretaker squat on a houseboat for this fart in a nursing home who ain't got around to unloading it yet."

"Lucky you," Quarell'd said.

Quinn used the federal narc who now worshiped the paranoia of hiding necessary work in the bureaucracies of law and order. The narc pulled in favors, vacuumed widely to obscure his specific attention. Coast Guard harbor logs showed Zep's houseboat and its slip were registered to a name Quinn didn't recognize, with a secondary address of a Virginia nursing home. The narc pulled five years of marina records as camouflage for his true target, and that caution gave Quinn a break: up until six months earlier, one of the marina slips had been rented for a sailboat owned by a William Penzler.

Penzler: If the houseboat and nursing home guy were legit, you'd have been able to con his one-time neighbor into letting Zep use the boat—and keep your hand hidden.

Quinn trained the binoculars on the houseboat: perfect to motor to the nearby Chesapeake Bay, where a corpse could be weighted for delivery to the deep, where even if the dead rose again, what was left could not testify.

Zep appeared inside the houseboat's glass-walled cabin at noon. He scratched himself, ate something, went below. An hour later, Quinn's binoculars tracked the hood walking from the houseboat, along the boardwalk to the marina gangplank, up to unchain his motorcycle and roar away. Quinn ate a sliced chicken sandwich, an almond Hershey bar, a green-skinned apple. Zep returned to the boat at two-seventeen, bearing a grocery sack.

A gold Cadillac parked beside the gangplank chain at four-eleven. The binoculars let Quinn make out the profiles of three men inside the car, but the sinking sun glancing off the windshield wouldn't let him see clearly through that glass. Quinn scrambled out of the sleeping bag, put the .45 in one gloved hand while the other held the binoculars on the Caddy.

At four-thirteen, Nezneck climbed out of the Cadillac's driver's side, buttoned his overcoat and lit a cigarette. He coughed puffs of fog.

Lieutenant Cleve Godsick stepped out of the front passenger door. He carried a black briefcase.

Detective Billy Bruce climbed out of the backseat. He leaned against the car.

Nezneck and Godsick left him there as they walked down the gangplank, along the dock's boardwalk to Zep's houseboat, two figures marching in the magnified circle of Quinn's watch. Zep ushered them inside the glass cabin.

Quinn swung the binoculars back to Billy Bruce leaning on the Cadillac: still there, waiting. Sentry duty. Rear guard.

Three, maybe five minutes later—Quinn didn't take his eyes out of the binoculars to check his watch—Nezneck led Godsick back to the car.

They'd left the briefcase: the bait prop.

At 4:31, the three creeps were in the Caddy, driving off toward the sunset.

Quinn ate his last sandwich and Hershey bar at five-fifteen, used the last of the coffee to wash down a hit of got-no-sleep-last-night speed.

Watchlights on poles spaced along the dock blinked on as the day grayed.

Sunset painted the sky.

Night swallowed the city. House lights twinkled against winter's cold in the horizon's neighborhood. All but one of the rocking boats in the marina were dark shapes; the glass cabin of Zep's pad glowed in the night, where above the sounds of distant traffic, Quinn heard the metronome of lapping waves.

This is the official night of love. Lorri is hiding in our bedroom, no doubt cuddling a bottle of vodka. Waiting. I'm alone in this ambush tower, shivering, cold. Scared. Trapped even as I set my trap. Lorri: Be my Valentine, and let me come back able to be yours.

The shape of a man appeared in the shadows near the gangplank chain. Headlights on a passing truck washed over him: Holloway.

My backup. Mr. Make Certain Man.

On time at 8:45. Just like I told you to be. Just like you'd expect everything to be.

Except it isn't. It won't be.

No other hunters had showed, no sniper climbing up to where Quinn waited, no reinforcements to hide belowdeck at Zep's, where he futzed inside the glassed cabin.

So it's just the three of us. Me, my Judas, and the man at my back.

You'll be the one, Quinn telepathed to the shape in the shadows by the chain. That's the smart, perfect, make-sense play. They know I'm paranoid. Won't trust Zep. So they gave me a backup I'm desperate to believe. Holloway and I will walk on board together. Zep will—predictably—go attention-grabbing *dramatic* because there's a stranger with me. I'd be keeping my eyes on Zep anyway, and when the positioning is right . . .

A bullet in the back of the head. From a man who probably was a Marine. An experienced pro. A taxpayer-trained killer, just like Penzler. *Bam!* One bullet to the brain, a boat ride, slide what was left of Johnny Quinn into the indigo waves of gone forever.

Wonder what their explanation will—would—be? Doesn't matter. Not an important question. Maybe shot mysteriously in the line of duty. Maybe a suicide if they can control the forensics. Maybe I just disappear, though best would be for them to have a body with a logical explanation. After all, Godsick's got pictures of Zep and me.

Nine o'clock.

Holloway stood in the shadows. Waiting. Watching for the man who wasn't there. For the plan that wasn't happening.

How long can you stand it? Wait before you know something is wrong, terribly wrong, and you've got to do something?

Then we'll see. Know. Then I'll run a new play. Put the fucking Marine in my gunsights again. This time he'll go for it and I'll blast him out of his shoes. Trap Zep alone, bring him into—

Holloway stepped over the chain and headed down the gangplank toward the houseboat.

No retreat. No surrender.

Quinn unzipped his parka to clear his holstered .38. Picked up his .45. Watched through the binoculars.

You're going to find out what's wrong and prove your cover's blown and your lies didn't work. But you won't even know how badly you miscalculated until it's too late.

Zep spotted the lone man walking toward his houseboat. He left the glass-walled cabin to stand on deck to see who it wasn't. Quinn's binoculars pulled the shapes of the two men in close and clear, though fifty yards away and in the tower shed, he couldn't understand the emphatic words Zep threw at the man standing on the dock beside the houseboat.

Zep's probably telling him so what if I'm late, but Holloway knows that's not how I—

Holloway charged onto the boat. Punched Zep.

What the—

Zep fell back against the far gunwale of the houseboat, a bobbing image in Quinn's binoculars. Zep thrust a hand inside his shirt. Holloway's back filled Quinn's view.

Quinn dropped the binoculars and ran, .45 in hand. Down the light tower stairs, stumbling, crashing, falling and tumbling down the last flight but rolling up to his feet.

Go! Go!

Running charging over the boardwalk, the slap of his shoes on the frozen wood. Cold and black all around. Cones of white light whipping past him and the lit boat looming close.

Gunshot!

Glass shatters!

Quinn leapt on board the houseboat as Holloway ripped the pistol from the hand of the man he fought. Zep yelled in broken-thumb pain as Holloway pushed him back against the cabin with its bullet-shattered glass wall. The Marine whirled to face the thump of hostile boarder.

"Don't shoot! Fucking drop the gun!" yelled Quinn, the .45 swinging back and forth from Zep to Holloway.

Zep, his hand on fire, his nose and mouth bleeding, crashed backward into a pane of the glass wall, which cobwebbed with his impact, almost shattering like its neighbor: *"No! No! This ain't the fucking shit that's supposed to happen!"*

"You lied to me!" Holloway yelled to Quinn. "You set me up. You didn't show!"

"Just calm down!"

"Quarell, man, he's beating on me, yelling where the fuck are you, what'd I do to you! Nothing, man, not yet, you fuckin' were supposed to come here. They said you would, not this fucking madman, shit and guns here on me. Man, *this isn't right!*"

Over his shaking .45 Quinn yelled to Holloway, "I didn't set you up!"

"The hell you didn't! You been out there somewhere, haven't you! Fucking ambush—"

"No! I thought you were—"

"Not me, man!" blubbered Zep, holding his broken hand. "Not guns for me, man. I'm just doing business. Payback. You fucking *both* fucked me and it's not fair, you fuckin' cops!"

"You know I'm a cop!" yelled Quinn.

Zep blinked.

Quinn risked it; moved while Holloway still had the pistol trained on him. Kicked the cobwebbed glass pane Zep leaned on.

That wall shattered. Zep fell back into the cabin, his moment of composure blown away as the man called Quarell pointed a fucking *cannon* at his face.

"Shit, yes, man! That was the deal! You cop, you fucked me! So fuck you! And those people, cool cops and connected guys, gonna help them set *you* up for a change!"

Holloway gentled his aim but didn't lower his gun; frowned.

"Set me up *how*? Tell me or I'll blow you the fuck away! Forget about jail. We'll witness ourselves clean and you'll be history!"

"Dirty you up, man! Here! I'll show you! Prove it to you!" The black briefcase Nezneck had brought lay on the cabin's table. Zep dropped his unbroken hand to it. "Fuckin' delivery scam, man. I knew you'd go for it big-time. Get your fingerprints, only yours, on a bag of smack, Jack, 'cause you'd have to know you'd have to look."

Zep clicked the first latch on the briefcase.

Quinn's mind raced: Nezneck, Godsick, they knew Zep, knew me—knew his record—former Weathermen arms and explosives dealer—pictures of us, like I'd walked Zep into a surveillance to build a case. What kind of case? What crime! Manster was a throwaway to get Holloway. They need a cop's body accounted for. Murder's messy. Suicide needs forensics covered. Killed in the line of—

Zep clicked the second latch on the briefcase.

Quinn dove at Holloway, drove both of them staggering and flailing across the narrow deck. They hit the low gunwale, flipped over and plunged into the icy river.

Wet cold slammed with bone-cracking fire ice. Two men intertwining and struggling in choking arctic blackness. Lungs burning, heads spinning, *where's up or down*, swirling and sinking as winter clothes soaked thick with leaden drowning water.

The bomb booby-trapped in the briefcase blasted the night.

Light flash in the turgid choking darkness showed Quinn and Holloway which way to go.

Kicking, clawing with lead-wrapped arms, they broke up to the surface, gasping—getting air that still trembled from the bomb's roar. Pieces of wood and other things floated on the surface around them as they struggled to the edge of the dock. Quinn got there first, reached back and helped Holloway pull himself to safety.

"G-g-g-go, gotta go! We can't get caught here!" cried Quinn.

They staggered, slipped, stumbled, sloshed, ran.

Behind them, the houseboat with its blasted-gone cabin bounced in the waves.

Ran, they ran, Quinn following the Marine over the dock, up the gangplank.

Sparks from a frayed electrical wire found wisps of butane from the broken stove line.

Blue fireball lit the night to silhouette two men stumbling over the gangplank chain.

Gone, they were gone, running in the shadows before the night's second roar rattled neighborhood windows. They vanished out of that flash of light, ran across the big road, two, three blocks—*Cold, so cold, shivering, head on fire, can't*—

"Here! Here!" Holloway forced his shaking hand to put

the key in the car door. He had the passenger door unlocked before Quinn got there, the car started before Quinn slammed that door on the winter night.

They tore their clothes off—shoes, socks, pants, shirts, underwear: everything leaden and wet with the water of death. Holloway grabbed a dry shirt and pair of jeans off the backseat, frantically wiped himself off with the shirt as he tossed the jeans to Quinn.

Fire truck Klaxon! Sirens!

Up the block: spinning red lights racing closer!

Two naked wet men dove beneath the dashboard, where the maximum-cranked heater fan finally began to blow warm air.

Jammed together, shivering flesh on shivering flesh, cramped, hurting.

Blasts of red and blue emergency lights lit their trembling hidden huddle, then the fire trucks and police cars roared past.

Teeth chattering, Holloway said, "*Now* can we trust each other?"

CHAPTER 54

"Maybe we've got a chance," Quinn told Lorri two mornings later as they sat parked along the sidewalk at National Airport, Quinn's engine idling, the defrost failing to keep the windshield unfogged. "Now that I'm not alone, with Holloway . . ."

"Thanks for remembering me."

"I'm sorry! I mean *we've* got. You know what I mean."

"Truth is, you're more right than wrong and that's my fault. *I'm* sorry! I've been so scared. Hell, I haven't been together . . . since before you went to burgle. Now even the booze isn't stopping me from shaking."

"You ought to stop," he blurted.

"Yeah, cut back, I have, I am, I will. I'm sorry!"

"Sorry won't help us."

"You really think Holloway can?"

"Him plus us plus something else I don't know about. Something's happening. They tried to kill me. They think they've neutralized Holloway. Why? Why now?"

"The bombing, people will have to pay attention because of the bombing!"

"America's been averaging a radical bombing a week since 1968. Homicide and the feds bought the cover story Nezneck created. The law thinks Zep was a boom-boom dealer who slipped."

"What do Nezneck and Penzler think?"

"They can't know. That's got to be driving them crazy. Especially if I play it cool."

"Will they try again?"

"Yeah, but they have to start over. Be twice as careful. Even not knowing about my Marine, they know I'm a hard target."

"How much safe time do we have?"

Quinn shrugged.

"So we just keep on like our life is normal?"

"And hope we get the chance to make it that way."

Suddenly, she wedged herself between the steering wheel and his chest—the horn beeped. They flinched, snuggled. She kissed him, unexpectedly opening her mouth, and for a moment he knew only the electricity of her tongue. Outside the car someone yelled *Woo-who!* Brakes squealed. She leaned into the crook of his neck.

Like old times, thought Quinn. Almost.

"Will you miss me?" asked Lorri.

"Yes. Sure."

"Love you."

"Me, too."

"Did Buck tell you what he wants?"

"He's doing a favor and wants my help."

"Are you going to tell him?"

"If I ask for a hand, Buck'll reach out. Right now, all I could do is pull him down, too."

She swung her slim legs out to the sidewalk, raised the handle on her stewardess case and rolled it behind her as she strode to the sliding glass doors. Quinn watched a businessman stare at her, his face alight with fantasies. The glass doors slid shut behind Lorri. Quinn swiped his glove over the fogged windshield and drove away.

Quinn sat alone at the long table in the Library of Congress cafeteria watching a gray-haired woman smoke an extra-long cigarette. Too late for breakfast, too early for lunch, too cold for tourists. The coffee in the tan mug in front of Quinn tasted like aluminum.

Buck walked through the doors beside a man undeniably stamped as his brother. Buck wore his D.C. uniform, the brother sported Capitol police gear. Both men wore sergeant's stripes. Their hard eyes judged the room in a heartbeat, two black rooks escorting a white knight and a pale queen. The brothers made the introductions, then left for fraternal time elsewhere. The man and woman sat across the cafeteria table from Quinn.

Dane said, "Are you tape-recording this?"

Quinn blinked. "Your turf, but you still asked. You are in serious shit."

"You didn't answer."

"No," said Quinn. "But there are other ways I could be fucking you. You either trust me or we say good-bye. Buck is my ex-partner. His brother with the three stripes on the force up here, you went to him on pure instinct and respect. You told him you needed to meet a D.C. street cop who was flexible but clean. Discreet. He called Buck. The brothers vouched for all of us, for you. Here we are. Can't say I'm the best man, but I came, badge and all."

"Your badge makes us nervous," said Vaughn. "So you know: we're not without clout."

"If you had the clout you need, we wouldn't be here."

Quinn shrugged. "Sorry for being a hard ass. These aren't my better days."

"What were?" said Dane.

Quinn watched her. Her eyes didn't push back and they didn't look away. He said, "Here's hoping the better days are coming."

She glanced at the man called Vaughn and Quinn saw they were a couple. A romance. With her in charge, Quinn decided as she gave her lover a nod.

"One of your kind is our problem," said Vaughn.

"And here I've been afraid I was a one-of-a-kind," said Quinn.

"We're staffers on the Senate Watergate Committee," said Dane. "A D.C. police detective named Billy Bruce has us boxed in a frame so tight we can't clear ourselves with the law or our own people. And the oddest part is, all he's pushing us to do is not investigate things that our committee doesn't care about anyway."

Quinn laughed.

Dane's eyes widened. Vaughn's jaw dropped.

CHAPTER 55

The Washington Monument rises 555 feet straight up from a grassy knoll in the center of the vast national Mall, with the Lincoln Memorial off to the west beyond the Reflecting Pool, and the ivory dome of the Capitol building on a distant hill where the sun rises. Wind strafed sleet through the city that gray March day. Quinn stood in a grove of trees fifty yards from the monument's entrance and watched a lonely taxi pull up to the distant curb, discharge two passengers, and drive away with a *whoosh*. The taxi's man and woman hurried through the sleet. No cars stopped in the horseshoe curve behind them; no one followed their wake across the icy sidewalk. Quinn waited until he was sure, then stepped out of the trees and hurried to the white marble obelisk.

The park ranger wore a plastic sheath over his Smokey the Bear hat. He stood inside the monument's entrance with a woman made plump by sweaters layered under her elevator operator's uniform. The orange lines of a space heater glowed by the operator's shoes.

"Hell of a day for sightseeing," said the ranger as he beckoned Quinn in from the storm.

"Tourists get what they find." Quinn stamped his feet. Nodded to the couple who'd been taking their time closing umbrellas, shaking off the storm. "Looks like I'm not the only one."

"Damn near," said the ranger.

The couple followed the elevator operator into her machine. The hippie-looking man in the parka brought his odor of wet jeans into the cage. The operator shut the doors and they all lurched toward the sky.

Dane eyed her watch as the elevator clanked against gravity. The brochure in Senator Martin's office claimed the ride up took seventy seconds. "I want to take my time up there. Can we just buzz you? That way you don't have to cruise all the way up for nothing."

Visions of the space heater glowed in the operator's eyes. "OK by me if it's OK by you all. Ain't hardly nobody up there now."

The cage jolted to a stop. The door rolled open to the four-sided observation level.

Dane stepped out of the cage without a backward glance. A sunken-eyed man in an overcoat checked her out, then swung his gaze back to the two portals overlooking the Reflecting Pool from the wall he faced. Vaughn turned right when he exited the elevator and saw the most beautiful woman he would ever know. She whirled when their eyes met, determined to stare out the portals as he walked past her. Her hair shone like ebony; she perfumed the dank concrete cold with the scent of coconut musk. Vaughn stood at the stairs that zigzagged down one level to a gift shop. The portals on his wall showed the wet dome of the distant Capitol. The bearded, shaggy-haired man in the parka circled round the elevator shaft toward Vaughn as that cage's motor and cables hummed its descent to the ground floor. The shaggy man looked down from a portal: Cars the size of Vaughn's typewritten name silently slid over slick gray ribbons of road cutting through the Mall's winter-green grassy plains. No vehicle parked, waited, watched. No punctuation marks of humanity dotted the pale lines of the sidewalks.

"We're clear," said Quinn. "Everybody showed up clean."

Five "tourists" came together.

"This may be the only time we can all meet together in one place," said Quinn. "Hard enough to get away from what we're supposed to be doing. Plus we have to worry about surveillance. But we had to rendezvous so we can see who we are."

"The legion of the not-yet-dead," muttered Vaughn.

"Don't trust the phones," said Holloway. "Not now, not in this town."

"Do we know anything more?" said Dane. She and Vaughn had shared Billy Bruce's warning about call girl questions. The veiled threats about other queries like the Presidential pardons, including Teamster Jimmy Hoffa's, the connection there to Mel Klise and the American Association for Justice, a linkage cop John Quinn extended to Lorri and Heidi, to CREEP, to mobster Nezneck and CIA question mark Penzler, who might be partners in ultrasecret plots against Fidel Castro.

"Nothing new since you appeared," said Quinn.

"We just keep going round and round and round!" sighed Lorri.

"What about Watergate?" asked Quinn.

"Our committee is still alive," said Vaughn, "but now everybody's focused on the House Judiciary Committee impeachment hearings. We're tracking the Howard Hughes money. I'm pushing on the Hughes-CIA-mob kill-Castro link. My staff counsel said he'll go to our chairman again.

But he also said that he didn't think an investigation like that would be 'effective' for us."

"Is Nixon going to skate?" said Quinn.

"I don't know about skate," said Dane, "but did you see him on TV when he went to the Grand Ole Opry? The crowd loved him! Mid-America, his 'silent majority.' Their kids coming home in body bags in the first war we're going to lose while college boys grow their hair long and ugly-up the TV cameras, then get the good jobs. Their daughters are going for that radical free-love sex and power that threatens rules they think Jesus wants. Even white folks who hate the Klan are scared by black-power rhetoric. Plus those Arabs holding us up at the gas pump, forcing us to wait in lines just to fill our God-given cars. Behind all that have to be the commies, shaking their missiles. The civil rights marches, the war protests. Change slammed Mom and Pop America like a tidal wave. Took them a while to realize how big it is, but now they're scared shitless. The only constant they can point to is Richard Nixon. Still there. Still *certain*. Defiant. You could read the gratitude in their faces, them singing while he played an upright piano and banged out 'God Bless America.' "

"Is out there the world," said Holloway, "or is this it?"

Vaughn said, "There is no real world."

"Why us?" whispered Lorri. "Why is this happening to us?"

"Why not?" countered Dane. "We were there."

"We put ourselves in the line of fire," said Holloway.

"Nobody's going to touch the CIA," said Vaughn. "Doesn't matter if they cut a corrupt, illegal deal with the mob to murder people."

"Nezneck and Penzler," said Quinn. "They've gotta be part of that game. The Agency will fight like hell to protect them—right up until they throw them away to protect the Agency. Then they'd bury the bodies rather than be exposed by letting anybody face possible murder conspiracy and corruption charges. Which Penzler and Nezneck know. Their lives are on the line if the CIA gets real heat. Or if their identities and dirty tricks get dragged out into the open."

"The Agency isn't in our Senate committee's jurisdiction," said Dane. "A House subcommittee only said they shouldn't have let themselves be used as dupes. A few skeletons popped up—a memo that said a guy working for a PR front of the Agency's convinced a *Washington Post* reporter not to write about the CIA, plus the wig and false ID's and stuff they gave Hunt. But nobody except Nixon's men when they were trying to build the cover-up has said that there might have been a CIA operation like a . . . a . . ."

"A honey trap," said Holloway.

Dane shook her head: "Nothing that the CIA was doing has been linked to Watergate. It's like all the Nixon dirty tricks occurred in a vacuum and aren't related to any CIA or intelligence or even racketeering shit. The Agency wants—"

"Don't think like that," said Holloway. "No agency is a monolith. The CIA is an infinity of agendas wrapped around legitimate goals. Penzler uses that. He's pure MICE, pure ego."

"No soul," sighed Lorri.

The Marine nodded yes to the woman whose makeup couldn't cover her fear. "If that's the way you see things. Being Agency lets him go all the way with who he is. My bet is they don't know how far he's gone. As long as he gets results, they don't want to know."

"Results can be hollow," said Quinn. "You spy because you can. Because somebody can, everybody must. But you create license. Just doing it becomes the only result you can trust. Maybe you get the atomic bomb secrets, but you can also end up with Penzlers. And plumbers. And me. And Nezneck and the mob.

"Watergate has got to be the key," argued Quinn. "We all know something that could put Nezneck and Penzler on the firing line. Each of us has pieces tied to the whole of Watergate. That's what's got Nezneck and Penzler so worried that they're finally trying to take us out—kill me, neutralize Holloway and you two Watergate investigators. We were 'problems' before, manageable problems not worth the cost of a final solution. But now, with Watergate ripping the lid off this town, they need to stop us."

"From finding out what?" asked Dane. "What's their giant secret?"

"I don't know," said Quinn. "But Vaughn trying to focus Watergate light on prostitutes and mobsters and dirty alliances, somehow I think that set them off. Add that to Holloway and me, our jabbing at them, it all reached critical mass for those two monsters. Everybody else in town is focused on Nixon, not the monsters hiding in his shadow, so if they can zap us, they think they can stay hidden and safe. And they're too smart and too ruthless to just sit back and hope for the best."

"They have to terminate our threat to them," said Holloway. "Permanently."

"We can just go!" said Lorri. "Get away! Run away! If we're not here, they won't care!"

"No!" said Dane. "We can find their fingerprints on something! Fight them into the Watergate record!"

"That's the problem," said Quinn. "Nezneck and Penzler aren't *in* Watergate! They're not street hoods or burglars or guys on official lists. They use button men to do their dirty work."

"Mostly," said Holloway. "There's Manster—"

"—and Pat Dawson," said Quinn. "We got nothing we can prove about either one of those murders. Or any other crime. They're buffered, protected by layers of other guys and official sanctions. As long as they stay off the street like puppet masters, we can't nail them with the law."

Dane added, "Plus, beyond the law, we don't have the clout or credibility to be believed politically."

"Then we have to be the law," said Holloway. "We have to become the politics."

"So we become just like them?" argued Quinn. "Then even if we get them, they win."

Dane said, "We've got to pull them out into the open.

Isolated. Show that they're dirty. Show how they're part and parcel of Watergate."

"Forget it!" said Vaughn.

They stared at him.

"Forget about Watergate. This is about us, not that. Watergate *was* a third-rate burglary. So what if it's about Howard Hughes and who he bribed and who he didn't. Or the CIA and honey traps and assassinations. Or Nixon and his creeps being so paranoid they were too afraid to trust J. Edgar Hoover to do their dirty work. Or the spooks from Langely and the Pentagon sneaking into the White House and secretly taping Nixon, the secret taper. Or the mob and why they killed Pat Dawson. Forget trying to understand or find out what parts go where. Forget about praying that the system solves Watergate and, hallelujah, somehow saves our ass, because it won't, it's the whole damn thing that's pressing on our ass. Watergate is business as usual, the all-American way this town works. Watergate is a thousand elements reaching critical mass and exploding. Watergate is a collision. We can't merely survive all that. Won't be enough. We've got to prevail over it. Stop it stone-cold dead so we can get free with a chunk of its heart in our hands so nothing comes back to bite us. And hell, to do that, we need one fucking powerful mojo bullet."

Bullet!

Quinn heard Dane trying to soothe the ranting kid, heard Holloway's impatient breath, the near sobs of Lorri, but *bullet*, he heard *bullet* and felt a cold blast of light slam into his forehead like a slug from a .45.

Quinn said: "Listen to me."

CHAPTER 56

Cherry blossoms lingered in Washington's trees the April morning Lorri bleached her hair blond. She saw them from the window of Quinn's apartment, wisps of pink in the landscape's concrete and chlorophyl swirl as an alien reflection stared back at her from the glass.

"You look good," said Quinn. "You look . . . great."

She'd put on bright red lipstick. Painted her fingernails a matching hue.

"But you recognize me."

"I can. But that's only me. Nobody else."

"So we'll get away with all of this?"

"Sure we will."

"Then what?" Her walk from the window was languid, liquid. She pulled his eyes with her. Weighed his silence. Smiled. "What's the matter? No more promises?"

"It's barely breakfast and you're—you've been drinking!"

"You forgot to say *again*. Drinking *again*. Or *still*." She flowed into the sunlit kitchen. "What do you think's keeping me afloat? I can't leap tall buildings in a single bound like you and our Marine, but if I keep the jangles smoothed, I can get from A to B without falling down."

"You've got to do more than stay on your feet drunk."

"You don't want me to quit. Not now. Can't risk that on top of everything else." She took a duty-free silver-plated flask from her purse on the kitchen table, unscrewed the cap for a modest swallow. "Want some? I'm always willing to share."

Quinn said nothing.

She took another sip, screwed the cap back on. "So do you still love me?"

"That's not the point."

"That's the only point I give a damn about."

"This isn't about us!"

"Really? We started everything. What's going to happen when we finish it?"

"What do you want from me?"

She slow-stepped to him like a street boxer sizing up a punch. "I want you to love me like you did. I want you to get mad at me for fucking up and trapping you here—but still love me. Sometimes I'm glad I got caught and stuck you in the damn Watergate-Nezneck-CIA-guy shit. Doing that's gotta be the worst even I could do, whore and trap you."

"You're not a—"

"You hate the word, don't you? Hard to save a girl when maybe she deserves what she gets." She drew a line across his shirt with a scarlet-tipped finger. "What happened to us, Johnny? You never even fuck me anymore, and everybody wants to fuck me. Hell, now I'm even a blonde. Don't you like that? Doesn't every man want a blonde?"

"This isn't some damn test."

"Sure it is. I know I'm a fuck-up behind a great face. Now maybe you do, too. Can't hide from that anymore. Pretend I'm who you want me to be instead of who I am. If you know that, if you still want to stick around, then maybe I'm not such a loser after all. And you know what I know in my heart? If it weren't for all this Watergate shit, there'd be nothing driving us apart. What scares me is that same Watergate shit might be the only thing still holding us together."

"Everything I'm risking."

"All the gunslinger jazz you do to 'save' me doesn't mean as much as just waking up beside the real me every ordinary screaming day. You still want to do that?"

Her fingernail plowed his chest.

"Should have jumped right in there, Johnny. Said something. Said anything."

He grabbed her hand. "Say I'm pissed off you're a drunk? Say I wish to hell you'd never done what you did? Say I'm scared shitless? About you! For you! Scared that we're not going to pull this off, that we're all going to die—"

She dug her nails into his hand. He swore and threw away their grip.

"Go ahead!" she cried. "Hit me! Hate me! Leave me! You can run!"

"You don't get off that easy!"

"At least I didn't go all the way, like your damn Pat Daw—"

He grabbed her shoulders.

Her fist pounded his chest. "Let go of me!"

"So you can fuck up some more? Screw up all over Holloway and Vaughn and—"

"And Dane, who's so damn smart!"

"*Dane?* What does she have to do with anything?"

"You're already seeing where you want to go next."

Quinn pushed her back into the table. "You're risking—because—"

"Because you're all I've got! You can do it! Leave me! Hell, even leave that damn ghost Pat you drag into bed with us. Have somebody good like Dane! I'll do what we have to do so we can save the fucking world! Anything you want! But don't lie about wanting to stay with me."

"There's nothing about Dane here," whispered Quinn. "Or Pat Dawson." And he knew that was true. "This is just us." And he knew that was true. "I love you."

"Say it like you mean it."

"You bitch!"

She slapped him.

Cocked her arm to slap him again but he caught it. She clawed his chest. Her face lunged toward his throat. He grabbed her blond mane, jerked her head back, her crimson mouth open in pain that shut her eyes.

Quinn let go.

She charged, her mouth latching onto his.

For a frozen heartbeat all he felt was terror. Then he pushed into her kiss, his fingers plowing her bleached blond hair as he devoured her face. He ripped open her blouse. Muscled her onto the table, shoved her skirt up. Her hands tugged his belt. Her purse hit the floor with a liquid metal *clunk* as he pulled off her panty hose. She stabbed him into her. He saw her contorted face smeared lipstick crimson as he knew his would be, her eyes open wide as she panted. Every time their flesh slammed together, he heard himself cry "I love you! Love you! Love you!" a savage chorus until she bucked and screamed "Yes!" and "Yes!" again, until their sound drowned every whisper in the world and that roaring silence let him come, let him *believe*.

Two hours later, he and Holloway sat parked on New York Avenue a hundred meters from the White House fence. They watched as with her newly platinum hair pulled in a bun Lorri marched along the opposite sidewalk, her blouse puffed out with a padded bra, her lips scarlet as she spun through the doors of the Sobel Building, a shoulder bag clutched to her side.

"She's OK," said Quinn. "She can handle it. Don't worry."

"I wasn't," said Holloway.

Outside their parked car felt glorious. Spring made even this block near the streetwalkers' turf feel fresh and clean. Another Nixon aide had been convicted, this time for perjury. The House Judiciary Committee had subpoenaed forty-two more conversations on Nixon's tapes. Across the continent in California, surveillance cameras recorded brainwashed media heiress Patty Hearst—now rechristened Tania and brandishing a machine gun—holding up a bank with her kidnappers-turned-comrades in the Symbionese Liberation Army.

Holloway said, "Does Lorri know not to take the elevator?"

"She'll be fine. Something like this is no problem."

"Sure," said the Marine. "They're not looking for her. Even if she gets caught on film, even though the perimeter team will ogle her, she isn't who she was. Nobody can make a link."

Ten minutes passed on their repeatedly checked watches.

Holloway stared at the street. "You and I are gunners. Dane's solid. Vaughn's a crazy kid."

"Can't call him a kid, he's about our age." Quinn shrugged. "He's who we got."

"Walking around with these beepers, it's like we're doctors. Or IBM typewriter repairmen. People see beepers on us, we stand out."

"Chance we take."

"More than a month getting set up, and we're still nowhere."

"We're still OK," said Quinn. "We're secure as long as Nixon isn't overrun. Our play all depends on timing. We can't go until Nixon goes, and we gotta be sure he doesn't pull something grand that'll wipe us out at the last moment. We got to watch him, watch all this, keep on top of it so when we move . . . Our lives depend on Nixon."

"Then we're fucked."

"So at least we can count on something. And on Nixon staying Nixon. How much time can you give this today?"

"Not much. Right now, I'm officially at lunch."

"Here she comes!"

Lorri slid into the backseat and passed over the shoulder bag Quinn had cut and rigged for a camera from the Red Squad caches.

"Like you said," Lorri told Holloway. "Different guy at the front desk, but a man in janitor's clothes matched your description. I shot pictures of them while I pretended to be looking for opera lessons."

"Let's hope the operation hasn't shut down," said Quinn.

"Why would they do that?" answered Holloway. "So what if Nixon says he turned off his taping system? That means people who meet with him in the Oval Office feel even more secure. That means the two other systems are all the more valuable."

Quinn said, "Hope so."

"Gotta go," said Holloway, opening the car door.

THAT NIGHT, MIST floated around the tires of Holloway's car as he stepped out to the parking lot in the Washington Navy

Yard. He closed his car door with a muffled *thunk*. Cicadas fell silent as he crunched across the pavement toward the only other vehicle in the lot, a Navy jeep parked outside the yellow glow of the lone light pole. A ramrod Marine sergeant swung out from behind the jeep's steering wheel, his spit-shined shoes sinking into the white ground fog. He nodded warily to the officer wearing civilian clothes.

"You've gone to a lot of trouble, Major."

"So have you, Gunny. I appreciate it. Are you sure I'm the right man?"

"You called your old Top over in Okinawa. He called me. I hooked a corporal at the Pentagon and he got me your photo spread before you and I even connected on the phone. Would have been easier if I could have returned your call. I know the number of the White House."

"Then you're one up on the world these days. You need anything else?"

"Hell, yes, sir. Check the regs: I can't do this. The capability does not exist within the command to which I am currently assigned. And even if it did, so many orders would have to be cut, we'd need to ax half the trees in Idaho."

"So what's our solution?"

"All this never happened. No way, no how, no paper, and next time, even for a maximum-vouched Marine like you— never happen. *Xin loi*, but I say again: there is *zero* next time."

"Are you sure you're covered?"

"Due respect, Sir: What kind of question is that to ask the man *who will be* sergeant major? And, roger: you are invisible, too, even though I copy you have stratospheric authorization for some aspect of what's not happening here tonight.

"What's also not happening," said the sergeant, "is me exceeding my wish to know. I can do what I do because men in the Corps who matter vouch for you and whatever 'command objectives' you say you've got. I may not know, I may not like, but I am a Marine."

"Semper fi."

"We are some stone certain that proud faith will not be abused, are we not, Major?"

"These are hard times, Sergeant. But I am that stone."

They heard the sounds of the swollen, fetid river fifty meters away. The city lay beyond them in darkness. Fog floated around their feet.

"Muggy night like tonight," said the Sergeant, "reminds me of where I wish I didn't know. Don't want other memories like that cropping up around here. Not from my hands."

"I say again: *Semper fi*."

The Sergeant nodded. "Believe I'll walk me down to the water. Permission to be excused?"

No salute, no waiting; the Sergeant marched away to where all he could see was a rolling darkness under mist.

When the Sergeant's back was well turned, gone from the parking lot, Holloway flipped the tarp off a wooden crate in the back of the Jeep. Chisel scrapes on the wood showed where identifying stencils weren't. Holloway carried the crate to his car, locked it in the trunk. His White House military ID and "command presence" would get him past the saluting, white-helmeted gate sentries without a vehicle inspection.

"All clear up there, sir?"

"Yes, Sergeant. All clear."

Holloway climbed in his car and drove off. Fog swirled in the darkness.

CHAPTER 57

Feels like I'm floating, thought Quinn as April's river swept steadily toward May. Swimming within the current. Toward. . . . Don't think about that.

Quinn finessed intelligence reports to pinpoint a bank opposite the Sobel Building as a target for "guerrilla theater disruption" by leftist radicals. The threat was mild enough not to involve the FBI's overburdened Washington field office, but strong enough for Quinn's superiors to get twenty-four-hour access to a locked-door alcove overlooking the front of the bank—and the entrances to the Sobel Building. Quinn convinced the bank guards that the pictures he showed them of Holloway, Dane, Vaughn and Lorri were images of undercover operatives who should also be allowed "secret" access to the surveillance post, no questions asked, no logs made.

They pooled their money, bought two-way radios and stored them in the surveillance alcove, along with a crate Holloway let no one inspect. They bought a repoed muscle Trans Am and a Ford from a used car dealer who owed Quinn's friend on the auto theft squad beaucoup favors. They stashed the Trans Am on a Capitol Hill street a five-minute walk from Vaughn's apartment: all of them had a key to it and to the Ford, which Quinn rented a driveway for in Foggy Bottom, close to Holloway's quarters and to the White House.

Quinn rendezvoused with Vaughn on the last day of May outside Ford's Theater with its perpetual crowd of tourists.

"Good thing you pulled me out of line," whispered Vaughn as they walked along the crowded sidewalk. "I don't have a ticket."

"You don't have a tail either. We'll cruise inside that office building, keep walking."

The line to get into history stretched along their right as they sought shelter from the bright sun. A transistor radio dangled from a teenage boy's belt as he stood in line with Mom and Dad, who clearly regretted having given that noise machine to him, which he kept turned on as the only saving grace of this why'd-we-have-to-go-there "educational" vacation.

Radio music swept Vaughn into its sound: heartbreak drumbeats and the plunked *twang* of an electric guitar leading a soulful chorus from the Beach Boys.

Couldn't help it. As they hurried past the kid, Vaughn softly sang himself into the song, a tender bunch of nothing about a kid trapped into a drag race by his own bragging and the girl who still loved him anyway and swore everything would be all right. Vaughn felt himself flush with embarrassment of such a . . . a juvenile act, but then, *damn*! Out of nowhere! The cop beside him sang along, too!

Don't look! they both thought. Don't let the other guy see I'm just as big a sap as him.

A car horn blared. The sound of the radio died, lost somewhere behind them.

"Remember driving your dad's car, warm night, radio on and nothing but no girl and nowhere better to go?" whispered Vaughn.

Quinn jerked open the building door. "That's not where we are."

Vaughn stopped on the sidewalk, in the warm sun, the air-conditioning from inside blowing over them as he said, "But weren't we there once? Just for a moment?"

Quinn led the way inside.

As they circled unobserved through the air-conditioned maze of corridors, Vaughn told Quinn, "Our last clean chance just died. We'll get some Hughes stuff in the final report, but nothing about the CIA and the mob working together to kill Castro. I begged and pleaded. Yelled. Cried. Said I could bring in new information, cops who might substantiate links to Watergate, local mobsters and fixers and CIA execs. I argued about how breaking open 'Cuban stuff' was one of the things Nixon threatened the Agency with so they'd block the FBI probe of Watergate, so therefore etc., etc., etc. I got the word this morning: any link to my speculations or unsubstantiated findings and 'abuses in the seventy-two campaign' is tenuous, so drop it. All that stays out of the report, with no referral to any outside agencies or investigative groups. Nobody wants a runaway investigation subpoenaing every human being who might know about the President's sins."

"Speak for yourself."

"I did. Nobody agreed. I tried bringing in the milk fund stuff and the testimony about Hoffa and mobbed-up Nixon crony Chotiner, who's dead now—"

"Convenient."

"Speak for yourself," said Vaughn. "We got no more cards to play on the Hill, so tell me we're jumping off real soon."

"We did that when we met."

"If we wait too long, we'll lose our chance. Don't you know how tight it is? This whole city is ready to blow. You can smell it. Feel it. *Electricville*. We've got to—"

"Keep it together," said Quinn. "We've got to—"

"Wait for it, yeah. I hope to hell we know it when we see it."

SIX DAYS LATER, Holloway was stalking through the White House when he spotted a target: a barely out-of-college man with burr-cut hair and a White House visitor ID clipped to his cheap suit. Handcuffs and a white knuckled grip secured the young man to a GI attaché case.

I've seen shavetail humps like you before, thought Holloway. Rigid face, jumpy eyes, tight mouth, clean boots pacing on packed red earth while the sun-leathered platoon watches from under battered helmets, waiting for you to lead the way across rice paddies, calculating the odds on your return and scoring them as laughable. There it is: you don't belong. So if somebody sent you to my jungle, you gotta be special.

"At ease, Lieutenant." Holloway watched the young man embrace that rush of familiar data. "And stand close: we got civilians all around us."

"Yes, sir!"

Holloway flashed his White House ID. "I'm the NSC military security officer. You are . . . ?"

"Special courier, sir! From CIC, Criminal Investigation Command, U.S. Army, Penta—"

"Lower your voice, son."

"Yes, sir! I . . . beg your pardon, but do you work for General Haig?"

Alexander Haig, Nixon's chief of staff. "If I didn't, I wouldn't be here."

"Sir, am I glad to see you! I went to General Haig's office, but his secretary said he wasn't there. She's not military, so I didn't think I should work with her on something like this."

"Good call, Lieutenant." Holloway led the young man to chairs in a corner. "Catch your breath. Sit."

"Thank you, sir!" The young man sank into a red velvet cushion. "Sorry I'm so nervous but . . . How do you stand it? Working here, handling what we're doing for General Haig."

"We didn't sign on for it to be easy, Lieutenant." *Hook him.* "That's why we need good men like you to work with us."

"Begging your pardon . . ." The lieutenant hesitated, uncertain what to call the clearly higher-ranking officer.

"Colonel," lied Holloway, gambling correctly that the junior officer had absorbed no more than the existence of the superior officer's ID. *Stay hidden. Flush him out.*

"Begging your pardon, Colonel, but this isn't why I went through ROTC. I thought I'd get . . . I don't know. Tank school, my father was with Patton, but I never signed on to be a . . . a cop."

"You've done fine so far. But, mister, what bothers you so much about our mission?" *And who the hell is "our"? What the hell is "it"?*

"Sir, due respect, but I don't know if I should report to anyone but the general."

"Son, if a junior officer can't confide in his ranking superior in this white-walled HQ, then the whole chain of command breaks down."

"That's just it, sir! The chain of command is what I feel I'm breaking!"

" 'Breaking'? By us following General Haig's orders?"

"But this! He ordered CIC to run an investigation of President Nixon—our Commander In Chief—an investigation of the President and any links he's got to . . ."

Holloway could barely hear the young man whisper, "... *organized crime!* Militarily, with the war, I understand why we should care about gold smuggling in Vietnam like he also ordered us to check out, but the *President* and ... That's like—"

"Unbelievable!" whispered Holloway. Recovering, he said, "Our mission here is highest priority. And absolutely classified. Lieutenant, tell me you haven't broken security."

"No, sir!"

"I'd like to take your word for that, but as vital as this is, as nervous as you are ... We don't want any questions raised, you being vetted, fed to the gumshoes to check out. I think you're fine, but ... Look, if you're unable to break security, then you haven't. You should have been compartmentalized out of most of it, but I have to be sure. To do that, right and right now, fast and straight to keep you clear, report what you know."

Scared, nervous, conditioned to obey, sitting the center of all command authority, hooked by Holloway's sincere and solemn lies, the young lieutenant whispered, "Nothing, sir! Nothing more than the overall mission! I'm scared to death to even know what we're doing! I'm from Indiana. We don't know about stuff like organized crime. But I saw *The Godfather*! To even be carrying this status report to the general, even though all it shows is the duty stations that CIC contacted about the mob."

"Do not mention that again!"

"Oh, God! I didn't mean to break security!"

"One time, just between us: you're clear. But from now on, just do your job. Report back only what you need to report. You came here, you delivered, you returned. Nobody has to know you couldn't complete your assignment without my help."

"Yes, sir! Thank you, sir!"

"Do you have the schedule of final report delivery?"

" 'Soonest' is what Ha—the general ordered, but I don't—"

"Never mind. I'll check with your CO."

"Sir, my orders are to ask: Any other subsequent instructions?"

Like looking over a rifle barrel as the wind blows jungle branches out of the way.

"Yes, Lieutenant: Give me an investigatory authorization form."

"I don't have—The sergeant didn't give me anything like that!"

"Ah, shit!" Holloway cupped his brow. When he looked up, his face was stone. "Straighten your tie, soldier. You and I have to go tell the general there's been a fuck-up!"

"Sir, oh, God, sir, I—"

"Both of us, son. I'll take the bullet for not riding your CO, but you know generals: they shoot all of the sons of bitches standing in front of them."

"Sir, I—I'm sorry! Is there . . . Can we . . . Isn't there any way we can—fix it?"

Holloway stroked his chin, obviously strategizing to save the younger man's head. "The general wants a specific individual investigated and covered in the final report. I needed to fill out your damn form, send it back with you soonest. But as long as your people acquire the target . . ."

"A warrant officer at HQ is the one who really runs things! He wants me to sign off on extra leave for his honeymoon. I can tell him I took a verbal order from the general's command that we have to ace without making any waves about paperwork."

"Then let's get you signed off and sent on your way, no questions asked."

"Yes, sir! Thank you, sir!"

"But first, don't you think you better know the name you're sticking in CIC's machine?"

The lieutenant frantically pulled a scrap of paper from his pocket, clicked his pen.

"Last name Nezneck." Holloway spelled it. "First name Joe or Joseph. Middle-aged, maybe older. Area of operations is Washington, D.C."

Holloway led the lieutenant to the desk of a Haig military

aide. Before they reached that power seat, Holloway picked up a nearby phone, faked a conversation while he watched the lieutenant deliver the sealed report, collect the aide's signature—and discuss nothing. Holloway fell in step beside the younger man as the lieutenant walked away from a mission accomplished.

"Outstanding, Lieutenant!" said Holloway. He walked the lieutenant to the West Wing exit. Stood at those white French doors as the young man retreated through the green June heat; stood so still his breath stopped, so still his heart silenced, a stillness so perfect that he vanished.

He caught Penzler three steamy nights later as the CIA rogue locked his car door in the parking garage beneath his condo building. Penzler heard a shoe scuffle on concrete— threw a briefcase at the man blur charging him through the gap between cars.

Holloway blocked the flung briefcase. Penzler's hands met as if he were holding a beach ball, then flew apart with an arc of gray light. Fire burned a line along Holloway's right arm. Drops of red flecked a nearby parked white panel truck. Penzler jabbed with the translucent dagger he'd pulled from a sleeve sheath, driving the bigger man out of the gap between the parked cars. Holloway's gloved left hand brushed a car's radio antenna—grabbed it, snapped it off! He whipped the antenna back and forth like a rapier as warm liquid trickled down his right arm. Holloway tripped over the briefcase, tumbled backward to the concrete floor as the blazing-eyed bearded knife man scampered close for the good thrust.

Roll! Somersault! Up!

Holloway flicked the antenna over the stabbing knife and slashed a red line beneath one of those blazing eyes. Penzler cried out, pulled back, his hands coming up to protect his face.

The Marine kicked him in the knee. Penzler wildly lunged with his knife—Holloway's leather glove grabbed Penzler's lunge, bent and twisted the spy's arm with quick, snapping power. The knife flew from Penzler's grip as Holloway punched the smaller man in the heart. Punched him in the face. That impact sprayed Penzler with Holloway's blood and knocked the bearded man flat on his back. Holloway slammed down on the skinny man, sitting astraddle Penzler's chest, pinning the spy's arms to the concrete with his knees like a school-yard bully. The Marine clamped his left hand around the bearded man's windpipe as awareness flooded back into Penzler's eyes.

"Know why I didn't kill you?" hissed Holloway.

"You still don't know how to have a good time."

"But I'm learning. That's why I don't want you to die before you see just how bad you fucked up. How stupid you are. Way things are now, I get to crush you and anybody, anything else I want! All thanks to you for being so stupid when you put me together with Jud."

"Your Green Beret fuck is history nobody knows!"

"Knows *yet!* Maybe he's gone. Maybe you got him. But now I've found the big secret about him. When I move with it, this whole damn town will kiss my ass and crush yours."

Holloway tightened his grip.

Penzler gurgled, his arms and legs thrashed. He windmilled a foot up to kick the Marine but his leg hit only a muscled back. Holloway closed his grip even tighter with his good hand and hammered the gloved fist of his wounded arm into Penzler's groin. The man pinned beneath the Marine bucked and trembled. Holloway eased his throat grip, said, "When you get slammed by that truck roaring out of nowhere, I want you to know it was me who sent it."

Then he punched the gasping spy's face.

Holloway scooped the dagger off the concrete: plastic, double-edged, razor-sharp, opaque, invisible to a metal detector. His blood smeared the blade. He looked at the man curled on the damp concrete. Glaze blurred those eyes; still, they stared back.

"Think there's any fingerprints on this?" Holloway asked their glare.

He laughed. Left that underground stench of dank concrete, car exhaust, summer heat.

CHAPTER 58

Holloway surprised Dane four weeks later when she arrived at work. He stood in the corridor beyond a clutch of male reporters hanging out near the Select Committee's cave. She spotted Holloway's pale face, thought, You're never supposed to be here!

The reporters laughed.

A heavy-breasted Clare with thick brown hair, creamy skin, a whimsical Italian mouth and swell legs under her short faux-silk summer dress strolled past the reporters on her way to her job for a Louisiana senator. The reporters swiveled their gaze to watch her as she passed by.

Dane pointed four fingers toward the stairway sign above a door in the corridor beyond the reporters. Holloway nodded to her just as the reporters turned back to tend business. They only saw Dane going into the cave to work.

Just another Monday in July.

Dane "went for coffee" ten minutes later. Bantered with the reporters as she walked past their huddle, disappeared into a crowded elevator. She found Holloway on the fourth floor.

"What's wrong?" she asked. "Are you waving me off?"

"No! You need to go today!" The Marine led her to a public corner where a man and a woman could create privacy. "Lorri—You know the airline let her go? Guess she missed too many call-ins for even a part-timer. Lucky for us. Last night on surveillance she spotted Penzler in front of the Sobel. She said he spent nine minutes inside—long enough for a quick recon—then left."

"Is she sure? Not that Lorri—I mean . . . She could have made an honest mistake."

"Quinn will print the film she shot. But she's got to be right. I'd taped her earlier recon pictures of the Sobel in an envelope inside my Sit Room desk. Finding them would have been hard. Two days ago, the envelope had been moved. As small as the Sit Room is, as busy, Penzler took a hell of a chance to black-bag me there, even if he did it in the dead hours before dawn."

"So he identified the Sobel. So what? How can he know about the taping?"

"Because he has to know! Because now he knows I got something *ultimate* from Jud. Penzler's already made his peace with my admirals. Now that Penzler knows the better questions to ask about Jud, he'll get a piece of data here, a secret squeezed out there. He'll figure or find out there's a taping system in the Sobel. Most importantly, he knows that I know. By now he probably also knows the Haig probe has put his buddy Nezneck in the badge machine. Trees are falling all through his forest. Penzler wants to stay safe, so he needs to get his hands on a huge shield to hide behind. Secret White House tapes are as big a shield as Hoover's files. Doesn't even matter what's on them, it's the threat of what *might* be there in the shadows. Ego freak like Penzler, a man with all his own crimes to hide, he hungers for power like the tapes. Besides, after what I did to him, no way will he let me grab power and use it against him first."

"As long as Nixon doesn't give up *all* his tapes . . . You can't stay at your apartment."

"I've got to act like I'm still an admirals' boy waiting for their envelopes."

"Soon as they're done with you, they'll throw you away."

"But they don't know I know that."

"You have to sleep sometime! You're safe in the White House, but if Penzler—"

"Pity the sapper team that hits my apartment."

"I don't want to. We can't afford a battle scene like that."

Is that what his real smile looks like? she thought as Holloway said, "Penzler will kill me, but not yet. First, for his ego, he has to defeat me and make sure that I know he won."

"What if he's not that crazy?"

"Then we are." Holloway sighed.

"You didn't come up here just to tell me what Lorri saw."

"Ever think about the end of the world?" Holloway rubbed his brow, his hand covering eyes that Dane feared were too shadowed; when he looked at her, she ached as she read their bloodshot map. "Not how you're personally going to die. That's not scary."

"What's wrong?"

"We can destroy the world in fifteen minutes," said the Marine. "That's how smart human beings are. Everything since World War II has been built around us being that smart. We got the bomb, the Soviets got it, the Chinese and French and British, India. And secretly the Israelis, with South Africa going to join the nuclear club in a few years. Supposedly, we all balance each other. They teach that theology to us from grade school and Main Street to Harvard, the service academies, the war college. Balance of power. Balance of terror. Nuclear holocaust won't happen because we're all so damn smart and organized. Everybody's got from-the-top-down command and control procedures.

"Not anymore," said the Marine major assigned to America's nerve center. "Not now. They took the bomb away from Nixon."

"What?"

"Secretary of Defense Schlesinger issued an order that now all commands—including nuclear strike authorizations—all commands for military action anywhere in the globe must be explicitly approved by him. Used to be the President could pick up the phone. Now, the President's been deprived of the ability for 'unwarranted' commands."

"Do they think he's nuts?"

"They don't know that he's not. They do know our Commander In Chief is desperate. What's a little war but a great diversion? Or how about troops deployed around Capitol Hill to preserve and protect 'order' while Congress 'runs amuck'?"

"We can't have a coup here!"

"We've never had a President driven from office."

"Yet," she said.

"If we're right, as long as Nixon's there, we've still got a chance. But time is running out. You've got to make your move today."

She nodded. "I was going to. Is that why you came?"

"Maybe. I don't know. I couldn't . . . I had to do something. Talk to somebody."

"Good thing I'm here."

"Yeah," said the Marine, his eyes looking past her. "Good thing."

Bring him back: "Has anything like this ever happened before?"

"You mean with Nixon?" Holloway glanced at this civilian to whom he'd welded his life. Took a deep breath. "Back in October, the Yom Kippur War, Kissinger wanted to send the Soviets a message—keep it secret from all our citizens but make sure the Soviets found out so they'd know Henry was serious. Kissinger jumped all our forces up a level of nuclear readiness, a higher alert than, say, the bloodiest days in Vietnam. American reporters found out, but what they didn't realize was that Nixon didn't authorize it and didn't know about it until he woke up the next morning."

"Did it work?"

"We're all still here. So far. That Middle East bloodshed ended up OK for us." His grin was slack. "If you want to send a message, nothing like going nuclear."

DANE WALKED FROM the Senate to the House through the steamy heat of that afternoon. The Senate and the House were jealously guarded domains few Americans could differentiate: for most citizens, all of it was just Congress, but the House and Senate cultures held Congress together because they worked apart and worked differently. An imaginary line drawn through the center of the Capitol building split Congress's turf; as late as the 1950s, janitors working for each side would push their brooms up to that border, then stop.

My ID gets me past police lines, she thought, but the only clout Vaughn and I have on this side of the Hill comes from what we can bargain.

Or what we can bluff.

To get through the milling reporters and the police guards, Dane flashed her old plastic-laminated Senate ID card, not her Select Committee leather-cased credential. Never reveal too much to too many. A receptionist in the main office directed Dane to an office a long walk away from the chaos outside the hearing room and main committee suite.

Dane entered that distant door, flashed her Select Committee credentials to a so-young woman receptionist. "Is she in?"

"Ah . . . No, she's over at the Library of Congress pulling some research."

Plan B, thought Dane. She asked the receptionist, "Is that her desk?"

"Yes, but—"

"I have to leave her this." Dane taped an envelope to the 'hers' glass-top desk, explained, "One envelope could get shuffled and lost in all this mess."

"You could leave it with me."

"That's OK." Dane stuck the second strip of tape across the envelope: somebody would have to work to get it off the glass. Hard to ignore, forget or snoop it. "No problem."

A glance at the envelope taped to the desk, then Dane turned to walk away—turned back, picked up a pen and on the envelope printed: To: HILLARY RODHAM, Counsel.

"WHY HER?" ASKED Quinn as he sat with Dane in the surveillance alcove that night.

"Why not?" she replied.

They sat on metal folding chairs, the alcove bulbs turned off. Below them on New York Avenue, a taxi rolled past the

Sobel. Didn't stop. They could see the red-yellow-green beat of a traffic light slicing the urban darkness.

Dane shrugged. "Vaughn and I figured that I should be the one to make the link. I decided to go woman professional to woman professional, and if we're going to keep control, we have to stay at staff level. I picked Hillary Rodham at random."

"What's she going to think about being so lucky?"

"All I said was a number of Select Committee staffers wanted to be sure that the House Judiciary Committee staff members knew we would help them with any information or data they might require that was or was *not* in the Senate report we're releasing this week. I said this 'contact' was informal, not authorized. Friendly. I enclosed Vaughn's and my business cards. I wanted to leave the note rather than deal with her and the questions she'd have if we met in person, and I got lucky."

"Sounds like bullshit."

"It was, it is, and I bet she's smart enough to know that. She hasn't called and she probably won't. But we reached out, made a link. Nothing improper, but when we need somebody there who knows, us, we can reach back to her. And if we turn up . . . she'll remember us."

"Sounds shaky."

"Luckily, the rest of what we're doing to stay alive is completely solid."

The cop laughed.

"You should go home," said Dane. "Get some sleep. Pulling double shifts—"

"Everybody is. You, too."

"Do I look as bad as you?"

"Worse."

Dane focused the tripod-mounted camera pointed to the building across the street. "Even with Lorri handling days, us splitting nights, a bathroom break or a blink, we could miss our moment."

"Then we're fucked," said Quinn.

Dane shrugged. "Well, it's nice to know there's some fun in our future."

They laughed together.

Settled back into their vigil.

"You know what's funny?" said Quinn. "After I realized Lorri and I were in deep trouble, I thought that the way to survive was to hide on the edges of everything—of Watergate and the mob and the CIA and politics. Not get in close and deal with it.

"Now I realize that was wrong. Not just for us, but . . . the big wrong. How we ended up in this hell storm. Us, the CIA, maybe everybody who once was innocent. We tried to cut deals along the edges of what was supposed to be. Deals to do what we shouldn't so we could get what we wanted. Deals to be practical. Deals to make it easy. Shortcuts. Deals to feel good or not be afraid. And the farther we went out on the edges of what was supposed to be, the more lost and in trouble we ended up. Until here we are. And fighting our way back toward the center of supposed-to-be is the only real way to survive. Maybe we'll die trying, but that's the only chance we have to live."

Dane frowned. "And that's 'funny'?"

"Guess it's gotta be. Guess the joke's on us." He shrugged. "Hell, I refuse to cry about it, so I might as well laugh."

They sat. Waited. Watched.

"Go home," she said again. "Get some sleep. See Lorri. We're all on beeper, I've got coffee, Vaughn will relieve me at midnight."

"Yeah. I should go home."

A van pulled to the curb across the street. Dane and Quinn leaned toward the window in their light-free alcove. Three women bearing mops and buckets and brooms climbed out of the van and shuffled inside the Sobel. Dane and Quinn settled back down in the darkness.

"He's a good guy," said Quinn. "Vaughn."

"Yes. I know all of you think he's . . ."

"Spacey? Weird?"

"Frivolous," she said. "But he's not."

"You wouldn't be with him if he were."

Say nothing about that, she thought. "You might think he's careless."

"Like any of the rest of us deserve to judge him on that count."

She let silence pass between them to acknowledge both his kindness and his confession.

"I should go home," he said. Then, "Bet you never figured on this."

"Which part?" She cleared her throat. "Lorri . . . I'm worried about her. She's a good woman—great, but . . ."

A Metro bus rolled past on the street below, breaks hissing, steel creaking.

"You don't get to decide who you fall in love with," said Quinn. "If you did . . ."

"It probably wouldn't be as much fun."

"Or the rest of it either." Quinn stared out at the night.

"Nothing ever stays what it was," said Dane.

A police cruiser drifted between their watch post and their target.

"I'm going home," said Quinn in the darkness beside Dane.

"Sure."

After a while, he left.

CHAPTER 59

July sizzled toward August. According to a Gallup poll, inflation replaced the energy crisis as the American public's major concern. The Senate Select Committee released its fist-thick green paper-bound report to go with 4,133 pages of Watergate evidence and hearing records. A minority report issued by committee Republicans claimed that the CIA had destroyed Watergate records and that there were unanswered questions about the CIA's Watergate role.

Dane went back on Senator Martin's staff but kept working in the cave. Vaughn remained on the committee payroll; mostly he packed boxes to go to the archives, watched the televised House judiciary hearings and listened as his fellow staffers schemed to be sure they had a role in the probable trial in the Senate of an impeached President.

The Supreme Court ruled that Nixon had to provide tapes subpoenaed by the Watergate special prosecutor. As the sun set on July, the House Judiciary Committee had voted three articles of impeachment against President Richard M. Nixon.

On August's first evening, Nixon cruised the Potomac in the presidential yacht, *Sequoia*. His family stayed ashore, but his multimillionaire friend Bebe Rebozo joined him on board for dinner, then wandered away on the yacht to let Nixon be alone, gliding with the river.

Dane and Vaughn took over most of the surveillance. Vaughn brought a transistor radio that he dialed away from the two rock stations he preferred to an AM station that prided itself on interrupting its regular broadcast for news updates.

"TV wouldn't do us any good," said Vaughn, "even if we had a portable. By the time the evening news rolls around, it could be too late."

"Time is killing us," said Dane. "We can't keep up this watching and waiting. If Nixon hangs tough, if he takes an impeachment vote by the whole House and demands his day in court, his trial by the whole Senate, a trial that he just might win . . ."

"You got a better suggestion?"

Dane stared out the window. Shook her head no.

"What would it take to make Nixon a quitter?"

Dane shrugged. "How about finding out at just the right moment that besides all the Watergate sins being stacked against him on Capitol Hill, the Pentagon can throw an investigation about him and the mafia into the fire?"

Nixon helicoptered back to the White House from Camp

David that first August Monday morning. That afternoon, Holloway and about a hundred other White House staffers filled the Executive Office Building's fourth-floor auditorium. They used all the chairs, stood in the aisles, shuffling from one foot to the other as the air-conditioning labored against the day's baking sun and their trapped body heat. Haig stepped to the podium in front of the closed blue curtains and spoke into the microphone:

"I have the tough task of bringing you some bad news. The President has been reviewing tapes. All except one are consistent with his previous explanations. The exception is of sufficient gravity to warrant a briefing."

After his explanations and praise for the White House staff, Haig read a statement from the President. Nixon's statement said he had not previously realized the implications of this "smoking gun," use-the-CIA-to-block-Watergate tape and so had told no one about it.

"This is a serious act of omission for which I take full responsibility and which I deeply regret," said the President's statement. "I am firmly convinced that the record, in its entirety, does not justify the extreme step of impeachment and removal of a President. I trust that as the Constitutional process goes forward, this perspective will prevail."

The White House staffers gave messenger Haig a standing ovation.

Holloway's beeper went off: Quinn's number code, but what phone number is that?

The Marine slid through the crowd, commandeered a phone.

"Not a safe line!" said Holloway when Quinn answered his call. White House staffers—some crying, some dead faced, some angry—streamed past the Marine.

"I'm on duty. We just got a general call-in. Crowd control, security alerts. I sold my captain bullshit about tracking radicals who were looking for an opportunity to go nuts. He won't nail me down to a post, so I don't have to go AWOL, but something is happening!"

"Yeah," said Holloway. "Meltdown."

CHAPTER 60

Tuesday morning. August 6, 1974. Newspapers screamed Nixon's "admission." A crowd gathered in the park across the street from the White House. At eleven that morning, Nixon convened a cabinet meeting. Navy stewards served coffee.

"I would like to discuss the most important issue confronting this nation," said Nixon, "and confronting us internationally, too: inflation."

But Nixon shifted to the topic of Watergate—and told the men who ran the government with him that he would not resign, though he expected the House to impeach him. He wanted the Senate trial. No one encouraged him. When he tried to talk about the economy and other crises, several cabinet officers balked, insisting that he not make long-range plans. Nixon disagreed. Forceful diplomacy from Kissinger moved the meeting to an unexploded close.

Tuesday afternoon, one of Nixon's sons-in-law confided to a Republican senator that Nixon had been wandering the halls of the White House at night, talking to the portraits of dead Presidents.

Holloway surprised Vaughn at the alcove that Tuesday night.

"You're not on shift until four this morning," said the Senate aide.

"I don't need much sleep. I can't anyway." The Marine peered through binoculars toward the White House fence. A steady stream of pedestrians gawked at the white mansion glowing beyond the black iron poles. "Look at them. Any other almost-midnight, most of them wouldn't be caught dead walking around downtown D.C."

"Most of them think walking around D.C. at night can make them dead."

Holloway smiled. "But not us."

"Naw, not us. We're going to live forever."

"Be optimistic, not cocky."

"I'm nervous, not cocky."

"At least you admit it. I was afraid you didn't really understand the stakes. Afraid you thought this was all rock 'n' roll or Saturday night at the movies."

"You think that because I never went to war or never carried a badge and a gun that I don't know this is real?" Vaughn shook his head. "I can't believe it's true, but I know it's real."

"And you can handle all of it?"

"I might trip and fall on my face, but I'll go all the way with all I've got."

"Those words came out pretty easy."

"How hard was taking your Marine oath? You can go through life taking what you get or choosing what you'll take. Marine oath, sitting here with you. . . . we're both volunteers."

"And you want to be here."

"Hell, no." Vaughn shrugged. "You come to an understanding about what you can do and what you will do. Most of the time you get there because of fear—you're afraid of how people will see you if you don't do this or if you do that. Mostly you're more afraid of rejection than you are of any consequences. That's why guys risk their lives in a war they don't agree with rather than, say, skip to Canada."

The shaggy-haired veteran of anti–Vietnam War demonstrations took the binoculars from the Marine who'd fought, bled, killed and commanded in that combat.

"When you realize that," said Vaughn, "you pick the way you stand. You say, 'I will do these things.' And 'I will fight these battles.' Then it's a matter of chance, of whether or not you get put in that position."

Vaughn scanned the Sobel with the binoculars.

"Here I am," he said.

"Think you're lucky this chance hit you?"

"Best luck I'll ever have is Dane." He kept his eyes focused through the magnifying lenses. "Nobody else sees as much of me as she does."

"Gotta love her for that."

"Yes," said Vaughn. "You do."

He handed the binoculars to Holloway. "I'm scared."

"You should be."

"Scared that we'll blow it. That Dane won't get away clean. That I won't make it."

"Guys like you don't die." Holloway shrugged. "And apparently I can't."

"It's not dying that scares me most. I wasn't joking about falling on my face. That's what I'm afraid of. That when it's really happening I'll freeze or panic or fuck it up." Vaughn raised his eyes to the Marine. "Still worried about having me on your squad?"

"Not with what I've seen."

Vaughn smiled. Looked out the window. "I came to this town to see the whole heart of things. It's out there now. You know what it is?"

"No."

"Me either."

They laughed.

Vaughn said, "What's out there is chaos and chance, choices and consequences."

"And us."

"Yeah," said the younger man. "Us."

WEDNESDAY MORNING NIXON talked with Haig about suicide. Haig ordered that all sleeping pills and tranquilizers be taken away from the President.

At 5 P.M. Nixon met with Congress's leading Republicans. They found a subdued President, one who with seeming calm listened to their report of certain impeachment and probable conviction in any subsequent Senate trial. He ushered them out of the Oval Office without committing to any course of action. Senator Barry Goldwater told the waiting cameras and microphones, "Whatever decision he makes, it will be in the best interest of our country."

Just before dinner, Nixon sent his secretary, Rose Mary Woods, to tell his family that he would resign. Nixon came to them, had a few tearful pictures snapped, talked about going home to California. Shortly after eight o'clock that night, he summoned Secretary of State Henry Kissinger to the White House's Lincoln Sitting Room, an upstairs cubbyhole where, surrounded by portraits of America's first President to be assassinated by a conspiracy, Nixon would often sit alone listening to Rachmaninoff. And drinking. Brooding. That White House night, the President and his foreign policy guru drank. Reminisced. Shed tears. Nixon made Kissinger kneel with him to pray.

As the clock reached 11 P.M., a shaken Kissinger managed to break free of his master and escape to his White House office, where Holloway and other aides anxiously waited. Kissinger poured forth the details of his intensely bizarre encounter. The phone rang: it was Nixon.

Holloway and other NSC staffers grabbed extensions of the phone to listen.

Nixon drunk, slurring and rambling, insisted that Kissinger "stay for good of th' country. And, Henry, please don' ever tell anyone that I cried and that I was'n' strong."

At midnight, Captain Nathan Holloway, USMC, couldn't stand waiting anymore. *Now is when. The hell with beepers.* Holloway picked up a supposedly-secure Sit Room phone, tapped out one of the numbers he'd seared into his memory.

One ring. Two—

In the phone, Holloway heard a sleepy Quinn say, "Yeah?"

"Squeeze the trigger."

CHAPTER 61

Holloway delayed leaving the White House: Once you go, you're gone. He begged a cot in the Secret Service locker room, dreamed about Jud being alive in some other hell. Dreamed about the jungle; about a soul-dead soldier with wheatfields in his eyes. Dawn broke. Holloway showered in the Old Executive Office Building, trooped back toward the West Wing. The heat and humidity and heebie-jeebies soaked his clean shirt before he'd made it back to the Executive Mansion. *Be out of this monkey suit soon anyway.* Breakfast in the White House mess was an exercise worthy of a crypt. Someone dropped a fork on a plate and the clatter froze every heart in the room.

The Marine officer stood in the cigarette fog and electronic hum of the Sit Room. His colleagues filled their duty stations with grim intensity: they refused to let the ship of state sink.

He left without saying a word.

Straight out the main entrance. Marine guards snapped to attention as he exited.

"Semper fi," whispered Holloway.

But those mere grunts did their silent duty and kept their eyes locked straight ahead.

Then Holloway saw them.

They hovered beyond the black iron poles of the White House fence, hundreds of ordinary Americans. In T-shirts and suits, cutoff blue jeans and cotton dresses. Long hair and crew cuts. Beards and beautiful breasts. Sunglasses and cameras. One lady carried an umbrella open against the August sun. Hundreds of watchers. Like crows on barbed wire.

Secret Service guards buzzed Holloway out of the gate. The crowd on the sidewalk parted, their eyes darting at him, their hands trembling as if with a hunger to reach out and pluck something from this man who'd been inside. But no one spoke to him. He disappeared into their multitude, forgotten as their eyes flicked back to that white mansion. He walked through them, and was gone.

DANE WALKED THROUGH the fourth-floor halls of the Old Senate Office Building toward Senator Gus Martin's office. Morning sun warmed the high-ceilinged salmon walls and mahogany doorways. She was ten steps from the brass elevator, her footsteps echoing on the marble floor, before she noticed it. As usual, the main doors to all the senators' suites on that corridor stood open. But this Thursday morning, Senate staffers idled in those portals. Dane saw the silhouette of a woman dart from a doorway at the far end of the corridor to the entrance to another senator's suite across and down the hall. That woman huddled with two male staffers from another member's office. Dane had taken only three steps before one of those men cut away from the huddle and quick-walked across the hall to the office of a senator from a different state and the opposite party; the quick walker whispered to a woman and man standing there—she hurried inside her workplace.

Rumors literally running through the halls, thought Dane.

"Is the senator in?" Dane asked Gus Martin's private secretary.

"First one here this morning. Said he didn't dare fall asleep." The older woman frowned. "You look like you need a vacation."

"Can I see him for a few minutes? Alone?"

"Byron's getting his morning beer and tomato juice. Figure you've got that long."

Senator Martin sat behind his massive desk. He looked up from the book he was reading as Dane entered and shut the door behind her.

"Do you ever read Basho?" asked the Senator. "Japanese

haiku. He gets the universe into seventeen syllables about a frog."

He closed the book, rubbed his eyes. "Can you keep a secret?"

Dane laughed. Couldn't stop. Choked, coughed and wheezed. A heavy paw on her shoulder eased her down to the leather couch. When her vision cleared, Senator Gus Martin sat across from her.

"Was my question that tough?"

She saw the concern in his eyes; shook her head.

"The leadership says that Nixon will announce today that he's going to resign tomorrow. Guess he wants to give us time to talk him out of it."

"Too late for talking."

"It can't be. Or you wouldn't be here to see me."

"I'm not going to cry."

Senator Martin became stone.

"Today, now, I'm supposed to do something. Make a phone call. Lie and pretend I'm calling for you. To make something happen. Something that must happen! If it doesn't . . . Then even if Nixon goes, the shit wins."

"Is this Select Committee problems?"

"Too late for any committee. Too late for anything but just us."

"You and I?"

"I never wanted you in this! Working for you is so special, you're—"

"I'm stubborn, pissed-off, Nazi-shot-up knees, no kids, dead wife. Loyal to men who don't give a big enough damn about why we're here. I got a temper—remember when I ripped a phone book in half because of some silly son-of-a-bitch thing? Plus, in case you haven't heard, I drink too much."

"You're my senator."

"And now is when you tell me."

"No. Now is when I can't. Our plan was I wouldn't even see you. I'd make the call myself. Say it was for you. There was a good chance that would work. But a good chance isn't enough. We've got to be certain. Or everything dies."

"So you want me to make a phone call?"

She nodded. Kept her word and didn't cry.

"Where's Vaughn?"

"He's on the line, too."

"Sam Ervin and I are friends. He's solid and smarter than Satan, so I could—"

"Nobody's that smart."

Gus Martin frowned. "So if it's not him I'm calling, not the prosecutors . . . Are you asking me to break the law?"

"There's nothing illegal about making the phone call, even if you know that what you'll say is a lie. Not if you don't know anything more."

"I'm the ex-judge, not you." Martin rubbed his chin. "I already know something. Knowledge can legally compel action, especially for a public official. Just ask Nixon."

"If you were like him, I wouldn't be here."

"You won't tell me your secrets. I'll tell you mine. My secret fear is that someday it'll be Nixon's hatchet face I see in my mirror." The Senator frowned. "You broke your plan with Vaughn and asked me to make this call. You had to know there's a damn good chance I'll rip up whatever you got going because for me that's the safe thing to do."

"Safe for you . . . deadly for Vaughn. And me."

His eyes widened. The second hand swept once around the clock on the wall, a circle past the clock's lights that signaled votes and quorum calls. United States Senator August Martin said, "So what am I going to say to whoever answers my phone call?"

CHAPTER 62

As Gus Martin dialed the phone number Dane gave him, Richard Nixon got a haircut.

At noon, the White House staff turned off the robot signature machine that scrawled Nixon's Presidential signature. The White House mess featured Mexican food. Press Secretary Ziegler announced that at 9 P.M., the President would address the nation. Crates were packed. Nixon autographed a photograph for his rabid supporter Rabbi Korff. Haldeman telephoned, but Nixon refused to take his call. Nixon vetoed appropriations for the Department of Agriculture and the Environmental Protection Agency, saying they were too inflationary. He ordered Haig to make sure that the President could walk outside from the White House to a meeting with congressional leaders in the Old Executive Office Building next door without running into anyone. Reporters were locked in the press room, staffers ordered away from windows. White House drivers sitting in their cars parked inside the black iron fence lay down on the car seats. Nixon walked alone through the summer evening. The crowd outside the fence watched him. Some sang "God Bless America." Some cried, some jeered, some applauded. Nixon walked alone.

As the President entered the Old Executive Office Building, a knock sounded on a condominium door a mile away in a posh building on Connecticut Avenue. The door swung open and the two people standing in the hall saw a beaming Mel Klise say, *"Holy cow!"*

"Hey, Mel," said Lorri, tight slacks, a leather tote bag slung over her shoulder: a blonde in sunglasses. "Sorry about this."

"Holy cow! I mean, *hey:* Glad to see you, but—"

The long-haired, bearded freak led the blonde into Mel's home, shut the door behind them.

"The Senator's not coming," said the freak.

"How the hell did you know—Hey! You're that cop! From my office burglary!"

"My name is John Quinn."

"Good to see you!" Mel said. "But I gotta tell you, tonight is not the best time. Mimi's not even here. I sent her to the movies, she loves the . . .

"You got the Senator to call!" whispered Mel. "He was never coming to get my help with the unions, but you got him to make the call and ask and hell, yes, I'd be home alone tonight for that! Son, my hat is off to you! You're the arranger, not me!"

The wispy-haired pro shrugged. "Come on in."

Lorri drifted ahead of the two men to a living room decorated with French art and an oil portrait of Mimi over the mantel. An alcove held a flat desk with two phones and three Rolodexes. The black velvet painting behind the desk showed dogs playing poker. Central air-conditioning chilled the room. Mel had made sure a tray of liquor bottles, ice and glasses waited by the couch for his expected guest.

"Can I get you guys something to drink? How you been?"

"Swell." Lorri wore her sunglasses. "We've been just swell. Vodka rocks. Or whatever."

"How about you, John?"

"You figure it out."

The gnome obeyed Lorri's gesture to top off the tall glass. "Better take it easy, kid."

Call it a laugh, then Lorri said, "Too late, I'm worn out."

"What am I thinking of?" said Mel. "Anybody could see that. You go down that hall and have a lie-down. You need anything, just holler."

She drifted from the living room. With her vodka.

Mel gave a bourbon over ice to Quinn. "If that's not right, I got plenty of other choices."

Quinn opened his hand so the tumbler fell to the carpet.

"Son, that was just plain rude."

Quinn hooked his fist into Mel's face.

"Get up, Mel. Sit. On the table."

Mel sat on the magazines spread over the glass and steel coffee table. "Do your business and get out before Mimi comes home."

So, thought Quinn, you got a heart after all. Something to shoot.

"All that depends on you, Mel." Quinn sat in the chair across from the bruised gnome. "See what you can arrange."

"What do you want from me? I'm no hard guy."

"No, but you make life easier for them."

"Business is business. You got a badge—if you got a problem, bust me."

"If I bust you or anyone else here, it won't be with my badge."

The sinking sun streaming through the windows lit the room with a thick golden hue.

Quinn drew his service .38 revolver from under the denim work shirt he wore unbuttoned over a black Hell's Angels T-shirt. He removed five of the pistol's six bullets. Holstered the revolver. The bullets jangled like gambler's dice in his hand.

"You can tell your friends that I beat you up," said Quinn. "That's on the way to being true. Tell them I stuck my revolver in your mouth and played Russian roulette until you cracked. That's Hollywood enough that they'll buy it, but just between you and me, I won't waste a trigger squeeze that doesn't splatter somebody's brains over your fine art."

"Wha-what friends?"

Quinn bounced a bullet off Mel's forehead.

"Nezneck," said the cop. "And his partner Bill Penzler, Mr. CIA spook-a-rama."

"I . . . I don't know anybody from the Agency named Penzler."

"Half a lie is better than none, huh, Mel? Let's not quibble about names. You might be right the way you said it. Maybe he uses different names. Fuck both of them. They're on the way to checkmated forever. There are only two questions for us here tonight."

Their hearts counted the silence.

Quinn bounced a bullet off Mel's chest.

"Wha-wha-what questions?"

"Question number one: Do you and Mimi want to take that hard ride, too?"

"Leave her out of this!"

"You married her. Not me. Package deal. That's the way Nezneck calls it. He puts everybody on the line. He calls the game, you arrange, I'm the player."

"Nothing's to happen to Mimi!" Mel licked his lips. "Maybe it wouldn't hurt to listen. That's what I do. For lots of people. Like a lawyer! So me, I listen, I help out, arrange—"

" 'Atta boy, Mel. Let's do what you do."

"What do you—What's the second question?"

"All the answers about Pat Dawson."

Mel closed his mouth.

The bullet hit him smack in the forehead but he didn't even blink.

"You remember her, Mel. You were in her address book. With a happy face beside your number. She had a great smile. Did you know she had a mom who still listens for the phone to ring? Did you know she had a son she loved who still goes to the window and waits for her to finally come home? People loved her, and she loved them. You got Mimi, so you understand that. Pat Dawson, she's nothing but cold now. She got on the wrong road and got stuck turning tricks for Nezneck or Heidi or maybe Penzler: doesn't matter who sent her out, Nezneck held the strings. Then he killed her. Ground her up in a garbage disposal. *Whoa!* Looks like maybe you didn't know that part! You got a garbage disposal? Mimi got one in her kitchen?"

Mel stared at the freaky cop.

"Think about it, Mel. Would I risk all this if I didn't have the hammer to beat Nezneck? And Penzler? And everybody else in this damn town? Even you wouldn't believe what I'm gonna get, me and my own private Marine. But there's one piece of business I don't have, and you're going to arrange things so I get it."

"Why me?"

"Because you're smart. Because you'd know. Maybe not all the details like the garbage disposal—that makes me glad, Mel. Gives you a little grace. But you'd have heard whispers, maybe smoothed some action, or just arranged to know. You would have made it your business. Because we both know Pat Dawson kissed something huge."

"Let's say you are a miracle man. Supercop. Let's say you can put Joe down, get around all his friends on your side of the law. Why do you care about whether Mimi and I walk or not? Why would you offer me an arrangement?"

"Because you were nice to Lorri. You helped her. You tried to save her."

Mel nodded. "OK. I'll buy that. But if she's with you, looks like I failed."

"I'm the best either of you gets," said Quinn. "Sorry about that."

"Still not enough," said Mel.

Quinn threw the bullet as hard as he could.

Mel ducked.

The bullet bounced off the far wall.

The gnome's eyes gleamed. "Why do you give a damn about Pat Dawson? If you can already put Nezneck down, why do you care about her?"

"Because that's my job," said Quinn.

Mel watched him.

"Because I made a promise."

Mel didn't blink.

Quinn whispered, "I need to stop seeing her when I sleep."

Sunlight thickened around them.

"Poor Pat," sighed Mel. "She had these great violet eyes! We had a few laughs. She entertained a soda pop executive with me one night. I didn't have any part in any tragedies. I never work arrangements so . . ."

"So you get blood on your hands. Yeah, you are like a

good lawyer. But no self-defense now. Use the words right and we'll pretend you're on the outside looking in."

"Aren't we all." Mel leaned forward. "We got a deal?"

"I got the bullets."

"But a deal's a deal. That's what happened to Pat. She broke the deal."

"With who?"

"History, that's who. That's how you gotta look at it.

"Nezneck works with some guys," said Mel. "You call it mob, I say business is business, and laws make that business, so what can you expect? These guys are like competitors who belong to the same chamber of commerce.

"Turn the clock back to poor JFK, after Dallas. Business grows or it busts. And business is flattening out. Union deals are tight, what with the feds banging away at my friend Jimmy Hoffa. The street stuff—I hear that while it was steady, it wasn't getting much bigger."

"Hijackings. Auto theft rings. Extortion. Gambling. Bank-rolling—"

"Whatever. The steady thing—and I never liked this—the steady thing was the powder trade."

"Heroin."

"Something the customer asks for you so you can't blame the businessman. It was big, but mostly in the ghettos 'cause nobody else except jazz musicians were looking to buy."

"Bullshit! I've nailed white junkies by the score."

"You wanna know, then listen. The wise guys missed the new drug dollars with the hippie kids. Hell, these fellows are all older, established men. They hate all you hippie types! Everybody knew marijuana and LSD were just fads. So they didn't pursue those opportunities until—but that's another story."

"And I know about black power kicking them out of the street action in the ghettos—numbers, heroin, the whole deal. I know about the Vale."

"What veil?" Truth rang from Mel's question.

So you don't know about that motel's gangster convention, thought Quinn. So Nezneck doesn't tell you everything.

Plus maybe you arrange to keep a little innocent ignorance. At least in your own eyes.

"Never mind," said the cop. "So they lost the monopoly on heroin, missed out on the new drugs, needed new money."

"Right!" Mel glowed like a proud teacher. "Then Joe— give the man credit, he's a genius—our own Joe Nezneck had a vision: *Let's make another Las Vegas*. Make it a place everybody wants to go to: moms and pops, grannies, high-rollers, kids. Family entertainment. Like Mickey Mouse world with casinos."

"Washington!"

"Forget about this town!" said Mel. "What isn't black is marble and boring. But drive past the Beltway, and Maryland is a whole state of beaches! Baltimore is in the rust these days, so D.C. is the nearest turf, and it's—"

"An open city."

"Bingo! Guys like Marcello and Meyer Lansky *loved* Joe's vision! You set it up from the get-go. Vegas will always be the model for a gambling strip, beach or desert. The gambling business out there is run by the gaming commission, so if you want to control the business, you need to control the gaming commission."

"There is no gaming commission in Maryland!"

"But there will be, if casino gambling goes. To get it off the ground, to control the commission, you need the person who would appoint the commissioners."

"The governor," whispered Quinn.

"Guys like that, they're all politicians." Mel shook his head. "You can't trust them. My associates learned that lesson with JFK. So when you make a deal with one of them—"

"Agnew. Oh shit, this is all about Agnew!"

"Hell, getting him on board was not going to be hard; he knew how things work. But making sure he wouldn't welch . . . Nezneck, the guys who were going to front casino development with Teamsters loans . . . Joe came up with the hook to keep the governor from welching."

"Pat Dawson."

Mel sighed. "Mimi's more than enough woman for me.

But guys are guys and that's their business. So you set a guy up with a beautiful broad, set up a place—"

"They filmed Agnew with Pat Dawson! Oh, shit!" whispered Quinn. "At Heidi's apartment across from the Watergate!"

"Easy to arrange," said Mel. "Who was Agnew back then? Just the nobody governor from the state across the street from D.C. Drove in from Annapolis for a GOP fund-raiser, met the right people. Then comes Miami and *wham!* Nixon stuns everybody by picking Agnew."

"And they had the vice president of the United States," said Quinn. "They owned him on film. They were in the White House."

"Well, *sure.* One of those simple twists of fate. But even without it, everybody needs money to get to the White House and stay there, so Spiro was just icing."

"Pat Dawson?"

"Pat was too hungry for a big score to be smart enough," he whispered. "I never knew for sure after she wasn't around anymore. But yeah, I'd heard she'd tried to up her end. Make trouble. She knew enough to know what she had, but not enough to know how to use it right, and she wouldn't let nobody arrange nothing good for her. Had to do it herself."

"No. Your pal Nezneck did it for her."

"She should have kept her deal!"

"Maybe she did," said Quinn. "Maybe she died trying to keep the real deal she had with herself."

Mel looked away.

"No wonder Nezneck needed to be sure that binder with pictures of women didn't get found by Watergate investigators," said Quinn. "The binder would have led to a call girl ring. To blackmail and maybe expose his honey-trap deal with Penzler. That would put them both on the line, but good investigators pushing through all that could make a link to Pat, to her murder, to Agnew and corrupting a whole damn country!"

"What you just said, I didn't hear that too good, and even if I did, some details, links. I'm not ever going to know."

"You were a bagman for CREEP. You carried mob money across town in an old grocery sack."

"How'd you know?" Mel shrugged. "That's a never-mind now. No matter what you know, you have nothing you can prove. Cash is cash and cash doesn't care. Maybe a few times, some friends and friends of friends wanted to help a little, needed a way . . . All I did was arrange help that was going to happen anyway."

Mel sighed. "It would have been so good for everybody. As popular as Nixon was, as much of a national figure as Agnew'd become, with the Democrats blowing themselves up like they do, Nixon's number two would have coasted into the Oval Office in the seventy-six election. Forget about a few casinos. Think of the patronage jobs! The contracts! Parking lots! Construction!"

Quinn said, "Think of Pat Dawson and her little boy."

Excitement faded from Mel's eyes. "I never knew till it was too late. I never knew any details. What's not my business, I don't want to know."

Quinn shook his head. "Maybe I can sleep now. But how the hell will you?"

"I don't make the rules, I just play the game that's out there. What else should I do?"

"Why'd you give this up to me?"

"You got bullets," said Mel. "We have an arrangement. Besides, times change. Two years ago, Nixon was like a god in the White House. If he can end up where he is today, maybe you're not crazy or full of shit. Maybe having a deal with you is good business."

"And if it's not? Do you think you can arrange to stay square with your friends?"

"I always have. I'll make sure that they understand that you knew the nut of this before you knocked me around, and that me telling you the rest was how I arranged to get you to blab about your action. Everybody knows I'd never go to any committee or court. And that the cost of my funeral is way over the top."

"That's sure something to be proud of."

"Yeah, and what the hell do you have?"

Quinn dropped the last bullet into Mel's shirt pocket. Handcuffed the gnome's ankle to the steel and glass coffee table. He found Lorri stretched out on a king-sized bed in a boudoir filled with framed pictures of Mel beaming at Mimi; one vacation shot caught them grinning from atop a camel.

"Lorri? Come on, honey. Wake up." Her sunglasses kept him from knowing when her eyes opened, but she stirred to his touch. "Did your pager go off?"

"Don't you have yours?" She stretched on the flowered bedspread.

"Yes, but we have to be sure. Did it?"

"No." The sunglasses turned from side to side. "Is this how an old married couple lives?"

"Come on, honey. We have to go."

She gathered her carry-on bag and shuffled to the living room. Quinn put her in the foyer while he roamed the apartment taking the voice diaphragms out of phones.

Mel called him to the coffee table, whispered, "Do you have to have her in this? When I say what I gotta say, nobody has to know she was here."

"They won't care. There was no way to cut her clear from this."

"You should have tried harder. Been smarter. You know I'll dime Joe just as soon as I can. Figure you've got an hour. Joe, that CIA guy you call Penzler—not that I know him. Now that you know what you know, plus whatever your 'hammer' and your 'I got a Marine' adds up to—those are serious businessmen. They'll tear this town apart. They'll have every tough guy they can buy, beg, borrow or steal hunting you."

"See you around," said Quinn.

"No, you won't."

CHAPTER 63

The sky bled.

Quinn stood with Lorri on the porch of a rowhouse in a D.C. neighborhood that had seen better times. He rang the doorbell next to the iron gate. A green awning hung over the porch. A picket line of tulips bordered the lawn near a black iron fence. With her platinum hair and ivory skin, only her sunglasses saved Lorri from looking like a pale flame. Quinn thought: I must look like something blown off a long dirt road.

The door beyond the bars opened enough for the gray-haired black woman to peer out.

"Please don't close the door, Mrs. Watson!" said Quinn. "You probably don't recognize me looking like I do now."

"You're the policeman who killed my son."

"Yes, ma'am, I am. John Quinn. When I came to apologize six years ago, you wouldn't talk to me. I know I've got no right but I had to come here now."

"Since when has 'right' ever stopped you?"

"Right is why I'm here. Why we're here. Please, will you let us come in?"

"Is she a cop?"

"No. She's innocent."

"So you gonna kill her, too?"

"Not if you give us a chance, let us in."

"Give me one damn good reason."

"I owe you the best I can do. And this is it. You're it."

"Do you even remember his name?"

"Cyrus. He loved you and he liked to laugh."

She stared at the two people who shimmered like ghosts in her darkening neighborhood. Unlocked the grate.

The house smelled clean. Window air conditioners hummed. Above the couch hung a framed high school graduation photo of a handsome youth whose face as a baby, as a boy, as full-grown man in a swinger's suit smiled from other framed pictures placed here, placed there. A worn easy chair faced the television, which was turned on to Richard Nixon's haggard image live from the not-far-away Oval Office:

"GOOD EVENING. THIS IS THE THIRTY-SEVENTH TIME I HAVE SPOKEN TO YOU FROM THIS OFFICE IN WHICH SO MANY DECISIONS HAVE BEEN MADE THAT SHAPE THE HISTORY OF THIS NATION. . . ."

"Thank you," said Quinn. "This is Lorri. We're in trouble."

"I'm sorry for you, miss."

"THROUGHOUT THE LONG AND DIFFICULT PERIOD OF WATERGATE, I HAVE FELT IT WAS MY DUTY TO PERSEVERE. . . ."

"We don't mean anything bad," said Lorri.

"We need a place to stay," said Quinn. "Just for a few hours. A place where no one would ever look for me."

"Have you gone stark raving crazy?"

"The world's gone crazy," said Quinn. "We're trying to stop that."

"You got people chasing you, don't you?"

Quinn had stopped en route to make three phone calls: to the alcove, where Holloway, Dane and Vaughn were crowded together to confirm "Nothing yet!" To his commanding officer, to lie about being "hard undercover." To his ex-partner Buck: "Get your wife out of the house to somewhere safe; tonight Nezneck will burn the city to get to me!" Now he told his ambushed host: "By now, all of hell is after us."

Doris Watson laughed. "And you expect me to help you? Hide you?"

"Your son said you were a religious woman—"

"I must be. You getting trapped here is the answer to my prayers."

"I HAVE NEVER BEEN A QUITTER. . . ."

"Give me one good reason not to throw you out—hell, not to find whoever wants you, call them up and say, 'Come on over, here's the sorry son of a bitch!' "

"BUT AS PRESIDENT, I MUST PUT THE INTERESTS OF AMERICA FIRST. . . ."

Quinn said, "The only reason I've got is Cyrus."

"You killed him."

"He and I did that together. I tried to save him. I tried to do right by him. I did my best."

"Girl," said Doris to Lorri, "you better shop for your coffin."

"Because Doris Watson wants to drive the hearse!" snapped Quinn.

The old woman glared at the bearded white cop.

Lorri's voice trembled. "All I want is for everything to be over! To be gone!"

"THEREFORE, I SHALL RESIGN THE PRESIDENCY, EFFECTIVE AT NOON TOMORROW. . . ."

Doris told the two white people standing in her living room, "You be gone the first of tomorrow. Then I'll be over and done with all of you."

She sat in her armchair. Lorri slumped onto the couch. Quinn stood beside her. Nixon talked to them from the television.

"IF SOME OF MY JUDGMENTS WERE WRONG—AND SOME WERE WRONG—THEY WERE MADE IN WHAT I BELIEVED AT THE TIME TO BE THE BEST INTERESTS OF THE NATION. . . ."

Quinn said, "I'm going to wheel my motorcycle under the porch."

Even with California plates he'd lifted from the police impound lot, Quinn didn't want any vehicle that might look linked to him to be seen by street stalkers. Not that they'd think to search this neighborhood, but with so much left to chance, he wanted to make certain of all that he could.

He went back into the house. Doris sat in her chair; Lorri slumped on the couch. He locked the grate and the inside door with the keys dangling from its lock. Quinn put the keys on the table beside Doris.

". . . TRIED, TO THE BEST OF MY ABILITY, TO DISCHARGE THOSE DUTIES AND MEET THOSE RESPONSIBILITIES THAT WERE ENTRUSTED TO ME. SOMETIMES I HAVE SUCCEEDED. AND SOMETIMES I HAVE FAILED. . . ."

"So even with your shiny badge and your big gun and your white skin, you're running outside the law tonight, aren't you?"

"Yes. No. I don't know."

"Feels damn naked, don't it? You and Nixon. Couldn't happen to two better men."

". . . IN LEAVING IT, I DO SO WITH THIS PRAYER: MAY GOD'S GRACE BE WITH YOU IN ALL THE DAYS AHEAD."

President Nixon disappeared from the TV.

Quinn asked Lorri, "Did he blow it for us?"

Lorri laughed. Hiccuped. Sighed. "No. Not yet."

The old woman felt the tension flow from her two guests. The young woman's eyes drooped.

"Miss, you go down that hall. There's a bedroom on the right. Both of you stay the hell out of there. My room's on the left. You can use my bed."

Lorri touched Quinn's hand as she stood.

"I'll stay out here," he said.

The woman who loved him walked away.

He sat on the couch, watching Doris Watson watch him. TV flickered on their faces.

"There shouldn't be any danger here now or ever for you," he said. "If you knew what a good thing you're doing, how much I appreciate it."

"I ain't doing this for you."

"I know, Lorri deserves—"

"I don't know what she deserves or what she doesn't. I'm sorry for her, but she's just along for your ride. And I ain't doing this for you, I'm doing it for me."

Quinn stared at her.

She leaned forward, snapped off the babble of television news commentators.

"Me doing this means I'm better than you. That's cold comfort to take to my grave. But it's something, and now it's more than you got."

A clock ticked somewhere in the house. Night filled the barred windows.

"You go to bed now," said Doris. "Tonight you be the one trying to sleep in there."

"I'm fine here on the couch."

"Who you afraid I'm going to call? You damn right, I could turn you out to face your monsters. Or call your buddies on the police. But that would take all this away from me. I'm gonna sit here and let it all be."

The clock ticked.

The air conditioner hummed.

"We just going to stare at each other all night?" asked Quinn.

"What else you want us to do? Talk about the mysteries of life? Life is no mystery—there it is and that's that. You do what you do, I do what I do. Once upon a time I believed I had to walk a certain way so that Jesus would come down and wash away my pain and my sins, lift me up to the heavens of milk and honey. Now I know there's nothing up there but sky."

His beeper stayed silent.

"I wish I could give you something more," he said.

"Me, too."

The clock ticked. The windows stayed dark. They sat where they were. Then Doris got up and turned off the lights except the lamp by the chair, where she came back to sit.

Deedeedeedee—

Beeper! Asleep, how long was I—it's dark, still—Doris, asleep in her chair. Beeper: the callback number signals *Alert*. Not *Go!*, but . . . I gotta go, get there and bring the team together. We had to keep a spread-out, scattered target until . . .

A light shone under the bathroom door at the end of the dark hall. Quinn tiptoed past the bedroom to his right, where a young man's things waited, and eased the bathroom door open.

Lorri stared at the mirror above the bathroom sink. Locks of dyed blond hair covered the porcelain like harvested straw; the hair on her head was chopped into a jagged crop. She held scissors and stared at her reflection.

"Look at me now." She spoke in a flat monotone. "Think they'll recognize me?"

"We . . . we have to go. Not panic, but . . . Now." Quinn stared at the stranger. He saw a woman's razor on the edge of the tub.

"You've got five minutes," he said, taking the scissors from her hand, grabbing a fistful of Q's hair. "Then we're ready."

They left Doris sitting in her chair. Her eyes said she saw the blood from shaving cuts on Quinn's bare cheeks just as he saw tears on hers. No one spoke. They closed the door.

CHAPTER 64

A murky gray sky covered the city when they joined Dane, Holloway and Vaughn in the alcove overlooking the Sobel Building.

"We spotted your buddy Billy Bruce across the street." Holloway checked his watch. "Thirty-four minutes ago. He didn't check in with the police barricades up by the White House. He's not one of those vultures camped out to eat history. He scouted the Sobel, the front of the bank—"

"But he didn't see us," said Vaughn. "The sons of bitches don't know we're here."

"We parked in the alley," said Quinn. "Came in the back. No surveillance. Their manpower is looking for a hippie cop and a long-haired blonde, not a buzz-cut biker and his woman."

"So they're going to do it?" asked Lorri.

"They have to," answered Dane. She registered the jagged blond locks on the woman beside her, the cop's scraped face and home-butchered haircut, Holloway's warrior gear. *Of course we look bizarre, that's this time.* "Nixon still hasn't given the tapes up, so Penzler knows that getting his hands on them makes him King Kong. Put what Nathan did and said to him together with what you and Quinn sold Mel, and Penzler and Nezneck will realize that we've joined forces to nail them both. With the world on fire, with Nixon going down, everything is up for grabs. They have to assume we're all after the same ultimate weapon."

"Damn, I hope they rip off those tapes!" said Vaughn. "If they don't, then we have to. I'd rather be the heroic public servants stealing from traitors and crooks."

"Interdicting," said Holloway. "Recovering. Preserving. Rerouting."

"Whatever," said Vaughn. "If the bad guys steal from the government spies, then it's OK for us to rip the tapes back from them. We'll be the cavalry. Lock them up. And use the tapes to deal our way safe."

Quinn caught Holloway's eyes focused into long gone from here.

"Remember," said Quinn, "we've set up the law to be on our side. So we use it. That's our play. We're not here just to save our sorry, should-have-stayed-straight hides. This is how we get back to who we're supposed to be. We're not going to be renegades anymore.

"Right?" said Quinn. Lorri and Vaughn and Dane responded with looks, with gestures, with agreement; Holloway stared like a stone statue. "I say again: no more renegade."

"If they're going to do it, they're going to make their move any second now," said Holloway as false dawn lit the sky. "They can't wait and neither can we. Dane, you and Vaughn—"

"No," said Vaughn. "She goes, I stay."

Quinn said, "That's not the plan!"

"None of us planned on being here," said Vaughn. "So what? Lorri driving one of our cars they won't recognize, Holloway in the other, you on your bike—Hell, you'll need all the musketeers you got to overwhelm them. Dane—"

"I'm going, too!"

"No," said Vaughn. "Quinn is right about that. We need someone inside the power machine. Someone to be our voucher."

"He's right," Lorri told Dane. "You know he is. You're the smart one. The good one. You'll know how to make the right people believe."

Holloway nodded to her. Dane kept her vow not to cry.

"Come on," said Vaughn. "You have to go now."

She hugged Holloway in his khaki T-shirt and combat pants, his worn jungle boots; Quinn, his barbered boyish face with blazing eyes; Lorri, pale, pixielike in her embrace.

"It'll be OK," said Lorri. She felt Dane's diagnosing eyes. "Hell of a time for me to go sober, huh?"

"We'll see you in a while," Quinn told Dane.

Then Vaughn took her hand and they hurried from the alcove, out a side door of the building, down a putrid alley to his battered car. He gave her the keys, said, "You've got my heart forever."

"Vaughn . . . I . . . you're so . . ." She found no words.

"Sure," he said. "I know."

Then he put her behind the steering wheel, slammed the door as she started the engine. The driver's window was open and he punched down the lock button. Forced a smile: "Rock 'n' roll."

Dane hit the gas. The blue Dodge tore down the alley into the morning light.

Vaughn reentered the building's side door, walked down the long hall toward the inside stairs. He glanced out the front door's glass to the Sobel across the street.

A U-Haul truck and a Cadillac pulled to a stop; parked.

Dane drove as fast as she dared. A black sedan pulled behind her. Her mirrors showed a male driver beside a second man riding shotgun. She blew through a red light. A car horn screamed, but the black machine in her wake obeyed the law and she raced through the city alone.

She parked beside the Senate Office Building. A Capitol Hill cop nodded to her staff ID after she spun through the revolving door. Her footsteps echoed in the empty marble halls.

Alone, she thought. I'm—

"Dane!" A male voice boomed behind her and she jumped, stumbled into the wall, her keys skidded down the marble as she whirled.

Gun on his belt, gun, white shirt, black bald head, somebody's behind him, too, and—

Stepping out of sunlight glaring through the hall window, smiling: "Good morning."

"Oh, shit! Sergeant Jones!" The shape behind the Capitol

Hill cop came closer: an elegant black woman with strands of silver in her hair. "I didn't expect you here!"

"None of us *expected*," he said. "This is my sister-in-law, Buck's wife. She didn't expect not to be home safe in bed neither. My family's already gone to North Carolina for the summer. All things considered, Buck figured she ought to hang out with me and my crew."

Dane could only nod.

"Best that we don't know what we don't know. The guard posts told me your insomniac boss is inside his office. I was thinking, all the history that's supposed to happen today, long as it's smart for me to pull some duty hanging around this hallway, you mind if my kin stayed inside the Senator's office with you and your man where it's gonna be . . . cool?"

"Vaughn isn't—Of course she's welcome! Thank you!"

The sergeant picked up her keys. "Buck told me that there's an all-officers' alert out for his ex-partner. Locate, report, surveil, do not approach. Official word is he's been Patty Hearst'd, an undercover officer snatched and maybe brainwashed by some bad-ass lefty white boys and girls. Armed and dangerous and shootable. Some FBI guy told Buck that a swarm of Uncle Sam's suits who aren't Bureau are kicking doors and staking out airports, the train station, bus depot."

Dane led Buck's wife inside an office he guarded and had her shake hands with a real United States senator.

In the surveillance alcove, Quinn handed a heavy revolver to Vaughn: "Can you handle this?"

"I've shot guns before," said the Senate aide. "I'm an all-American boy."

"There are six in the opposition out there and you've got six shots, a .357 Magnum, highway patrolman model."

"Highway patrolman," muttered Vaughn. "Perfect."

"They're still inside," said Holloway, who stood at the window overlooking the Sobel and the parked Cadillac and U-Haul truck. "Smart of them to leave Godsick out front. Crowds gathering up the block across from the White House, all the extra cops and security. He's got the lieutenant's badge in case they're checked out."

"But why don't they have an army?" said Lorri. "Besides that snake-eyed creep Godsick, there's only Nezneck and Penzler, the other cop Bruce and two guys we don't know."

"All their armies are looking for us," said Quinn. "We let them know we were running loose, so they have to find us . . . fast."

"Besides, they don't want a crowd that will attract the hordes of press just a couple blocks away," said Holloway. "And they don't trust each other enough to let the other one grab the big prize alone. How do you figure the two strangers?"

"They don't look like feds," said Quinn, joining them at the window. "Figure them for Nezneck's. Penzler's running off the books: the last guys he'd trust are government issue."

The D.C. cop handed Lorri the snub-nosed .38 revolver he'd taught her how to use; he kissed her softly. Quinn grabbed a handheld radio with an earplug, said, "I'm gone."

CHAPTER 65

The doors to the Sobel Building across the street opened nine minutes later. One of the two young gunmen Holloway didn't know scanned the sidewalk while his partner propped open the Sobel's doors. D.C. detective Billy Bruce opened the U-Haul cargo box and pulled down the loading ramp. Nezneck and Penzler came out into the morning light, got an OK nod from Lieutenant Godsick. Penzler beckoned four men with handcarts to roll boxes out of the Sobel and stack them in the truck. Holloway recognized the cart men: patriots from Gallaudet. At least we were right. Penzler compromised enough bona fides to scam you, not kill you. The deaf patriots worked for twenty minutes, filled three quarters of the U-Haul's huge cargo box with brown unmarked cardboard boxes.

You didn't even have to get every tape, thought Holloway as he watched Penzler nod dismissal to the deaf patriots. You just had to get enough.

As Detective Bruce padlocked the U-Haul doors, Holloway slipped one arm through a duffel bag's shoulder strap, radioed the others: "They're done! Nezneck's driving the Caddy. His two cops and one of the gunners are getting in the Caddy, too. The other gunner is climbing into the truck—he's driving. Penzler is riding on the passenger side.

"They're pulling out! Caddy's leading. They're headed east on New York Avenue! I say again: they did not turn down Fourteenth! I'm launched!"

Not down Fourteenth. Not toward Virginia. Not toward the CIA. Not out of our free-fire zone.

Holloway ran from the alcove; the duffel bag swinging from his shoulder, he raced down the steps. The wall of heat and humidity hit him as he exploded out the bank's door.

Don't see me! he willed to the policemen walking post one hundred meters away in front of the White House fence. Keep your eyes on the history vultures gathering in the park across the street, must be a thousand of them.

He made it unchallenged to the parked Ford, threw his duffel bag on the front seat and peeled away. The White House and the mob of ordinary Americans fell from his mirrors.

"Mobile!" he yelled into his radio. All his windows were rolled down, and the AC turned off so the engine had all its power. Urban summer flowed into the car as he sped through the waking streets, a caustic, emerald thickness that felt right, felt like where he belonged. "Where is everybody?"

Lorri's voice on the radio: "We're on Mass Ave. and Eighth, headed toward Capitol Hill!"

She sat in the Trans Am's passenger seat, a sheaf of maps in her lap, the .38 under her thigh; Vaughn drove the muscle car, his eyes riding the bright aluminum mirror of the U-

Haul's cargo box three blocks beyond his windshield.

"John's a block behind us!" radioed Lorri. Her lover rode his motorcycle. A helmet and smoked visor hid his face. A clamp held the radio to the bike, an earplug let him hear reports; lifting the radio to transmit while controlling the bike would be tricky.

"Don't crowd them!" ordered Holloway. The Marine in the Ford blew a yellow light and raced to catch up to this dawn's secret parade.

"We know what to do!" radioed Lorri. She unfolded the map. The aluminum box of the U-Haul was easy to track; now and then they glimpsed the sleek Cadillac leading the way.

Lorri told Vaughn, "If they're leaving town and not going to the CIA, maybe John was right when he figured Nezneck will head to PG county."

Vaughn saw her smile for the first time that morning as she said, "I hope so."

"Me, too," he told her; If they don't go anyplace "official," we've got a chance.

"All this . . ." Lorri struggled for the right word, ". . . all this badness won't stop even if we get Nixon's tapes, make Nezneck and Penzler and those cops pay for what they've done. Even if we get away with it, we'll still be stuck with who we are."

"But at least we'll have done what we could," said Vaughn. "That's something."

"Something," she whispered.

The machines they followed streamed up Capitol Hill. The car that carried Lorri flowed past Union Station. She glanced to her right, saw the multi-imaged reflection of the Capitol dome caught in chessboard plate-glass windows of the nearby Teamsters headquarters.

"Yeah," she said, an unfamiliar lightness filling her with warmth. "That's something."

Vaughn glanced at the Capitol dome, the magnet that had pulled him to Washington; at the Senate Office Building where he knew, he just *knew*, Dane was waiting and safe.

"Where are you?" came through the radio that played no Beach Boys, no Beatles or Hendrix, no Dylan or Van Morrison, no Springsteen. No mercy, No "Don't worry, Baby."

"Going around Stanton Park," Lorri radioed Holloway.

"I see you!" he said. "I'll catch up. We'll start leapfrogging. Quinn, hang back."

Engine throbbing between his thighs, road slamming under his wheels, Quinn swore and knew that was all he could do.

Nixon ate a breakfast of grapefruit, wheat germ and milk in his White House bedroom.

Synchronized red lights stopped traffic on the city streets.

Holloway unzipped the duffel bag. He pulled out a web belt with bulging pouches and cinched it around his waist. A .45 automatic rode in a Marine pilot's shoulder holster beside his heart; he knew the pistol's twin rode under Quinn's shirt.

"You didn't get any flack vests," the cop had told him so many nights ago.

"Didn't want one," Holloway'd replied, seeing "What about us?" and other unasked questions in the cop's eyes even as the Marine silently cursed himself with should-haves.

Won't matter, vowed Holloway. I won't let that matter.

The lights turned green.

I should have written Sandy a letter, he thought as he drove past the Trans Am carrying Vaughn and Lorri, swung between them and the shiny U-Haul bouncing over chuckholes toward the Robert Kennedy Memorial Stadium. But what would I have said? . . . And what will they tell Dad?

The Cadillac passed the stadium, headed over the bridge toward suburban Maryland. Holloway turned on the car radio to the live-from-the-White-House continuous broadcast so he could track Nixon even as he followed Penzler and Nezneck. Come on, Nixon! Be who you are: don't give up the tapes and make our play worthless! And Penzler and Nezneck: don't look behind you. Holloway knew the Caddy crew would be watching the U-Haul. What else would they see?

Metro buses crammed with commuters rumbled away from the sidewalk toward where this unnoticed parade had been. Lorri saw the faces and figures of "real" people, saw them reading newspapers at the bus stops or checking their lipstick in the mirrors of cars. They cruised past a man in a Japanese compact who was brushing his hair. Radio babble from other cars darted through their open windows: Nixon was resigning. Due to leave any minute. Some prankster had sent a moving van to the White House. They showed it on TV.

No! she wanted to say to the people going the other way. We're over here! We're here!

Watch the U-Haul. Read the map. Work the two-way radio. Sit on the gun. We're here.

I am Q, he thought as the motorcycle rumbled against his groin: I am Quarell. John Quinn. American. I am a police officer. Somebody had to.

The megalopolis of Washington, D.C., was a toddler on that morning of August 9, 1974. Vacant lots, groves of trees and farm plots appeared along their unfolding easterly route with a frequency that would be lost before the millennium. Suburban tract houses became scattered farm homes set back from the road; traffic thinned.

"Heads up!" radioed Holloway. "They're turning right!"

"It's a long, winding road!" radioed Lorri as her finger traced the route. "Some county or state highway that goes off the map!"

A Coca-Cola truck roared past them, then the lane emptied beside their strung-out parade.

"They've spotted us!" radioed Lorri. "They must have!"

"Not yet!" came back Holloway. Fields tall with corn flashed past his windows. The road snaked with curves. "But they will soon. What does the map show?"

"Nothing!" she radioed. "It shows shit! No named suburbs. Just empty space. There's a big horseshoe curve a few miles ahead, then—"

"Stay back!" Holloway punched the gas pedal to the floor. The Ford surged toward the shiny U-Haul, closer, closer . . . "If they get where they're going, there will be more of them!"

Closer, the aluminum cargo box loomed closer . . .

"What are you doing?" screamed Quinn to the hot wind racing past him. He was a mile or more behind Vaughn and Lorri's Trans Am, and they were behind Holloway. Quinn fed gas to the motorcycle and charged over the blacktop highway.

RICHARD NIXON MET his Chief of Staff General Haig in the White House's Lincoln Sitting Room. Haig gave his boss the letter addressed to Secretary of State Henry Kissinger: *I hereby resign the Office of President of the United States.*

A pen scrawled: *Richard Nixon.*

Holloway blew past the U-Haul—Don't look! Don't make eye contact with the driver even if Penzler's sitting on the other side and can't see who you are! White lines on the blacktop flashed toward Holloway's windshield as he roared past the Cadillac. Don't look at those guys either!

God, don't let any civilians drive this road today!

The Ford shimmied, fishtailed—Holloway pulled back to the right lane. Pressed the gas pedal. A double yellow stripe centered the road rushing toward Holloway. His Ford flew by a broken-off warning sign. Coming, it's got to be soon.

The road banked and curved to the right, a tire-crying 180-degree bend . . .

. . . fishtailing out to a straight leg of the horseshoe, rows of corn to the right as Holloway's brakes screamed and burned, the Ford shuddering, slowing . . . Scrub field off to the left, a big sign: FUTURE SITE OF ASPEN HOMES ESTATES. Fifty open meters then a windbreak of trees. Beyond the trees he glimpsed silhouettes of townhouses hulking like monopoly pieces in precise lines; two low white wooden guardrails over a culvert for a ditch flanked the road—Stop! Gotta stop before that bridge!

Empty! Keep the damn road empty!

Holloway cranked the steering wheel. The Ford slid sideways on the highway—stopped across both lanes just before the culvert and the ditch. He left the motor running—

Pulled the once-crated war rifle out of the duffel bag, an M16 with a blunderbuss XM148 forty-millimeter grenade launcher mounted under the barrel. He bailed out of the Ford, web belt slapping as he dashed down the slope of the road embankment to the man-high rows of corn, crashed into them, dropped to the dirt and radioed:

"Vaughn! Close up! We're going to take them on the road! Cut them off after they make the horseshoe curve! I blocked the road beyond that! You block the highway behind them! Both of you bail out on the high side, the open field! Take cover! I'm opposite side of the road, up front, in the corn! We'll have a crossfire!"

I'm coming! Quinn gunned his motorcycle. Wait! I'm coming!

Plowed dirt and the acrid scent of green corn filled Holloway as he fought his breath back down, down: slow, silent. He sank his prone body into the brown earth, a khaki smear hidden in the tall rows of corn. His thumb clicked the M16 down from full auto to selected fire. A bird chirped. This is it. This is where I belong.

The Caddy came round the bend—a blur, a flash of brake lights as Nezneck reigned his fat-cat machine to a stop twenty meters from the empty Ford. The U-Haul barreling around the curve shuddered, its brakes groaning as the rental truck bore down on its escort. Holloway thought luck might give them a rear-end crash, but the U-Haul stopped five meters short of the Caddy's bumper.

In the White House, Richard Nixon, wearing a white shirt, maroon-patterned tie and blue suit, led his family into the East Room, where more than a hundred White House aides had gathered. Nixon entered after the traditional, "Ladies and Gentlemen, the President of the United States." The crowd stood, applauded, cried and cheered for four minutes. Nixon stepped to the microphone:

"YOU ARE HERE TO SAY GOOD-BYE TO US, AND WE DON'T HAVE A GOOD WORD FOR IT IN ENGLISH. THE BEST IS *AU REVOIR*. WE'LL SEE YOU AGAIN . . ."

*   *   *

HOLLOWAY WATCHED THE shapes of the men in the Cadillac as Nixon's words blared from the improvised car blockade: the Marine had left the car radio turned on as loud as it would go.

Not just tracking Nixon. Fucking with Penzler and Nezneck. You don't know what's up, Holloway telepathed to them. You can't be sure.

A hired gun stepped out to the road on Holloway's side of the Caddy. The gunman carried a pump shotgun. He stood beside Nezneck's car, his eyes on the empty Ford blocking the road.

"SURE WE HAVE DONE SOME THINGS WRONG IN THIS ADMINISTRATION AND THE TOP MAN ALWAYS TAKES THE RESPONSIBILITY AND I'VE NEVER DUCKED IT. . . ."

Holloway put the U-Haul's passenger door in the sights of the M16: Come on, Penzler. Get out. Climb down from that metal box and see what's what.

In the course of events, I am the officer in charge. I am the judge. I am the jury.

But the driver climbed out of the U-Haul. He walked from the truck toward the Caddy; the Teamster carried a WWII carbine sporting a banana-curved magazine packed with bullets.

But fuck you, we got you! Position, surprise . . . will.

Tires screamed in the distance. Even Holloway looked as a Trans Am skidded out of the curve to make a roadblock fifty meters behind the U-Haul. A man and a woman bailed out of that sleek muscle car and ran for cover in the plowed field.

"WE MUST BE STRONG HERE, STRONG IN HEARTS, STRONG IN OUR SOULS, STRONG IN OUR BELIEF, AND STRONG IN OUR WILLINGNESS TO SACRIFICE . . ."

Eyes hungry for the muscle car's scrambling occupants, shotgun man threw his weapon up to his shoulder—

The M16 in the cornfield punched three holes in that hired gunman before its *crack crack crack* reached the road. The shotgunner fell. Holloway stamped holes in the Caddy as the men in it scrambled out the driver's side. Holloway swung his aim to the carbine man, but that sniper had jumped behind the U-Haul. Holloway emptied the M16 magazine into the truck's passenger door, knew he'd missed Penzler. The Marine slapped in a fresh ammo mag.

Quinn raced his motorcycle toward the curve in the road. He heard his mind screaming, "Radio me! Why won't somebody radio me!" Heard the staccato crack of gunfire slice through the roar of his engine. He leaned into the curve and turned the throttle wide open.

Pistols roared at the cornfield from behind the Caddy. Slugs sliced cornstalks.

Way off! thought Holloway. They haven't zeroed my location yet.

He heard the whine of a motorcycle. Saw Quinn whip around the curve. Saw the motorcycle racing toward the back-end roadblock of the Ford.

Holloway spotted the carbine poking beyond the U-Haul, a long-distance weapon pointing, *tracking* Quinn. Carbine with what? Fifteen rounds? Even if the gunner was a bad shot: target hurtling toward him, Quinn on a motorcycle, no steel U-Haul protecting him, a shot hitting even just the bike would knock him off balance and crash him at top speed to the highway.

Can't wait for Lorri-Vaughn amateurs with handguns, even if they try, won't—

The man or the mission. The tapes or Quinn.

Fuck it: we are *the mission!* Holloway slid his finger off the M16's trigger.

"EVERY JOB COUNTS UP TO THE HILT, REGARDLESS OF WHAT HAPPENS. . . ."

*   *   *

HOLLOWAY SQUEEZED THE trigger of the M79 grenade
launcher mounted under the M16 rifle and slammed a
baseball-sized bomb into the mirror-bright U-Haul sheltering
the carbine-killer.

The grenade exploded—Measure that fucking hole!

The truck erupted in a ball of flame.

Quinn wrestled his motorcycle around the Trans Am,
braked a skid toward the fireball for as long as he could, then
turned the wheel toward the cornfield. The motorcycle flew
off the road.

The explosion snapped cornstalks above where Holloway
lay. The fireball devouring the U-Haul truck swamped him
with heat and the stench of melting metal and burning rubber.

Burning gas and debris rained down on the Cadillac.

A screaming Detective Billy Bruce charged from behind
the Caddy's fins, blasting his pump shotgun at the corn.

Buckshot cut Holloway's back. He rolled, flipping the se-
lector switch to full auto and saw the charging Billy Bruce
knocked to the earth by a burst of M16 slugs.

Lorri spotted him first: a wispy-bearded guy in a suit running from the burning truck, running across the open field
where she lay with Vaughn. Fire and smoke hid the running
man from the cornfield and Holloway. Primal rage rocketed
her to her feet, screaming as she fired all six bullets in the
snub-nosed .38 at Penzler.

Rolling, kneeling, slapping a new magazine in the M16,
Holloway heard Lorri's salvo.

He saw the Caddy suddenly lurch forward and spin a circle
as it hurtled back the way it had come, racing on the far side
of the fireball. He had the rifle to his shoulder, leading where
he thought the Caddy would emerge from behind the burning
truck when a bullet whined past his head. He hit the dusty
earth as the Caddy roared out of the smoke and flames, Nezneck at the wheel, snake-eyed Lieutenant Godsick blasting
out the rear side window with his revolver—blind shots,

sure, but enough to make Holloway duck and waste a full auto mag on even wilder fire.

Detroit's golden horses roared the Caddy toward the Trans Am blocking the highway.

Lorri's gun *clicked* in her hand. Twenty yards away, cutting across her horizon, the wispy-bearded man kept running.

"I missed!" she said. "Every damn time!"

Vaughn swung his eyes from the fleeing Penzler to the Caddy roaring toward the Trans Am roadblock. The creep cop who came after me, he's down, but Nezneck is in there! Nezneck is the blackmail puppet master, the guy most vulnerable to the law. Vaughn swung his eyes toward the birdlike man he knew was Penzler, the fleeing CIA man he knew Holloway would chase into hell.

The Caddy punched into the Trans Am, knocked it out of the way enough to roar by, enough to crumple both bumpers. The Caddy powered forward on the open, empty, free road.

Quinn groaned. His helmet had popped off. He rolled upright on the patch of corn his motorcycle had flattened. He saw the fireball consuming the rental truck and knew what that meant. He saw two crumpled forms near the front of the burning truck. Quinn watched Holloway slap a fresh magazine into the M16, squeeze off rounds that slammed into the fleeing Cadillac. And across the road, running toward Quinn—*No!* Running toward the battered Trans Am: Vaughn. And Lorri.

"No!" screamed Quinn.

Vaughn yelled to Lorri, "I'll—"

Lorri yelled louder, "I'll drive!"

She had the Trans Am roaring, dropping into gear before Vaughn could slam the passenger door shut. They peeled out after the fleeing Caddy.

Holloway swung his aim off the Caddy. The U-Haul burned. Nixon radioed from the blockading Ford:

"NEVER BE PETTY. ALWAYS REMEMBER, OTHERS MAY HATE YOU. THOSE WHO HATE YOU DON'T WIN UNLESS YOU HATE THEM. AND THEN YOU DESTROY YOURSELF. . . ."

Where's Penzler?

Quinn plucked his motorcycle off the ground. The engine still hummed. Can't catch them, not fast enough to swing around—a horseshoe, a curve. Geometry, fucking high school! He pointed the bike through the corn, the straight, bisecting line, cranked the throttle: fuck the cornstalks leaves slapping his face, the dirt berms tossing his bike from side to side. He raced between two sentry rows, everywhere green slapping at him, no sky but *go!*

"We'll get them!" Lorri yelled as she wrestled the steering wheel hard to her left and the Trans Am slid into the curve. "We have to! We're faster!"

Vaughn tore his eyes from the Caddy racing beyond their windshield to her chopped blond hair, her blazing eyes as she fought to stay in her seat and steer. He saw pride, fierce pride that she was here, that she was doing something straight from the heart, straight to the heart.

And so am I, thought Vaughn.

"Can't risk them beating us!" yelled Vaughn. "Hold it steady!"

"It's a damn curve!"

Vaughn stuck his head and shoulders out the open side window, shot at the fleeing Caddy with the booming .357 Magnum. Each blast almost ripped the heavy gun from his grasp, but he held on—to the gun, to the car, to his precarious perch in hot wind pushing against his face.

"Out of the curve!" yelled Lorri. "I can catch them! We can catch them!"

The Trans Am fishtailed as Vaughn dropped back into his seat, empty gun, hand digging in his jeans' pocket for more bullets while their momentum hurled him from side to side.

On his racing motorcycle, Quinn winced, flinched, corn leaves slicing his face—Sky! There's blue sky up ahead!

Lorri said, "Look!"

Vaughn saw the rear window of the Caddy disintegrate.

"But I'm not shooting!" he whispered.

Shotgun buckshot cobwebbed the windshield in front of Vaughn and Lorri into a million rainbows. Vaughn was aware of crying tires and busting glass and the steering wheel ripping free to spin in the hands of the beautiful woman driving his machine, how curiously slow and heavy was the air and how nobody screamed.

Holloway charged up the shoulder of the road, M16 ready, barely glancing at his latest body count of three dead. The road stank of fired metal and burning tires, seared human flesh, melted plastic and vaporized recording tape, of gasoline and voided bowels and blood on blacktop. He smelled his sweat, cordite from the hot weapon in his hands. Black smoke swirled across the horizon of plowed field, distant trees in front of new houses.

But Penzler, where is—

There! Running across the cleared earth toward the trees bordering a new housing development: fifty meters, but "every Marine a rifleman" and such a shot was everyday *Semper fi* work: Select fire to semiauto, shoulder weapon, set the running man in the iron sights—

Houses. Target's background is houses. Homes. Civilians. Old people. Kids and parents home to watch history on TV in living rooms with walls that were like book pages to M16 slugs.

Holloway screamed and charged after the fleeing spy.

Penzler never looked back, never stopped running and made it to a grove of trees.

Nixon left the White House with his family, arms linked with his wife and Vice President and Mrs. Gerald Ford. They walked across the lawn through a crowd of Secret Service agents, military aides, White House staff, reporters, friends, walked to a waiting Marine helicopter.

Holloway charged into the half moon of trees ten steps behind the fleeing Penzler. Five . . . The bearded CIA executive stopped, whirled—pistol searching.

The Marine major swung his rifle in a butt stroke that swiped Penzler's gun arm—the spy's pistol hit the ground. The M16 backstroke creased wispy white hair. Penzler staggered—barely grabbed the rifle Holloway thrust into the spy's guts as if it were tipped with a bayonet. Penzler stumbled backward, spun, pulled the rifle as the Marine let it go. Penzler fell to his hands and knees, his butt facing Holloway like a dog.

Holloway slammed his boot into the spy's tailbone.

Penzler sprawled facedown on the dirt, the war rifle pinned beneath him. Clarity and his breath fought their way back through blinding stars of pain, and he felt the press of his own pistol against his right temple, the weight of the Marine on his back pinning him to the earth.

"No! You need me!" cried Penzler. "I can fix everything for you! From the inside! Nezneck can't do that, not like me! The admirals and the Agency won't allow a mess, no new scandal, and they'll let me, they'll make us fix it and I know how and I'll give you Nezneck, too! I'm the only one who can get you what you all want!"

Engines roared in the distance . . .

Slowly, oh so slowly, the Marine eased his weight up and Penzler slowly, oh so slowly, rolled onto his back beneath the Marine. The cold bore of the gun plowed a furrow as it slid along Penzler's turning head from his right temple, across his forehead, stopping when Penzler stopped turning, when he was on his back with the Marine on top of him like a lover, the gun bore pressing into Penzler's left temple.

Penzler looked Holloway in his mad eyes and smiled.

Quinn raced toward the sky—exploded from the corn rows, the wheels of his motorcycle finding traction and rocketing him onto the pavement. He tried to turn the bike ninety degrees, but the machine slid out from under him, careened off on its own as he tumbled on the blacktop. He stopped his rolling with bleeding hands, pushed himself up to see the Cadillac racing toward the city while the muscle car behind it spun out of control and the laws of the universe flipped the Trans Am end over end, crashing and rolling along the highway into a crumpled twist of steel and glass and other things.

On the White House lawn, Nixon mounted the steps of the helicopter. He turned and waved with a swooping right hand, then again, both hands flying out to his sides in a wide

V as he grinned and both hands gave the two-fingered salute—Winston Churchill's WWII gesture for "victory" the gesture also used by antiwar demonstrators to mean "peace."

Nixon turned his back, the door closed, the helicopter lifted off the White House lawn.

At the U.S. Capitol complex, the Senator, who'd insisted that any champagne celebration be in honor of a random intern's birthday and not from joy over Nixon's departure, watched Dane stand at the window of his office, her face to the sky where the TV showed Nixon's helicopter chopping its way to freedom. Senator Martin feared the tears streaking her cheeks were not for America's profound moment.

Crying, thought Penzler as he stared up into the face of the man who had him pinned with his own gun pressed against his head: he's crying.

"I can fix anything," whispered Penzler.

Nathan Holloway saw his own reflection in that man's eyes. Said, "You're too much trouble."

Squeezed the trigger.

Nixon flew out of Washington in the Marine helicopter, headed east to Andrews Air Force Base near Maryland's rural Prince Georges County.

On the highway beneath that sky, Quinn staggered toward the wrecked car. Nixon's helicopter chopped to tomorrows that revealed how KIA Detective Bruce and Officer Quinn thwarted Pagan-allied Weathermen bombers. A police Internal Affairs investigation validated Quinn's report and noted that the police action, with its "peripheral distracting turmoil," contributed to the single-car accident that killed a stewardess and twisted the body of her Senate aide boyfriend, though lab tests showed a suspicious alcohol level in that woman driver's blood. Along with files about the call girl ring Lorri brushed, a Pentagon report on Richard Nixon and organized crime vanished into the smoke swirled by Nixon's chopper, smoke that swirled around the tragic death of CIA executive William Penzler, whose deserted sailboat was found drifting in Chesapeake Bay. Penzler's body washed up at a naval radar base, where Navy forensic spe-

cialists ruled it a gunshot suicide, then released the remains
to Penzler's colleagues for immediate cremation. From that
smoke came the transfer of Major Nathan Holloway, USMC,
to Saigon, where months later a helicopter plucked him off
the American embassy's roof in that city's last hour. From
that smoke too came Lieutenant Godsick's transfer from IAD
to Motor Pool, and negotiations by various federal agents, a
deputy D.C. police chief and a U.S. senator that promoted
John Quinn to Detective Sergeant, Intelligence Squad. Dane
told Quinn: "What *they* want is to get back to business as
usual." Then she walked away in the marble Senate corridor.
"It's OK to just say good-bye," Vaughn told her before he
wheelchaired onto the west-bound airliner. "Hell, a busted
heart deserves a busted body." After Watergate, Nezneck was
as visible as the haze of his cigarettes. And on the highway
of Nixon's last day as President, as a truck burned, *because
someone had to,* John Quinn fell to his knees before a car
wreck, his raised hands grasping at the helicopter sky but
catching only smoke.